Gone

with the

Nerd

Vicki Lewis Thompson

St. Martin's Paperbacks

GONE WITH THE NERD

Copyright © 2005 by Vicki Lewis Thompson.

Cover photo © Phil Hefferan

ISBN: 0-312-99858-9
EAN: 80312-99858-5

Printed in the United States of America

St. Martin's Paperbacks edition / August 2005

St. Martin's Paperbacks are published by St. Martin's Press, 175 Fifth Avenue, New York, NY 10010.

10 9 8 7 6 5 4 3 2 1

For Cooper Scott Thompson,
a really cool California dude.

Acknowledgments

As always, my books are blessed with help from incredible people. Special thanks to Guy Bordelon for giving me insights into the Bigfoot phenomenon, the St. Martin's marketing department for its heart-warming enthusiasm, my family for continued support, my agent Maureen Walters for her steady guidance, and my editor Jennifer Enderlin for awesome input.

Gone

with the

Nerd

Chapter One

Two blocks from the restaurant, Zoe Tarleton knew she was screwed. Slowing for the light, she grabbed her cell phone from her purse and speed-dialed her lawyer. "Flynn, forget the restaurant I told you. It's a fuster cluck of reporters out front."

"So I see. I'm two cars ahead of you."

Zoe braced herself on the steering wheel and pushed up to see over the yellow Corvette in front of her. Sure enough, there was a white Honda Civic idling in traffic with Flynn at the wheel. One of the richest entertainment lawyers in Hollywood drove a ten-year-old sedan. And that's why she needed him. Flynn Granger was the only nerd she knew.

"I'm assuming you mentioned this meeting to Leon?" Flynn sounded resigned.

"I had to. He wanted to schedule an interview and I had to tell him why I couldn't do it." And her agent, Leon Borowsky, had alerted the new publicist, Sandi. Good old

Leon alerted the publicist every time Zoe stepped out her front door, even when she'd specifically told him not to, like now. But she had a movie out and Leon had a thing for the new publicist, which meant he'd gladly turn Zoe's every breath into a photo op.

"Okay." Flynn switched to his lawyer's voice. "New plan. We'll drive past and go to a different restaurant."

"They'll recognize my car if I drive past. As slow as traffic's moving, I could still get waylaid." Even if she put up the top, that wouldn't save her.

"Switch cars with me."

"Now?"

"Right now. You have about five seconds before the light changes."

Zoe didn't pause to think. Still clutching her cell, she flung open the door and ran past the Corvette. She and Flynn bumped into each other, mumbled apologies, and whirled toward their respective destinations. She made it into his car just as the light turned green.

With zero time to move the seat, she stretched her legs to reach the pedals and used the steering wheel to balance herself. The Corvette driver leaned on his horn during the nanosecond she needed to release the emergency brake and put the Civic in gear, but finally she was in motion, gliding down the street in Flynn's nerd car.

Another horn blared from somewhere behind her, and she realized that Flynn wouldn't have fit in her Boxster without adjusting the seat, so he must have taken longer to get situated. But he was moving now. She could see him in the side-view mirror, his prescription sunglasses glinting in the light, his dark hair ruffled by the breeze.

When he picked up a little speed, the end of his brown tie flapped into view. He needed to lose the tie and roll back the sleeves of his dress shirt. Then he'd be at one with that sports car.

Even so, he looked good driving a ragtop, surprisingly good, macho even. But he'd never buy one. According to him, cars were transportation, not toys or status symbols or—heaven forbid—compensation for sexual inadequacies. Cruising the coast highway with the top down and the radio up wouldn't occur to Flynn as a way to spend some quality time.

Perched forward on the seat, Zoe concentrated on not crashing Flynn's car into the vehicle ahead of her. Flynn didn't have a scratch on his Civic. Even the inside was immaculate—not a gum wrapper, empty CD case, or soft-drink container to be found.

He was anal as the day was long, but that was fine with Zoe. That same meticulous attention had been applied to her studio contracts, and she gave thanks every day for a thorough lawyer like Flynn.

The car smelled like Flynn, too. No pricey aftershave for this guy. He was an Aqua Velva man. She'd learned that one day when she'd had to use the powder room adjacent to his office and had found a bottle of Aqua Velva on the counter. Taking off the cap to sniff, she'd immediately recognized the familiar mint scent she associated with Flynn.

Speaking of Flynn, she wondered if he was still connected via cell. She snagged hers from the seat where she'd tossed it. "Zoe to Flynn. Come in, Flynn."

"I'm here, crammed in like a sardine."

Zoe smiled. Only Flynn would complain about being behind the wheel of a freshly washed black Boxster. "Yeah, but you're stylin'."

"Not my goal."

"I know. Listen, thanks for trusting me with your car."
She thought it might be harder for him to loan out an
economy car he'd carefully maintained for ten years than
for her to let him drive the Porsche she'd owned for less
than six months, a car that had no sentimental value and
was maintained by a member of her staff.

"No problem. Okay, we're getting close to the restaurant. Lock the driver's door. The others are already locked."

"I will, but don't worry. They'll never look for me in
this car."

"Lock it anyway."

Zoe searched for a power switch. "How?"

"There's a button on the door frame along the edge of
the window. Take your finger and push it down." He
sounded amused.

"Oh." She locked herself in. "I thought there was a
switch somewhere."

"I know."

"You're trying not to laugh, aren't you?"

"I'm not laughing."

"Yes, you are. Almost. So I haven't been in a car with
manual door locks in a while. So sue me."

"As your lawyer, I don't think that's legally possible."

"You are so laughing." She checked in the side-view
mirror again and there was a big grin on his face. Driving a
sports car while showing off his pearly whites, he looked
rakish and daring, two words she never would have associated with Flynn previously. Probably a trick of the light.

As she'd predicted, she slipped right past the restaurant
without a single person recognizing her. No one moved; no
cameras flashed. Flynn was not so lucky. Everyone on the
sidewalk had been waiting for her Boxster. Zoe watched in

the mirror as the crowd surged forward, creating a momentary halt in traffic.

Zoe could hear their shouts of frustration through the cell phone connection. "They're not happy," she said to Flynn.

"Nope. Not happy." Eventually the Boxster continued on down the street, but Flynn was no longer smiling.

"You okay?" She hadn't considered how the mob scene might have affected him. He wasn't used to that kind of pressure.

"Sure, I'm fine. But I don't know how you stand it."

"It's the price of fame. I'm willing to pay it, most of the time. I just wish Leon hadn't decided to turn our meeting today into a media feeding frenzy. Maybe he's ticked because I wouldn't tell him why I was meeting you." Or maybe Leon was making points with Sandi the publicist so he could score, but Zoe decided not to mention that possibility to Flynn.

"For that matter, you didn't tell *me* why we're meeting," he said.

And she knew how he must have hated that. Flynn liked to have all available info before he did anything. "I will tell you, but not on the phone. Any ideas where we could go?"

He paused. "How about Venice Beach? You park by the boardwalk and stay in the car with the air on. I'll get us some hot dogs and we'll eat in the car."

"Flynn, I wanted to buy you a nice meal."

"Why, so you could soften me up?"

Bingo. He was too smart for her, but then, she'd always known that. Normally she liked that he was smart. "Okay, hot dogs in the car then."

"What do you like on your hot dog?"

"Everything."

This time he really did laugh. "Somehow I'm not surprised."

Later, as Flynn ordered the hot dogs—one with everything and one with only ketchup and mustard—he speculated as to what Zoe wanted from him. Maybe she needed to find a way around her current studio contract in order to do some work for an independent production company. If so, he'd have to burn the midnight oil to find a loophole for her. But she could have asked that over the phone.

Maybe she planned to fire him and wanted to tell him personally out of consideration for their five-year association. God, he hoped not. The timing couldn't be worse, now that he was seriously thinking about marrying Kristen. He wanted to present a healthy financial picture when he proposed, and Zoe was his biggest client.

He had his game plan regarding Kristen all mapped out. He'd booked a hotel on Catalina Island for her visit next week. Assuming all went well, he'd propose to her there and ask her to take a year's sabbatical from Harvard and live with him in LA. He thought she'd agree to that.

Carrying the hot dogs in a bag and two bottles of chilled water in his other hand, he approached the Civic from the passenger side. Zoe looked so out of place in the driver's seat of that car. With her pricey sunglasses and her red hair cut in the trademark shaggy style she'd made famous, she belonged in a Boxster.

She was his complete opposite—a person who basked in the limelight and loved all the luxuries her star power could buy. Her seaside home in Malibu would make three of his town house in Pasadena, and the town house wasn't exactly a hovel. But he did live below his means.

Like Zoe, he'd grown up poor, but unlike her, he was determined to squirrel away enough cash to guarantee he'd never be poor again. Zoe spent most of what she made, on either herself or others. Although he'd never seen her tax returns, he knew what she earned because he reviewed her contracts. And because he had a fair idea of her lifestyle and a good estimate of real estate values in Malibu, he could safely say that Zoe wasn't putting away a whole lot for the future.

He tapped on the window with a water bottle to get her to unlock the passenger door.

She leaned over and pulled up the button. "See how fast I learn?" she said as he climbed into the car.

"I shouldn't have laughed." He handed over her hot dog and one of the water bottles. "I'm sure you're not the only person who expects power locks to be standard."

"No kidding. Come to think of it, you might be the only car owner in LA with manual locks." She pushed her sunglasses to the top of her head and smiled at him. "But the car switcheroo worked great. Thanks. And thanks for the food."

"Not exactly Spago, though, is it?" He set the bag with his hot dog on the floor of the car so he could open the glove compartment and replace his prescription shades with his regular glasses.

"I don't always eat at fancy restaurants, you know." She braced the water bottle between her knees and unwrapped her hot dog.

"No?" He snapped the glove compartment shut and put on his glasses. The first object in his line of vision was her water bottle, which was propped between two of the most photographed knees in the world. Zoe had great legs, and right now she was wearing a denim micromini that showed off a good part of those assets.

Flynn hadn't spent much time admiring Zoe's legs, because their meetings had always taken place at either his office, where she was on the other side of his desk, or a restaurant, where those legs were under a table. He'd never sat in a parked car with her where he had the perfect position to ogle. And he shouldn't be ogling, not even a little bit. In another week he'd probably be engaged.

"Sometimes I order from fancy restaurants and eat at home," she said.

As he brought his attention abruptly back to her face, he had the uncomfortable feeling that she'd caught him staring. "Which pretty much cuts out Taco Bell," he said, trying to sound cool.

"Pretty much." She laughed and opened her mouth for her hot dog.

Flynn was bombarded with an explicit sexual image. Never in his wildest dreams had he expected this hot dog–sharing experience to make him think of oral sex. He'd come up with the suggestion as something quick and easy, something unlikely to attract anyone's attention, so Zoe would have the opportunity to talk with him privately.

Maybe that was the problem. He'd never been in a totally private setting with Zoe. Outside the car the usual hurly-burly crowd of Rollerbladers and beach bums mixed and mingled, ignoring them completely. In the air-conditioned interior of the car he and Zoe seemed to be in their own little world, wrapped in a disquieting intimacy. That had to explain why he was watching her eating a hot dog and thinking about sex.

Worse yet, he was responding. He tucked his own water bottle between his legs and hoped the coolness would have some effect. Then he pulled his hot dog out of the bag at his feet and unwrapped it. Unfortunately, he couldn't seem to eat it without noticing that the bun cradling the hot dog could easily represent something other than a bun.

See, that's what he got for having a girlfriend who lived three thousand miles away, one he hadn't seen in six months. Despite their busy schedules, they should have found a way to get together. He hadn't thought he was feeling sexually needy, but this whole episode was proving him wrong.

"Are you busy this weekend?" Zoe asked.

With his thoughts still firmly in the gutter, Flynn choked on his hot dog.

"Oh, dear. Drink some water." She twisted the cap from her bottle and handed it to him.

He took her water and drank. Surely she hadn't been angling for a date or anything. Flynn was the last person in the world she'd want to be seen with socially. Besides, she had a romantic interest. According to all reports, she and her costar in the new movie were an item. Pictures of her with Trace Edwards were plastered all over the supermarket tabloids.

After coughing and clearing his throat, Flynn readjusted his glasses and glanced over at her. He was back in control. "Sorry about that." He gave her his unopened water. "Here. We'll trade."

"If you insist, although I'm sure no self-respecting germ would dare invade your system." She took the water. "So, as I was saying, I have a proposition for you."

The discussion wasn't improving. He tried to stay

calm but decided against another bite of the hot dog at this juncture. "Such as?"

She turned to him, bringing all the beauty of that fabulous face into play. Those turquoise-blue eyes had bewitched millions, and those full lips had made grown men weep with longing. If Helen of Troy had launched a thousand ships, Zoe could launch five thousand, easy.

"I desperately need some help," she said. "I'm hoping you don't have any plans and can spend Friday night through Sunday night working with me."

A man would have to be made of stone to refuse a woman who looked like Zoe. Flynn wasn't made of stone. But first he had to make sure of the details. He pulled an ultrathin PDA from his breast pocket and flipped it open.

He loved this little technological toy, partly because it was state-of-the-art and sheathed in space-age titanium, but mostly because Zoe had given it to him for Christmas. It was a perfect gift, which meant she understood him, and that was gratifying. "Are we talking about day after tomorrow?"

"That's right. I know it's short notice."

He checked his electronic day planner. "It is, but I don't have anything pressing. Nothing I couldn't cancel." Kristen had a conference in Chicago, so he'd planned to spend the weekend running errands. He shouldn't be so happy to be spending time with Zoe, but he'd work on that problem. He closed the PDA and returned it to his pocket. "What do you need?"

"I've booked a little cabin in Long Shaft, and I wondered if you would go there with me so that I can—"

"Excuse me—*Long Shaft*? Where the hell is that?"

"Northern California. We'll fly to Sacramento and then you'll rent a car. Can you go?"

He felt as if he'd walked into the middle of a movie. Nothing made sense. "Why? Why would you want the two of us to go to a cabin in a place called Long Shaft? And what kind of a name for a town is that, anyway?"

"Long Shaft is an old mining town. This place is totally off the map, and I don't want anyone to know we're there. I . . . uh . . . need some coaching."

"On what? Trust me, I'm not a dramatic coach, and I can't think of a single thing I know how to do that would come in handy in your line of work, unless you've suddenly accepted a role that involves contract law."

"No, that's not it." She seemed uncertain, as if she couldn't figure out exactly how to explain herself. "I don't suppose you saw two copies of a script lying on the passenger seat of the Boxster."

"No. I was too busy making sure the paparazzi didn't vandalize the car."

"I'm auditioning for a part next week. It's a romantic comedy with some action/adventure thrown in, and the female lead is a chemist."

He still didn't get it. "I passed chemistry, but I wouldn't say that's my area of expertise. If you're looking for a chemist, maybe you should consider someone from UCLA. I can't imagine that you'd have to be secretive about it, either. Any chemistry prof down there would love to—"

"It's not the chemistry part that I'm worried about. So long as I follow the script I'll sound like I know my chemistry. It's the character of Vera who worries me. She isn't like any of the others I've played. As you might have noticed, all my roles so far have been glamorous and sexy."

"And that works, Zoe." It was working on him right this minute. The conversation was weird to begin with. All their meetings until now had centered around contract clauses and legalese, and he didn't think she'd ever been dressed quite this provocatively for those meetings, either.

He had trouble concentrating when she smelled so good and looked so incredible. She did amazing things for a low-necked blouse. He'd known that all along, but he'd never allowed himself to fully acknowledge Zoe's sexual appeal. Today he couldn't seem to help himself.

"I'm in a rut," she said.

"It's a damned nice rut, too. You're a top earner at the box office. Why would you want to mess with success?"

She took a deep breath. "Because I'm tired of low-budget movies where I carry the whole thing but get no respect for my work."

He'd become so engrossed in how a deep breath affected her cleavage that he had trouble absorbing her comment. Belatedly he realized that this was a damned serious topic that could have life-changing results. She was his top client and he needed to focus.

Clicking back to lawyer mode, he started gathering information. "What kind of respect are you after?"

"The kind that comes from working with A-list actors like Nicolas Cage, who might take the male lead, and Steven Spielberg, who's directing."

"I see."

"That's the league I want to be in. I finally figured out that if I keep playing myself in these throwaway films, I'll never get there. This project, if I bring it off, could win me a Golden Globe."

No doubt about it, she was shifting gears and he needed to stay alert. "Have you talked to anybody at the studio about this?" He could imagine some major resistance to this idea of hers.

"I have, and basically they don't expect me to have a good audition for the part because this isn't normally what I do. They want somebody like Holly Hunter or Jodie Foster."

"That's tough competition."

She leaned her head against the seat and blew out a breath. "Tell me about it. That's why the studio is willing to let me go for it and fall on my face. If I'm no good, they don't have to cast me, so they're playing along, certain I'll be awful."

"How about Leon?"

"Leon thinks I'm out of my mind, but he expects me to go down in flames, too, so he's not terribly worried. I'm determined not to fail. And I want you to help me get inside this character's head, show me how to act the way she'd act so I can nail the audition."

"I don't understand how I can do that."

"It's very simple." She paused. "No offense, Flynn, but I want you to teach me how to be a nerd."

Chapter Two

From Flynn's expression, Zoe knew she should have found a more delicate way to broach the subject. No guy really wanted to be called a nerd even if he knew that's what he was. "I apologize. I've offended you."

"Not at all." The tight lines around his mouth said otherwise.

She scrambled to find some way to repair the damage. "You're not a complete nerd," she said. "I mean, there are lots of cool things about you."

"Name one." Behind his black-framed glasses, his gray eyes gleamed as he issued the challenge. He looked well and truly pissed.

She searched frantically for an example and remembered the image of him driving the Boxster, but of course that was her cool car, not his. "Well, you . . . um . . . wear prescription sunglasses instead of attaching that flip-up kind to your regular glasses." It was the best she could come up with on short notice. "That's very cool!"

He snorted. "Even a dweeb like me wouldn't wear the flip-ups. But prescription glasses aren't cool. To be cool I'd have to wear contacts, so I wouldn't need prescription shades in the first place. But I think contacts are too much trouble."

"Actually, I like your glasses." She surprised herself by saying so, but it was true. They gave him a sincere, scholarly air that she found endearing. "They suit you."

"You mean they suit my nerd image."

"There's nothing wrong with your look. You're true to yourself. You know who you are."

His expression softened. "I think you do, too. And you're definitely not a nerd."

"I can learn to be a nerd. By playing someone very different from me, I'll prove I have what it takes to work with top directors and actors. Getting this part would be an excellent career move."

He studied her for several long seconds.

"You don't see me doing it, either, do you?" How depressing to think that no one believed in her acting ability. She did, though. At sixteen she'd deliberately taken the part of a hard-drinking, meddling old biddy in the school play. She'd nailed that role, too.

But from the day of her first Hollywood audition, she'd been typecast as the bombshell. She loved the fame and fortune, but she hated the assumption that a glamourpuss was automatically an airhead who couldn't act. Because of that prejudice she never got to work with the big names and she'd never win any awards. She craved both.

"I don't know if you can do it or not," Flynn said.

"Neither do I," she admitted in a moment of brutal honesty. She'd played herself for so long she might be unable to change. Maybe she'd lost that nugget of genuine talent she'd had back in high school. "But I have to try. Will you help me?"

"Why can't we just work on this at your house? Why go all the way up to this Long Shaft place?"

She took it as a good sign that he was asking questions instead of turning her down flat. Maybe she had a shot at making this work, but she'd have to be straight with him. "A couple of reasons. First of all, this won't be easy, so I will need maximum input from you. I'm talking about total immersion, an all-weekend marathon."

Flynn blinked as if she'd said something shocking.

Then she figured out why. He might think total immersion meant being her boy toy for the weekend in addition to coaching her on all things nerdy. Although Zoe didn't play the game that way, the tabloids had helped give movie stars that kind of rep, so Flynn could easily misunderstand her intentions.

"The cabin has two bedrooms," she said quickly. "I wouldn't want you to get the wrong idea about what I'm asking."

His startled expression disappeared. "I assumed there would be two bedrooms."

No, you didn't. "Of course."

"I mean, you and Trace Edwards are practically. . . ."

"Yes, we are. Practically." Practically nothing to each other. Their high-profile dating was all about publicity. She'd started worrying that Trace was getting emotionally involved, though, and she needed to find a way to call a halt to that, because she felt only friendship for the guy.

"And as for me," Flynn continued, "as it happens, I'm committed to someone."

Knock her over with a feather boa. "Is that right?" She stared at him in astonishment. "You never said! Who is she? Anybody I know?" Come to think of it, she had no clue about his private life, except that he was single. Of course he must date, but she'd never thought of him as having a steady girlfriend. The idea added a whole new dimension to Flynn's personality.

"You wouldn't know her. She's a law professor at Harvard."

"Perfect!" How fake and jolly that sounded, but she didn't dare say what she really thought, that two law professors in the same relationship sounded as exciting as test-driving a golf cart. "You must have tons of things in common." Tons of boring things.

"Uh-huh."

"Do you have a picture?" She found herself feeling a wee bit territorial, which was stupid. Flynn certainly had a right to a life apart from his dealings with her.

"No picture. But she's coming out here for a visit next week, so I'm sure we'll take pictures then. Maybe you'd like to meet her."

"That would be nice." Not really. The more Zoe thought about this development, the less she approved. Long-distance courtships usually ended with someone moving. She didn't want that someone to be Flynn. "You're not thinking of living back there, are you?"

"No. At least not at the moment."

Well, that sucked. He hadn't promised to stay in California until hell froze over, which was the kind of statement of intent Zoe was looking for. Imagining Flynn leaving her life was unsettling. Extremely unsettling. She'd never realized before how much she counted on his solid presence.

"So what's the other reason for heading off to Long Shaft?" he asked.

"Oh." She'd become totally derailed by the prospect of Flynn involved in a cross-country love affair. "Vanity, mostly," she said. "I don't want anyone to know how hard I worked at this."

He nodded. "In case it doesn't go well."

"Or in case it goes extremely well." She struggled to hide her irritation. Honestly, nobody had faith in her. "Either way, I don't want them to see me sweat. Using you as a coach would be our little secret. I hope you're okay with that."

He stared at her. "You think I'd want to tell everyone I'm the guy who taught you how to be a nerd?"

"Um, no, guess not. Good point." She hadn't appreciated before how touchy this subject might be. "So here's my plan. We fly up on different airlines and go to the cabin separately."

"Won't you be recognized and followed?"

"I'm working on that. First of all, Leon won't know a thing about this. Most of my public mob scenes are courtesy of Leon and the new publicist, Sandi. I'll be recognized on the airplane, but I'm taking some nerd clothes and I'll change in the airplane bathroom."

"Nerd clothes."

"Yeah, you know—polyester, drab colors, out of style . . ." She trailed off as she realized that she'd just described his white shirt, mud-colored slacks, and brown and white striped tie. "Functional stuff," she amended. "Sturdy clothes."

Amusement glinted in his eyes. "Now you're getting the idea."

And suddenly the tables were turned. He was the one passing judgment, and she felt the need to defend her choices. "But clothes can be a fun thing! They can lift your spirits! Colors have an effect on people. They've done studies on it!"

"I'm sure they have, but if you want to transform yourself into a nerd, you'll have to give up worrying about your clothes. Because we don't care. It's not a priority with us."

Zoe blew out a breath. "You're right. And I will give up worrying about clothes this weekend." She couldn't imagine it—packing a suitcase with things she didn't care about—but she'd try. Even her nightgowns would be boring, not that Flynn would see that, but she wanted to stay in character all the time, even when she was buck naked, not that Flynn would see that, either. . . .

But they would be living in the same cabin. At some time, they would each be naked. Maybe not at the same time and definitely not in the same room, but there would be disrobing going on. It was an interesting thought. More than interesting. She wondered what kind of a body Flynn had, and she'd *never* wondered about that before.

"Okay, so you're changing into nerd clothes in the airplane bathroom. Then what?"

She pulled her thoughts away from Flynn, naked, to deal with Flynn fully clothed and sitting next to her in the car. They had more details to settle. "If I'm dressed differently, I should make it through the terminal okay, and a friend's picking me up at the airport and taking me to the cabin."

"You have a friend in Long Shaft?"

"Strange as it sounds, yes. We were both cheerleaders at the same high school in Sacramento. And our last names are close in the alphabet, so we ended up together on class seating charts. She's relocated to Long Shaft, and she's the one who suggested the cabin. It's rented in her name."

He nodded. "That makes sense."

"She's been very helpful. She's volunteered to help keep the residents from knowing who I am." Zoe felt lucky to have reconnected with Margo Taggart after all these years. The last few months of e-mails and phone calls had been like old home week. Margo had followed Zoe's career with enthusiasm, apparently, and was only too happy to do this favor.

"Sounds as if you've thought of everything."

"I have your airline ticket and the car rental arrangements tucked inside your copy of the script." She mentally crossed her fingers. He seemed to be going for it.

"My copy?"

"I thought we should both have a copy to read. That way you'll know what I'm going for. I also thought . . ." She hesitated, not at all confident that he'd like what she had in mind. "It would be so great if you'd read through some scenes with me."

He stiffened up immediately. "I'm no actor, Zoe. Not even close. There's a reason I got into contract law. I had no desire to be a trial lawyer and spend hours in the courtroom."

She didn't try to argue with him about whether he could act or not. Chances were he'd be terrible, but that was okay. "It doesn't matter. I just need someone to read the lines so I can deliver mine in response."

"So no pressure to read them well?"

"None whatsoever. We can read a page or two once we get there. If you really hate doing it, then we'll stop." At least she had him debating whether he'd read the script out loud with her instead of debating the merits of going, period. "So you'll go to Long Shaft with me?"

He didn't answer right away. Finally, he nodded. "I will, on one condition."

"You name it." Victory! "If you want your hourly rate, I'll gladly pay it."

"That's not the condition. I wouldn't feel right charging an hourly rate when I'm not giving you legal advice. My condition is that I get to tell Kristen what we're doing. I think she has a right to know."

"Kristen is her name?"

"Yes. Kristen Keebler."

"Like the crackers?"

"Uh-huh, although she's not related to that Keebler, and she hates that reference. She was called Kristen Crackers all through school. I'm sure she'll be happy to get rid of that last name when we . . . well, assuming that we . . ." He paused and cleared his throat.

Marriage. Yikes. "You're really serious about her, huh?"

"I am. She's heading to a conference in Chicago this weekend, so I'd like to call and tell her about this before she leaves."

Zoe didn't like the idea at all. She didn't know Kristen Crackers and hadn't the foggiest if she could be trusted not to blab. "How about telling her after we get back?"

"I don't want to take that chance. What if, in spite of your disguise, somebody recognizes you and takes a picture of us together? You know what the tabloid headlines would look like. And Kristen would be completely unprepared. She'd feel betrayed, and I wouldn't blame her. For that matter, I think you should tell Trace, too."

"I'm definitely not telling Trace." He'd been acting possessive lately, and unless she told him all about the project, he might throw a jealous fit and bring in an army of reporters to break up whatever he might think was going on. She should clear the air with him, but not right now. He'd get suspicious of her reasons.

"That's up to you. It's your relationship on the line. But I have to tell Kristen. That's my condition." He pressed his lips together and set his jaw, which made him look almost soldierlike.

In the five years she'd known Flynn, she'd noticed in passing that he was an attractive guy—thick dark hair, squarish jaw, good cheekbones, and a well-proportioned nose. But at the moment he looked more than okay. He'd morphed into absolutely hot.

She'd never seen him take a resolute stand before, and as he stuck up for his lady love he was extremely cute. Zoe felt a pang of envy and wished she could be the woman whose tender feelings he was protecting.

Yet she was reluctant to have him give away their hiding place. "I don't mean to insult Kristen, but after many years in the business I've seen how normal people get goofy when it comes to movie stars. I would hate for her to accidentally spill the beans during the conference cocktail hour."

"She won't. I'd trust her with my—"

"Okay, okay." Now Zoe was truly envious. No man had ever said he'd trust her with his life, not even in a script, and she didn't want to hear Flynn saying it about Kristen, either. She was starting to take an unreasonable dislike to the woman. "So tell her. But can you keep the details vague?"

"No."

Zoe sighed. "Oh, all right. Tell her everything. Read her parts of the script if you want. Take pictures with your cell phone and beam them to her cell phone. Just so you understand that she could sink the whole project with one careless word."

"It won't happen."

"Then we have a deal?" She held her breath.

"I guess so, if you're convinced I can help. I have serious doubts about it, myself."

Turning off the motor, she handed him the keys. "I have no doubts whatsoever." She picked up her cell phone from the dash. "Come on. Let's get your script and tickets from the Boxster. Then we can each be on our way. I can't speak for you, but I have plenty to do before Friday."

"I have a few loose ends to tie up myself." He took the keys and opened the car door.

"Flynn, before you go." She put out a hand to stop him and ended up touching his arm. He felt warm and surprisingly muscular under the fabric of his dress shirt. When he turned back toward her, she immediately ended the contact. She really didn't want him to get the wrong idea. "Listen, thank you. Thank you so much. I appreciate this more than you know."

He smiled at her. "You can thank me at the Golden Globes. Until then, we don't know if I'll be an asset or a liability."

"You're already an asset." And she was only beginning to understand how great an asset he was. Funny how much more appealing a man looked when some other woman had staked a claim. Not that Zoe was romantically interested in Flynn. But he was far more intriguing to her than he had been a couple of hours ago.

Flynn dodged a Frisbee as he walked over to the Porsche with Zoe to get his copy of the script. Venice Beach was its usual crazy self, filled with bodybuilders and bathing beauties of every sexual persuasion. Most members of the crowd were hooked up to their own private music system, but a few old boom boxes hung around pouring rap into the atmosphere and obliterating the sounds of the surf and the gulls wheeling overhead.

Flynn stood out like a sore thumb in the array of color and noise, but he liked the place anyway. He'd never stopped to examine why, either. It might be the same reason he'd specialized in entertainment law. It wasn't his world, but it sure was fun to watch . . . from a safe distance.

That safe distance had just been eliminated in regard to Zoe. He still couldn't believe he'd agreed to spend the weekend with her. But at least now he knew exactly what she thought of him. He was her token nerd.

He hadn't been called a nerd since college. Yeah, he supposed the label still fit, but he'd stopped thinking of it years ago. Was Kristen a nerd, too? Probably, which was why they belonged together. Still, he wasn't entirely happy knowing Zoe's true opinion of him, even if her opinion was pretty much on target with the truth.

The weekend should prove . . . intriguing. At least he wouldn't be immersed in some Hollywood pleasure palace, which might have freaked him out. Instead he'd be staying in a place that would feel reasonably familiar if it lived up to its name. It might turn out to be something like the ratty Arizona mining town where he'd grown up.

Only these days his hometown was a cutesy tourist trap, and his retired father regularly dressed as a gun-slinger and joined his buddies to stage shoot-outs on Main Street for the greenhorns. His mother wore hoop-skirts and ran a bed-and-breakfast. Their Wild West schtick earned them a comfortable living, which was a good thing, because the mine had gone bankrupt and left them with no retirement income.

Flynn had tried to give them money, but they wouldn't take it. He supposed in their shoes he wouldn't have, either. But their situation was another reason that he was so big on saving money. If he had to stage shoot-outs or run a bed-and-breakfast in order to make it through his golden years, he'd starve to death.

Zoe reached the car and turned back to him. "Keys?"

He reached in his pocket, pulled them out, and handed them to her.

"Thanks for putting up the top. This sun turns the seats into little hot plates. I would have roasted my tush getting back in."

"No problem." He'd never considered doing anything else. You didn't leave a Porsche sitting at Venice Beach with the top down. Anything could happen. But he supposed not roasting Zoe's tush was also a consideration. The world's male population would likely thank him for protecting Zoe's tush.

As she beeped open the locks and leaned down toward the passenger door, he got a full view of that valuable fanny and his mouth went dry. He'd better get a grip. Once they were tucked inside that cabin together, he'd be spending a lot more time within touching distance, and he absolutely could not be caught reacting. He'd just told her he was in a relationship, for God's sake. Now he needed to make sure he acted like he was committed to another woman.

Zoe turned and handed him the script she'd picked up from the seat of the car. "Here you go. I'll try to glance through it before we get there, but I might not have time. You might not, either."

Flynn looked at the title page. "*The Billion-Dollar Pill.* What's it about?"

"I read the treatment. She's working on a drug that combines weight loss, antiaging, and sexual performance in one pill."

"Whoa."

"Yeah, it's kind of a spoof. I need to be an over-the-top nerd. Anyway, the company she's working for thinks she might sell out to a competitor, so they hire a bodyguard, supposedly to protect her but really to keep an eye on her and make sure she doesn't try to smuggle the formula."

"Interesting." And he'd be reading the part of the bodyguard, no doubt. "Is she going to smuggle it?"

"No, she's very ethical and she's insulted by the sur-veillance. Plus, she thinks the bodyguard might be a dou-ble agent trying to steal the formula. Then they become lovers, which complicates the whole thing."

He wondered what kind of scenes she'd want to read aloud. Probably not a love scene. If she picked a love scene, he was in serious trouble, but she wouldn't pick a love scene.

They'd probably read an opening scene, not a love scene. She wouldn't expect him to get into that mushy stuff. "Sounds like a good story," he said.

"It's my ticket, Flynn. I feel it in my bones." Her en-thusiasm for this career move was contagious.

"I think you're right." Maybe at first he'd been insulted by her request for geek tutoring, but that had worn off. Now he felt damned good knowing that she'd turned to him. Beginning Friday night, he vowed to be all the nerd she needed.

Chapter Three

Flynn didn't have a chance to look at the script again until he was on the plane to Sacramento. The first scene opened with Vera Parsons working late at night in her lab as her bodyguard Tony Bennetti showed up for the first time. Flynn tried to picture himself reading it with Zoe.

TONY

I'm Bennetti. I guess Peterson told you I was coming.

VERA

He told me. And it's a total waste of company funds and your time.

TONY

Looks to me like you need babysitting. The door was unlocked. I could have been anybody.

VERA

I was expecting you. But you bring up a valid point.
You could still be anybody.

Tony looks her over with an obvious male appraisal.

TONY

Yeah. Maybe I'm some weird guy who gets turned on
by flat-chested women wearing white lab coats and
sensible oxfords. Maybe all I can think about is throwing you down on that table and steaming up your
wire-rimmed glasses.

VERA

See this beaker of liquid? One flick of my wrist
and you'll be needing a genital transplant.

TONY

No shit?

VERA

No shit. Now go sit somewhere where I can't see you,
hear you, or even smell you. I have work to do.

Flynn stared at the page. He was very afraid this
movie was all about sex. And Zoe wanted him to do a
read-through with her. Closing the cover of the script,
he stared out the window of the plane at the fading afternoon light. He'd told Kristen this was strictly a business
trip. Which it was. So how come he already felt guilty as
hell?

Probably because Kristen trusted him so completely.
That would be his buddy Josh's doing. A year ago, before

Flynn and Kristen had ever met, Josh had been doing the matchmaker thing. Flynn guessed that Josh was still at it, telling Kristen that she'd latched onto a paragon. Flynn hated to think what Josh would make of this weekend, if he knew.

Zoe flew first class and bought herself two seats for the privacy. So maybe it wasn't the nerd thing to do, but she didn't want to carry this transformation too far. With two seats to herself, she didn't have to worry about a nosy neighbor and she had a chance, finally, to start reading the script.

As she scanned the first scene, she started to laugh. The flat-chested part would be hard to pull off, but she'd packed an Ace bandage and would practice binding her boobs. She'd special-ordered some glasses with clear lenses, and luckily they were wire frames.

She flipped to the second scene, which took place in Vera's apartment after she and Tony had left the lab.

TONY

Someone followed you home.

VERA

It was you, and you were tailgating.

TONY

I stayed close so that the car tailing you couldn't get between us.

VERA

It was probably one of my neighbors coming home from the convenience store, but you have to turn it into a stalking incident to justify your existence.

TONY

Suit yourself.

VERA

Tomorrow I'm calling Peterson. Either he gets rid of you or I'll go on strike. I can't live like this, being shadowed at every turn.

TONY

I was completely quiet while you were working.

VERA

You were not. I could hear you breathing.

TONY

Not used to hearing a real man breathe, are you, babe?

VERA

I'm going to bed.

Vera walks toward her bedroom.

TONY

Since that didn't sound much like an invitation—

VERA

It most certainly wasn't!

TONY

Where am I supposed to sleep?

Tony hoists his duffel bag over his shoulder.

VERA

That's not my problem.

Vera walks into her bedroom, cries out, and backs into the living room. Tony draws his gun and moves into a crouch.

TONY

What is it?

VERA

Someone's . . . someone's been in there.

Vera glances at him in horror.

You have a gun?

TONY

The better to shoot the bad guys, little girl. Now stand back and let me do my job.

Zoe closed the script with a smile. A flat-chested chemistry professor with an attitude. For the first time in years, Zoe was excited about a part. And her preparation would begin now.

Taking her carry-on from the seat beside her, she headed for the bathroom. She was Superman, ducking into a phone booth. But halfway through her quick-change act, stripped to her underwear, she wondered what she'd been thinking. The plan had sounded logical when she'd described it to Flynn. She'd pictured airplane bathrooms as being bigger.

Maybe they used to be bigger, before deregulation. After all, what about the Mile-High Club? That involved two people doing something very aerobic in here. She glanced around. No way. Two midgets, maybe, but if Flynn happened to be standing there, they'd never in a million years be able to—

Holy crap, where had that thought come from? The script must have started her thinking about sex, and of course Flynn would be reading the part of Tony, so that explained why a picture of Flynn in the airplane bathroom with her had surfaced. And thoughts weren't deeds, or something to that effect.

Scmeone tapped on the bathroom door. "Ms. Tarleton? Are you okay?"

Cripes. Naturally they'd be worried about her. Movie stars were probably considered loose cannons, capable of all sorts of weirdness. The airlines might have banned smoking in the bathrooms, but that left snorting a few lines of coke or swallowing a handful of happy pills.

"I'm fine!" she called through the door. "Be out in a sec."

She was aware of the flight attendant standing right outside the door, listening. Because Zoe tried so hard to be quiet putting on the beige polyester pantsuit, she fell down. Well, not all the way down, which was impossible in the minuscule space, but she banged around a lot.

"Ms. Tarleton?" The flight attendant sounded very worried now.

"Ha, ha," Zoe said. "Dropped my bowling ball."

"Your *bowling ball*?"

Zoe unfastened the latch and stepped out, nearly colliding with the flight attendant, who seemed to have no sense of humor whatsoever. "That was a joke. I decided to change clothes and that was the only place to do it."

"Oh." The flight attendant gave her a once-over. "Nice . . . uh . . . outfit."

"Thanks." Holding her carry-on in one hand, Zoe straightened her jacket with the other. She'd bought the outfit at a resale shop and it was two sizes too big for her. She'd had to cinch up the waist of the pants with a safety pin. Instead of her cute little pointy-toed shoes, she now wore crepe-soled lace-ups, only they weren't laced up. Some things could not be accomplished in an airplane bathroom.

Trailing her shoelaces, she made it back to her seat and managed to finish the job by turning sideways and propping her feet on the empty seat beside her. When she noticed the flight attendant still staring with her mouth open, she gave her a big smile. "Ah, now I can be comfortable again."

The attendant closed her mouth. "Right. It must be tough maintaining that image all the time." Then she bustled away.

No, it was *this* image that would be tough to maintain. Zoe hadn't felt so frumpy since fourth grade when she'd been forced to wear her cousin's hand-me-downs. Soon after that Zoe had started babysitting to earn money for her own clothes. She'd looked good ever since, if she did say so herself.

But this weekend wasn't about looking good. She had to keep reminding herself of that, especially because she would be not looking good in front of a guy. That really chafed. Maybe she had no romantic designs on Flynn, but greeting him while wearing this pantsuit would not be easy on her ego.

Then she thought of something. What if Flynn liked her *better* in these nerdy clothes? After all, he'd told her two days ago that clothes didn't matter to him. That meant he wouldn't care what she wore, might not even notice that this outfit bagged in all the wrong places. Considering that, she felt relieved.

Taking a mirror from her purse, she did her best to check her outfit, although she could only see parts of herself, not the whole presentation. The clothes were okay, but she needed to do something different with her hair. A bun would be good, but she'd never accomplish that with all the layers. A ponytail might be possible.

Pushing the button located above her head, she summoned the still-wary flight attendant. "Do you have a rubber band anywhere? I'd like to put my hair in a ponytail." Philippe would kill her for subjecting his oh-so-artistic and expensive cut to the tortures of a rubber band, but tough times called for tough measures.

The flight attendant looked at Zoe as if she'd landed from Mars. "Uh, let me see what I can find." Soon she returned holding a handful of twist ties. "This was the best I could do."

"That's great, thanks." Zoe took the twist ties, put two together, and managed to get most of her hair into the ponytail. Twist ties might be even better, more geeky, as if she cared so little how she looked that she'd put her hair up with the same things she'd used to hold her sandwich bag closed.

As the plane touched down she tissued off most of her makeup and pulled her clear-lens glasses out of her purse. One last look in the mirror convinced her that she'd never looked this ridiculous, not even in fourth grade. Nobody would guess she was a world-famous movie star, and that was exactly what she was after.

She exited the plane, walked the length of the terminal, and even retrieved her luggage without a single person stopping her for an autograph. It felt strange. In one way being anonymous was liberating, but in another way she missed being recognized. Perhaps she was more addicted to fame than she cared to admit.

Margo had wanted to meet her in the terminal, but Zoe had thought getting picked up right outside Baggage Claim would be less obvious and allow her a quick getaway in case someone noticed who she was. Except no one did notice. She hadn't realized how critical clothes, hair, and makeup were to her star image. That was humbling.

Pulling her rolling suitcase behind her, she stepped out of the terminal and looked for Margo's green Taurus. Zoe had been thinking your ordinary factory green, but when a car arrived with a paint job no factory would ever offer, Zoe knew in her bones Margo was behind the wheel. Apparently Margo still loved the neons.

Zoe put on a big smile and waved as if she'd just spotted her limo arriving. Who cared if Margo had decided to paint her old car the color of a glow stick? Zoe was determined to concentrate on the friendship, not the trappings.

She wished they'd been closer in high school. If she'd known Margo better back then, she would never have accepted Rob's invitation to the prom without checking with Margo first. But Rob had been on Zoe's dream list all through high school, and how was she to know he was a liar when he swore Margo had dumped *him*? The jerk.

When the fifteenth high school reunion notice had arrived at the studio, Zoe had seen Margo's name as committee chair. The guilt pangs had been as sharp as if the prom had happened yesterday. Zoe hadn't meant to steal Margo's boyfriend, but she'd been the reason Margo had missed her senior prom.

Zoe wasn't about to attend the reunion, but she'd gotten in touch with Margo anyway. And Margo, forgiving person that she was, didn't hold a grudge about Rob and the prom. She'd moved on and was engaged to a great guy. Zoe looked forward to meeting him.

Reminiscing with Margo for the past several months had been fun. Zoe hadn't kept track of any of her high school friends, and once she'd moved her folks to LA, no one had an easy way to contact her. Margo was a blast from the past, a chance to feel seventeen again.

Margo tooted the horn and swerved over against the curb. Leaping from the car, she pranced around to the sidewalk in pink UGG boots. Although Margo's makeup was perfect as always, Zoe worked to hide her shock at what fifteen years and at least fifty extra pounds had done to the Margo she remembered.

Her former classmate sported an eighties perm, a pink vinyl mini, a tight silver blouse, and a rainbow of plastic bangle bracelets. She would have made Abba proud. "Zoe!" She hugged her fiercely. "Are those your nerd clothes? Awesome!"

Zoe hugged back. So what if Margo had put on some weight? Zoe understood the battle of the bulge after a girl turned thirty. If not for her personal trainer and a cook who could do wonders with a low-carb menu, she'd be a balloon in no time herself.

No doubt working in a diner put Margo constantly in the path of greasy, fattening food. Zoe was lucky enough to be in a different place. Besides, appearance was unimportant between friends. Margo had a big heart and loved reliving old times. Zoe cherished that.

"Let me get your suitcase." Margo grabbed Zoe's rolling bag, opened the back door of the car, and heaved the suitcase onto the seat.

"Hey, I could have done that."

"Absolutely not." Margo slammed the door and grinned at her. "You're the star!"

Zoe put her finger to her lips. "Shhh."

"Oh, right. Sorry about that. But I doubt that anybody heard me. I'm just so excited to see you again that I forgot for a minute that you're trying to stay anonymous."

"No problem." Zoe smiled back at her. "I'm probably being paranoid."

"We'll vamoose outta here, and then it won't matter." Margo yanked open the passenger door, which creaked on its hinges. "Climb into my chariot. I just got her painted last week, in your honor. She's showing her age, but what with saving for the wedding, I can't afford a new car."

"Good grief, Margo, you didn't have to get your car painted just for me."

"You coming was a good excuse. Don't you love the color?"

"It really pops." Zoe sat on the lavender terry-cloth seat covers and reminded herself that this car would add to her disguise. "Speaking of the wedding, how is Bob?"

"Oh, the same sweetie as always. He's so excited to meet you, but he's on shift work this weekend, so we'll have to see how it goes."

"I'm excited to meet him, too." Seeing Margo happy with her fiancé would go a long way toward making Zoe feel better about that ugly business with Rob.

"You hungry?" Margo asked as she got behind the wheel, closed her door, and turned the key. The engine coughed, wheezed, and finally caught. "We can swing into a drive-through before we head out."

"No, I'm good." Zoe wanted to make sure they got to

the cabin ahead of Flynn, who would be landing any minute.

"All righty, then." Margo checked her makeup in the rearview mirror before pulling away from the curb. "Long Shaft, here we come. I stocked in some groceries, like you asked me to, so you can fix something once you get there. I'd love to treat you to a meal at the Sasquatch Diner, but you might not want to take a chance on eating in public."

"Sasquatch Diner. Cute name."

"It's sort of a town theme. You'll see. But I don't think you should eat there first thing. See if your disguise works. Love the twist ties in your hair. Nice touch."

"My disguise worked great in the airport. Nobody had a clue who I was." Zoe wasn't as thrilled about that as she'd anticipated.

"Nobody's gonna hear it from me, that's for sure. And I'm the only one besides you and your lawyer who knows you're here."

"Well, that's not quite true. Flynn, that's my lawyer, thought he should tell his girlfriend."

"Uh-oh. You didn't say he had a girlfriend."

"I didn't know until I asked him to come here for the weekend. He insisted Kristen had to know about it. She lives in Massachusetts, but right now she's at a convention in Chicago, and I'm worried that she'll mention it to someone and word will leak out."

"I think you have reason to be worried," Margo said. "You don't even know this person. Is he telling her exactly where you're staying and everything?"

"Yep. All of it. He was afraid if the paparazzi showed up and got a picture of us together, then she'd freak if she saw it in the tabloids."

"Yeah, she probably would. I mean, any woman would

get nervous knowing that her boyfriend's spending the weekend with you. It's only natural."

Guilt from the past whispered in Zoe's ear. She might be forgiven for Rob, but she doubted Margo had forgotten it. "This weekend is totally platonic," she said. "Flynn is the last guy I'd ever want to be involved with, so Kristen has nothing to worry about."

"She'll worry anyway."

"I suppose so. Well, she'll have e-mail and phone contact with Flynn all weekend, so that should help."

"I just hope she doesn't shoot off her mouth and ruin your plan."

"I hope not, either, but Flynn refused to come unless he could tell her, so there's nothing I can do at this point."

"Guess not." Margo drummed on the steering wheel. "I guess he's crucial to the plan."

"He really is." Zoe was still assimilating the new version of Margo. Although she'd packed on some extra pounds, she obviously paid attention to her grooming. Not a single one of her silver-toned nails was chipped, and her brows were perfectly shaped. She wore a medium-sized diamond solitaire on her left hand.

"Have you set a date for the wedding?"

"I'm thinking the first Saturday in June, if that's not too much of a cliché." Margo sounded worried. "Do you think that's too obvious, a June wedding?"

Zoe was touched that Margo wanted her advice. "I'm no expert on weddings, but it's a beautiful month, especially in Northern California." She wondered if there was any way she could go without making the wedding all about her instead of Margo. Maybe not.

"Then if June has the Zoe Tarleton seal of approval,

I'll go with that," Margo said. "So what's it like kissing Viggo Mortensen, anyway?"

"Not bad."

"*Zoe*. What do you mean *not bad,* like it didn't affect you at all! Come on, spill. You can tell me. Were you ready to melt?"

"That was a while back. I'm not sure I can—"

"Oh, come *on*. You don't forget things like that. I mean, *Viggo Mortensen*. Of course he wasn't so famous back then, but still. I'll bet you were a little puddle by the end."

"Okay, I was a little puddle." That wasn't exactly true. Sure, she'd had fun, and because her character was supposed to be hot for Viggo's character, she'd worked up some steam, but it was all in a day's work.

At the very beginning of her career she'd fallen hard for a costar. The resulting affair and train wreck of a breakup had broken her heart, but worse, it had been splashed all over the tabloids. She'd decided right then to stick with fake publicity romances and not let herself in for that kind of misery again.

"I knew it! Viggo Mortensen is a god. He can have me any day of the week. Okay, so is Halle Berry that beautiful or is it all camera angles and makeup?"

"She really is beautiful. Even without makeup."

"That is so not fair!" Margo laughed. "Makes me want to kill her!"

"I know what you mean. I just found out that without my makeup I don't turn a single head. By the way, have you heard from any of the other girls on the squad? Who's coming to the reunion?" She'd much rather talk about their classmates than Hollywood stars.

"Mandy Estevan, who's now Mandy Ochoa, is coming."

"I remember Mandy! She was so good at the splits. So she married Richard Ochoa. How about that. How about Suzanne Guthries? Or Crystal Hildebrand?"

"I think Crystal said she'd be there. I can't remember if I've heard from Suzanne. I'll have to check. Listen, do you ever hang out with Matt Damon and Ben Affleck?"

"Um, sometimes." Zoe didn't remember Margo being fixated on Hollywood gossip when they'd talked on the phone. Instead they'd ragged on teachers they'd hated, tests they'd flunked and yearbook pictures they'd like to destroy.

"Are Matt and Ben funny when they're together? I picture them as cracking jokes with each other all the time."

"They like to joke around, yeah. Sort of like Jeff and Darin used to in English. Remember the time—"

"They've been friends forever."

"So they're still buddies?" Zoe was glad to hear it. She should have maintained a long-term friendship like that, but her lifestyle hadn't made it easy to do. "I always liked Jeff and Darin."

"To heck with Jeff and Darin. I was talking about Matt and Ben. They wrote *Good Will Hunting* together and wouldn't sell it unless they could both be in it. That's loyalty. How about J-Lo? I saw a picture in *People* of you two coming out of a hair salon together. Are you friends with her?"

"Not close friends. We go to the same salon." Zoe realized she'd be quizzed all the way to Long Shaft, so she gave up her fantasy of riding along with eighties tunes and pretending to be teenagers again.

Margo wanted a glimpse into her star-studded life, and that was an understandable reaction. Zoe couldn't really blame her. Margo lived in a tiny town where not much went on, obviously. Zoe was her contact with the world of glamour and excitement. For the next half hour Zoe answered Margo's endless questions as darkness fell and they wound their way up into the pine country.

About ten miles outside Long Shaft the lighted billboards started appearing. *Long Shaft: Home of the Giant Sasquatch! Long Shaft Trading Post: THE Place for Bigfoot Souvenirs! Keychains, Dolls, Bumper Stickers, Posters and More! The Sasquatch Diner: Big Meals for Bigfoot Hunters! Stay at the Bigfoot Motel: More Sightings Than Anywhere Else in Town!*

The billboards were decorated with crude drawings of a large, hairy creature who didn't look the least bit like the creature Zoe remembered from *Harry*, the comedy about Bigfoot. This Bigfoot looked very unfriendly. Hostile, even.

As the billboard parade continued, Zoe's uneasiness grew. "Is all this for real?" she finally asked.

"What?" Margo continued driving down the two-lane road, which finally brought them to the edge of town and the granddaddy of all the billboards. It read: *WELCOME TO LONG SHAFT, The Bigfoot Capital of the World!*

"This *Bigfoot Capital of the World* stuff."

"Well, we do have a lot of sightings. As to whether it's more than anywhere else in the world . . ." Margo shrugged as she pulled into town and passed the Bigfoot Motel, the Sasquatch Diner, and the Long Shaft Trading Post. "Couldn't prove it one way or the other by me. But it's Long Shaft's claim to fame now that the mine is closed."

"So have you, um, seen Bigfoot personally?" Zoe got the impression Margo believed in this mythical creature, and she didn't want to offend her.

"Sure." Margo slowed down for the town's only traffic light, which had turned red, although no one was coming the other way. "There's a whole family of them living near here. I've seen the male twice, the female three times, and the baby once. I hold the town record for sightings."

Zoe peered at her, trying to discover if she was kidding around. "You're serious."

"Of course! Number six was just last week, about midnight. I heard heavy footsteps and looked out the window and there the male was, walking through the trees. Plus I knew what it was, even without the howl or the smell."

"What howl?" Zoe kept waiting for the punch line. She'd never met anyone who believed in Bigfoot, let alone someone who'd caught a glimpse of an entire family group. This had to be a joke.

"You'll know it when you hear it. Sort of like a mountain lion, only more volume. And they stink something fierce, too. Like about ten skunks letting loose."

Zoe stared at Margo. Talk about bizarre. Maybe the whole town, including Margo, was staging some kind of hoax. If so, she didn't want to play. "Um, how close is your place to the cabin you rented for me?"

"Not far. About half a mile down the road." Margo glanced over at her. "But don't worry. I know the pictures on the billboards are scary, but that's designed to pull in the tourists. They wouldn't be as attracted to a cuddly version. The California variety of Bigfoot is huge, but I'm convinced they're harmless."

Zoe took a deep breath. She could hardly wait for Flynn to get here. Solid, dependable, logical Flynn. She was absolutely positive that Flynn wouldn't believe in Bigfoot.

Chapter Four

Finding the cabin in the dark wasn't easy, but Flynn had an excellent sense of direction. When he pulled into the small parking area in front of the place, he found a neon green Taurus sitting there and lights on inside the cabin. If his Civic had been a huge step down for Zoe, riding in the Taurus must have been ground zero.

Taking his overnight bag, the script, and his laptop case from the passenger seat of the rented car, he closed and locked the vehicle. He'd downgraded from the luxury class Zoe had ordered. She might not like that, but he couldn't see wasting the money on a Lincoln Town Car. Besides, if she wanted to learn the art of being a nerd, she'd have to start appreciating thrift.

Speaking of that, he hoped she hadn't spent much on this cabin. Calling it quaint would be generous. Dilapidated was more like it. The peeling paint and sagging front porch struck a chord, though. His folks had lived in company housing like this for years. Now that they'd bought the bed-and-breakfast, they maintained its appearance, but his dad had never seen the point in sprucing up something he didn't own.

If Flynn owned this particular shack in the woods, he'd make some changes. Huge pine trees grew right next to it, which spelled out fire hazard, wind damage, and roots in the plumbing. Sure, the trees smelled nice, but they were way too close for his peace of mind. Thankfully, structural damage wasn't his problem unless a storm toppled one of the trees onto the cabin while he was in it.

With the strap of his laptop case over one shoulder, he carried the overnight bag in one hand and the script in the other. Slowly he climbed the creaking steps and walked across the narrow porch to the front door. The sound of voices, one belonging to Zoe and the other to her friend Margo, reminded him that he didn't want to do this. Given a choice, he'd get back in the car and leave. But Zoe would never forgive him, and he couldn't afford to lose her as a client.

With a sigh, he glanced around, delaying the moment when he'd have to go inside. Maybe he could sit on the porch for a while. Or maybe not. A couple of flimsy rocking chairs looked as if they'd collapse under the weight of anyone over twenty pounds. The place was a lawsuit waiting to happen, if you asked him, which nobody had.

Finally he stopped stalling and rapped on the door.

The conversation inside ceased. "That must be Flynn," Zoe said clearly, and footsteps approached.

When she opened the door, he stared. Then he closed his mouth tight so he wouldn't laugh. Her nerd outfit was *way* over the top. He'd have to teach her a little subtlety, or she'd never get the part.

She must have figured out that he was trying not to

laugh, because she became very indignant. "Nobody recognized me in the airport, so there!"

"I believe you." He wondered if he would have recognized her in the airport. Yeah, he would have. One look into those trademark blue eyes of hers, even with the wire-rimmed glasses disguising them, and he would have known. Plus there was the faint dimple in her left cheek and the scent of her favorite perfume, some designer fragrance that reminded him of hot tropical nights.

"Come on in." She stepped back and motioned to the woman standing in the middle of the cabin's living room. "Flynn Granger, this is my friend from high school, Margo Taggart."

"Hi, Margo." Flynn put down his overnight bag and shook Margo's hand, which made her plastic bracelets click against one another. Margo was a shock. He couldn't figure out how a woman like her fit into Zoe's life. If they were truly friends, then his whole picture of Zoe was wrong. Flynn didn't know a lot about women's clothes, but he could spot a fashion disaster in progress.

"So you're the guy who's going to teach Zoe how to be a geek," Margo said.

"That's right." He thought it a little ungracious of her to point that out, but maybe she didn't mean it unkindly.

She surveyed him, her gaze lingering on his carefully knotted necktie. "I'm sure you'll do a great job."

"Thanks." He decided to take it as a compliment. "That's my goal." Glancing around, he took a quick inventory of his surroundings. The inside matched the outside, and in this case that wasn't so good. The theme seemed to be Early Salvation Army, with a tattered couch in a brown floral print, a scuffed coffee table, and two beige armchairs.

A mottled brown carpet camouflaged whatever had been spilled there over the years. The room's only saving grace was a stone fireplace, but there wasn't any wood stacked beside it, probably because it was still too warm this time of year to think in terms of a fire. Flynn wondered if Zoe would adapt to these bare-bones accommodations, considering that she was used to a luxury beach house.

"I guess I'll be getting on home, then." Margo turned away from Flynn and focused her attention on Zoe. "If you need anything, you have my phone number."

"I'm sure we'll be fine. And thank you so much." Zoe walked over and gave her a hug.

"You're quite welcome!" Margo beamed at Zoe. "Don't forget to try the blueberry cobbler. Our cook Fiona at the diner made it last night. You're lucky to be here during a full moon, because that's the only time she makes it."

"Why is that?" Zoe asked.

"Nobody knows for sure, but it's like this ritualistic thing every full moon. Ray—that's her husband, who owns the diner—says that's the only time he gets sex, too." Margo winked. "But Fiona won't explain it even to him, and they've been married twenty-eight years, so I guess we'll never find out."

Flynn shook his head. "That's weird."

"Anyway, around here we all wait for the full moon. Ray, he has two reasons to wait, but the rest of us are after the blueberry cobbler. It's out of this world. My Bob just loves it. See you guys later." She whisked out the door, closing it behind her.

Once she was gone, Zoe let out a long heartfelt sigh. "She believes in Bigfoot."

"Who does?"

"Margo. And if she doesn't believe, she's doing a great job of pretending to. It's a big deal around here. Didn't you see the huge sign at the edge of town?"

"Well, yeah, of course. This is a logical place for Bigfoot sightings, up in the mountains."

Zoe smiled. "I'm so glad you're here. I didn't dare make fun of this concept while I was with Margo."

"Who said I was making fun of it?"

She paused a beat. "You're not?"

"There have been some credible eyewitnesses over the years. With all that evidence, it seems logical that something's out there creating all the hubbub. Cryptozoology is a fascinating subject."

"Crypto-whatzit?"

"Cryptozoology, the study of mysterious animals like Bigfoot and the Loch Ness Monster." Seeing the sign at the edge of town had reminded him of how he'd devoured those accounts as a teenager.

"*Flynn!* I was counting on you to be the sane person around here."

He shrugged. "Sorry. I think Bigfoot's cool. I've been reading the accounts about Sasquatch for years."

"Then this place should be right up your alley." She didn't sound happy about that. "Margo told me there's an entire Bigfoot *family* living around here. She's spotted the daddy twice, the mommy three times, and the little baby Bigfoot once."

"No kidding?" Flynn felt his old interest stir. If Margo's sightings were legit, he wouldn't mind talking to her about them.

"According to her, she holds the town record for number of sightings. Which means she's not the only Long Shaft resident who believes in Bigfoot."

"They keep track?" Flynn's excitement grew. A fascination with Bigfoot wasn't something he'd reveal ordinarily, but if he'd accidentally landed in the middle of a major Sasquatch area, he wouldn't be able to resist checking it out.

"I'm sure it's all a big hoax. They need tourist dollars, so this is their gimmick. There's no such thing."

He wondered if she was afraid of the possibility. That thought touched off a wave of unexpected tenderness, followed by the urge to protect her from things that go bump in the night. "Of course they could be seeing something else and imagining it's Bigfoot. Maybe it's a large bear."

"A bear?" Her eyes widened.

Whoops, wrong explanation. He'd scared her even more. "Probably not a bear, now that I think about it. I doubt there are any bears left in this area." He knew squat about the bear population here, but he could BS with the best of them.

She didn't look reassured. "I've heard bears are making a comeback."

"In national parks, maybe. I can't believe they're common in a populated area. I'm sure it's everyone's active imagination. They want to see Bigfoot, so they see Bigfoot." But he sincerely hoped it was more than pure imagination. He'd love to catch a glimpse himself. "It's easy to look through the trees when it's getting dark and imagine a shadow is something menacing."

"According to Margo it's more than shadows. The other night she heard heavy footsteps. Plus they howl. And they smell."

Oh, wow. But he decided to downplay this, because Zoe was looking very nervous. "Well, maybe they have a prankster in Long Shaft. Or maybe it's one of the business-men in town dressing up for the good of the economy."

"Well, that's certainly possible. Long Shaft could use an economic boost."

"That's for sure. It could use a tourist attraction, some light industry, a Del Webb retirement community, and a McDonald's franchise."

That made her laugh. "It is a sad little town, isn't it? And I'll bet someone is dressing up pretending to be Big-foot, like you said. They probably carry a tape-recorded howl and a stink bomb with them."

"Sounds logical to me." Not really, but he'd settle for that reasoning in order to calm her down. There was noth-ing particularly logical about some guy dressing up in a furry suit running through the woods setting off stink bombs to boost the town's economy. Negotiating with Wal-Mart to build a discount store, now that was more like it. So maybe Bigfoot lived in the neighborhood. What a concept.

"Because there's no chance Bigfoot really exists," she said more firmly.

"Probably not." He wasn't about to recite all the stories he'd collected and probably still had stuffed away in a box somewhere in his closet.

"I'm glad you agree, because I'm one of those people who don't like monster movies. Never did, never will." She took a deep breath. "Now that we've settled the nonex-istence of Bigfoot, do you want to eat first or unpack?"

"I vote for unpacking. I like to know right away where I'm going to sleep." He thought of Tony's dialogue as he said that.

"Fair enough. I'll show you where your bedroom is." She started down the hall.

He picked up his overnight bag and followed her. "Have you read any of the script?"

"Uh-huh. It sounds like fun. But unlike Tony, you won't have to bunk down on the couch."

"I didn't get to that scene." He'd been a little afraid of what he might find if he read any more. Following the trail of Zoe's perfume down the hallway and watching the sway of her hips, he wondered if he should beg off on the script read-through altogether. Even in that ill-fitting pantsuit, she looked sexier than any other woman he knew.

Even Kristen, whispered a devil lodged in his brain. He tried to picture how Kristen looked in a pantsuit. Couldn't do it. He tried to imagine Kristen naked. Couldn't do that, either.

"How much of the script did you read?" Zoe asked.

"Just the first scene."

"In the second scene she discovers an intruder has been rummaging through her bedroom. She'd meant to send Tony packing, but the idea that someone's broken into her apartment makes her reconsider and let him sleep on her couch."

Flynn would bet a guy like Tony wouldn't stay there long. He'd be off the couch and in Vera's bed in no time.

"Here's your room." Zoe gestured toward an open door.

Walking in, Flynn decided he'd stayed in worse. A single bed covered in a thin blue spread sat against the far wall under a small window, with a nicked dresser on the opposite wall near the door.

"Long Shaft doesn't have much to choose from," Zoe said. "I hope you can make do."

"This is fine." He walked into the room and set his overnight bag and laptop on the bed. "But are you okay with everything?" Still holding the script, he turned back to look at her. "I mean, you have a house in Malibu. This is a far cry from—"

"I'm on a mission," she said. "I need to stay far away from the public eye this weekend, so I can get ready for that audition with your help." She gestured toward the script in his hand. "I want the part of Vera, and I'd willingly camp in the wilderness to get it, except that I'm deathly afraid of bears."

"I'm glad we're not camping." Flynn smiled at her. "I'm not crazy about bears myself."

"And given the choice, I prefer an indoor bathroom."

"Same here."

"You see? Compared to roughing it in the wilderness, and I've done plenty of that on location, this is a five-star resort!"

"It'll be fine, Zoe."

She looked relieved. "I'm glad. How did you like the Town Car?"

"I, uh, traded down for a midsize sedan."

"You didn't! I wanted you to try the Town Car. I thought it suited you, and that you might even like it well enough to—"

"Buy one?" He tossed the script on the bed. "Zoe, are you ashamed of my transportation choices?"

She flushed. "*Ashamed* is not the right word. I don't care what you drive. But appearances are important in Hollywood, and you might get more business if you drove something . . . more substantial."

It was a hot button with him and he knew it, but he reacted anyway. "I hope clients hire me for my knowledge of contract law and not for the type of car I drive. If anything, they should be happy that I'm careful about money, because it means I'll be careful about other things, like the fine print in their contracts."

"But do you have to turn it into a religion? Couldn't you get a new car every five years, just for the hell of it?"

He'd been seriously thinking of buying a new car, something with a little more zip. He'd already done quite a bit of research on the Internet, but he wasn't about to admit that now. "My car runs great. I don't need a new one."

She threw up her hands. "Okay, I give up. I'll go unpack my stuff. Oh, and your bathroom is across the hall."

"Are we sharing?"

"No. There's one attached to my bedroom." She looked guilty. "I took the master suite, such as it is."

"Which you should! You're paying for this."

"I was trying to make it up to you by reserving the Town Car."

"Zoe, I didn't want the Town Car, okay? I'm happy with the one I have. I won't be driving it much anyway. We need to stay here and work, right?"

"Right. Which reminds me. What's wrong with my outfit? I could see you were trying not to go into hysterics over it."

He wondered if she realized how cute she was, standing there in her ridiculous outfit and nerdy glasses while trying to convince him to buy a new car, and repentant because she'd taken the better bedroom. The twist ties in her hair were especially endearing. He was charmed, and he didn't want to be. "We'll talk about the outfit over dinner."

"About that, I should warn you that I can't cook."

"Neither can I."

She shrugged. "Oh, well. How hard can it be? We have groceries. We're two intelligent people. We'll find a way to turn that into food."

"I'm sure we will." Flynn had a warm feeling settling into his chest, and he thought he knew what it was. Because they were sharing this experience, he and Zoe were starting to bond. He didn't think bonding with Zoe was a good idea. It could lead to all sorts of problems. But he didn't know how to stop it from happening.

Now that Zoe had Flynn physically in residence for the weekend, she'd begun having all kinds of crazy fantasies. She'd had no idea that he'd appeal to her in that way, but he did. What an inconvenient time to start thinking about sex.

Besides, Flynn had a girlfriend, a Harvard lawyer girlfriend. He'd already said he'd trust Kristen with his life, so it sounded like true love for sure. Zoe wasn't about to start messing with Flynn's happily ever after.

Still, she thought about him the entire time she pulled her clothes—way too many for only a couple of days—out of the suitcase and draped them over whatever surface presented itself. The job was more difficult because her glasses kept sliding down her nose, and finally she took them off.

She wasn't used to unpacking, because normally she had someone around to do it for her. The process of dealing with clothes was boring anyway. She wondered how Flynn unpacked.

Wait a minute. Brainstorm. She needed to know how Flynn unpacked. What was she doing in here when she could be observing Flynn being nerdlike? She could take notes! So maybe she'd enjoy observing him. So what? It was part of her job.

Grabbing a legal pad she'd shoved into her suitcase at

the last minute, she rummaged in her purse and finally found a pen. In seconds she was standing at the open door to Flynn's room, ready to observe.

He didn't see her right away. He was too busy arranging his underwear in the top dresser drawer. She made a note: *Are there neat nerds and sloppy nerds?* She'd have to decide which her character was. She thought maybe a neat nerd, from what she'd read of the script.

Then he looked up and spied her standing in the doorway. "What's up?"

"I suddenly realized that I need to know how you do things. You can tell me stuff all you want, but if I watch you going about your normal routine, I'll pick up the habits you don't even know you have."

"Uh, okay." He didn't look thrilled by the prospect, but he didn't tell her to leave, either.

"You're putting everything away, aren't you?"

He glanced at her. "I guess you think that's anal. It's only a weekend."

"I'm here to learn, not judge. Why do you put everything away? Why not live out of the suitcase for a couple of days?"

He paused, a belt in his hand. "I guess because I like knowing where everything is." Coiling the belt, he put it in the drawer.

"You would know that. It would all be in the suitcase."

"Jumbled up."

She thought of the mess in her room. Flynn would hate that. "So jumbled up is a bad thing." She noticed that his underwear drawer contained knit boxers, which she found sexy. But then, she seemed to have sex on the brain when it came to Flynn.

"For me, jumbled up doesn't work." He took out a

small black bag and put it on top of the dresser. "My shaving kit," he said, acknowledging her unasked question.

Zoe scribbled on her legal pad. "Let's say you're a woman."

"Let's not."

"I know you're not, but I have to make this gender switch. If you were a woman, you'd have all your bras and panties neatly stacked in a drawer, with no holes or stretched elastic spoiling the mix. Does that sound right?"

"Zoe, I can't even get my mind around the idea of neat stacks of bras and panties. On this one you'll have to go with your instincts." He went back to his suitcase and pulled out a couple of white shirts, which he shook and hung up in the tiny closet.

"How do you stand on wrinkles?"

He paused. "I don't like them, but if you're talking about nerds in general, that's all over the map. Some don't give a damn about whether their clothes are wrinkled."

"I'm going to play Vera as if she cares about wrinkles. I think she's an exacting person. I think she likes her world to be orderly. That's what bothers her about having Tony around. She doesn't have a good place for him in her neat little life."

"That sounds right." He returned to the suitcase, took out a pair of slacks identical to the ones he was wearing, and hung them in the closet.

"I'm guessing not much variety to the wardrobe," Zoe said.

"Variety takes too much thought."

"Gotcha. You have to save your brain for the important things, like complicated contracts. Or, in Vera's case, the formula that will combine weight loss, antiaging, and sexual stamina."

"That's such a crazy concept." Flynn unzipped a small outside pocket in his overnighter.

"I know. I—" She forgot what she'd been about to say. Inside the zippered compartment was a box of condoms.

Chapter Five

Flynn zipped the pocket closed so fast he pinched his finger. He hoped to God Zoe hadn't seen what was in there, but she'd stopped talking right when he'd opened it, so she probably had. How awkward.

If he acknowledged that he had condoms, then he'd have to explain why. Last weekend in a flash of efficiency he'd packed his overnight bag for the Catalina Island trip with Kristen. Of course he'd brought along a full box of condoms. He was planning on a fair amount of sex.

When Zoe had come up with this plan, he'd just grabbed the already packed bag, because his traveling wardrobe was the same as his everyday wardrobe and packing for one trip was the same as packing for another. With one glaring exception. And he'd totally forgotten about the telltale box in that outside pocket.

He really didn't want to go into all that with Zoe, so he'd pretend this little moment hadn't happened and steer her focus back to his girlfriend. Without turning around, he reached for his laptop. "I'm not sure if my wireless connection will work up here, but I'd like to try e-mailing Kristen before dinner."

"Um, sure. It should work. Cell phones do."

From the sound of her voice, he would bet she was still processing that glimpse of condoms, damn it. "Great. Then I think I'll set myself up in the living room and give it a try."

"All right."

He took the laptop out of its case and turned to her, forcing a smile. Yeah, she was looking at him very strangely. She'd seen the condoms, all right. "I want to let Kristen know that I made it here and that everything's . . . fine," he said.

"Okay." She backed away from the doorway, a gleam of speculation in her eyes. "I'll look over the groceries Margo bought and see what might work out for dinner."

"Great. That would be great." He walked briskly into the living room, sat on the brown flowered couch, and flipped open the laptop. He could hear Zoe banging around in the kitchen and recognized the aimless clattering. She behaved in the kitchen the same way he did, flailing around without a clue how to make food happen.

She must be confused as hell by those condoms. He'd made such a production out of his relationship with Kristen that bringing condoms on this trip looked sleazy, as if what Kristen didn't know wouldn't hurt her. Even without the Kristen angle he must seem damned cheeky and presumptuous with that box in his overnight bag.

He didn't like looking sleazy, cheeky, and presumptuous, especially not to Zoe. Maybe he should simply explain, but he wasn't sure how to begin the conversation. They didn't know each other that well.

Eventually he realized that he hadn't even bothered to turn on the laptop, let alone call up his e-mail. Bad sign. He was already so distracted by Zoe that he was neglecting Kristen. He'd fix that right now with a long, cheery message.

Powering up the laptop, he was able to connect to his Internet account, so he could stay in touch with both Kristen and his conscience. Maybe before he e-mailed Kristen he should do some Bigfoot research, just to be current.

He found plenty of Bigfoot sites, which was encouraging. The idea hadn't died. As he logged onto one, eerie music poured out of his laptop and he immediately hit the mute button.

"Was that you?" Zoe called from the kitchen.

"Some crazy pop-up ad. It's gone now."

"It sounded like the soundtrack for some creepy movie I would hate."

"Yeah, you never know what you'll find on the Web these days." What he was finding right at this moment got his adrenaline flowing. Zoe might not believe in Bigfoot, but a whole lot of other people did, and they were only too happy to talk about it. Flynn read eagerly.

Someone reported clocking a California Sasquatch at 35 miles per hour. That was damned precise. Casts of footprints too big to be human, too human to be a bear, had been made. Large bipedal creatures estimated to be fourteen feet tall had been seen running out in the open, and not far from here, either.

Margo claimed to have seen a whole family of them. That was beyond cool. Maybe he should take a walk in the woods at night and see if he got lucky. Maybe—

When Zoe cried out, he threw the laptop down and ran

into the kitchen, his heart racing with anticipation that she'd spotted something outside.

"M-mouse," she said, pointing a shaky finger toward a small alcove that held a table and four chairs. "I'm s-sorry if I scared you, b-but it startled me. And I s-suppose we don't want it in here."

Flynn was so incredibly disappointed she hadn't seen a Sasquatch peeking in the window at the far end of the alcove that he forgot that he didn't like dealing with mice. He blew out a breath and settled his glasses more firmly on the bridge of his nose. "No problem."

Surveying the area, he considered the options. The kitchen itself was narrow, with a sink and an old refrigerator along the wall on his left and an ancient stove and a counter with cupboards underneath on the wall to his right. Beyond the stove was a back door.

He needed something, some helpful instrument to facilitate the situation. Then he spied a broom propped in the small space between the refrigerator and the sink counter. He reached for the broom.

"Don't kill it."

He hadn't made it that far in his thinking, but beating the mouse to death with a broom didn't sound like a good idea, for either him or the mouse. "We'll relocate it."

"To where?"

"Outside." Except he was remembering the main thing about mice, the thing he didn't like. They moved very fast. Right now the little fur ball remained stationary, staring at Flynn with whiskers quivering and eyes bright as drops of motor oil. But the mouse could turn into a gray streak in a split second.

"There's a back door."

"I saw that." And Flynn needed it to be open. Zoe was standing fairly close to the door, but she looked frozen in place. Besides, he wanted to be the hero. Solving this mouse situation might make her forget the box of condoms he'd inadvertently introduced into the equation.

Keeping his attention on the little gray rodent, he edged over toward Zoe. "If you'll move back a little, I'll see if I can get the door open without scaring the mouse."

"I can open the door." She stepped a fraction closer to the door and the mouse.

"Let me. Just stand back."

"I'll do it." Sounding determined, she slipped a little closer to the door. "Between Bigfoot and bears, I'm beginning to feel like a wuss. I may not like scary movies, but in real life I can be brave if I have to. And it's only a little mouse."

"Yeah, but they move fast."

"I know. You get the broom ready to head him off in case he tries to go anywhere besides out the door."

Flynn couldn't very well wrestle her out of the way. "Okay."

"Going toward the door." Zoe spoke softly as she cleared the stove and reached for the door handle. The mouse didn't move. "Opening the—damn it, it's locked." She fumbled with the lock, obviously not wanting to take her eyes off the mouse.

"I think he moved a little."

"The lock's sticking. I'll have to get closer and concentrate on it, which means I can't pay attention to the mouse."

"I'll let you know what he's doing." Feeling like the goalie on a hockey team, Flynn clutched the broom and waited.

Zoe flicked the lock back and forth and pulled. The door didn't budge. "What if it's painted shut?"

"Then we think of something else. This mouse is outta here."

"I think we should name him." She tugged harder on the door.

"Name the mouse? Why on earth would you want to do that?"

"So he's not such a foreign creature." She'd started puffing with the effort of trying to get the door open. "See, if we personalize the mouse, he won't seem so *other,* and we won't be so freaked out."

"I'm not freaked out." Which was a lie. The idea of sharing the cabin with a little scurrying thing that could go anywhere, that could bite him in the middle of the damned night, for crissakes, was giving him the willies. Bigfoot was one thing. A little hyperactive mammal was something else again.

"Well, I'm freaked out. A little. We'll call him George."

"George is moving."

"Hee-yah!" Zoe gave a mighty pull and wrenched the door open, but George dashed past her, past the broom Flynn wielded like Wayne Gretzky, if he did say so himself, and made for the living room.

"Get the bedroom doors!" Flynn yelled as he ran back to the living room with George still in his sights. The little mouse ran under the coffee table and—naturally—under the ugly couch.

Zoe slammed both bedroom doors and reappeared in the living room. "Well?"

"Under the couch."

"We'll lure him with cheese and shoo him out the front

door. When I was taking inventory I found some cheese. Keep watch. I'll be back."

"He won't get past me." Flynn crouched down, peering with narrowed eyes at the opening under the couch.

Moments later Zoe came back, her hand brimming with chunks of cheddar cheese. "We'll make a trail leading out the front door. George will go from piece to piece and finally find himself on the porch. We slam the door, and *voilà*. No George."

Flynn had his doubts about the plan, but he didn't have a better one at this hour of the night. "Go for it."

Zoe opened the front door, letting in the sounds of the night. Flynn couldn't remember the last time he'd heard crickets, or the breeze through the top branches of tall pines. Now if he could manage to hear the howl of a Sasquatch, that would really make his night.

"Here you go, George." Zoe dropped pieces of cheese in a line from the front porch through the open door to the edge of the couch. "Din-din is served." Then she backed up and came to stand beside Flynn.

"Now what?"

"We watch from a safe distance and see if it works."

"Then I'll get us a couple of kitchen chairs." On his way to accomplish that mission he noticed the groceries spread out on the counter. "Want some wine?" he called out.

"Sure!"

"Should we eat some of that cheese?"

"Better not," Zoe called back. "We don't want to confuse his little olfactory glands by putting cheese in places we don't want him to go."

Flynn pictured George running up his pants leg to get the cheese and heartily agreed. "I see a can of nuts. I'll bring those."

"Great!"

Making the mercy mission into one trip gave Flynn a sense of efficient accomplishment. He stuck two wine-glasses in his hip pockets, shoved the bottle opener in his front pocket, hooked an arm through each of two chair backs, and then picked up the wine bottle in one hand and the can of nuts in the other.

When Zoe saw him she laughed. "You look like a street performer about to start his act."

"Trust me, once I unload this stuff there's no act. I'm still worried about the read-through of the script, considering that I'm way out of my depth. Maybe we should discard that plan. It could leave a really bad taste in your mouth for this role, and I wouldn't want that." *Nice segue, Granger*. He patted himself on the back.

"I'm not at all concerned. I just need Tony's lines read. You'll be fine."

So it hadn't worked. He gave up the fight for the time being. She helped him unload, and soon they were sipping a fairly good Merlot and munching on an assortment of salted nuts.

"Do nerds care about wine?" Zoe asked.

"This nerd does." He took another swallow. He was aware that he was drinking on an empty stomach, which might not be the wisest move, but it tasted good after all the stress of this trip. He lifted his glass. "Not bad. Not bad at all."

"I sent Margo a list of brands, and this was at the bottom, but it's fine. I'm sure she tried her best to get what I asked for."

"So you've known her ever since high school?" Flynn was still having a tough time making all the pieces fit.

"Not continuously. And don't get me wrong—we

weren't best buds in school. We were on the same cheer squad and knew some of the same people."

"So why are you hooked up with her now?"

"She's reunion committee chair. You know how some people weren't close in high school, but later on they find they have a lot in common? That's how it is with Margo and me."

Flynn questioned that Zoe had a single thing in common with Margo but decided not to say so. Sometimes stars like Zoe got lonely, and a simple friendship with someone who wasn't in the business was exactly what they needed. He wouldn't tread on that.

Zoe helped herself to another glass of wine. "Did you e-mail Kristen?"

"Um, no." And he felt guilty. He'd been more interested in researching Bigfoot than getting in touch with the woman he planned to marry.

"I guess George interrupted you."

"Yeah." And his laptop still sat on the couch, open and running. He suspected he'd been bumped from the Internet by now after all this period of inactivity, but he was burning battery life. In order to fix that, he'd have to approach the couch, which could compromise the George plan, so he vowed to get the laptop plugged in at his first opportunity.

"I think it's great that you've found someone special," Zoe said. "How did you meet her anyway?"

"Went back to visit my old roommate, Josh. He fixed us up."

"And it was love at first sight."

"I'd say *like at first sight* instead." But Flynn had sensed a kinship they could build on. They'd managed to keep the relationship alive in the past year with Flynn making several trips back to Harvard. The sex was good and he liked the companionship. No question, Kristen was a logical choice.

"If you're thinking of marriage, then I guess you've progressed beyond the liking stage."

"Yeah." He believed that, although he hadn't told Kristen he loved her. The timing had never seemed right, and it wasn't the sort of conversation to have over the telephone, when you couldn't kiss each other afterward.

"Selfishly I'm hoping you won't move back to Massachusetts."

"I hope I won't, either." He poured himself some more wine. It was tasting better with every sip.

"But it's a possibility? I hate hearing that."

"I have to be fair. My plan is to give Kristen a year to decide if she likes Southern California. If she doesn't, I can't force her to live there. And I would be fine in Massachusetts. I spent all those years going to Harvard. I'm used to it."

Zoe turned to him. "Flynn, *used to it* is a long way from liking it. She shouldn't expect you to be miserable, either."

"I wouldn't be miserable. I could teach at Harvard. They probably need someone with practical experience in the field of entertainment law."

"Do you hear yourself? You're settling, Flynn!" She looked into his eyes. "Admit that you'd miss Hollywood."

The wine was getting to him, forcing him to be more forthcoming than he might have been otherwise. "Yeah, I'd miss it." He'd miss Zoe, to put an even finer point to it. Maybe he hadn't seen her regularly, but he had to admit she'd always hovered on the edge of his thoughts. Knowing there was a file in his office marked *Zoe Tarleton* had given him a thrill, a reason to feel good about life.

"It's none of my business, but I think you should let Kristen know that your life is here." She sighed and took another gulp of wine. "Listen to me, being self-serving. I want you to stay, so I'm trying to convince you to deliver an ultimatum to Kristen. That's not right. I apologize."

"No apology necessary." Not in the least. God, her eyes were incredibly blue, and knowing that she needed him to hang around was a real high. "I'm glad I've been of value to you."

"You have, Flynn. You've been extremely valuable."

He was convinced that the wine was causing this moment when their eyes were locked and sparks seemed to be shooting off of both of them. "What happened to your glasses?"

"They were sliding all over the place while I was unpacking, so I took them off."

"You probably need the screws tightened." The wine was coaxing him to lean over and kiss her, which he most certainly wasn't about to do. They'd been discussing his life with Kristen, so how could he be thinking of kissing Zoe?

She smiled at him. "I'll bet you have one of those little kits with the tiny screwdriver inside and little spare screws."

"Yeah, I do. I can fix your glasses. They just need to be screwed . . . tighter."

"That would be nice." She had a dreamy, come-closer expression in her eyes.

"No problem. Glad to do it." Damn. He wanted to kiss

her. He justified his unacceptable urges by reminding himself that she made a living being kissable. A close-up shot of her lips was guaranteed to make any guy in the Free World ditch his significant other and long for the ecstasy promised by Zoe's mouth.

So he could be forgiven for thinking of kissing her. Any normal male would be engulfed by her natural sensuality. He felt himself drifting toward those smiling lips.

"George is coming out."

Apparently she hadn't been as mesmerized by the moment as he had, because she'd caught a movement from the corner of her eye. Well, of course she hadn't been mesmerized. He wasn't her type. He was her Rent-a-Nerd. He would do well to remember his place in the scheme of things.

He turned to look, and sure enough, George had ventured out to sniff the first piece of cheese.

Zoe's voice was low and filled with excitement. "This is going to work."

"Could be."

Sure enough, George wolfed down the first piece of cheese and moved to the next.

"He's just like Pac-Man," Zoe said.

"I used to love that game." Flynn watched George moving steadily toward the door.

"Me, too." Zoe drank her wine and watched George move laboriously through piece after piece. "It's what gave me the idea to try this."

"Well, it's working like a charm." Flynn poured himself a touch more wine.

"Let's drink to ridding the cabin of George without bloodshed." Zoe raised her glass and smiled at him.

"I'm for that." Flynn clicked his glass with hers and drank. Damn it, this cabin was feeling cozier by the minute. Good thing Zoe was so far out of his league. He'd been with her less than two hours, and he already felt as if he'd betrayed Kristen.

"George is out!" Zoe bounded from her chair and slammed the door on the tiny mouse.

"I'm e-mailing Kristen," Flynn said, and retrieved his laptop.

Omigod, Zoe Tarleton is actually spending the weekend in Long Shaft! I can hardly believe this is happening. Who would ever think that a big star like her would end up coming to a little place like this? But she's here, she's really here! No one is supposed to know about it, of course. But I know, and I'm completely stoked! I know everything about her. I've done lots of research. You might say I'm a secret fan. I think she should stay here awhile. In fact, maybe she should stay here forever and ever. . . .

Chapter Six

While Flynn got on the Internet to type in his love note to Kristen, Zoe returned to the kitchen, closed the back door, and looked for something they could fix for dinner without burning down the cabin. She felt as if they had a third person on this trip and she didn't like it, even though she'd agreed that Flynn could communicate with Kristen.

This whole Kristen business was kind of weird anyway. Flynn could have e-mailed his lady love earlier, while Zoe had unpacked groceries. At least fifteen minutes had gone by before she'd spotted George, plenty of time to type a message. Yet apparently he'd been fooling around with something else instead.

Also, and this was the salient point—what the hell was he doing with condoms on this trip? Ever since she'd seen them in that little compartment of his suitcase, she'd been second-guessing herself. Maybe it had been a box of something else. Maybe he'd saved a condom box and was reusing it for . . . something.

No, that was nuts. Nobody, not even Flynn, would save an empty condom box and reload it with some other doodad. Besides, Flynn didn't have doodads. He had his basic wardrobe and a shaving kit. That was it.

Except for condoms. No matter how she turned the situation around, examining it from all angles, she came up with the same conclusion. Flynn thought there was a chance he'd get lucky this weekend.

Once she accepted that fact, another one came bounding along on its heels. Flynn wasn't nearly as committed to this Kristen person as he'd implied. Kristen might be a safety net, a way for him to protect himself until he decided how he wanted this weekend to go. That made him a lot more complicated than she'd thought.

So now what? The idea of a weekend fling with her favorite nerd had crossed her mind more than once in the past few hours. She'd dismissed it because of Kristen. Also, she didn't see Flynn as the weekend fling type, and she might end up ruining a perfectly good lawyer–client relationship. Flynn was the best in the business, which was why he got clients even if he did happen to drive a nerd car.

"So what do you think we should fix for dinner? Something with olive oil?"

She turned to find him leaning in the doorway. Looking down at the bottle in her hand, she realized she'd spent quite a while fixated on Flynn instead of scoping out a dinner plan. "That's what I was thinking," she said. "Something with olive oil."

"Like what?"

She thought quickly. Olive oil had to do with Italian cooking. She knew that because of the fabulous dipping sauce at her favorite restaurant. Glancing at the pile of groceries she'd unloaded from the bags Margo had carted in, she noticed a package of angel-hair pasta. "Spaghetti?"

"Spaghetti sounds good. But I don't see a jar of sauce. How can you have spaghetti without sauce?"

"Maybe we have one of those envelopes of dry ingredients you mix in with tomato paste." Zoe rummaged through the pile on the counter, but no little packet showed itself. "Here's a can of tomatoes," she said brightly, holding it up. "We could mush them up and add a lot of salt and pepper."

Flynn looked doubtful. "In a pinch, maybe, but I think more goes into spaghetti sauce than that. Maybe some of the olive oil. Is that garlic?"

"I guess so." Zoe picked up the tiny bulblike thing and held it to her nose. "Probably garlic. And this is definitely an onion." She picked that up, too.

"It looks like Margo thought we'd make our own sauce."

"She probably did." Zoe didn't relish the idea of admitting to Margo that she couldn't pull that off. She'd look like a spoiled rotten diva if she did that. "I have an idea. Let's get creative. We'll open up the tomatoes, mash them up a little, add some of the garlic, and some of the onion. We'll keep tasting until it seems right."

"I have a better idea." Flynn looked immensely pleased with himself. "I'll go back online and find a recipe for spaghetti sauce. Then we can get the exact measurements we need."

"C'mon, Flynn. Let's try this on our own. We might come up with a whole new taste."

"More likely something totally inedible. Look, we

know we're both bad in the kitchen. I'm sure I can find some good recipes. I'll Google *spaghetti sauce*. Be right back."

"But the thing is, I'm not into recipes," she called after him. "That's the reason I—" She gave up protesting when she heard the sound of his laptop booting up. She should have known he was a recipes kind of guy.

But she had a little time to maneuver before he showed up with his Googled spaghetti sauce formula. She could get the jump on him and show him that innovation had it all over following directions. He would be so amazed. She liked the idea of amazing Flynn.

First she found a big kettle, filled it with water, and dumped in the pasta. After turning the burner on high, she located a can opener and a pan for the tomatoes. There. She had the pasta on one burner and the potential sauce on another one.

Next step, mush those tomatoes into a pulp. The utensil drawer had the kind of potato masher she remembered her grandmother using, so she took it out and began pulverizing the tomatoes.

Now this was what she called creative cooking! She'd bet Julia Child started out this way, forging a path to creative cuisine. Zoe poured in some of the olive oil, which seemed like the right move at this point. The tomatoes were sticking to the bottom of the pan and olive oil was good lubrication. She'd learned that from massage.

Massage made her think of sex, which she hadn't had in ages. One bout of watching her love life dragged through the scab sheets was quite enough. She wasn't only worried about her feelings. Her parents had suffered, too. They were simple people who'd never anticipated having an international star for a daughter.

They still weren't comfortable with it. Her mother had once confided that they wished Zoe had become a school-teacher or a nurse. That way they wouldn't have to cringe every time they passed the magazines in the grocery store checkout aisle. Whenever the gossip was flying, they stopped shopping completely and bought takeout, and they hated takeout.

Zoe had passed the stage of feeling guilty about that, but she didn't go out of her way to stir up the gossipmongers, either. An affair wasn't worth the angst of wondering when the tabloids would get the story and her parents would be back to take-out menus.

Too funny—one of Hollywood's biggest sex symbols wasn't having any sex because she was a scaredy-cat, afraid of the repercussions. But what if she happened to be in a situation where no one would ever find out? Hmm. *Whatever happens in Long Shaft stays in Long Shaft.*

She shouldn't be thinking about that now, though. She had cooking chores. Garlic was definitely an Italian kind of spice, but this thing looked too big to throw in as is. Luckily, the big piece broke apart into smaller pieces. Cool. She tossed in four of them. They seemed kind of hard and crusty, but the cooking process would probably soften them up.

She'd always wanted to experiment like this, but her mother was a follow-the-recipe kind of person like Flynn. Her roommates had bought into the same propaganda, insisting that recipes were the only way to go. Finally Zoe had decided to leave the cooking to those who loved reading the fine print. She shouldn't have let herself be intimidated, because this was turning out to be a blast.

"Sorry I took so long. I found several, so I had to narrow the search." Flynn came into the kitchen still gazing at the screen of his open laptop. "I don't have a printer, so you'll just have to read it on the—" His nose twitched, as if smelling the food cooking. He glanced up. "Zoe, what are you doing?"

She smiled at him. He was so far behind the curve. "Making spaghetti."

"How? You don't know what you're doing."

"Does it look like I don't know what I'm doing?"

"Yes."

"Look again. I have pasta there and sauce here. Everything's under control." she turned away from the stove to relocate the onion in the pile of groceries still on the counter. "I have good instincts."

"Do your instincts tell you when a pot is boiling over?"

She spun around and discovered foam coming out of the kettle where she'd dumped the pasta. "Omigosh." Dropping the onion, she reached for the kettle.

"Zoe, don't!"

"It's making a mess!" She grabbed it off the stove, discovering too late that the handles were blazing hot. As she twirled around, she dropped both pot and contents with a clatter into the sink. The pot wobbled and fell over, discharging all its contents.

"Did you burn yourself?" Flynn shoved his laptop onto a clear space on the counter and turned to her. "Let me see."

"I'll be fine." Her fingers stung, but her pride stung worse. She'd been so sure that she could handle whipping up a gourmet feast. She wanted to blame Flynn for coming in at the wrong moment and distracting her, but she knew the pot would have boiled over regardless.

"Let me look at your hand." Flynn reached for her.

"I'm okay. Really." She put both hands behind her

back. Then she heard a now-familiar hissing sound and glanced quickly at the stove. "Oh no!" Her sauce mixture was bubbling over, too.

This time, as she made a move to get it, Flynn grabbed her arm. "Wait! Get a pot holder first!"

"I don't have one! I don't know where they are!"

"Let me." He shoved a finger into the knot of his tie and loosened it enough that he could wrap the end around the handle of the pan. After moving in to the back of the stove, he turned off both burners.

Gathering the tattered remnants of her pride, Zoe took stock. All might not be lost. "If I can get the pasta back in the kettle and add more water, I can finish cooking that while I cut up the onion for the sauce." She opened a couple of drawers and finally found the silverware. A fork should do the trick.

"Zoe, I think maybe—"

"I'm sure this will work." Her fingers still smarted, so she tested the handle of the kettle before trying to hold it. The handle had cooled. Holding the kettle steady, she began scooping the pasta back inside.

She got most of it, filled the kettle with water, and put it back on the stove. This time she turned the burner to medium instead of high. She'd miscalculated the first time. A girl couldn't be expected to know everything right off the bat.

Time to check out how Flynn was handling this, though. He was awfully quiet. Glancing in his direction, she discovered him standing in the same spot as before, staring at her in disbelief. He hadn't even bothered to fix his tie.

"I suppose this all seems a little unorthodox to you."

"You could say that."

She had to give him credit for not laughing, because he looked as if he really wanted to. The corners of his mouth were twitching. "It's just that recipes are so boring," she said.

"And so nerdlike."

That stopped her in her tracks. "Oh." She'd been so intent on doing her own thing that she'd forgotten the main reason she was here—to immerse herself in nerd behavior. Yet the first time her resident nerd had tried to demonstrate that behavior she'd sabotaged him.

"Vera would follow a recipe," he said gently.

Much as Zoe hated to admit that, she knew he was right. She surveyed the chaos she'd created. Vera's kitchen would never look like this, with groceries piled helter-skelter, a mess on the stove and another mess in the sink. Tony's kitchen would always look like this. She was modeling the wrong character.

"But I admire your grit," Flynn said. "Most women I know would have burst into tears after an episode like this. You weren't about to give up. I'm impressed by that."

"Maybe I'm just bullheaded."

"I would believe that."

That made her smile. "Hey, you didn't have to agree with me."

"So prove to me that you're not bullheaded. Look at the recipe."

Zoe decided to accept defeat gracefully. "Okay, I'll look at it."

"And let me see your hands."

"They're really fine. Honestly." But she held them out, because she was currently demonstrating that she wasn't stubborn as a mule. Secretly she was afraid that she was at least that stubborn.

Flynn cupped her hands in his and peered at her fingers. The contact had the strangest effect on her, as if she'd popped an antidepressant. Her nerve endings quivered and she felt anticipation, as if something wonderful were about to happen.

"Stay right there." He let go of her hands, reached over to the counter, and picked up a squeeze bottle of mustard, which he began shaking.

She moved so that she stood between Flynn and the stove. "Hold it, buster. If you're about to put mustard in my spaghetti sauce, you'll do it over my dead body. I may not be the Galloping Gourmet, but I know there's no mustard in spaghetti sauce."

"I'm not putting it in the sauce. I'm going to squeeze some on your fingers."

"My *fingers*?" She tried to make sense of that. Maybe he was more innovative than she'd given him credit for. "Flynn, are you kinky?"

He glanced at the mustard bottle, then back at her. "With mustard? What kind of kinky thing could you do with mustard?"

"You tell me. You're holding the bottle."

"I was going to put it on your burn. What did you think I was going to do with it?"

"I had no idea." She put her hands behind her back again and stepped into the little alcove, out of range of Flynn and his squeeze bottle. "And I'm not sure I like your idea, either. It sounds weird and messy."

"Trust me, it's great first aid. Back in college I spilled hot coffee in my lap. Somebody suggested mustard, and I never blistered."

She had a sudden mental image of Flynn smearing mustard on parts of him she'd never given much thought to before, parts she was certain he wouldn't want getting blistered.

He flipped open the cap on the mustard. "Hold out your hands and let me squeeze a little on the places that are red. It'll take the pain away, too."

"But if you put mustard all over my fingers, how will I cook?"

"I, ah, guess you'll have to let me take over."

"Oh, *now* I get it. This is your devious method to get me away from the stove."

"I swear, that's not the point." He advanced toward her. "Just see how nice it feels. You'll be amazed."

She backed up another step. "I'm not about to be put out of commission by a mustard bottle. I started this spaghetti meal and I'll finish this spaghetti meal."

"Just try it. I'm not trying to take away your cooking rights. I'm trying to keep you from suffering."

"I'm not suffering." Her fingers did hurt a little, but she hated to give up her spaghetti project. "If you'll please bring the laptop over, I'll work with the recipe you found."

"Okay, but the offer stands." Flynn put down the mustard and walked over to get his laptop.

"I appreciate the thought, Flynn." She knew men hated it when you wouldn't take their advice. "It's good to know about the mustard, in case I ever really burn myself, like you did." She was dying to know the details of his mustard incident. "I'm sure that hurt like crazy, being in such a tender spot and everything."

He brought the computer over, but he didn't quite meet her gaze. "It was, um, not quite in *that* tender spot, fortunately."

"Oh." She wouldn't have pursued it, except there were those condoms in his suitcase to consider. A guy who packed condoms on a weekend trip when he'd made it clear he was taken . . . well, that kind of guy deserved to have his tender spots discussed. "When you said the coffee landed in your lap, I was afraid that meant something more delicate was in danger."

"Uh, no." He coughed. "Can you see the screen okay?"

"A little to the left. That's good. Thanks." She forced herself to stop thinking about his package and look at the recipe.

Sure enough, she was in big trouble. She was supposed to cook the onion and garlic in the oil first and then add the canned tomatoes. Plus she was supposed to peel the garlic and mince it. She had no idea how that was accomplished.

But she was committed to this sauce, and she'd make it work. She'd chop up the onion and throw that in, plus add the water that was called for. The stuff was kind of thick and gooey, so the water would help.

"Got it," she said to Flynn. "You can shut down the laptop, now."

"You're sure?"

"Sure I'm sure." She found a knife and a chopping board and started hacking at the onion.

"You committed that to memory pretty fast."

"The recipe's no longer than the blocks of dialogue I have to memorize all the time. Not as interesting, though."

Flynn closed the laptop and set it back on the table. "How close is the recipe to what you've been doing?"

"Pretty close." She sniffed as her nose and eyes started running from chopping the onion. At least this reaction was familiar, because some of her actor friends used cut onions when the scene required tears. With her, though, the emotions building in the character usually did the trick.

"Is that the onion making you do that or are you upset?"

"Onion." She sniffed again and kept chopping.

He walked over. "Here." He took a soft cotton handkerchief from his back pocket and gently wiped her nose.

It was the sweetest gesture. No one had wiped her nose since she was five years old. She appreciated everything about the moment—Flynn's careful but firm touch, the freshly washed scent of his handkerchief, and the cozy feeling of being cared for. In fact, she was feeling cozy all over, in that warm, getting-ready-for-sex kind of way that she hadn't experienced in like forever.

"Thank you," she said. "I didn't know guys carried handkerchiefs anymore."

"My dad always does. I remembered the times his handkerchief came in handy when I was a kid, so a few years ago I decided to return to the tradition."

"So you carry it more for other people than for yourself. That's nice." And it fit his personality. Flynn was the kind of guy a woman could count on in a crisis, as he'd proved several times recently. Zoe hadn't thought she needed that quality in a man, and yet she found it very appealing out here in the woods where Bigfoot might be lurking behind every tree.

Maybe that sense of safety was another reason she felt like having sex. Getting involved with an actor was dangerous to her privacy, but nothing about Flynn seemed dangerous. He would be the perfect guy to let loose with, even if he did turn out to be on the predictable and boring side. She'd been so long without that it probably wouldn't matter if they never went beyond the missionary position.

But she was getting way ahead of herself, thinking about what position they might use, when they probably wouldn't use any at all. Scraping the onion into what she hoped would be their spaghetti sauce, she redirected her thoughts to the script.

She needed to put aside everything else until they'd made some headway there. She'd forget about Bigfoot, too. There was no such thing anyway. Margo was probably making up all those sightings as her claim to fame.

Even so, Zoe couldn't help glancing to her left through the darkened windowpanes to the pine forest beyond. When two eyes stared back at her, she forgot to breathe.

Chapter Seven

As Flynn tucked his handkerchief in his hip pocket, Zoe moaned and grabbed his arm. Startled, he turned quickly and found her staring out the kitchen window, her face white. Her lips were moving, but he could barely hear what she was saying. Finally he figured out the words. *Baby Bigfoot.*

His heart began to race. Wrong time to be without a camera. He had to be cautious, though, because she might have seen a bear instead. As much as he'd love to catch a glimpse of Bigfoot, he had no interest in being mauled by a bear.

But hard as he tried, he couldn't see anything outside except shadowy pine trees. Either he needed a new prescription or she'd imagined it. He sighed with disappointment. "I don't see a thing."

She continued to grip his arm. "It ducked down behind that bush. But I saw two eyes. The light from the kitchen reflected off two eyes. I'm sure of it."

He didn't want to mention it might be a bear. He didn't even want to admit that to himself. "Maybe it was a raccoon. I'm sure they have raccoons around here."

"Then we're talking about a five-foot raccoon."

Or a bear that stood five feet at the shoulder when it was on all fours. Flynn quickly calculated other possibilities for a pair of eyes in the woods. "Paparazzi?"

"God, I hope not. That would almost be worse than a bear. I think we should check this out."

"Yeah, me, too." If it really was a baby Bigfoot and he didn't see it because he was worried about bears, he'd never forgive himself. "I'll go."

"I'll go, too."

He figured it was a token offer. "No, you stay here. I'll go."

She took a deep breath. "No, we'll both go. But I wish we had a flashlight."

Flynn had an unwelcome vision of *Blair Witch Project.* "I do. On my key chain." He paused. "Except I didn't bring my key chain. In order to be more efficient, I only brought my house key."

"Then I guess we just go." Zoe started for the back door.

"Wait. There's a fireplace. Maybe there are matches or something. Let me go check."

"Good idea. I'll look for candles."

Flynn didn't find matches anywhere near the hearth, but he did find a pistol-style butane lighter that worked. He took it triumphantly back to the kitchen. "I found a flamethrower. All we need is a candle."

"No candles."

"Then I guess this is it. I'll go first." As he opened the back door in a great show of bravado, he tried to remember if bears were afraid of fire. He thought they were, but a puny butane lighter might not qualify. A bear would probably laugh at his little flame and eat him up anyway.

He wondered how many Bigfoot investigators had run afoul of bears. A guy had to take chances in pursuit of a phenomenon like this. Sniffing the air, he detected only a woodsy smell. Even a bear would smell a little bit, but Bigfoot would smell a *lot*.

Thinking more and more that Zoe had imagined the eyes, he left the safety of the cement stoop and started walking toward the bush. Pine needles crunched under his feet, but otherwise the forest was still. Not even the crickets were chirping. The bush was about ten feet from the light shining through the window onto the ground. He paused at the edge of the additional light spilling out of the open door and tried to see into the shadows.

Then Zoe closed the back door and he stood in darkness as she came up behind him, her crackling footsteps loud in the silence. "See anything?" she whispered.

"No."

"*There.*" Her voice was low and urgent. "Something moved behind that bush."

The hair stood up on the back of his neck. What the hell was he doing out here armed with a butane lighter? He had zero information about what was behind that bush, but whatever it was, a butane lighter wasn't going to stop it.

Zoe shifted position and nudged his arm with her breast. "Maybe we should call out."

He was sure the breast nudge was an accident. She wouldn't have deliberately done that, but the contact re-minded him of his role as he-man protector. It also reminded him of what spectacular breasts she had, truly works of art. Ever since that day in the car, he'd become slightly obsessed with her cleavage. He had a sacred duty to keep that cleavage from harm.

So he pulled the trigger on the lighter and pointed it in the direction of the bush where Zoe had seen something with eyes. The flickering flame looked beyond puny. "Who's there?" he said, doing his best to sound bold and commanding, even though his knees shook and his flame was ridiculous.

Something snorted, and he backed up so fast he stepped on Zoe's foot. She yelped, but not loud enough to drown out a new sound coming from behind the bush. *Giggles.*

He mentally reviewed his research about Bigfoot, but nothing surfaced about giggling. Roaring and howling, yes. Giggling, no. He took a deep breath. "All right, who's back there?"

"Luanne Dunwoodie." The voice was definitely girlish. Then the owner of the voice stood up. In the meager light of the butane lighter she looked to be a perfectly normal kid of about ten or eleven, stick-figure skinny and dressed in jeans and T-shirt. Strands of hair had escaped from the blond pigtail that hung down her back.

She was laughing at Flynn. "You look funny holding that lighter thing."

Flynn supposed he did, so he doused the flame, holstered the lighter in his pants pocket, and straightened his tie. He needed to remember that he was a lawyer and should act accordingly. No way would he suddenly morph into Indiana Jones.

"We didn't know what or who was out here," Zoe said. "You scared us to death, Luanne."

Flynn winced. "Speak for yourself. I was calmly investigating the situation."

"And breathing like a freight train in the process," Zoe said.

"Was not."

"Was, too."

Luanne's grin faded. "Whoops. My bad. I didn't mean to scare you guys, but I just *had* to find out who'd rented the cabin. It's a miracle that somebody wanted it. Normal people never come to Long Shaft."

"We needed a break from the rat race," Zoe said evenly. "Right, Tony?"

"Tony?" Flynn stared at her in confusion. "I'm not—"

"I know, darling. You're not used to having me call you Tony. I apologize, and I won't do it again. I didn't mean anything by it. Don't worry, you're still my candy-coated snookums." Zoe stepped forward and held out her hand to Luanne. "My name's Vera Parsons, and this is Tony Bennetti."

"Hi. Glad to meet you." Luanne shook Zoe's hand while glancing sideways at Flynn. "Um, you guys don't have the same last name?"

Zoe winked at her. "Not yet."

Flynn broke out in a cold sweat. Surely Kristen wouldn't find out about this conversation, but he didn't like the idea of masquerading as Zoe's candy-coated snookums, even in front of a kid.

Word could get around. He hadn't pictured interacting with anybody in Long Shaft, so he hadn't visualized how they'd identify themselves if they happened to meet someone. He got it now. Zoe had given Luanne names from the script.

"Where do you live?" Zoe asked.

"Right over there." Luanne pointed to her left through the trees.

Flynn couldn't see anything, not even a light. "There's a house over there?"

"Oh yeah. You can't tell because the 'rents are watching TV with all the lights off and the curtains closed. They do that every night, retreating to their cave. It's very Neanderthal. I've tried pretending I'm Ayla from *Clan of the Cave Bear,* but the TV doesn't look much like a fire. And Frankenstein is out on a date. Otherwise you'd hear his obnoxious sound system blaring at about a million decibels."

Flynn blinked. "Frankenstein?"

"Otherwise known as Jeff. He's tall and sort of clumsy, so I call him that, which makes him crazy, which is my goal. Anyway, if you walked in that direction, eventually you'd smash right into my house. In fact, I wish you would." She grinned. "I'll bet that would boost them out of their matching La-Z-Boys."

"And do your parents know you're over here?" Flynn hoped not. If they did, the next neighborly move might be a knock at the door and a fresh-baked coffee cake. Then again, he was getting extremely hungry. A fresh-baked coffee cake would go good right now.

Luanne avoided his gaze. "Sort of."

"They don't know," Flynn guessed. "You sneaked out."

"I'll be back before they know it. The screen in my bedroom comes out real easy. I would make an awesome cat burglar."

Zoe exchanged a glance with Flynn. "I don't know if it's such a good idea, roaming around the woods at night by yourself."

"My thoughts exactly," Flynn said.

"I've been going out the window since I was nine." Luanne's chin lifted. "A girl has to make her own excitement around here. Long Shaft is terminally boring."

Flynn couldn't stop himself. "Have you ever seen Bigfoot?"

Luanne shrugged. "Sure. Big deal. I mean, what's the point? Some big hairy stinky thing. Ask me if I care." She looked at Zoe. "Has anyone ever told you that you look like Zoe Tarleton?"

If Flynn expected Zoe to freak out, he was in for a surprise. She handled it like the consummate actor she was.

"People mistake me for her all the time," she said. "I'm flattered."

"I *love* Zoe Tarleton." Luanne raised her arms heavenward. "Oh, dear God, If I could meet her for *one second,* my life would be perfect." She let her arms flop back to her sides and studied Zoe again. "Are you absolutely positive you're not her? You really do look alike."

Zoe laughed. "Thanks. I'm sure if she ever heard that, she'd be extremely insulted."

"Maybe. No offense, but she wouldn't be caught dead in clothes like that."

"I'm sure she wouldn't."

"She's a goddess. I have all her movies on DVD, except this last one, which isn't out yet. Long Shaft doesn't have a movie theater, so I have to order them online and watch them on my parents' suckola TV." Luanne sighed dramatically. "That tells you how dead this place is. *Nothing* ever happens here."

Flynn smelled something burning and decided that was as good an excuse as any to ditch this precocious preteen. "Luanne, we need to go. We left our dinner on the stove." Or what he hoped would be their dinner. He didn't have huge expectations.

Zoe gasped. "Yikes. Luanne, we really do have to run. Besides, you should head home before you get in trouble with your parents."

"They'll never know. My brother didn't get caught, either. He started climbing out his window when he was eight, and he's about as graceful as a spastic elephant. If he could get away with it, I'm golden." She gazed longingly at the cabin. "You guys got some cards? I know some really neat games."

"Sorry." Zoe gave her a smile as if to soften the rejection. "No cards."

"Okay. See you around, then." Luanne turned with obvious reluctance and started back through the woods.

Zoe lowered her voice. "I feel terrible. Maybe we should invite her in."

"Not on your life." Flynn took charge, grabbing Zoe's arm to steer her toward the back door. "She already thinks you're a Zoe Tarleton look-alike, and she's too smart for her own good. Give her a little more exposure to you and she's bound to figure out you're in disguise. And then all hell will break loose."

"You're right." She sighed. "But can you imagine being her age and being stuck in a place like Long Shaft?"

"Yes." Flynn thought of his own teenage years in a sorry little mining town a lot like this one. "It's a fantastic motivator."

Fifteen minutes later, as they sat at the small table in the kitchen, Zoe was driven to brutal honesty. "This is the worst spaghetti I've had in my entire life."

Flynn topped off her wineglass. "Alcohol helps."

"Not enough. I accidentally bit into one of those pieces of garlic. Did you know I was supposed to peel and mince that stuff?"

"I know nothing about the care and feeding of garlic."

"Me, either, but I think I'll be tasting this for three days. I'll have to swish a whole bottle of mouthwash before we start working on the script."

He looked wary. "About the script. I really know nothing about acting. I could foul you up instead of helping."

"I need to hear the lines said out loud. Your delivery isn't critical right now." She pushed aside her plate. "I've eaten enough of this rubberized pasta to get me through until breakfast."

"We could try some of the blueberry cobbler Margo raved about."

"I'll have to pass on that cobbler, but you're welcome to have some. I don't have any place to work out this weekend and I've already had pasta, which wasn't any less fattening just because it tasted like Play-Doh. Adding dessert would require twenty minutes on the treadmill, and I didn't pack one."

Flynn shook his head. "I don't get this weight thing. You look fine."

"I look fine because I work out with a personal trainer five days a week. I inherited the fat gene from my mother's side of the family. If I didn't have a regular maintenance program, I'd look like Margo in no time."

"Impossible."

"Not. But have some cobbler if you want."

"No, that's okay." Flynn pushed his plate aside. "I'm not really hungry for it, either."

"I'm not surprised. That pasta could kill anybody's appetite."

"It wasn't so bad."

"You don't have to be nice. Next to this dreck, Chef Boyardee would be a gourmet treat. Come on, let's try a scene from the script."

"I don't know about this, Zoe."

She figured all he needed was a little push to get him over his stage fright. "Bring your wine. Just one itty-bitty scene." She picked up her glass and stood. "Flynn, I really need you."

He gave her a startled look.

"To read the part of Tony," she clarified.

"We should rinse the dishes."

"Oh." She hadn't rinsed a dish in years. She'd finish eating, push her plate aside, and somebody else would deal with that.

He must have picked up on her surprise, because he immediately qualified his statement. "I meant *I* would rinse the dishes."

"That's silly. We'll each do our own." She picked up her plate and went over to the sink. But even with hot water, which was probably playing hell with her manicure, she had trouble getting off the pasta that was cemented on the plate. And then there was the spaghetti pot to worry about and the saucepan caked with that awful sauce. She'd forgotten how much she hated doing dishes.

"Here, let me." Flynn reached in and took the plate.

She was pretty sure he hadn't intended it to be a sexual thing, and yet having him move in like that and take the plate out of her hands, thereby relieving her of having to scrub off the last ickiness, was positively gallant. She wanted to melt into those strong arms and express her gratitude. Aqua Velva was suddenly her favorite scent in the world.

"You go ahead and start looking over the script," he said. "I'll take care of this."

So that's what living with Flynn would be like. He'd sweep away the nasty chores she didn't want to do. He might even be the kind of guy who would change a baby's diaper. She'd never thought in terms of babies, let alone dirty diapers, but Flynn was the sort of man who made a girl consider those options.

"Okay," she said, feeling extremely cooperative toward whatever he had in mind. "Thank you."

"No problem." He unbuttoned his cuffs and rolled up his sleeves.

Now *that* was appealing, watching a man roll up his sleeves in order to do housework. The fact that he still wore his tie made it even cuter. Zoe remembered seeing her dad doing dishes when she was growing up, but now her parents had a maid who took care of that.

They'd protested the maid, but Zoe had talked them into it. Her mom still cooked, but at least she didn't have to clean anymore. Somehow Zoe also had convinced them to live in a nicer house, one she'd helped pay for, by telling them that success meant nothing to her if she couldn't have them close by to share it.

"Do you have a housekeeper?" she asked Flynn, curious now that she saw how efficiently he attacked the dishwashing job.

He glanced up from the sink. "No. Why?"

"Everybody I know has a housekeeper."

"So you think I need one of those, in addition to a better car?"

"I didn't say that. I just wondered if you did or not."

He shrugged. "Never saw the need for one. I'm neat and I don't have a huge place. I don't mind doing it myself." He gazed at her. "Are you going to stand there and watch me?"

Well, she wanted to. It was a turn-on. But she couldn't let him know, especially when they hadn't discussed the condoms vis-à-vis Kristen Crackers. "Nope." She picked up her wine from the table. "I'll get my script and start looking it over. Meet you later in the living room. And don't forget to bring your script."

"I'd rather do a hundred dishes than read that part, Zoe."

"It'll be *fine*. And a huge help to me."

"All right." He sighed in resignation. "I'll bring my script."

"Thank you. I really appreciate it." Giving him a smile, she left the kitchen and went to her bedroom to grab the script. In her bathroom she took the time to swish a little mouthwash, just in case. Then she picked up the script and her glass of wine, put on her wire-rimmed glasses, and headed for the living room.

She put her wine on the end table beside her before sitting down on the sofa, the script in her lap. She had to keep sliding the glasses back up her nose, but she kept them on to remind her of the role as she paged through, searching for a good scene to read.

Flipping through, she got interested in one where Vera was fighting off a potential kidnapper in a ski mask who had come through her bedroom window. But Tony wasn't in that scene. She paged to the next scene, in which Tony arrived in the bedroom and the kidnapper escaped by diving out the window into the padded bed of a pickup truck spattered with mud that covered the license plate.

With no opportunity to chase down the kidnapper, Tony ended up alone with a disheveled, nightgown-clad Vera who was riding an adrenaline high. As Zoe scanned the scene, she heard Flynn leave the kitchen and go back to his bedroom to get the script. She glanced up as he returned carrying the script and his glass of wine.

He didn't look happy. "In first grade I was cast as an eggplant in a skit about vegetables," he said. "I forgot my line and stood there frozen to the spot in my purple suit until someone came and led me away." He cleared his throat and sat on the sofa about three feet away from her. "Just so you know what you're getting into."

She gazed at him and did her best not to laugh. "What kind of line would someone give an eggplant?"

"Bake me, fry me, I'll be gone. I'm also great with Parmesan."

She tried not to crack up. She really tried. But the image of a little Flynn in big glasses and dressed as an eggplant was too much.

"I'll never forget that damned line as long as I live."

"I'm sure you won't." She took off the glasses, which had seriously slipped down her nose, and wiped the tears from her eyes. Then after looking at Flynn again, she had to swallow a new burst of laughter. "Now that I've heard it, I'll never forget it, either. Too bad we didn't have an eggplant in the grocery bag. You would have known exactly what to do with it."

"No, I wouldn't. I've avoided eggplant entirely ever since. On the rare occasions I go into a grocery store, I see those big purple things and start to shake."

"Poor Flynn." She had the urge to touch him, but she controlled it. She still didn't know where they stood.

"Traumatized by a vegetable. Have you gone in for eggplant therapy?"

"No, but I'll bet there is such a thing somewhere in LA."

"I'll bet you're right. All my friends think I'm weird because I don't have a personal shrink."

Flynn smiled. "Now that *is* weird. Don't tell me you're well-adjusted."

"I think I am. But then, what do I know?" She crossed her eyes and stuck out her tongue.

That got a laugh out of him, which gratified her immensely. She was an entertainer at heart, had been ever since playing the part of a turkey in her preschool Thanksgiving skit. Had she been the one in the eggplant costume, she would have given the crowd a song and dance to go along with the dopey line.

She vividly remembered the moment when she'd figured out that people got paid to act. Sitting on Santa's lap at the age of seven, she'd accidentally pulled off his beard. Discovering he wasn't Santa really sucked, but learning that he got money for pretending to be Santa had been a turning point in her life.

From that moment on, all she'd ever wanted to do was act. She'd started with the soaps, moved to a sitcom, and finally earned her stripes on the big screen. She secretly longed to do Broadway, but she was afraid no one would take that plan seriously. Landing this role would open doors, though.

Flynn reached in his pocket and pulled out a small plastic case. "I can fix your glasses now, if you want."

"You know what? I won't need them for the scene I found." She laid the glasses on the coffee table. "So we can deal with them later."

"What scene is that?"

"Right here." She showed Flynn the page and quickly described the setup.

He glanced over the script. "It's in her bedroom?"

"Yes. Knowing how she'd behave in her chemistry lab is easy. But I need pointers on how she'd react when she's been through a scare like this, when her defenses are down."

Flynn swallowed. "I don't think I'm up to this."

"Oh, sure you are. Just use your imagination. Tony's been roused from a deep sleep, so he's sort of rumpled, and lots of adrenaline is flowing for both of them. You can do it."

"I'm not so sure."

"Okay, maybe you need a little help to get in character."

He glanced up. "Like what?"

She studied him for a few seconds, trying to picture him as more Tony-like. "For starters, you could take off your tie."

Chapter Eight

I thought you said it didn't matter if I'm in character?" Flynn didn't want to be in character. Tony was high-octane, the kind of guy who would jump at any chance to take a woman to bed, especially a woman like Zoe.

As long as Flynn kept his tie on, he wouldn't turn into Tony. Besides, most sexual encounters began when a guy loosened his tie. A loose tie led to everything becoming loose. Flynn wanted to stay tight.

"You admitted you're not very good at this," Zoe said. "I'm trying to help. In fact, I should do the same thing." She reached for the twist ties holding her hair into a ponytail.

Flynn began to panic. That was another sexual signal, when a woman took her hair down. He reached for the eyeglass repair kit. "Let's fix those glasses and get it out of the way. Then we know for sure it's been done."

"I don't want to take the time right now." She tossed the twist ties on the coffee table and shook her hair free. Glossy red strands reflected the glow from the table lamp. "Ah, that feels good. I wonder if I should put on a nightgown?"

"No! I mean, that will only take more time. Let's read." Flynn decided if he let Zoe get any further into character she'd want to rehearse the scene in her bedroom.

"Then you'll take off your tie?"

"Yeah. Sure." Still worried that she might reconsider the nightgown, he unknotted his tie and stripped it from under his shirt collar in record time.

"The first couple of buttons, too."

His heart pumped faster than the Civic's four-cylinder on an uphill climb. "Okay." This was insanity. What next, his belt?

"That's good." Zoe picked up the script. "You have the first line."

Grateful not to be going deeper into Tony-land, Flynn grabbed the script and recited his line. *"Damn it all, he's gone."*

"More feeling."

He didn't bother to remind her that his delivery wasn't supposed to matter. *"Damn it all! He's gone!"*

"Much better." Zoe cleared her throat and began to pant. *"Oh, Tony. Dear God. I've never . . . no one's ever tried to . . . do that, before."*

"You mean kidnap you?" Flynn did his best to ignore the way Zoe's breasts rose and fell with her rapid, shallow breathing.

"Kidnap me? He was trying to rape me!"

"You're kidding."

Zoe sat up, ramrod straight and indignant. *"Obviously you find the concept unbelievable."*

"I find it unlikely."

"Why? Because I'm not that sort of woman?"

"There is no sort of woman, Vera. Rapists aren't turned on by lust. They want power over another human being. They don't care much what she looks like. For what it's worth, I don't think he was after your body."

"He was so! He . . . grabbed me."

"Where?" Flynn began to sweat. He didn't like where this was going, or rather, he liked it too much.

"Here." Zoe put down the script so she could clutch both breasts. *"And he squeezed me, hard."*

Flynn stared at Zoe, unable to tear his gaze away from the sight of her cupping her breasts. Her hair was tousled and her makeup was almost nonexistent, but there was a healthy flush on her cheeks. She looked like a woman who had recently had a good roll in the hay.

"Your line," she said, still looking at the script. Then she glanced up and caught him staring. "Okay, I know what you're thinking."

He hoped to hell she didn't.

"Vera is supposed to be somewhat flat-chested, which will make this part funnier. I'll have to bind my breasts when I'm in costume, and when they shoot the love scenes . . . I'll have to hope they use really dim light."

Flynn gulped. "Um, yeah. Exactly what I was thinking." Wrong. He'd been thinking that he'd give a year's income to see her executing this move with no costume whatsoever. Nada. The thought of her scarlet-tipped fingers wrapped around her bare breasts was enough to give him a woody. And that was the last thing he needed right now.

It took all his willpower, but he managed to return his attention to the script. With an effort he even found his place. *"I think grabbing your boobs was unintentional."* Oh, dear God. These lines were killing him.

"Unintentional? Come on, Bennetti. I may not have a wild and crazy sex life, but I've never known a man to unintentionally grab a woman's bazookas. It's always intentional."

"Okay, okay. So your kidnapper wasn't above copping a feel while he was trying to get you out the window and down to the truck. But he wanted your brains, not your body." Flynn fervently wished he could say the same.

"So you think the break-in the other day and this man grabbing me tonight are related?"

"For a genius, you aren't very smart, baby doll."

Zoe glanced up again. "No, no, Flynn. You have to say that with more swagger."

She was lucky he could still speak the language. The vision of her holding her breasts was still dancing in his fevered brain, teasing him with possibilities he had no business imagining. "Like how?"

"Like this." She curled her lip and cocked her head at an angle as she delivered the line, putting special emphasis on the *baby doll* part.

She looked so damned cute doing it that he laughed.

"C'mon, Flynn, be serious. Try it again."

"I don't know how any guy uses that term with a straight face."

"I know it's not your style, but—"

"Not even close." He should get back to the script and stop looking at her mouth before he landed himself in trouble. Who was he kidding? He was already in trouble. Her perfume set off reactions where he didn't even know he had reactions. The distance between them seemed to have shrunk, but he wasn't sure if she'd moved or he had.

Her voice softened. "For what it's worth, I'd probably hate it if a guy called me *baby doll*."

"Yeah, it's really patronizing." While he was trying to remember how to breathe, somehow his hand ended up curved around the nape of her neck and he was pulling her toward him.

"Yes."

He wasn't clear on exactly what that *yes* pertained to. Her silky hair tickled the backs of his fingers as disjointed thoughts skittered through his brain. She smelled incredible. He'd never kissed a movie star before. This wasn't in the script. To hell with the script.

She slid her hand along the side of his jaw. She wouldn't do that if she didn't like what was happening. He closed his eyes. Zoe Tarleton was waiting for him to kiss her. Or maybe she'd kiss him first. Either option was totally acceptable.

From his bedroom, his cell phone rang. Not only did it ring; it played the special little tune that worked on his conscience like a cattle prod. He squeezed his eyes tighter, hoping he was imagining things. He wasn't, damn it. Opening his eyes, he gazed down at her. "Let me get that."

Her expression promised him all the joys of heaven. "You could let the message service get that."

"I . . . can't." With a groan he pushed away from the sofa, away from a temptation he should be resisting, away from a moment that he'd forever regret losing.

He caught Kristen right before the happy little tune switched to message mode. "Hey there."

"Hey yourself." She sounded so glad to hear his voice.

Guilt sat on his shoulders with the weight of a hundred hippos. "How's the conference going?"

"Dull. I wish I hadn't agreed to be here. Then I could have come out there earlier."

"I wish you could have done that, too." Then his life would be in order. He could have given Zoe a legitimate excuse, and he wouldn't currently be sitting in a cozy little cabin in the woods with the sexiest woman on the planet, a woman who wanted him to kiss her.

"I'm still thinking of ditching part of this deal. I know you're tied up right now, but maybe you'll get finished early. How's the nerd tutoring coming along?"

"Fine." Flynn definitely didn't want to talk about that. "Would you believe we're sitting in the Bigfoot Capital of the World?"

"Bigfoot? You mean that monster thing?"

"Yeah. Some people think it's real." He decided not to admit that he was one of those people.

"There are kooks everywhere, Flynn. But I'm sorry you have to spend the weekend right in the middle of a townful."

"Yeah, me, too. But I have to keep the client happy." He glanced toward the doorway and discovered Zoe standing there, shamelessly eavesdropping. She didn't look particularly happy, either. If keeping her happy was his intention, he was doing a crummy job so far.

He turned away from the doorway. "Uh, Kristen, could I call you back in a few minutes? I need to take care of something here."

"Actually, I'm heading down to the bar to have drinks with some of my colleagues. Maybe I could fly out there tomorrow night, though. How would that be?"

Uh-oh. "Um, it's a ratty little town. I don't think you'd like it."

"I wouldn't be coming there to see the town. And I promise not to get in the way."

"I'm sure you wouldn't." Flynn had no idea how he'd deal with Kristen showing up in Long Shaft. "But it's not your kind of place. And don't forget, nobody's supposed to know Zoe's here." He peeked over at Zoe, who had moved past mildly unhappy to royally pissed.

"I know," Kristen said. "It was just a thought, anyway. I'll talk to you tomorrow."

"Good. Have fun with your friends."

"Fun is what I have with you," Kristen said. "This is strictly an obligation."

"Same here. Talk to you tomorrow." He disconnected the call. Then he turned to face the music. "I should probably explain."

"Oh, you think so?" Zoe crossed her arms over her impressive assets, which strained the top button on her ugly beige jacket.

He stood there wishing the button would give and hating himself for wishing that. He wanted to strip her naked and push her down on the twin bed that was so conveniently within reach. The immediacy of his lust astonished him—he'd never felt this kind of urgency with Kristen or with any other woman.

The only impediment to his lust was Zoe, who was glaring at him with a fierceness that was intimidating. Her expression was the exact opposite of the one she'd worn a few minutes ago, before Kristen's phone call. She sure could switch directions fast. He'd have to remember that.

"Did I misunderstand, or did Kristen say she might come to Long Shaft?"

"I'm sure she won't."

"If she gives us away, I'll—"

"She won't give us away." He didn't want Zoe to know how worried he was about that.

"If you say so, but I'm not reassured. And there's another thing we need to discuss."

"Okay." He had a pretty good idea what that was.

"What's up with the box of condoms, Flynn? Are they part of your plan to keep the client happy? If so, you flatter yourself. I don't need sex from you. I can get sex any time I want it. Matter of fact, there's a waiting list, and guess what? You're not even on it!"

"The condoms are for Kristen."

"*Kristen?* How does that work? I thought you said she wouldn't be coming here?"

"She won't."

"In that case, I hate to break it to you, but you don't need condoms for phone sex. They haven't figured out a way for sperm or STDs to travel through that cable. I'm not saying it won't ever be possible, but as of now, you—"

"I packed them when I was getting ready for the Catalina Island trip with Kristen, okay?"

She looked confused. "But that's not until next week."

"I like being prepared." And how he cringed at being forced to reveal what an anal geek he was.

Gradually, understanding replaced the confusion in her eyes. "Let me get this straight. You packed for the trip with Kristen, and when I asked you up here for the weekend, you grabbed the already packed suitcase, forgetting about the Kristen condoms?"

"That's about the size of it."

"Oh." She gazed at him as if lost in thought. "Then why were you so hot to kiss me a few minutes ago?"

There was the really tough question. And *hot* was the operative word, all right. He wasn't proud of his lack of control. "Unfortunately, I seem to be attracted to you."

"Is that right?" She perked up a little upon hearing that. "Is it a new thing or an old thing?"

Another tough question. "An unrecognized thing. An unacknowledged thing. A thing that has been lying dormant and then suddenly popped up." Whoops. What an incredibly bad choice of words.

"I see."

"In any case, I can guarantee that I didn't count on that when I agreed to this trip. I should have factored it in, but I didn't."

"So you want me, but you don't want to want me."

"That's right. I'm committed to Kristen." Then he remembered he wasn't the only person who was involved with someone else. "For that matter, what about Trace?"

She looked uneasy. "Well, yes. There's Trace."

"Damn right there's Trace." He allowed himself a little male indignation on the part of the wronged Trace Edwards.

"My relationship with him is . . . complicated."

"Meaning what, exactly?" He hoped she wouldn't say they had an open relationship, where they could sleep with anybody who took their fancy. He knew that happened in Hollywood, but he didn't like thinking that Zoe subscribed to such a philosophy.

She hesitated.

Flynn decided he had to know what the deal was with Trace. It was important. "Does he care what you do with other guys?"

"Yes, he cares. And you're right. We're each committed to someone, so there can't be any fooling around. Those Kristen condoms threw me, but I'm back on track, now. We'll both be careful from now on."

He wished she wouldn't keep referring to them as Kristen condoms, as if they had his girlfriend's name on them, along with a label that warned against using them for any other purpose. He wouldn't be using them for any other purpose, but still, they were there, in case of an emergency.

And what sort of emergency would that be, Flynn, old man? The kind where Zoe's driving you so crazy you can't keep your pants zipped another minute? God, he hoped he was up to the task of resisting her for the next thirty-six hours. He should have brought a framed picture of Kristen to put on the dresser.

"Flynn, if we're going to manage this, you have to stop looking at me like that."

He snapped out of his lustful daze. "I wasn't looking at you any particular way."

"You were, too. You were looking at me as if you wanted to eat me up with a spoon."

He groaned and ran a hand over his face, as if he could somehow rub off his lustful expression. "Maybe we should just go to bed."

"Do you think that would work? It's worth a try. We might be awful in bed. We probably would be awful in bed. Most couples don't hit it off right away. So we'd have a disastrous experience and be over this problem in a jiffy."

Instantly he was aroused. He didn't think there was a chance in hell they'd be awful in bed, not with the kind of energy they would each bring to the project. "I meant go to bed individually, each in our own rooms."

"Oh." Pink tinged her cheeks. "I misunderstood. I certainly hope you don't think I was being too aggressive for making that suggestion. I was only trying to consider all the possible solutions to our problem."

"I don't think you're being too aggressive." Part of

him, the part currently in charge, wouldn't mind if she'd be more aggressive. "But I doubt it would work."

"You think we'd have fun in bed, don't you?"

"Yes." *Fun* didn't even begin to describe what he thought they'd have.

She nodded. "Me, too. Okay, I'm leaving for my own bedroom now and closing the door. Sleep well."

As she started out the door, an eerie howl filled the night. "Yikes!" Zoe raced back to him and hurled herself into his arms.

Flynn held her tight as the howl came again, sending a chill through him. He had no doubt Bigfoot was out there in the woods, and this could be his chance to see the mythical creature he'd studied so eagerly as a kid. On the other hand, he had a trembling Zoe in his arms and she needed his comfort.

To hell with Bigfoot.

As the second howl died away, Zoe shuddered. She wasn't proud of herself for clinging to Flynn like the peel on a banana, but that howl had totally freaked her out. With the side of her face flattened against his chest, she could hear his heart beating fast, so he might not be all that copacetic with it, either.

"I'm afraid to ask what that was," she said, not moving an inch.

"It's the trademark howl of a Sasquatch."

She tightened her grip on Flynn, noticing in the process how nice that felt, to be hugging her lawyer. Who knew? "I really didn't want that information."

"Sorry."

"It could be a hoax, right? A local businessman running around in a furry suit with a tape recorder under his arm?"

"Possibly."

"You don't sound as if you believe that." She desperately wanted to believe it, even if that meant she had no more excuse to hug Flynn.

"I can't picture a sane person wanting to try it, Zoe. For one thing, you might get shot by someone trying to make a name for himself. For another, if you got caught you'd never live down the humiliation. How many business owners would run that kind of risk just to boost tourism? It's not logical."

"But is a Sasquatch logical?" She liked this—wrapped tight in Flynn's arms, feeling cozy and safe while they discussed the potential existence of Bigfoot. His voice rumbled in her ear, and his body heat was taking away the shivers of dread. Also, she liked the way he stroked her back—firm enough to let her know he was there, yet gentle enough to be soothing.

She wondered what his hands would feel like if he was going for a sexual response. From the way he was touching her now, she suspected he'd know exactly how much pressure to exert. The perfect pressure. Oh, baby.

"Sasquatch is about as logical as the pyramids," he said.

"Huh?" She would have to think a little faster to keep up with this guy.

"We still don't know how the Egyptians built those things, but there they are, solid evidence of an unbelievable architectural feat. Same with the structures the Incas built. Did creatures from outer space land and give them some help? That's one explanation."

She could get used to this business of cuddling with Flynn. "Do you believe in aliens?"

"I pretty much do. Think of the vastness of the universe. I don't know if other beings have made it to this planet yet, but we can't be the only place that supports life. Which leads me to Bigfoot."

"Bigfoot's an alien?"

"That's one possibility."

Flynn's thought processes intrigued her. She never would have expected her sedate, conservative lawyer to believe in Bigfoot and aliens. "Flynn, do you subscribe to the *Enquirer*?"

"No." He chuckled. "Do you?"

"No. But what you said sounded as if it could be a headline story. I thought you might have read it there."

"I subscribe to the *Wall Street Journal* and the *Harvard Law Review*."

"Now that I would believe. That's more like the Flynn I know."

There was a long pause. "You think you know me?"

A subtle change in his tone caused her to look up. She found herself gazing into gray eyes filled with good old-fashioned lust. His dark-rimmed glasses made that lust seem even more potent in a still-waters-run-deep sort of way. As a test, she eased her hips forward, and encountered more evidence that Flynn was fired up and ready to go.

Her heart started racing again, and not from the threat of Sasquatch. Now that she understood what was going on with her nerd mentor, she ought to move away. But she couldn't make herself. A completely aroused Flynn was a new and delicious concept she wanted to savor for a moment.

His voice grew husky. "I've been thinking about that idea you had."

"I've had a dozen ideas recently." But she knew which idea he was talking about.

"I've had a hundred."

"Show-off." So much heat was being generated by the places where her body touched his that she wouldn't wonder if their clothes started to smoke.

"All my ideas involve getting naked with you."

Her mouth grew moist. In point of fact, *moist* was her middle name at this very moment. And what a coincidence: here they were in a bedroom, a bedroom stocked with condoms.

Then she remembered why they had condoms and who they were intended for. Not her. Her conscience began to shoulder its way forward through her misty fog of selfish desire. Flynn belonged to someone else. He'd made that point and they'd been about to retire to separate bedrooms when that ungodly howl had sent her running for safety.

But the howling was over, at least for now, and she needed to be a good girl and stop tempting Flynn. He didn't want to want her. He'd said so himself. Yet he was only human and she'd been rubbing up against him for a good ten minutes. She knew the effect she had on men. It was the quality that had made her a box-office favorite.

So she did the decent thing and backed up . . . at least an inch.

"Don't." His arms tightened around her, eliminating that inch.

"I have to. This isn't right." *It's perfect, but not right.*

"Then why does it feel so good?"

"Whether or not it feels good is beside the point." She put more effort into her escape plan and wiggled out of his arms.

"Zoe . . ."

"I'm sorry, Flynn." She edged toward the door. "I shouldn't have thrown myself at you like that. It's not fair."

He took a step toward her. "I've lost track of what's fair."

She backed toward the door. "We're not doing this."

He followed her. "I think we are."

"No." She held up her hand like a traffic cop. "You'll hate yourself in the morning."

He took her hand and began kissing the tips of her fingers. "Maybe, but I can't seem to make myself care about that right now."

The feel of his lips mesmerized her. They were incredibly soft, tantalizingly warm, and so supple she swallowed a groan of longing. Those lips belonged to Kristen "Crackers" Keebler, the woman with a rightful claim to the condoms and the man who'd bought them. Zoe had broken Margo's heart fifteen years ago by stealing her boyfriend. History would not repeat itself.

She pulled her hand free. "No, Flynn. Good night." As she walked down the hall toward her bedroom, his sigh of resignation followed her.

"Thanks," he said as she reached her bedroom door. "I think."

She almost turned around. But he was part of a couple and she refused to be the "other woman." Been there, done that, bought the T-shirt. Walking into her bedroom, she closed the door.

A noise outside made her pause to listen, and her chest tightened in fear. Someone . . . or some*thing* . . . was running through the forest. Something very big. And a terrible smell was making its way through the chinks and crannies of the cabin. Damn! She couldn't go back to Flynn's bedroom like a scared rabbit. She knew what would happen if she went to him for comfort.

So she stood there holding her breath and shaking uncontrollably as the crackling, crashing sounds gradually died away. Sheesh. And Luanne had said nothing ever happened in Long Shaft.

Chapter Nine

When he heard something charging through the woods and smelled the foul odor, Flynn hurried out into the hall, prepared to defend Zoe if necessary. He expected and fervently hoped that she'd come tearing out of her bedroom and rush to him for protection. No such luck.

Whoever or whatever was out there was moving away from the cabin, not toward it, which muted the danger factor. Zoe had probably decided to tough it out rather than risk another close encounter with Flynn. He was impressed with her resolve.

Or, and this was a depressing thought, maybe she wasn't all that motivated to have sex with him. He'd been so carried away by the excitement of bodily contact that he might have imagined her response. All that heat could have been coming from him and bouncing off of her, making her seem as hot as he was when she was actually being polite.

Any minute now he'd start feeling guilty for suggesting they get horizontal, but so far all he felt was a high level of frustration because they hadn't done that. A walk outside would help clear his mind and get his buddy to relax. Yeah, he definitely needed a walk to cool down.

Oh, who was he kidding? With Zoe forbidden to him, he wanted to investigate the area and look for evidence to indicate what had run past the cabin just now. He'd heard the rhythm of two feet hitting the ground, not four, so he doubted it had been a bear. And there was that smell.

He wished to hell he had a flashlight. In the morning maybe he'd drive to the nearest hardware store and buy one. They needed a flashlight in case of emergencies, not to mention potential Bigfoot sightings. The cabin should have come with one, but it hadn't. He was stuck with the butane flamethrower for now.

Retrieving it from the hearth where he'd replaced it after the Luanne incident, he started to leave. Then he remembered that Zoe might be startled if she happened to look out her bedroom window and see him roaming around in the dark pointing his flame every which way, so he walked down the hall and tapped on her door with the tip of the lighter.

"Who is it?"

"Bigfoot." Cheap shot, but he couldn't resist. Who did she think it would be?

"Not funny."

"I know. Sorry. Listen, I'm going outside to look around."

"Then I'm coming with you."

He didn't think that was wise. Too much togetherness in the dark wasn't a good thing. "That's okay. Maybe you should stay here and—"

She opened her door, cutting off his protest. "I'm go-

ing. I'm supposed to be observing you, remember?"
She'd changed out of her ugly beige suit into a ragged
gray sweatshirt and faded sweats the color of bile.

The new outfit did nothing to calm his libido. He
wanted to grab the hem of her sweatshirt and yank it over
her head. "I don't see how following me around outside
applies to your research."

"Sure it does. Vera is a scientist, which means she's
curious about everything. Just like you, she'd want to
look for clues about whatever it was that ran past here a
while ago."

"So you heard that?" He thought maybe her outfit was
mismatched on purpose as part of her nerd wardrobe. The
sweatshirt had a picture of Einstein on the front, along
with the Theory of Relativity formula. Flynn envied the
old guy his venue. Draped over Zoe's breasts, Einstein
looked almost three-dimensional.

"I'd have had to be deaf not to hear it," she said.
"Sounded like an elephant jogging on its hind legs." She
threw out the comment with bravado, but she looked a little nervous. "And the thing was smelly, too."

"You really can stay here. You don't have to go with me."

She swallowed. "I'd rather go with you than stay by
myself, okay?"

"Okay." He couldn't very well force her to stay. He'd just
have to watch himself and not get into any cozy situations.

"Flynn, we can handle this," she said, as if reading his
mind.

He gazed at her and wondered if she had any concept
of her sex appeal. She wouldn't have to do anything more
elaborate than stand there to drive a guy insane. He
couldn't believe he'd never realized how vulnerable he
was to that, but then again, they'd always been in his of-

fice or at a crowded restaurant. Here in the middle of the woods was a whole different story, a test of willpower he hadn't counted on.

Her breathing changed as she held his gaze. "You don't think we can?"

"Yeah, we can." He didn't want to admit he was losing control. He'd get it back. She was an international star who lived in a galaxy far, far away from him. He gestured with the butane lighter. "Let's go see what we find."

Zoe wasn't crazy about going outside, but she was even less willing to be alone inside. She hadn't pictured this weekend turning into some scary thing like *Friday the 13th,* but that's how it was shaping up. She hadn't figured on the sexual aspect of the trip, either. But she was on top of that problem, ready to call a halt at the slightest sign of trouble. She would not compromise Flynn's relationship with Kristen.

She followed him outside and closed the door. "It's getting chilly out here."

"Want to go back for a jacket?"

"No, that's okay. It feels good."

He sighed. "Sure does."

She felt terrible. Because of her, he was in an unwelcome state of arousal. Too bad he was taken, though, because standing in the forest with the great smell of pine all around them, an almost full moon, and about a billion stars overhead, she had the urge to start hugging and kissing.

Nature had that effect on her and she hadn't combined Flynn and nature before, so she hadn't realized how well he fit into the mix. Making film after film in the past few years, she hadn't taken vacations. Any time she'd been in a natural setting like this, she'd been working.

"I want to make this search systematic," Flynn said.

"Right." She was working now, she reminded herself, working to understand the thoughts and actions of her chosen nerd. He wanted a systematic search. When she got back inside, she'd write that down. Good info. "Meaning what?" she asked.

"The sound came from over there." He pointed the butane lighter to his left. "So we'll conduct a grid search, walking a pattern of lines lengthwise and then crosswise, so that we cover the area."

She glanced at the wooded section he'd pointed to and tried to picture walking in a line through any of it. "I don't get the idea. It's full of trees."

He gazed at her. "So you walk around them."

"Well, I know that, but which way?"

"All the way around."

"Hm." She glanced doubtfully at the forest and back at Flynn. "This could take a really long time. We're talking tedious."

"I know. You should probably go back inside. I don't mind doing it by myself."

She wasn't keen on that plan. "What about postponing this until morning? Then you'd be able to see what you're doing."

He adjusted his glasses and looked up into the night sky. "Now that the moon's up, I think I'll be able to see okay. By tomorrow morning the evidence could be gone, compromised in some way."

"Wouldn't want that." In point of fact she'd love that. No evidence would mean she could convince herself she'd imagined the sound of that lumbering giant. She was helping him look for something she hoped he wouldn't find.

He blew out a breath. "Zoe, just go on inside. In fact, go get the key and bring it back to me. That way you can lock yourself in and feel safe."

"No way, José. If those things are aliens, a silly old lock won't keep them out." Out here in the dark she was ready to believe every creepy story she'd ever heard.

"I don't *know* that Bigfoot's an alien species. It's only one theory. If you locked the door you'd be perfectly fine, and then I can conduct this search without putting you through a boring ordeal."

She shook her head. "Nope, I'm staying and I'm walking."

"That makes no sense. I'm probably less protection for you than a locked door, when it comes to that."

"So I'm not being logical. We both know that's your strong suit. Lead on, Flynn. Let's walk that line."

"Okay, if you insist. Come on over this way."

She followed him several yards away from the cabin. Glancing back at it, she wondered if she'd made the right choice. She could be inside that cozy little place where lights glowed and doors locked. Instead she'd thrown her lot in with Flynn out here in the wilderness.

She realized that she loved nature, but she liked it best when it was on the tamer side. Like city parks. When they'd been standing next to the cabin, nature had seemed a little friendlier than it did when she was face-to-face with the forest primeval.

"We'll walk side by side about three feet apart, until I tell you to stop," he said. "If you see anything, we can use the lighter to see it better."

Zoe tried to quiet the jumpy little squiggles in her tummy. "What am I looking for, exactly?"

"Anything unusual. Recently broken branches. Footprints."

"What kind of footprints?"

"Like a human's, only bigger. Maybe around twenty inches or so."

"Twenty?" She gulped. "How b-big are these guys supposed to be?"

"Some have been reported at fourteen feet, but that's . . ." He paused and took a closer look at her. "You're scared to death, aren't you?"

She shook her head and tried to stop shaking.

"You are so. Don't torture yourself. Let's go back to the cabin and I'll get the key so you can lock yourself in."

"No. I want to do this." She clenched her hands into fists and willed herself to be calm. Flynn wasn't afraid. Instead he was fascinated. That's what she had to go for—total fascination. She'd had no idea learning to be a nerd would be so scary, though.

Okay, she had the answer. She would pretend this was a scene in her latest film, not reality. That would be the reverse of her usual thought process, where she had to convince herself that the scene was real. Funky. She could do this.

Stepping about three feet away from him, she started walking, keeping her eyes on the ground. Twenty-inch footprints. *Oh . . . my . . . God.* If she saw one, she'd freak out, scene or no scene.

Of course she saw one. "Flynn!"

He came quickly and snapped the lighter to produce a tiny flame. Then he drew a quick breath and crouched down with a murmur of delight.

Zoe was not delighted. Pressed into a patch of soft dirt was a humanlike footprint, but no human had made that print. Her entire forearm and hand would fit lengthwise inside it, no problem.

She stood staring at it in the wavering flame of the butane lighter. The longer she stared, the more light-headed she became trying to process what she was seeing. She didn't realize she was squeezing Flynn's shoulder until he doused the flame, stuck the lighter in his pocket, and stood up.

"It's okay," he said, drawing her into his arms.

Her whole body was stiff with shock and she could barely make her lips move. "What . . . what *is* that?" It was a silly question. There was only one answer.

"Don't be afraid." He pulled her close. Then he took off his glasses and slipped them into his other pocket.

"What are you doing?" Another silly question for which there was only one answer.

"I'm commemorating the moment." He leaned down, his breath warm against her mouth.

She wasn't supposed to allow this. For some reason it was a very bad idea. But in the face of a twenty-inch footprint, she couldn't remember why.

Flynn had promised himself not to kiss Zoe, but she looked paralyzed with fear. If he could distract her, then maybe she'd be able to share his excitement in finding the footprint. Besides, he really did want to celebrate this huge discovery, and kissing Zoe seemed like the only move that would satisfy the demands of the occasion. It beat a bottle of champagne by a country mile.

He'd never kissed a frightened woman before, and at first it was a challenge. She was literally petrified. Her mouth had no give to it, and when he opened his eyes to check, he discovered hers were wide open and staring back at him. But she wasn't resisting, either, which she would have if she'd been her usual spunky self.

So he decided to keep going and hope for the best. Closing his eyes again, he put more effort into the kiss. Eventually her lips started to thaw. Encouraged by the small bit of warmth and movement, he tilted his head and went deeper, exploring gently with his tongue. He peeked again and discovered her eyelids were drifting downward.

After that, the shift to full participation came quickly. One second she was a plaster mannequin from a window display and the next a fiery lover in an X-rated movie. She ignited with a groan, grabbing his head in both hands and taking his breath away with a no-holds-barred kiss.

He figured this was her way of dealing with fear. Because he'd wanted to calm her fears, he had an obligation to go along. Any guy would do the same, especially if that guy happened to be flying high on his first personal evidence of the existence of Bigfoot. Besides all that, Zoe smelled terrific, like flowers and honey and sex. Definitely like sex.

She kissed him as if she couldn't get enough, so he kept on giving. She inspired him to shift position and discover different and wonderful ways to connect mouths and tongues. The pace was more frantic than his usual style, but Zoe's energy seemed to demand that. He didn't mind at all.

Gulping for air, she stopped long enough for a breathless question. "Do . . . all nerds . . . kiss like this?" Then she cut off any possible answer by zeroing in again.

He knew the answer to her question, but it brought up a subject he didn't want to think about right now. Kristen was a passive kisser. She didn't like to get too carried away. He'd told himself she was withholding her full-throttle response until he'd fully committed to her. Apparently Zoe didn't need that kind of reassurance.

She was completely into this kissing business, and consequently, so was he. As his control slipped even more, he began to consider whether he dared explore what lay behind Einstein's Theory of Relativity. To reach under that portrait of Einstein and touch her breasts would commemorate this moment even more completely. And damn, she smelled so good!

While still maintaining the mouth-to-mouth, he created space between his body and hers so he could slip his hand under the hem of her sweatshirt. She didn't stop him. In fact, he heard a distinct sigh. Sighs were good.

His heart beating even faster than when he'd first seen the footprint, he explored her cotton-covered, fully insured breasts. Each one filled his cupped hand to overflowing. How she'd ever convince a director she could pull off the flat-chested thing was a mystery to him.

As he teased her nipple through the cotton, she moaned and arched toward him. Oh, happy days. With that kind of gold-plated invitation, he searched for the catch of her bra. A sexy woman like Zoe would definitely be wearing a bra that hooked in front. But he, normally proficient with front-fastening bras, couldn't find it.

She lifted her mouth from his long enough to murmur, "Nerd bra, back hooks," before she returned to kissing him with enthusiasm.

Nerd bra? He'd had no idea there was such a category. Reaching behind her back, he undid the hooks easily. And then . . . nothing but glorious sensation. Her skin was silk, her nipples tight and begging to be sucked. Did he dare?

Hell, yes. He might never get a chance like this again. He started bunching the material of her sweatshirt to gain access.

Leaning away from his kiss, she lifted her arms over her head.

Such a vulnerable gesture of surrender. He went crazy with lust. In seconds he'd whipped both the sweatshirt and bra off and tossed them on the ground. For all he knew they'd landed right on top of the Bigfoot print.

He'd thought earlier of making a cast of it, but who cared now? He was gazing at Zoe, topless in the moonlight. Nothing was more important than that. Her nipples puckered in the cool night air. If this were a movie scene, primitive drums would be beating in the background.

He fought back an intense urge to back her up against the nearest tree. You didn't do that with a multimillion-dollar star. The bark would scratch her skin.

But he wanted a better angle. "Come here." Slipping his arm around her waist, he managed to maneuver them both to their knees without falling over. The pine needles crackled, and somewhere in the distance an owl hooted.

"We could go inside," she murmured.

"I know." He kissed her with all the longing he felt. Inside were condoms. Out here he had a built-in chastity belt. Breaking off the kiss, he sat down and managed to pull her, laughing, into his lap.

"We could go inside," she said again.

"I know." Instead he settled her crossways on his lap, where a major erection lived. He wasn't letting that bad boy out to play, either. He'd drawn some sort of ragged line in the sand for his ever-present conscience, and keeping his package covered was part of that internal bargain.

"That's better." He had the angle he needed to enjoy every square inch of her breasts.

"I think you're sitting on the footprint."

"That's the way it goes." He dipped his head and took his reward for negotiating a tricky compromise between complete surrender and total self-denial.

Chapter Ten

Media alert! Man loses forty IQ points at his first glimpse of Zoe Tarleton's tits! He's actually going to perform mammary worship out in the woods? They should be more careful. What if they plopped down in a bunch of poison oak?

I guess they don't care. Look at them going at it like they're the only two people out here. Little do they know. They'd be peeing their pants if they saw me standing barely thirty feet away. But they're way too busy to look.

Me, I'm all about looking. The way she's moaning and wiggling, you'd think he had the best technique in the universe. She's probably laying it on thick for his benefit. That "ooh, ooh, baby" routine sounds fake to me.

Then again, maybe she's really turned on. Maybe she'll let him boink her right there on the pine needles. She might get a butt full of pine needles before this is over.

I wouldn't mind catching that show, now that I think

about it. It's like watching a train wreck. I can't look away. And why should I?

Zoe hadn't had outdoor sex—with the exception of scripted scenes in a movie—for years. She doubted they'd have full-blown outdoor sex now, either, but what they were having was most excellent. She had very sensitive breasts, and Flynn had a very gifted mouth. Good combo.

Mm, wonderful combo. He was bringing on some major developments, developments that made her squirm in his lap and wish he'd add another dimension to the mix. Her tush registered what was happening under the fly of his pants, which was exciting to contemplate.

The more she wiggled and moaned, the harder he became. She suspected he wasn't planning on doing anything about that, being condomless right now. But she was getting desperate.

"Flynn . . ." His name came out as a groan, and she discovered talking wasn't all that easy when she was breathing so fast. "You're driving me . . . crazy."

His breath was hot against her damp skin. "What do you want, Zoe?"

Oh, God, he was going to make her say it. She didn't know if she could.

He nipped lightly at her breast. "Tell me," he murmured.

A cool chick should have no trouble asking for what she wanted, but when it came to sex, Zoe wasn't cool at all. She sucked in a breath. "I want . . ." But she couldn't finish the sentence.

Kissing his way back to her mouth, he hovered there, brushing his lips over hers. "What? What do you want?"

Need trumped modesty. "Your hand down my pants."

She quivered in his arms, astonished that she'd said it out loud.

"My pleasure." In one efficient movement he slid his hand under both the elastic of her sweats and the elastic of her panties. When he connected with her main event and joined the party already in progress there, she groaned again, even louder this time.

She learned quickly that Flynn was talented right down to his fingertips. If she'd ever been stroked better than this, she didn't remember it. He had the rhythm, and she had the shakes. Between his hot mouth on hers and his clever fingers inside her panties, practically no time elapsed before she was in final countdown.

This was so superior to a vibrator. She'd almost forgotten the pleasure of being given an orgasm instead of having to round one up for herself. She had to do something about her nonexistent sex life. Then all thoughts evaporated as she went ballistic with an orgasm that ranked at least 8.5 on the Richter scale.

She wrenched away from his kiss so she could yell. This was one perfect climax, and the world should know about it.

Laughing, Flynn peppered her face with kisses. "You should probably keep it down."

Zoe let out another bellow of satisfaction and clung to him, panting as he took his hand out of her underwear. "They'll just . . . think . . . it's Bigfoot."

"No, they won't," he said, still laughing.

When she opened her eyes, she could see the white flash of his teeth in the moonlight. "Why not?"

"There's a huge difference between the howl of a Sasquatch and the yell of a woman coming."

"What are you, some kind of expert?" With her arms

looped around his neck, she lay there in that lovely aftermath state she'd sorely missed. How great to feel squishy as a handful of warm pasta. What a miracle climaxes were. Instant stress reducer. She didn't want to move, ever.

"An expert on which, the Sasquatch howls or women coming yells?"

"Both."

"I've . . . been present at a fair share of climactic moments."

"Nice." And now that she'd discovered one of his methods for giving a woman the Big O, she longed to experience the full range of his abilities in that department. But she mustn't get greedy. Once was more than she should have allowed herself.

"I'm not bragging or anything."

"I didn't think you were. You're not the bragging type." Which made his sexual quotient that much more interesting. "So what about the Sasquatch howls? Why can you identify those?"

"I've heard tapes."

She began to get the picture. "You've studied all about Bigfoot, haven't you?"

"Some. When I was a kid."

And she'd bet he'd been fascinated back then. He'd shown signs of still being fascinated. She wondered if they'd managed to obliterate the footprint she'd found. "You mean to tell me that we're sitting on the realization of a childhood dream, the evidence of which we might have mashed completely with all that scooting around?"

He smiled. "I'm sitting on a childhood dream. You're sitting on me, and that's plenty of compensation for a mashed footprint."

"I don't see how it can be much compensation. All things considered."

"That's okay."

"Flynn, I'm well aware that it's not okay. You have to be uncomfortable." She paused, evaluating his condition from the evidence pressing against her bottom. He was sporting quite an erection.

Although she had an idea of what to do, suggesting what she was thinking about suggesting was bolder than she'd ever been in her life. Besides, it might constitute trying to steal someone's boyfriend. She was already on shaky ground in that area.

Some people didn't think oral sex counted, but Zoe thought it counted double. After all, look at the hullabaloo over that incident with Hugh Grant a few years ago. If Zoe engaged in such an exercise with Flynn, she would be another step down the slippery slope that could lead to stealing him from Kristen.

Somehow she had to segue from this highly charged situation to the platonic relationship they'd had before he'd stuck his hand down her pants. Maybe she should act as if he'd done her an ordinary favor, something equivalent to picking up her dry cleaning or taking her car in for an oil change. That might work—treating this as a normal interchange between two friends.

"I appreciate what you did for me just now," she said. "Thank you so much."

He sounded amused, although he managed to keep a straight face. "You're welcome."

She took a deep breath. "So what do you say, Flynn? How about some of that blueberry cobbler?"

Then she had to bite the inside of her lip to keep from laughing as she thought about the masturbation scene in

American Pie. Blueberry cobbler might work about as well, except the juice would make a terrible mess. Blueberry stained something awful.

Flynn cleared his throat. "I think I'll take a pass."

"You're sure? Margo said it was really yummy." Talk about wholesome conversation. She sounded like June Cleaver. No one listening would ever suspect that Flynn had just put his hand down her pants.

Unfortunately, her attempt to distract him from sex wasn't working, judging from the fully inflated condition of his Johnson. Maybe he'd associated blueberry cobbler with the scene in *American Pie,* too, and so her suggestion was turning him on worse instead of helping him get control.

"You go ahead," he said. "I'll be along later."

She had a strong suspicion he planned to stay out here and finish what she was reluctant to. It looked as if she'd feel guilty regardless. "That's just not right," she said.

"If you're worried for my safety, don't be. The Northern California Sasquatch isn't menacing. There are no documented reports that one has ever—"

"You deserve more than a hand job in the woods, Flynn."

He coughed, and his penis stirred beneath her. "What . . . what makes you think that's what I had in mind?"

"Women's intuition."

"Maybe I was going to walk around a little until the situation resolved itself."

She gazed up into his face. He looked so much more accessible without his glasses. "No, you weren't."

"You can't know I wasn't."

"I can so."

His eyebrows lifted. "How?"

"That wouldn't be logical. If you don't take care of the problem, it will . . . um . . . keep popping up, so to speak."

"God, Zoe. Just forget about it, okay?"

"I should help you out."

His penis flexed again, but he shook his head. "No. Thanks anyway."

"You're sure?"

His smile was tight. "If you really want to help, you'll get up and go into the cabin."

"And not look back, right?"

"Right."

"If you insist." She got her legs under her and put both hands on his shoulders. "Give me a boost."

He slid his hands under her bottom and hoisted her upward. As she pushed herself to her feet, her breasts rubbed against his face and he drew in a sharp breath.

"Sorry." She located her sweatshirt and bra lying on a carpet of pine needles. "Didn't mean to make things worse." Stuffing the bra in the pocket of her sweats, she pulled the sweatshirt over her head.

"It's my own fault," he said. "I knew kissing you was a mistake, but I did it anyway."

"To stop me from being scared?"

"Yeah, that, and . . . I kind of lost control there for a minute because I was so excited about finding that footprint."

Zoe glanced around the area. "I really think you are sitting on it."

"I think I am, too. Now go on inside, Zoe."

"Okay." She started toward the cabin.

"Zoe?"

She turned back, thinking he'd changed his mind. Her

heart started beating faster as she imagined how she'd engineer this. She should probably have him stand up, so that she could get on her knees. If he stayed sitting down, that could be very awkward, but if he leaned against a tree, then—

"What's a nerd bra?"

Not what she'd expected him to say. She had this all worked out in her mind, and he was talking about bras. Pulling it out of her pocket, she studied it in the moonlight. Yes, it was boring, but Flynn hadn't seemed bored by it. Quite the contrary.

"That's what I call it," she said. "I figured a nerd wouldn't spend time worrying about the sex appeal of her underwear while she was researching something like this ultimate pill, so I bought plain ones that hooked in the back, so I'd be more in character."

"Oh." He swallowed. "I just wondered."

"There's that curiosity again." She made a mental note. Nerds were curious about all kinds of things, even bras. She wanted in the worst way to ask him if Kristen wore this kind, but that would be prying.

Truth be told, she could be curious, too, and she was *very* curious about Flynn's girlfriend—what she looked like, whether she was skinny or plump, sexy or not. A guy like Flynn should have a sexy girlfriend. He was one hot-blooded man.

She took a step back toward him. "Flynn, I really think you should let me take care of—"

"No."

"We're out in the middle of the woods. I wouldn't tell anyone. It could be our little secret."

"Thank you, but no."

"Then I guess I'll go read the script." She stuffed the bra back in her pocket and turned around.

As she walked toward the cabin, she tried to remember if she'd ever heard of a guy rejecting an offer of oral sex. Nope, not really. In her experience, this was a first. She'd never heard any of her girlfriends mention this phenomenon, either.

No doubt about it, a fully aroused man who could say no to a blow job was probably harder to find than a Sasquatch footprint. And to think she'd encountered both in one night.

With a groan, Flynn levered himself upright. He couldn't remember the last time he'd had such a painful hard-on. Maybe never. He grimaced as he recalled his conversation with Zoe. She'd totally read his mind. In the anonymous shadow of a tree, he could solve his problem, at least for now.

Solving it for the rest of the weekend was another matter entirely. He could hardly keep making trips out to the woods, but he couldn't think of any other way to get through the next forty-eight hours. His case of lust was a hundred times worse now that he'd nuzzled her breasts and shoved his hand down her pants.

The consequence of that behavior was making a serious dent in his slacks. And wouldn't you know—Zoe had tried to distract him by mentioning the blueberry cobbler, and immediately he'd thought of the masturbation scene in *American Pie*. He hadn't thought of that apple pie scene in years, but with Zoe around, everything became a sexual reference.

Time to get some relief. He reached into his pocket for his glasses—not that he'd need them for this activity, but he didn't want to trip over a branch while he was searching for the right spot. If he fell face-forward in this condition he might nail himself to the forest floor.

Stepping into the deep shadow of a nearby pine tree, he started to unzip. Then he heard footsteps crackling across the pine needles. They were coming from the opposite side of the tree, and they were heading in his direction.

His first thought—that Zoe had circled back—died as he measured the heavy footfall. From the rhythm he could tell it was a two-footed animal and not a four-footed one. The fine hairs on the back of his neck quivered.

Had Bigfoot returned? He glanced toward the cabin and wished he'd reminded Zoe to lock the door. The footsteps were coming his way, though, and not going toward the cabin, so she was in no immediate danger.

He, on the other hand, could be. He was close to the tree, but not close enough to hide behind it. Dry pine needles were everywhere underfoot. Moving would give away his position, so he was stuck right where he was. Maybe the shadow of the tree would disguise him.

He had no reason to be afraid, not really. He could stop shaking any time now. Everything he'd read about the Northern California Sasquatch had emphasized that they were not dangerous. But still—coming face-to-face with a creature fourteen feet tall, a creature with the strength to annihilate him, would be unnerving. A rogue Sasquatch wasn't entirely out of the question, either.

One good thing was happening, though. As the footsteps grew closer and louder, Flynn's erection wilted. No problem in that department anymore.

Whoever—or whatever—was coming toward him was almost here, maybe only about five yards from the tree.

Flynn's breathing seemed unnaturally loud, so he held his breath. And of course he was wearing a white shirt, which would make him more visible in the dark.

Maybe he should take off the shirt. Yeah, right. And do what? Eat it? He tried to gauge the direction of the wind, but there seemed to be no wind at all. Bigfoot had a highly developed sense of smell, and . . . wait a minute! Bigfoot was supposed to stink! Flynn couldn't smell a thing. But then again, he wasn't breathing. Of course he couldn't smell a thing.

The footsteps approached the tree, came around the tree . . .

"Whoa!" A tall kid in baggy jeans with his shirttail hanging out slid to a halt beside the tree. "You scared the pee out of me, dude!"

Flynn let out his breath. "Likewise." A kid. A teenager. Probably Luanne's older brother, Jeff, alias Frankenstein. He had his hair waxed into little spikes all over his head, and a heavy silver chain hung around his neck. Apparently Jeff liked walking around the woods at night just like his sister.

"Sorry about that, man." The kid looked him over. "I'm going to take a wild guess that you're staying in the rental cabin for the weekend. Am I right?"

Flynn nodded. "I'm going to take a wild guess that you're Jeff."

"You've heard of me already? Awesome!"

"Luanne came by earlier."

"Oh. Well, don't go believing whatever she said. She's got an imagination that won't quit. I'll bet she was all *'He's so weird, I call him Frankenstein.'* "

Flynn tried not to smile.

"She said that, didn't she? She's such a brat."

Flynn decided to change the subject. "She said you were out on a date."

Jeff looked startled. "Uh, yeah. Yeah, that's right. Just got back a little while ago. Thought I'd, like, take a walk."

"Me, too." Flynn realized this could have turned out much worse. Jeff could have come along a few minutes later. Or several minutes earlier.

"I heard there was a Bigfoot sighting tonight," Jeff said. "So I thought I'd check it out. You spot anything?"

"Nope." Flynn wasn't about to describe how the footprint had been obliterated. "Heard something, though."

"Yeah? Cool! Like what?"

"Something big running through the trees, and a howl."

"Awesome." Jeff shoved his hands in his pockets and rocked back on the heels of his running shoes. "Did it sound like a Bigfoot howl?"

"It sounded like the recordings I've heard." Now that Flynn wasn't thinking about sex, he was once again eager for Sasquatch news. He was even a little sorry he'd sat on the footprint, although he wouldn't change what had happened. If only he'd sat down a yard to the left or right, though, he could have had both the footprint *and* the make-out session.

"Wish I'd been here," Jeff said.

Flynn was eternally glad Jeff hadn't been around. "Have you sighted very many yourself?"

"Just once. I was, like, parking with my girlfriend Janice. We were . . . well, you know. And I smelled this disgusting smell, which I knew couldn't be Janice because she always smells great." Jeff's eyes glazed over. "Does she ever smell great. I read in school about pheromones, and I think that's what Janice has going on. Dude, every time I'm around her I want to—"

"So you smelled something disgusting." Flynn didn't want to hear about Janice and her pheromones. He had enough problems with Zoe's pheromones, and he didn't want to be reminded of the havoc that a woman could create simply by smelling good. Zoe did, too, and it drove him nuts.

"Yeah, and I'm all *'what's that smell?'* So I poked my head up and looked out the window. This big hairy thing was walking away through the woods."

"Amazing." The story gave Flynn goose bumps. First the footprint and now this. He wasn't inclined to put stock in Margo's claims, but Jeff was providing even more evidence. "How long ago was that?"

"Last summer, on July nineteenth. I know it was July nineteenth because that's the night I finally talked Janice into . . . uh . . ." He paused and massaged the back of his neck. "Listen, dude, if you run into Janice while you're here, I'd appreciate it if you'd, like, keep this conversation to yourself."

"Sure."

"The thing is, she doesn't know I saw Bigfoot. I told her it must've been a skunk letting loose."

Flynn nodded. "Because you didn't want to scare her."

"Damn straight I didn't! Not considering the excellent progress I'd made to that point. If she'd thought I'd seen Bigfoot, she would've been all *'yikes, I'm putting my clothes on right now!'* " Jeff glanced at Flynn. "Am I right, dude?"

"Probably." The conversation had taken a turn that wasn't helping Flynn at all. Any reference to sex made him think of Zoe. He should be thinking of Kristen. He should be fantasizing about Kristen. At the moment he couldn't remember what she looked like. Pathetic.

"Well, guess I'd better get going," Jeff said. "I have to be at work early. We got a new shipment of Bigfoot action figures at the trading post and the boss wants them unpacked pronto. Like, people are clamoring for them. Not."

"I should leave, too." Although Flynn wasn't sure he was ready to face Zoe's pheromones.

"Yeah, your wife is probably all *'where's that husband of mine? I hope Bigfoot didn't eat him.'* "

"We're not married," Flynn said without thinking.

"Oh. Well, that's cool. You don't need, like, a marriage certificate to spend the weekend together. I can't figure out why anyone would want to spend the weekend in Long Shaft, though."

"I was curious about the Bigfoot sightings."

"You came here because of Bigfoot? Awesome! Come on down to the trading post in the morning and I'll give you a discount on a Bigfoot action figure. They're supposed to be, like, for kids, but I think one would look great on your desk. A conversation piece."

"How did you know I have a desk?"

"Dude, no offense, but you have *office geek* written all over you. Nothing wrong with that. You probably make a whole lot more money than me. Bye." With a wave, Jeff loped off through the woods.

Flynn turned toward the cabin with a resigned sigh. With luck, Zoe had gone to bed. Then he had a vivid image of her in bed, wearing some filmy nightgown. Or maybe she didn't wear anything at all.

Chapter Eleven

Teeth brushed and nerd pajamas on, Zoe propped a pillow against the headboard and leaned back as she picked up the script she'd brought to bed with her. She was also wearing the wire-framed glasses and had stuck a pencil behind her ear, although she didn't know if that was a nerd thing to do or not. She'd have to ask Flynn in the morning.

Tonight they shouldn't have anything more to do with each other. To that effect she'd closed her bedroom door. She thought Flynn would respect a closed door. He seemed like that type of guy.

And speaking of Flynn, where the hell was he? Unless he was making a big production out of his endeavor in the woods, he should be finished and back inside by now. She'd told herself not to think about it, but she couldn't help thinking about it.

Who could blame her? Flynn Granger, her conservative, buttoned-down lawyer, was currently out among the pine trees masturbating. That didn't fit her picture of him at all. It wasn't dignified.

Well, that wasn't her fault. She'd worked up the courage to suggest doing the job right, but he'd rediscovered his scruples. That was for the best. She really didn't want to poach on Kristen's territory. As wonderful as it might feel in the short term, she'd hate herself for it in the long term.

There was only one solution—to get back on track and concentrate on the reason she'd brought Flynn up here. She needed to read more of the script and get into character. Vera Parsons probably wouldn't have asked Tony Bennetti to put his hand down her pants. Zoe didn't know how Vera would react in a sexual situation, and she needed to know.

Pushing thoughts of Flynn out of her mind, she opened the script at the point where she and Flynn had stopped reading. Tony and Vera were still in the bedroom dealing with the attempted kidnapping. Now Zoe remembered the scene. She'd been trying to coach Flynn in how to play Tony with a little more swagger.

VERA

Don't call me baby doll.

TONY

I call all women baby doll.

VERA

Which is exactly why I don't want you to call me that.

TONY

Why not? Because you're not a woman?

VERA

Because I'm a scientist.

TONY

Is that some extra category? Last time I looked, that wasn't one of the answers on the form down at the DMV.

VERA

My gender is totally irrelevant!

Tony draws closer to Vera.

TONY

Gender is never irrelevant.

Vera's resistance weakens as Tony moves in.

VERA

It's . . . irrelevant in this case.

Tony leans down, preparing to kiss Vera.

TONY

I thought so, too. But you're getting to me, baby doll.

Tony kisses Vera. Vera responds at first, then pushes Tony away.

VERA

That was completely unprofessional!

Tony grins, extremely proud of himself.

TONY

I'm a bodyguard, not an escort service. When it comes to women, I cherish my amateur standing.

Tony turns and leaves the room.

Zoe sighed. So that was how Vera reacted to being kissed. She pushed the guy away. That wasn't exactly how Zoe had behaved a little while ago when Flynn had planted one on her. At first she'd done nothing, but at the moment when Vera would have shoved, Zoe had pulled.

And that was only the beginning. Matters had progressed rapidly after that, with Zoe inviting all sorts of things to happen. Vera would be scandalized by that scene on the forest floor.

Zoe heard the front door open and glanced up from the script. "Is that you, Flynn?" Maybe she should have locked the door, after all. But then she'd have been in the position of getting up to open it wearing her pajamas. True, they were ugly pajamas, a gaudy yellow and orange plaid, but she thought Flynn might get turned on anyway. He had a short fuse. Well, so did she.

"It's me," Flynn said.

"Is everything . . . okay?" She didn't know a polite way to ask if he'd successfully masturbated and could sleep better now.

He started down the hall, his footsteps steady. "Zoe, I didn't do what you think I did out there."

"Why not?"

His footsteps stopped in front of his bedroom door. "Because . . . because I met Luanne's brother."

"Frankenstein was out walking in the woods?"

"Yeah. Jeff. He's a nice kid."

Zoe thought about what had been going on in the woods prior to her coming back to the cabin. "We dodged a bullet, huh?"

"You could say that, although he thinks we're here for a romantic weekend, so maybe it wouldn't have mattered."

A romantic weekend. Zoe couldn't remember the last time she'd had one of those, and she wished she could be having one now. With Flynn. "So are you turning in?"

"It's probably a good idea."

"Probably." She could feel the tension building between them, even through the closed door. She wanted to be with him, and she was almost certain he wanted to be with her.

"Good night, then."

She felt so sorry for him. He must feel incredibly frustrated. She wanted him to have some sort of peak experience that would be the equivalent of her climax in the woods, something a little fun and kinky that wouldn't compromise his honor.

"Flynn, you're welcome to the cobbler. I'm not planning to eat any of it. You can have the whole thing."

He sounded like he was choking and laughing at the same time. "I don't want the cobbler, Zoe."

"Well, I don't blame you. It would be very messy."

"Good God, you really are talking about what I was afraid you might be talking about. Now I'm not going to be able to look at that cobbler without thinking of sex."

"Sorry. I was only trying to help."

"Please don't help." He cleared his throat. "So you don't want to eat the cobbler?"

"Absolutely not. It would go right to my hips. You're welcome to it, really."

"Then I'm going to put it down the garbage disposal, because God knows I won't be able to eat it, either, now that you've superimposed *American Pie* onto it. I'd just as soon get rid of it."

"Take all the time you need to do that."

"For the last time, I am not going to masturbate with the cobbler!"

"Okay." Zoe couldn't help grinning. If she had a tape recording of that statement, she could blackmail Flynn forever. And she'd thought he was stodgy. Not even.

She listened to him stomp away and soon after heard the loud grinding of an ancient garbage disposal. Too bad about the cobbler. She'd have to tell Margo they ate the whole thing, to save Margo's feelings. Obviously the cobbler, made only during a full moon, was supposed to be a treat.

Maybe the full moon was having an effect on her and Flynn. The moon had been officially full the night before—Zoe kept track of such things—but tonight it had seemed almost full. In some magazine or other she'd read that the full moon had an effect on people, as well as the ocean tides, but she couldn't remember exactly what it was.

She'd bet Flynn would know. When she heard his footsteps coming down the hall again, she decided to ask him. "Flynn?"

"What?"

"Do you know if the full moon has an effect on people?"

"You mean like werewolves? I don't believe in that. Werewolves are in a different category from a Sasquatch, in my opinion."

She loved hearing him talk. She'd never realized that before, but going to his office had been a treat to her ears. His voice had good resonance, the kind that actors worked to get and Flynn had naturally. He'd be good at voice-overs, not that he'd ever consider getting into that cutthroat field when he was making so much money as an entertainment lawyer.

So his wonderful voice was a bonus attribute, destined to be appreciated by clients . . . and lovers. But she wouldn't go there. "I meant does the moon pull at people the way it pulls at the ocean? I thought I heard that, but now I can't remember the particulars."

"I see what you mean. We're ninety percent water, so yeah, I guess we would be affected by the gravitational pull of the moon. Why are you asking?"

"I thought that might explain . . . our little problem."

He was silent for several seconds. "I don't think that's it."

"You don't?"

"No."

"So what is the reason why we're suddenly attracted to each other?"

"I think it's because we're finally alone together. Good night, Zoe." He closed his bedroom door.

Zoe stared into space and thought about that. What if she and Flynn were destined to be lovers, but they'd never figured that out because they'd never been alone? And now they were alone, and Flynn was committed to someone else. She wasn't, but he didn't know that.

She wouldn't tell him, either. He was barely holding on to his commitment to Kristen as it was. They had two nights to get through, and this one was almost in the can. Daytime would be a piece of cake, so tomorrow night was the big hurdle.

They could always go back to LA tomorrow, which would guarantee nothing would happen between them.

But she instinctively believed Flynn was the key to her getting this part. Maybe she was being selfish, but she really wanted his help. She wanted more than his help, but she'd control herself. The more she got into Vera's character, the easier that would be.

As Flynn undressed, he thought about the cobbler, and not as a masturbation aid, either. Something about that cobbler hadn't seemed quite right. The smell was a little off, and when he'd run water through the disposal, foam had bubbled up out of it.

That could have been a problem with the disposal, which looked like it had been installed right after the invention of electricity. Or it could have been the cobbler. A woman who only made the stuff during a full moon had to be a strange person. Maybe she added strange ingredients to the cobbler.

In any case, Flynn was glad that he and Zoe hadn't eaten the cobbler. Food poisoning would put a serious crimp in their plans. They needed food they could actually eat, though. In the morning he'd take a drive into town, buy a flashlight, and pick up some groceries.

He climbed into the uncomfortable twin bed and discovered it was too short. The bed Zoe was using would fit him better. He felt his mind sliding into the possibility of sharing that bed with her and yanked it right back out of that quicksand. The mere suggestion of sharing her bed had his penis stirring restlessly.

So he had a bed that was too short for him. So what? The length of the mattress wouldn't matter, though, because he probably wouldn't be able to sleep anyway. Maybe he should check out the script so that he'd know in

advance exactly what he might be in for if they had any
more read-throughs.

Propping himself up with a lumpy pillow against the
rough plaster wall at the end of the bed, he picked up the
script for *The Billion-Dollar Pill*. Now there was an invention he didn't need. His weight always stayed the same, his
health had been excellent all his life, and his libido was in
fine shape. At the moment he wished his libido would go
into temporary hibernation.

He flipped to the scene he'd been reading with Zoe and
continued on past where they'd stopped. Oh, great. Tony
kissed Vera. That meant the fun and games were about to
start.

If he could steer Zoe to the next scene, in which Tony
did some of his investigative work trying to find out who
was stalking Vera, that might not be so tough to read. Oh,
wait. Vera wasn't in that scene. Zoe would want to skip
over to the next one, and Flynn didn't like the looks of it
at all. Tony and Vera were back in the lab, alone again.
That was trouble.

VERA

You're making me nervous.

*Vera moves around the lab checking test tubes, typing
notes into her computer.*

TONY

I'm not doing anything.

VERA

That's the problem. You're not doing anything.

TONY

I'm guarding your body. But if you'd rather I did that standing up, fine with me.

Tony stands.

VERA

You shouldn't have kissed me last night. Now I can't concentrate.

TONY

I can concentrate just fine.

VERA

Of course you can! All you have to do is watch me! How hard is that?

TONY

Some parts are very hard.

VERA

If that's some sort of double entendre, I'm not going to acknowledge it. I have work to do. I wish . . . I wish you weren't here.

TONY

I'd love to accommodate you, toots, but you're so oblivious you'd let yourself be kidnapped. These jokers want that formula.

VERA

I wouldn't give it to them.

Tony comes forward and leans on the lab table.

TONY

Yes, you would. I'm guessing it would take about five minutes of torture before you'd—

VERA

Torture? You're not serious.

TONY

You have really soft skin, Vera.

VERA

You're trying to scare me.

TONY

Yeah, I am. I don't like thinking of you tied up and at somebody's mercy . . . unless that person is me. I'll bet you'd like the kinky stuff.

VERA

Don't project your warped sexual appetites on me.

TONY

Oh yeah, you'd like it. I can see it in your eyes.

VERA

Can you see in my eyes that I'm going to report you for sexual harassment?

Tony runs a finger down Vera's arm and she shivers.

                          TONY

No, you're not.

Vera tries unsuccessfully to concentrate on her com-
puter screen.

                          VERA

You are so incredibly arrogant.

                          TONY

And it turns you on, doesn't it?

                          VERA

Yes.

Flynn closed the script, slapping the pages together
so loud that Zoe probably heard him in the next room.
But he couldn't read anymore, not in his current state. If
he'd known the story was all about sex, he would never
have agreed to come up here with her. Oh, hell yes, he
would have, because he'd been too dumb to realize the
dangers.

He'd stupidly thought that once he'd decided Kristen
would be his future, no other woman would ever appeal
to him because lusting after someone else would be
counterproductive and illogical. His current counterproductive and illogical obsession lay a short walk down the
hall in a bed that would be much more comfortable than
this one.

She would let him into that bed, too. She didn't seem
overly concerned about compromising her relationship with
Trace Edwards. Flynn didn't admire that lack of loyalty, but
he couldn't very well condemn it when he was nearly as

guilty, maybe more guilty. He'd initiated their kiss, after all.

And the fondling. He had to take full responsibility for the fondling. Maybe he hadn't anticipated that the fondling would extend to giving her a climax, but he should have. She was a passionate woman. He knew that from her movies.

Throwing back the covers, he got out of bed and grabbed his laptop. He'd write a tender e-mail to Kristen, that's what he'd do. While writing to her he would picture how wonderful next weekend would be. Maybe she was more passionate than he remembered.

But as he sat on the edge of the bed, fingers resting on the keyboard, he couldn't think of a single thing to say to Kristen. He had a hundred things he wanted to say to Zoe and even more things that he wanted to do to Zoe, but when it came to Kristen, his mind was a blank. Snapping the laptop closed again, he put it back on the dresser and took off his glasses. Then he turned out the light and stretched out on his too-short bed.

Lying in the dark with his hands propped behind his head, he listened to the sounds of the forest. They were normal sounds now—the wind through the tops of the trees, the hoot of an owl, the scrape of a branch against the roof of the cabin. No Sasquatch howls.

For hours he drifted between oblivion and wakefulness. He was a guy who liked routine, and his routine had been seriously compromised. He also liked his own bed, his own sheets, his own pillows.

Sometime in the early morning he thought he heard soft footsteps near the cabin, but he was too exhausted to get up and investigate. Maybe Luanne was out skulking around again. Or maybe some creature of the night, like a raccoon, was prowling the perimeter.

Or maybe it was his imagination, still on overdrive from seeing the Sasquatch footprint and then making out in the woods with Zoe. With a sigh he turned on his stomach, hooked his toes over the edge of the mattress, and went to sleep.

Chapter Twelve

Zoe slept well, probably as a result of the orgasm Flynn had provided the night before. She'd love to thank him for that, but the subject was better left closed. The sun was up, but the trees filtered the light coming in the window. Zoe was used to full-blast sunlight at her place on the beach.

This felt different, more fuzzy and intimate, like a movie shot slightly out of focus. Outside the cabin the birds were chirping their little hearts out. What a happy sound. Morning might be a good time to make love, although she'd never settled in with a guy long enough to find out. She wondered if Flynn was awake.

She imagined creeping into his bed when he was still half-asleep and seducing him. Of course she didn't have the nerve, and besides, it was the wrong thing to do. But all her thoughts about sex made her too restless to go back to sleep, so she climbed out of bed and got dressed in the sweats and sweatshirt she'd worn the night before.

Amazing how comfortable she felt in such geeky clothes. She'd never in a million years walk down Rodeo Drive in an outfit like this, but out here in the woods fashion didn't matter. It was more liberating than she would have thought.

Leaving her feet bare so she wouldn't make so much noise walking around in the cabin, she left her room. Flynn's door remained closed, so maybe he was still asleep. Or he could be awake with a morning woody.

She'd heard that could happen with guys, especially frustrated ones. But she couldn't dwell on that possibility or she'd get herself worked up again. Today they would behave like brother and sister.

Although she'd like some coffee and it was even something she knew how to make, she decided against starting it yet. Brewing coffee might bring Flynn out of his room, and then they'd have the whole sexual thing to deal with again. For a little while she'd enjoy the peace of this hazy sunlit morning.

Maybe she'd go out and sit on the front porch in one of the rockers. Being here incognito meant she could do that kind of thing without attracting attention. She ought to take advantage of it.

Opening the door carefully so she wouldn't wake Flynn by her exit, she stepped out on the porch. The weathered boards were a little scratchy on her bare feet, but no worse than sand and seashells. She loved going barefoot, always had. Summers as a kid she'd never worn shoes. She used to weep when school started each fall and she had to imprison her freedom-loving toes.

Shivering slightly in the chill of early morning, she took a deep breath, and the smell of fresh pine needles made her nose tingle with pleasure. Under that scent lay something more subtle, the musty aroma of all the dry needles carpeting the forest floor. That scent brought back a memory of last night's episode with Flynn, and more than her nose started to tingle.

The birds she'd been hearing continued to warble as they hopped from branch to branch of the trees that nearly touched the sides of the cabin. If she lived here, she'd hang up a bird feeder so she could watch them more closely. But who was she kidding? She'd probably starve the little critters by leaving town and forgetting all about her bird feeder.

This cozy spot was giving her a false sense of living an ordinary life. She was miles away from an ordinary life. Even this weekend wasn't turning out to be particularly ordinary, considering Bigfoot. She wondered if the footprint was still there or if Flynn had obliterated it when he'd dropped to the ground and pulled her down with him.

In daylight the idea of Bigfoot running around in the forest seemed ridiculous. And yet she'd heard the heavy footsteps and the howl. And she'd seen that oversize print.

Staring out at the place where the footprint had been, she groped behind her for the nearest rocker, sat down, and began to rock. A faint buzzing noise told her there were bees somewhere in the vicinity. A little trickle of uneasiness ran through her. She hadn't thought about the possibility of bees when she'd decided to come up here.

Oh, well. Bees didn't normally sting if you didn't bother them. If she did get stung, though, she had no idea where the nearest emergency room might be. . . . Okay, then she just wouldn't get stung. If she saw bees, she'd avoid them.

The rocker creaked a little bit and she smiled, thinking of what her friends would say if they could see her rocking away on a porch while wearing the equivalent of bag-lady clothes. Well, they wouldn't see her this way, and her reputation as a cool chick would remain intact. This was peaceful, though. At least it had been before she'd heard the bees.

Maybe she should go in. No, damn it, she wasn't going to run inside because she heard a couple of bees buzzing around. That was being paranoid. They really didn't sting unless provoked or if they were stepped on, which she'd accidentally done that one time. Then there were killer bees, which was a whole other story. But surely she wouldn't have that kind of bad luck.

A bee flew past and she flinched. Then she blew out a breath, impatient with herself. What a baby. The bee was probably on its way to suck nectar, or whatever it was bees did. She wasn't entirely clear on the process, but she admired the results.

She'd think about honey instead of bee stings. Honey ladled over a buttered English muffin straight from the toaster was one of life's miracles. Picturing how the butter and honey combined as they sank into the warm craters of the muffin made her tummy growl.

Another bee flew by, and another. Goodness, now there were quite a few bees, and they were circling her chair. Maybe she shouldn't stay out here, after all. A bee sting would not be good, not good at all. And where were all these bees coming from?

She stood up, and the bees seemed to multiply as they continued to mill around. Now the buzzing seemed angry instead of industrious. But they had no reason to be angry with her. She hadn't done anything. Except she'd read that killer bees didn't need much of a reason to be upset. They had a bad attitude from the get-go.

"Look," she said. "I only eat honey once in a while, okay? And I really shouldn't have it at all, I suppose, so if that's your beef, I'll give it up right now. I'll take the pledge. Call off the troops."

Instead more bees arrived, and she finally figured out they were coming up from a knothole in the porch floor. She was afraid to make any sudden movements because there were too many and she might bang into one and get stung.

Oh, dear God, what should she do? A bee sting probably wouldn't kill her, especially if Flynn could get her to the emergency room fast enough, but several bee stings . . . she didn't want to think about what that might do to her. She might not make it to the audition next week.

What was a person supposed to do when surrounded by bees? Even in the chilly air, she began to sweat. She couldn't just stand here.

Very carefully, she took a sideways step toward the door. The bees buzzed louder, and now there seemed to be hundreds of them. They started landing on her clothes and in her hair.

Her heart began to race as the bee population grew. "Go away." She discovered she was hyperventilating, too. Definitely getting scared. Really scared.

"Look, I'm not your queen, or your hive, and I can do absolutely nothing for your honey production."

The bees continued to buzz around her.

Finally she couldn't think of anything else to do but call for help. And she only had one avenue for that. She waited until no bees were near her mouth, opened wide, and used her best voice projection. "*Flynn! Help!*"

She heard a loud thud, as if he'd fallen out of bed, then a scuffle and quick footsteps as he ran out of his bedroom.

"Don't open the door!" she yelled. "I have a trillion bees out here!"

He sounded out of breath. "What kind of bees?"

"Hell if I know! They're not carrying ID!"

"Killer bees?"

"It's possible! Flynn, I'm allergic! Can you do something?"

"Yeah! Hold on!"

Immediately she felt calmer. Flynn was on the job. She couldn't imagine that he'd know any more about bees than she did, but he was smart. He'd think of something. In the meantime, she would show no fear. Maybe bees could smell fear, which would cause them to attack.

So far, no attack, and for that she was very grateful. To most people, this was only a swarm of bees, but to her, they could mean the end of all her plans. A few little bee stings and it was good-bye audition, good-bye nerd role, good-bye Nicolas Cage and Steven Spielberg.

The door opened, and Flynn came out wearing his glasses and his flannel pajamas, neither of which would win him points for hottie of the year. But his rumpled hair and morning beard created a manly effect that almost trumped the glasses and pajamas.

Even more exciting, he waved a flaming torch and smoke billowed all around him. He looked like a cross between the Nutty Professor and Indiana Jones. He was her hero.

He blinked in the sunlight. "Jesus! Where did all the bees come from?"

Zoe spoke without opening her mouth much, in case a bee might be flying by and mistake her mouth for the entrance to the hive. She couldn't even imagine how a sting inside her mouth would affect her, and she didn't want to find out. "Under the porch."

"Damn." Flynn swept the smoldering torch in a wide arc. "Go away! Get out of here!"

The smoke and flames seemed to have an effect. The bees grew calmer and drifted away until only four or five continued to buzz around Zoe. With great caution, Flynn moved the torch closer to her, and the last bees left the porch.

"Quick," he said. "Get inside. They might come back."

She dashed through the door and he followed, the torch still in one hand. Wrenching aside the fireplace screen, he tossed the torch into the fireplace, where it continued to crackle and burn.

Smoke poured into the room. Swearing, Flynn dropped to his knees on the hearth. As he and Zoe coughed and choked, he reached into the firebox and pulled a squeaky lever. At last the smoke spiraled up the chimney.

Zoe collapsed onto the sofa and wiped her watery eyes. "Whew. Thank you. How did you know to use fire and smoke?"

"Read it somewhere." Flynn coughed and replaced the fireplace screen. "I'm glad it worked. Sorry about the smoke in here. I didn't stop to think about the flue being closed. I just wanted to get rid of the torch before it burned my hand."

"I'll take smoke over a hive of bees any day."

"Did I hear you say you're allergic?"

"Apparently. I stepped on a bee on location about three years ago. Didn't you see the story in the *Enquirer*? They had me as good as dead."

"Sorry. I don't read the *Enquirer*. I didn't know." He gazed at her with obvious concern.

"It shouldn't be a problem here, though. Bees don't normally go after people." The adrenaline rush left her a little shaky, so to calm herself she watched the rolled papers in the fireplace blacken and curl as they burned. Something about the material he'd used looked familiar. "What did you use for the torch?"

He followed her glance to the fireplace. "My copy of the script. It was the first thing I could find."

"Oh." She couldn't very well be upset with him after the way he'd gallantly saved her, but using the script was awfully convenient. Maybe he thought that would end any future read-throughs with her. If so, he was wrong. "That's okay. We can share mine."

"Uh, Zoe, maybe we should discuss that."

"What's to discuss?"

"I read a little more of the script last night, and there's a lot of sex in it."

"I know." She folded her hands and tried to look wise and scholarly. "I want your feedback on those scenes. With so much sex in the script, it's crucial for me to be on target with my nerdy reaction to sexual situations." She gazed at him and discovered that she wasn't scared anymore.

And exactly like last night, the absence of fear made room for other emotions. Like lust, for example. His pj's weren't what she'd call sexy, but he was probably naked under them. At the moment, that was enough to charge her batteries.

"After last night I would think you'd know my reaction to sexual situations."

She thought about what had transpired so far. "I've been a little too close to the forest, if you know what I mean. I haven't been analytical enough. I need you to break it down for me. Deconstruct the process."

He swallowed. "I see."

"I realize we have a slight problem, but this is important to me. Considering the stakes, I'll keep this strictly professional. However, I can understand if you don't think you'll be able to do that."

His gray eyes revealed the struggle going on. He obviously wasn't sure he could control himself, but he'd die before admitting that. He cleared his throat. "I have a suggestion."

"What's that?"

"Let's schedule the read-throughs during the daytime. Humans are naturally stronger and more logical when the sun's shining. At night their defenses come down. They can more easily make errors in judgment."

"All right. That works." She would have said that differently though. In her view, during daylight hours humans maintained their protective armor. At night their more vulnerable selves showed up. She cherished the moment when Flynn had kissed her. It had been a pure, uncomplicated gesture.

He nodded. "Okay then. I'll shave and get dressed. Then we can . . . uh-oh." He gazed out the window toward the porch.

"Please don't tell me we've attracted paparazzi already?"

"No, not yet anyway. But the bees are back."

• • •

Flynn hated like hell to get Margo involved, but he didn't think they had a choice. "We'd better call your friend."

"I guess so." Zoe didn't seem any happier about doing that than he was, but she stood and headed for the kitchen, where the cabin's only phone hung on a wall. "She'd know who around here takes care of things like relocating bees."

"I hope they have somebody in Long Shaft who can handle it. If we have to wait for a company from Sacramento, it could take all day." He followed Zoe into the kitchen, all the while wishing she'd worn a different outfit. He'd pulled off that Einstein sweatshirt and breached the elastic of those sweats. Such events were tough to forget.

"Yeah, a local pest company would be better." She paused beside the small bulletin board on the wall beside the phone. Margo had tacked up a slip of paper with her number scribbled on it. Zoe stared at the number and sighed.

"What's wrong?"

"I just hate to have someone come out to remove the bees. There will be paperwork of some kind, even if we don't have to pay for it. I've introduced us to Luanne using the names Tony and Vera, but we can't be Tony and Vera if they ask us to sign something verifying they've removed the bees." She glanced over at him. "You don't have some secret way to lure them out, do you?"

"Nope. I got lucky with the smoke thing. If you're allergic, we can't take a chance on having them around. Maybe there won't be any paperwork. If it's a small local operation, there might not be." *And if you don't make the call soon, I'm liable to grab you and kiss you, so do it.*

"Okay. I guess we have to try." She picked up the receiver and punched in Margo's number. After some time, still holding the receiver to her ear, she turned to Flynn and made a face, rolling her eyes and sticking out her tongue.

"What?" He remembered how good that tongue felt in his mouth. He wanted to kiss her until they were both out of breath.

"There's no answer. Not even a machine. Who doesn't have a machine these days?"

He controlled his urges so he could focus on the problem. "Your friend Margo, apparently. Could she be at work?"

"Quite possibly. And I don't have that number, damn it." She opened a drawer beside the phone and rummaged around with one hand while she continued to listen to Margo's phone ring. "No phone book. No advertising flyer from the Sasquatch Diner. How do they expect to get tourist business if they don't leave flyers in the rental properties?"

Flynn didn't think the fine citizens of Long Shaft were promo geniuses. "I guess I'll have to drive down there."

Zoe hung up the phone and leaned her hips against the counter. "By yourself?"

"I think I can manage. I've been driving by myself for some time now. I even have my own driver's license." He definitely shouldn't be thinking about lifting her up on the counter, which was the perfect height for—

"I didn't mean it like that. I just . . . would feel silly

hiding out here while you drive into town to talk to Margo. She's my friend. I should handle it. I can make myself up so I look completely different from Zoe Tarleton."

And she'd still be his fantasy. But he wondered if she was afraid to stay because of the bees. He couldn't blame her for that. "If you keep the doors and windows shut, you shouldn't have a problem. I'll make it a fast trip."

"I'm not worried about the bees. Well, maybe a little bit. But mostly I was thinking that . . . well, Margo works at a diner." She sounded wistful.

"And you want to get something to eat?"

"Desperately. All we have here is bread and eggs. I might be able to manage toast, but I like my eggs over easy, and if I try cooking them, they'll be splatted all over the pan. Spatulas and I have never been on good terms. And frying pans pretty much hate me."

Flynn believed that Zoe would make a mess of breakfast. So would he. He wouldn't mind having breakfast at the diner, either, which would accomplish several objectives. He would be uneasy leaving her alone in case a bee somehow found a way in. Besides that, a trip to town would break the sexual tension between them.

But he was worried about Zoe being recognized. "Are you sure you should risk it?"

She gazed into his eyes. "Think fluffy omelets." She lowered her voice to a husky murmur. "Think golden waffles with ripe, sweet strawberries on top and a luscious swirl of whipped cream. Think hot, rich coffee and cinnamon rolls filled with plump, juicy raisins. Think—"

"Okay, we'll go." He was getting harder with every word coming out of her mouth. He turned and marched down the hall to his bedroom before she could catch a glimpse of the bulge in his pajama bottoms. Soon they would have other people around, and maybe, just maybe, he wouldn't be quite so tempted to rip her clothes off.

Chapter Thirteen

Zoe and Flynn managed to slip out the back way and dash to Flynn's rental car without attracting attention from the bees. Zoe glanced at the porch once Flynn was in the car and they'd slammed both doors. The bees were clumped all over the rocking chair where she'd been sitting.

"This is beginning to feel like that old Alfred Hitchcock movie," she said, "except it's the bees instead of the birds that are taking over. I had to watch that movie in my film history course and I never forgot it."

"Yeah, I remember seeing it on TV." He glanced over at her. "Don't think about it."

"Okay. Let's talk about my disguise. How do I look?"

"Um . . . different."

"Nerdy enough?"

"Well, I have to say, the red plaid skirt with the purple flowered blouse is not subtle. Nobody would ever accuse you of having any fashion sense."

"That's good, isn't it?" Once they were out of range of

the bees, she rolled down the window so she could enjoy the fresh air. She knew to use the handle instead of looking for power buttons thanks to driving Flynn's Civic.

"Are you sure you want to do that?" Flynn asked. "Maybe this is bee season in Long Shaft."

"I can't live my life in a bubble, and this mountain air is a treat."

"Okay, then I'll roll mine down, too, so if a bee flies in it'll have plenty of room to fly out again."

"We won't find any bees," Zoe said. "They're all at a bee rally on our front porch." But she didn't want to talk about bees. "Let's get back to my outfit. I get the feeling you're not sold on my look."

"I have to admit it's a little extreme. And the floppy hat is a great idea for hiding your hair, but did it have to be neon orange?"

She leaned her arm out the open window and enjoyed the sun on her skin. "I didn't want it to *match*."

"You might have overdone that angle."

"I wondered, which is why I'm asking you. I found most everything I brought up here in a resale shop. Well, except for my plaid pj's."

Flynn started drumming his finger nervously on the steering wheel. "Let's not talk about your plaid pj's."

She glanced over and discovered a muscle in his freshly shaven jaw was working, too. If he was this touchy about anything remotely sexual, he had a bad case of the hots for her. That didn't bode well for his relationship with Kristen.

Zoe was beginning to think his attachment to his girlfriend was superficial at best, if he could be rattled this easily. But she'd humor him and stop talking about her plaid pj's. Sheesh. There was nothing sexy about those.

"I'm trying to decide what outfit to wear for the audition," she said. "Out of the three you've seen, which one screams *nerd* to you?"

"Truthfully? None of them. The one you have on now screams *color-blind*. A nerd would have to be oblivious to show up in something that weird."

The negative feedback didn't bother her at all. This was why she'd brought Flynn up here, and she was glad he was being honest. "So what do you think about Vera, from what you've read so far?"

"I think she'd wear something neutral and tailored."

"Damn. I didn't buy anything like that, unless you count the beige pantsuit, which doesn't fit very well."

"Vera would want her clothes to fit. She's exacting, and exacting people like clothes to fit, but most nerds aren't going to want to be bothered with a bunch of different color combinations."

"Like you," Zoe guessed. He was dressed in a white shirt and beige slacks again. But he'd left off the tie, and the top button of his dress shirt was undone. Maybe he was getting into the casual spirit of Long Shaft.

"Like me."

"I should have taken you with me when I looked for the clothes. I didn't think of that. I figured I'd know what a nerd costume would be, but I—Flynn, is that Luanne up ahead, standing by the side of the road?"

"I think so." Flynn's mouth compressed into a thin line. "Don't tell me she's *hitchhiking*." He veered to the side of the road and stopped the car.

Luanne sauntered up to the passenger side and peered in. "Hi! Can you guys give me a ride into town?"

Flynn leaned across Zoe and pulled off his sunglasses. "Luanne, what do you think you're doing?"

"Going into town."

"By hitchhiking? Do you have any idea how dangerous that is? Do you realize how many sickos are out
here waiting to pick up some unsuspecting young
woman? Don't you read the papers? Don't you have any
common sense? Walking in the woods is one thing, but
this is—"

"Wait, wait." Luanne made a T with her hands. "Let
me say something."

"I can't imagine what you can say." Flynn's body vi-
brated with outrage. "This is a terrible thing. I think your
parents need to know that you—"

"Let her talk," Zoe said. What an interesting interlude.
As Flynn leaned over her, his blood up because he imagined he'd caught Luanne hitchhiking, Zoe was enveloped
in the heat rolling off him, which brought out the scent of
his Aqua Velva coupled with a nice male aroma. She liked
that he was so concerned about a kid he'd met once. He'd
make a good daddy, not that she should care.

Luanne shot her a grateful look. "Thanks, Vera. So, I
was walking into town, like I always do on Saturday
morning to see what movie magazines have come in at
the trading post, because I can never get Frankenstein to
bring me any, when I heard a car. I looked back and saw it
was you guys, so I stuck out my thumb, sort of as a joke,
although I really wouldn't mind getting a ride."

Flynn hesitated. "So this is an isolated incident?"

"Well, not totally isolated."

"Aha!"

"Sometimes the Peabodys come by and I get a ride from
them. They live down past the cabin where you're staying.
They don't have kids, but they have a wiener dog named
Low Clearance. We call him Low Clear for short. He—"

"That's not hitchhiking," Flynn said. "I'm talking

about standing there with your thumb out, waiting for whoever shows up."

"I never do that."

"Are you sure? Because if you hitchhike down this road, ever, and I mean *ever*, I don't care how wholesome and homespun this town is, you could get kidnapped and killed."

Luanne took a deep breath and rolled her eyes. "I *know* that. I've known that ever since I was old enough to take walks by myself. I never get in a car with strangers. But you're not strangers."

Flynn let out a little *humph* of disapproval. "We're almost strangers. You really don't know much about us."

"I know your names, Vera Parsons and Tony Bennetti."

Zoe subdued a pang of guilt. The disguise might be necessary, but she didn't like lying to this kid.

"I know you're not married yet," Luanne continued. "And I know you didn't bring a deck of cards on your vacation, which is probably because you have other things to do." She delivered the last part with a smirk.

Flynn sighed. "Okay. Climb in."

"Thanks." Luanne opened the sedan's back door and got into the car.

"Buckle up," Flynn added.

"Of course." The seat belt snapped into place. "You must think I'm a total idiot."

"No, he doesn't." Zoe decided to step in again. "He's just a careful kind of guy. And that's a lot better than a careless one."

"I guess you're right." Luanne was quiet as Flynn put the car in gear and pulled back onto the road.

There was no other traffic. Apparently the Peabodys and their wiener dog were on a different schedule this morning. Zoe wondered if the Peabodys let Low Clear run around in the woods at night. With Bigfoot in the area, she wouldn't let any pets outside, if she had pets, which she didn't because she was away from home so much.

Then Luanne spoke again. "Um, Miss Parsons?"

"You can call me Vera, Luanne."

"Thanks! How about Mr. Bennetti?"

"*Tony*'s okay with me," Flynn said.

"Great! My mom says I always have to ask first. So, Vera?"

"Yes, Luanne?"

"Don't take this wrong, but . . . that outfit's really strange."

"I don't bother much about clothes," Zoe said. "I have more important things to think about. I live in my mind." She wasn't sure exactly what that last sentence meant, but it sounded intellectual.

"That's cool, but I think when you have a boyfriend— not that I've ever *had* a boyfriend—but when you have one, which would be Tony, then I think you have to spend time in your body, too. Just my opinion. I'm only a kid."

A soft snort of laughter came from the driver's side of the car.

"Am I right, Tony?" Luanne said. "Or do you really like that outfit? 'Cause if you love it, then I'll butt out."

"Tony likes neutral, tailored outfits," Zoe said.

"Most of the time," Flynn said. "There can be exceptions."

"Yeah, like lingerie," Luanne said. "Neutral and tailored definitely don't work for lingerie. I wish we had a Victoria's Secret in Long Shaft. I mean, I don't need it *now*, because like I said, I don't have a boyfriend. But when I get one, I'm up the creek without a paddle when it comes to lingerie."

Flynn cleared his throat. "It's a little early to be worrying about—"

"Victoria's Secret has a catalog," Zoe said. "You can go that route."

"No, she can't," Flynn said.

"Yes, I can," Luanne said. "That's an awesome idea. I don't know why I didn't think of it." She leaned forward as far as the seat belt would allow. "Is that what you do, Vera? Order from the catalog?"

Zoe realized her mistake. A nerdy woman who dressed in red plaid and purple pansies, then accented the look with an orange floppy hat wouldn't shop at Victoria's Secret. "No, I don't," she said. Which was true. Whenever she needed underwear, the Victoria's Secret nearest to her house invited her in after hours for an exclusive shopping spree.

"Maybe you should," Luanne said. "I'll bet Tony would appreciate it. Where are you from, anyway? If it's a decent-sized city, they'll have some other places where you could find clothes, like Wet Seal and Caché. 'Cause I'm not kidding. If you fixed yourself up, you'd look a *lot* like Zoe Tarleton."

"I seriously doubt that." Zoe was glad Luanne hadn't pursued the question of where they lived because that would mean another lie, but she didn't like the new direction of Luanne's thoughts any better.

"You would! Take off your hat, and let me look at your hair."

"I don't want anybody to see my hair this morning. I slept on it wrong."

"Don't be silly. Nobody has worse hair than me." Luanne snatched the hat off Zoe's head.

Thanks to Philippe's excellent cut, Zoe's freshly washed hair fell out in artful disarray, looking very much like it had on her latest cover shot for *People*. She held her breath and waited for Luanne's reaction.

Luanne stared at her for several long seconds. "Okay, you're going to think I'm insane, but you look so much like Zoe Tarleton that my brain keeps saying you really are her, and you're up here in disguise. And I would believe that, too, except Tony isn't Trace Edwards, and if you were hiding away somewhere it would be with Trace, because he's your boyfriend." She sighed dramatically. "So that means you're not Zoe, unfortunately. Life is so unfair."

"I'm sorry," Zoe said. "I wish I could be her."

"I wish *I* could be her! Can you imagine being a famous movie star like that? You can have anything you want, and to top it off, Trace Edwards, who is a god, is your boyfriend? She is the luckiest person in the entire world."

"I guess that's true." Zoe wondered if lusting after a Golden Globe Award made her an ungrateful woman who didn't appreciate all that she had. Most women would give anything to be in her shoes. They would be deliriously happy knowing they were a huge box-office success and that they had the attention of a movie idol like Trace Edwards. She, however, wanted more artistic respect, and she didn't want Trace at all.

Even more perverse, she had the hots for her lawyer, who had a serious girlfriend. Zoe hoped she wasn't the kind of person who only wanted what she couldn't have instead of cherishing what she did have.

"Luanne," Flynn said, "I have a question."

"What's that?"

"You . . . how can I put this? You don't sound like other girls your age."

Luanne laughed. "You mean because I don't talk like this?" She took a deep breath. *"I was, like, needing a ride, and you go, 'What are you doing, hitchhiking?' And I'm all, 'no, I never hitchhike,' and you go, 'You'd better not!'"*

"Exactly," Flynn said. "Why don't you talk like that?"

"Simple. I'll be a famous actress someday, and when I accept my Oscar, I want to sound elegant. So I work really hard not to fall into those habits. Whoops, we're at the trading post! You can let me off here."

"Then how will you get back home?" Flynn asked.

"No problem. Somebody will give me a ride. Getting to town is the hard part. Getting home is easy. Everybody's in town on a Saturday morning."

Zoe could see that. The parking lot in front of the Sasquatch Diner was packed with old cars and pickups that made Margo's neon Taurus look like a limo. Prosperity had not blessed Long Shaft.

As Flynn stopped the car, Luanne unlatched her seat belt and opened the back door. "Thanks," she said. "And Vera, ditch the hat. I don't know what you were worried about. Your hair looks great. Just like Zoe Tarleton's. Bye, you guys. See you later."

"That was almost a disaster," Flynn said as he drove the half block to the Sasquatch Diner.

"But you saved me by not being Trace Edwards." Zoe busily tucked her hair back up inside the hat. No point in taking unnecessary chances.

Flynn found the last spot in the diner's parking lot and

slid the car expertly into the opening. "Incidentally, speaking of Trace, I really wish you'd tell him you're up here with me."

"That would be a bad idea."

He paused before opening his car door. "Because he wouldn't like it?"

"Probably not." She met his gaze. "But you don't have to worry that I'll ever tell anyone what goes on between us. Trace won't find out, and neither will his friends. You don't have to worry about gossip or losing clients as a result of spending the weekend with me."

"I wasn't really thinking of that. I was more concerned with your relationship. Are you comfortable keeping this weekend a secret from him?"

"Think of it this way—last night we found a Sasquatch footprint in the dirt and after that we made out in the woods. I don't think we want to tell anyone about either of those things, do you?"

He swallowed. "When you put it that way, I guess not."

"Then we're agreed. What happens in Long Shaft stays in Long Shaft."

He continued to hold her gaze, all the while obviously working to maintain his serious expression. It wouldn't hold. He ended up laughing.

"You see, Flynn, you take life way too seriously."

"You could be right about that." He opened his door. "Now let's go get us a restaurant-cooked meal."

The smells of the ancient diner registered immediately as Flynn held the door open for Zoe. He'd spent many hours in a café like this back in high school because there had been no other place in the small mining town to hang out.

Years of cooking grease and cigarette smoke had settled into the plaster and the cracked vinyl upholstery. If anyone ever created an aromatherapy candle labeled Greasy Spoon, it would smell like this.

Flynn kind of liked it, but he didn't see the Sasquatch Diner as Zoe's kind of place. On a high shelf behind the counter stood football trophies and photos of an earlier, more prosperous Long Shaft. But the pictures and trophies took a backseat to the Bigfoot souvenirs—mugs, key chains, T-shirts, stuffed animals, and bumper stickers. Twenty years ago Flynn would have bought one of each.

A handful of customers were in the diner, and they all looked up when Flynn and Zoe walked in. Silence reigned for a couple of beats, and then everyone returned their attention to their plate, coffee mug, or conversation. Everyone, that is, except Margo, who came rushing out from behind the counter.

Besides a black vinyl miniskirt and her UGG boots, she wore a tight T-shirt in hot pink with the diner's logo on the front. It featured a scary-looking Bigfoot about to bite into an overstuffed hamburger. Flynn had the insane urge to buy a T-shirt for Zoe as a memento of the weekend.

Yeah, like she'd ever wear it. It wouldn't even work as her nerd outfit for the audition. Vera wasn't a T-shirt-wearing type of woman.

But Zoe was, he realized with a start, even if she hadn't figured that out yet. She might think she was strictly Rodeo Drive, but after seeing her in the Einstein sweatshirt, he could picture her lounging around her Malibu beach house wearing a Sasquatch Diner T-shirt and short shorts.

Yes, short shorts, even though last night and today she'd been wearing sweats. This was his fantasy, and in his fantasy he wanted to see her legs. He was truly pathetic.

As Margo came toward them, her permed hair caught up in a side ponytail, she looked perky enough to break into a cheer routine at any minute.

"Hi there!" Margo glanced at Zoe. "Great outfit!"

Zoe lowered her voice. "Flynn thinks it might be a little overdone."

"Nah. You know what you're doing. Did you come to eat?"

Zoe nodded. "And we need to check with you about something."

"Sure, sure. Take this booth over here." Margo ushered them to a place by a grimy window that looked out on the street. "I'll get you some menus."

As Flynn sat down, the ancient wood creaked.

Zoe took the opposite seat and leaned toward him. "Not exactly five-star dining," she murmured.

"Still want to eat here?"

"Are you kidding? Nothing that comes out of that kitchen could possibly be worse than last night's spaghetti."

"Not that I'm agreeing with you, but I thought I'd go find a grocery store before we leave and see if they have any microwave dinners."

"Flynn, there's no microwave. I checked."

"Most of those meals can be cooked in a regular oven, too."

Margo bustled over and slapped a laminated menu down in front of each of them. "Here you go! Fiona's in a good mood, so feel free to order any of the breakfast items."

Flynn caught sight of a dark-haired woman wearing a hairnet, peering out the kitchen door. It wasn't her fault that she had an angular face that made her look sinister, but Flynn was less enthusiastic about the meal after a glimpse of Fiona. "What happens if the cook's not in a good mood?"

"You're better off with the cornflakes. But as I mentioned last night, we're in that grace period right after the full moon, so we have blueberry cobbler, Fiona's willing to make anything on the menu, and her hubby got his monthly ration of sex. Which reminds me, have you tried the cobbler yet?"

Flynn said "No" at the same time Zoe said "Yes."

"So you've had some, Zoe?" Margo looked pleased.

"Uh-huh." Zoe glanced at Flynn. "But not much."

"Oh, come on, Zoe. Indulge yourself and have a regular serving when you get back. My Bob adores that cobbler. Trust me, you won't find anything like it in LA. Fiona has a gift."

Flynn thought of how the disposal had foamed up when he'd run the cobbler through it. Maybe the cobbler was as terrific as Margo said, but he was still suspicious, and just as glad they hadn't eaten any of it. Fiona's full-moon cooking jag was plain weird.

"I'll eat more tonight," Zoe said. "But we need to talk to you about the bees under the porch. A whole hive of them."

Margo frowned. "How annoying."

"More than annoying," Flynn said. "She's allergic."

"Uh-oh. I didn't know that."

Zoe laughed. "I'm always so worried about the stories that show up in the *Enquirer,* thinking everybody sees them, but I guess they don't. Flynn didn't know about the bee allergy, either. It was a big story about two years ago. I had a pretty bad reaction."

"Then we have to get rid of those bees. I'll get right on it. And I'm *really* glad you didn't get stung. So can I bring you coffee while you're deciding what to order? Juice?"

"Coffee sounds great," Flynn said.

"Be right back." Margo hustled off.

Zoe consulted the menu. "Eggs Benedict," Zoe said with reverence. "That sounds so good, but I'd better not."

"You'd better." Flynn adjusted his glasses and peered at the menu. "That's what I'm having. No telling where our next meal is coming from, or how it will taste. This may be our one and only restaurant outing. The more we come in here, the more likely somebody will recognize you."

"I guess you're right." Zoe pushed her menu aside. "Maybe I'll go for a run in the woods later."

"I could go with you."

Her eyebrows lifted. "You run?"

"Of course I run. It's a law in Southern California. Last week I saw two people arrested for not running."

Zoe smiled at him. "You're a funny guy. I never realized that before. So do you really run, or are you making that up?"

"I really run. Listen, I don't think you should smile while we're in the restaurant."

"Why not? Do I have something stuck in my teeth?"

"No. But that smile is famous. You could create the perfect disguise, but once you smile, I think people will recognize you."

"That's silly." She did it again. "My smile looks like everyone else's."

"Nope."

"It does. I have lips and teeth and gums. Nothing special."

"That's not true. You may have the same components, but the way they're arranged is very special. You knock people out with that smile."

She gazed at him for a long moment. "Tell me about Kristen's smile."

He knew what she was doing and he should appreciate it. "It's nice." He couldn't picture it right now, but he was sure she had a nice smile.

"What does she look like?"

"Oh, brown hair, about five-six, a hundred and twenty-five pounds."

"That sounds like the info on her driver's license. What does she *look* like?"

He knew what Zoe was after. She expected him to rave about how beautiful Kristen was, how he adored her lips, her eyes, her everything. Instead, he was horrified to discover he couldn't do that. Sure, she was attractive, and a man in love would call her beautiful without being prodded. He needed to rethink this Kristen business, and soon.

"She's athletic," he said. "She runs, too." It was something they shared. They had so much in common, so why couldn't he be more excited about her?

"Interesting." Zoe's gaze was speculative. "I'm probably stereotyping, but I didn't think . . ." She paused as if revising what she'd been about to say.

"That nerds would run?" he finished, pretty sure that's what she'd had in mind. And he would pursue that topic, because he didn't want to continue discussing Kristen's attributes and give himself away.

Zoe shrugged. "I thought physical exercise wasn't all that important, that mental gymnastics were the whole deal."

"Exercise didn't used to be important, but after I hit thirty, I realized that if I didn't do something, I was asking for health problems. I do it to avoid medical bills."

"I see." Rummaging in her purse, she pulled out the pad she'd used last night to take notes while he was unpacking.

"What?"

"I'm starting to get the nerd mentality." She jotted down a few things on the pad. "It's not so much what you do as why you do it. I run because I want to have a killer body. You run to avoid future medical bills. Your reasons are pure logic, and mine are pure emotion. Ego, to be exact." She finished writing and glanced up. "Am I on target?"

"I think you're being too hard on yourself." Damn. As uninterested as he was in Kristen right now, he was totally fascinated by Zoe. She looked outlandishly cute in her wild outfit and glasses as she made notes on nerd behavior. "Running to get a killer body is part of your job," he said. "People expect you to look amazing, so you have to oblige."

"But I also like looking amazing. That's ego. Even if I weren't . . ." She lowered her voice as one of the customers walked by on his way to the cash register. "Even if I weren't in this profession, I'd want a good body."

Twinges of a sexual response alerted Flynn to the need for a different topic. "Margo must have a local person in mind for the bees. She didn't say anything about calling Sacramento."

"No, she didn't. So maybe—" Zoe stopped talking as Margo arrived with their coffee and a bowl full of cream packets.

"Have you decided?" She set down the mugs and the cream.

"Eggs Benedict for both of us," Flynn said.

"Coming right up. And the bees should be gone when you get back. Somebody's headed out there now to take a look."

"That's fabulous," Zoe said. "Thanks, Margo."

"Yes, thank you." Flynn had to admit that Zoe's unlikely friend was coming through in the crunch.

He was starting to realize that life wasn't quite as neat and tidy as he'd like it to be. At first he'd thought Margo wasn't Zoe's type, but she might turn out to be the perfect friend for Zoe. And as much as he wanted to be in love with Kristen because she was everything he wanted and needed in a woman, he wasn't in love with her.

Instead he was becoming obsessed with Zoe, which was completely impractical. She'd never in a million years want a long-term relationship with her token nerd. But he seemed to have no choice about his lust. He'd always scoffed at the idea of being buffeted by out-of-control emotions, and yet that was the situation here in Long Shaft.

He remembered her comment before they'd come into the diner. *What happens in Long Shaft stays in Long Shaft.* He'd thought she'd meant it as a joke. What if she'd meant it as an invitation? And what if he accepted?

Chapter Fourteen

The eggs Benedict were runny, the sauce tasted like glue, the ham turned out to be Spam, and the English muffin underneath it all required a steak knife. Zoe ate it anyway, because she couldn't have done better and she needed the protein. To compensate she drank gallons of coffee, which was the best thing about the meal.

Flynn doctored his eggs Benedict with ketchup.

"I can't believe how gross that looks," Zoe said. "Like your meal is hemorrhaging."

"Ketchup is the answer to any culinary problem."

Zoe drained her coffee mug. "Maybe we should have ordered the cornflakes."

"If we have to do that, we might as well buy a box at the store when we get the microwave meals."

"Good idea. After tasting the eggs Benedict, I'm really glad you put the cobbler down the disposal."

"Me, too. I didn't tell you, but it made the disposal foam up. No telling what was in that stuff."

"Yuck." Zoe still felt guilty that she had lied about eating it, but Flynn might have saved her from a serious stomachache. "Well, I've had enough coffee to float a battleship, so if you'll excuse me, I need to make a trip."

"Don't smile at anybody on the way there. We've collected our share of looks from the other customers. I think several of them are trying to place you."

"I doubt it. We're strangers in town. That's all it is." She stood up and walked to the back of the diner where a sign pointed to the restrooms. Sure, customers glanced her way as she passed, but part of that might be her outfit. She should have worn something that didn't poke out a person's eye. Apparently it was possible to overdisguise yourself.

On the way out of the bathroom she found Margo standing by the door.

"I wanted to talk to you for a minute," Margo said.

"Sure." Time for more lies. "By the way, what a great breakfast!"

"Glad you liked it." Margo nodded as if she'd expected the praise.

"Listen, as long as we have a private moment, do you think anybody's starting to recognize me? Flynn's worried about it. He seems to think people are staring, but I said it's only because we're strangers in town."

"It's because they think you're a hooker."

"A *what*?" Zoe backed up a step.

"Joe Pasternak from down at the gas station overheard you say that even if you weren't in this profession, you'd want to have a killer body. He decided you were a prostitute."

Zoe groaned. "Lovely."

"I told him you weren't, but I fumbled around trying to

come up with a different story, so he still thinks so. He's spread the word."

"I suppose it doesn't matter. It's better than having them find out who I am."

"Well, Syd from the trading post did mention that you looked like Zoe Tarleton, only sleazier. So you probably have to be careful."

"I know." Zoe glanced back to where Flynn was sitting. "I might have made a mistake coming in here, but we didn't have your work number, and I thought it would be fun to come and see the diner." She wasn't going to admit she couldn't cook.

"Yeah, it's a pretty cool little diner. Did you see my picture on the wall?"

"No! Where is it?"

Margo pointed to a spot above one of the booths. There was Margo's high school yearbook picture, the eight-by-ten. She'd chosen to have it taken in her cheerleading uniform with the megaphone as a prop.

The contrast between that Margo and the one standing in front of Zoe was a shock. Senior pictures were always taken in the fall, so at that point Margo had been going steady with Rob. Zoe told herself that Margo might have slid downhill even if she'd ended up with Rob, but the guilt was still there.

"They wanted a picture of me to put up on account of all my Bigfoot sightings," Margo said. "That was the only one I had. There's a little sign underneath that says I'm the top Bigfoot spotter, and they have a space where I can change the number each time I have another sighting."

"That's terrific!" Zoe knew she sounded patronizing and couldn't figure out how to avoid it.

"I know it's not in the same league with a movie marquee."

"Margo, I have zero Bigfoot sightings and you have . . ." She searched her memory for the number Margo had thrown out last night.

"Seven," Margo said. "I saw the big male last night. If you'd been looking, you would have seen him, too. He went right by your place."

"I didn't see him." Zoe thought about the footprint. "Have you ever found footprints?"

"Oh, sure. I made that plaster cast that's hanging behind the cash register."

Zoe looked over and saw the cast, which was the same color as the wall, so she'd missed it before. It looked exactly like the footprint she'd seen last night. She shivered. "That's very convincing."

"You'd better believe it is. Bigfoot is definitely out there." Margo nodded wisely. "I'm trying to get a good picture, but what I've taken is too blurry. Someday I'll get that picture, and the world will sit up and take notice."

"I'm sure it will. That would be historic, Margo."

"I'm saving for a better camera. That will help. Well, listen, I have to get back to work, but I wanted to warn you about something. My guy called in about the bees, and he found an actual man-made hive under there. So he notified the landlord, who said no way, nohow, was that there yesterday. So somebody left it since then, probably during the night."

"On purpose?" Zoe felt a little chill. "Why would anyone do that?"

Margo gazed at her for a couple of seconds. "Think about it."

"I can't imagine why anyone would do that. It makes no sense, unless it's just vandals."

"Oh, I don't think it's vandals. I think it's someone who's targeting you personally, someone who feels extremely threatened by you."

Zoe's eyes widened. "Flynn's girlfriend?"

"Bingo."

Zoe shook her head. "That's impossible. She's in Chicago."

"How do you know that?" Margo glanced over at a booth where someone was signaling for her attention. "Be right there!"

"She's in Chicago," Zoe said again, unwilling to believe a woman she didn't know was after her. Yet thinking about what had happened with Flynn last night, Zoe had to admit that Kristen had a reason to be upset.

"What evidence do you have that she's in Chicago?" Margo sounded like an actor on a TV cop show.

"Flynn . . . Flynn talked to her. She was talking to him from the conference."

"Cell phone calls can come from anywhere."

"But she's a lawyer. She's a nerd." Nerds weren't stalkers. Were they?

"So what if she's a nerd? In fact, if she's a lawyer, even more reason to think she did it. Lawyers research things. After she found out about this weekend, she would have dug up everything about you. That would be nerd behavior, right?"

"I guess so." Zoe couldn't fault Margo's reasoning.

"And she would have found that old *Enquirer* story, which is probably available somewhere. So she'd know about your allergy. You need to watch your back, Zoe."

"I have a hard time believing she'd go to such lengths."

"Maybe I'm wrong, but I don't think I am. I wanted to warn you."

"I appreciate that."

"Anyway, I really have to get going before the customers call out a lynch party."

"Wait." Zoe wasn't ready to let go of the only person interested in protecting her from a potential threat. "The best way to prove this one way or the other is to find out if she's still registered at that hotel."

"Which hotel?"

"I don't know, but I can find out. I wouldn't dare call, though. Flynn might catch me doing it."

"So get me the name of the hotel. I'll call and see if she's there."

"Okay. I'll do that." Zoe watched Margo walk away. Then she looked over at Flynn, who was glancing in her direction. What should she tell him?

Nothing. He would go up in smoke if she so much as hinted that Kristen might be plotting to harm her. He might not be madly in love with his girlfriend, but he'd resent the hell out of Zoe making her out as some psycho woman.

She walked back to the table and smiled at him. "Ready to leave?"

"I'm ready. But I'm curious about what Margo had to say. You looked upset."

She thought quickly. "There's a chance they were killer bees, after all." Which could be true. Nobody had said they weren't. "I'm very lucky I didn't get stung." Also true.

She still had a tough time imagining the bees were a special message from Kristen. Even so, as she picked up the bill Margo had left, she memorized the number of the Sasquatch Diner, so she could call with the name of Kristen's hotel when she got the chance.

"I can pay for my own breakfast." Flynn stood and pulled out his wallet. "In fact, let me buy yours, such as it was."

"No, no." Zoe waved his money away. "I invited you up here. My treat." Then she remembered what else Margo had told her. "You can't be seen paying for me, anyway. Everyone here thinks I'm a hooker."

Flynn blinked. "Come again?"

She told him about the overheard remark. "So they think my profession is actually the world's oldest profession. You need to let me pay, which will make them wonder, because logically a prostitute wouldn't be buying the meal."

"Good Lord." His color high, he adjusted the position of his glasses. He didn't seem terribly comfortable being associated with a suspected lady of the evening, even in broad daylight. "And who do they think I am, your client?"

"I don't know. Maybe they think you're my pimp." With a wink, she turned and walked up to the cash register.

A pimp. Now Flynn was doubly glad he'd switched from the Town Car Zoe had rented to a sensible sedan. He didn't know any pimps, but he'd seen movies and he knew they were supposed to drive big expensive cars. Pimps also were supposed to dress in flashy clothes, so he was saved on that score, too.

No, people wouldn't think he was Zoe's pimp, but they might think he'd hired her for a weekend of sex. And a weekend of sex was exactly what he wanted, although he didn't plan to allow himself the luxury.

That didn't stop him from thinking about it as he held

the door open for Zoe and escorted her out to the car. Every customer in the place had watched their exit, and he wondered how many of the men envied him. Zoe's wild combination of colors and wire-rimmed glasses couldn't disguise her incredible body.

Once they were both in the car, Flynn backed out of the parking space. "I'm sure there's some kind of grocery store on this street."

"I'm sure there is. By the way, have you talked to Kristen today?"

"No, not yet." And he felt guilty about that. But with the bee problem and hurrying to come into town so they could have breakfast, he hadn't had much time. He needed to have a serious discussion with Kristen, because he was beginning to doubt his commitment to her. Yet he couldn't imagine having that discussion while Zoe was nearby.

"Don't you think you should check in with her?"

"You mean now?" He scanned the ragtag buildings lining Long Shaft's main street and spotted the Bigfoot Food Mart about midway down on the left.

"You brought your cell phone, right?"

"I always bring my cell phone." He'd been first in line to buy one the minute they'd become available.

"So call her while we're in town. I'm sure the signal will be better than out in the woods."

"She's probably in one of her sessions. She was giving a talk this morning."

"Then you could at least leave her a message."

"I could." And that might be better. He could leave a message to let her know he hadn't forgotten about her. If he left messages all weekend, then on Sunday night when he got back to LA he could have the necessary discussion about their future.

Pulling into a diagonal parking space between two battered pickups, he turned off the engine and reached in his shirt pocket for his PDA. He'd programmed Kristen's conference schedule into it. He'd be able to make sure she wasn't in a position to pick up.

Yep, she was right in the middle of her talk. *Assuming she hadn't ditched the conference and was on her way to Long Shaft.* He slipped the PDA back in his shirt pocket and reached for the cell phone clipped to his belt.

"Chicago's a great city," Zoe said. "I stayed at the Hilton on Michigan Avenue last time I was there. Is that where Kristen is?"

"No, she's at the Sheraton on Lake Shore Drive." He speed-dialed Kristen's cell. Her well-modulated voice on the recorded message raised his level of guilt. She sounded so calm, so civilized. An animal like him, a guy who couldn't keep his hands off Zoe, didn't deserve a woman like Kristen.

"Oh, well, that's nice, too."

"What?" He glanced at Zoe as he waited for the beep to begin recording his message.

"I meant the Sheraton's a good place to stay."

He had a sudden image of sharing a luxury hotel room with Zoe. He wouldn't care what city they were in because he wouldn't leave the room, and if he had Zoe figured right, she wouldn't want to, either.

That wasn't a good thing to be thinking about while he left his message for Kristen. His voice clogged up at first, and he had to clear his throat before continuing. "Hi, Kristen. It's me. I came into town for some breakfast and thought I'd give you a call. I hope your talk went great. I'll check back later. Take care. Bye." He ended the call and slipped the phone back in the holder clipped to his belt.

"What was her talk on?" Zoe asked.

"Research techniques."

"Research techniques?" Zoe's voice sounded slightly strangled, like she might be trying not to laugh.

"I know it sounds boring, but in actuality it's extremely . . . boring." He glanced over at her, feeling more like a louse every minute. "I shouldn't admit that. I'm being very disloyal, but she outlined her talk for me over the phone last week and I nearly fell asleep."

Zoe gazed at him. "Research can be important. I suppose she's very good at it."

Something was going on with Zoe, but he couldn't tell what. Her expression had always been open, but now it wasn't. She seemed to be hiding.

He wanted to know why. "What's with the sudden interest in Kristen?"

"I've always been interested in Kristen, ever since you told me about her this past week."

"I know, but now you seem even more interested."

"I just don't want you to forget about her this weekend, that's all. I know she's important to you. You should keep in contact."

"But you're not keeping in contact with Trace."

Her expression became even more secretive. "That's not really necessary."

"Why is it necessary for me and Kristen and not for you and Trace?"

She waved a hand in the air. "You know Hollywood relationships. They're not the norm. We're separated a lot by work, and when we are together the media is all over us. It's not easy to have the level of intimacy that you're able to have with Kristen. Trace and I aren't close enough for me to feel I need to keep in constant touch with him."

"You don't love him." Flynn hadn't meant to say it. Usually he guarded his comments better than that. "Sorry. That's none of my business."

"You're entitled to your opinion."

"Yeah, but I don't have to blurt it out. What do I know about your emotions concerning Trace? Nothing. I have no right to make a judgment."

"You could assume I didn't love him after what happened last night."

"No, I couldn't, Zoe. People are more complicated than that." He braced both hands against the steering wheel and blew out a breath. "Tell you what. Let's table this discussion while I go into the food mart and hunt down some food that's easy to fix."

"Do you mind if I sit in the car? I just realized the food mart might stock magazines with me on the cover."

"Then you probably shouldn't come in."

"I'll try to stay out of trouble."

He wondered if that were possible. She looked like trouble sitting there with a big purple pansy decorating each breast and glasses that made her seem more impish than scholarly. The blouse was buttoned up to her neck and the plaid skirt covered her knees, but that didn't matter. Nothing could disguise the sexual light shining from Zoe Tarleton. That was why she'd made millions.

"I won't be long," he said.

"I'll be here." She smiled at him.

"If anyone comes along, don't smile."

"I still say you're wrong about that. No one's going to recognize me because of my smile."

"Humor me. Don't smile."

"Okay." She scrunched up her face and crossed her eyes. "How's this?"

He laughed. "Perfect. Hold that pose." He knew she wouldn't, but at least he'd tried. He left the car determined to make this a power shopping trip.

When Flynn walked into the food mart, Zoe pulled her cell phone out of her purse and punched in the number of the Sasquatch Diner. A man answered, and Zoe decided he must be Ray, Fiona's recently satisfied husband.

Zoe watched the front of the food mart in case Flynn made an unexpected return. "May I please speak to Margo Taggart?"

"May I ask who's calling?"

"It's Zo—Vera. Vera Parsons."

"Zovera?"

"No, just Vera." Zoe didn't know if Margo would recognize the name she'd decided to use. "Tell her it's her friend from high school."

"Are you the person who was in here a few minutes ago? The one in the flowery blouse and plaid skirt?"

"Um, yes." Zoe crossed her fingers and hoped that wouldn't keep Ray from putting Margo on the line.

"The reason I ask is that some of us got to talking, and we think you look a lot like Zoe Tarleton."

Zoe's heart started pounding. "I get that all the time," she said. "I'm sure Miss Tarleton would be horrified by the comparison. I'm definitely not her."

"Oh, we know that!" Ray chuckled. "Anybody can see you're not a famous movie star."

Zoe wasn't sure she liked being dismissed so quickly as a loser. But she didn't have time to chat about it with Ray. "Is Margo available?"

"Sure. I'll get her. But my associates and I were talking, and you would make a perfect look-alike. Have you ever thought of creating a role for yourself as a Zoe Tarleton impersonator?"

"Not really." Zoe glanced at the door to the food mart. If Flynn shopped fast, he could be out any minute. "Listen, I don't have a lot of time, so if you could get Margo, I would appreciate—"

"Certainly. I'll be happy to flag her down. But back to this impersonation idea—we're in the market for tourist attractions in Long Shaft. I think Hollywood look-alikes are a viable concept, don't you?"

"Ray, I really do need to talk to Margo."

"How did you know my name was Ray?"

"Margo told me." *And she also mentioned that you got lucky recently, but let's not go into that.*

"Oh. Anyway, here's Margo. Please think about the impersonation idea. Even though you're pretending to be someone else, it's still an honest way to make a living." His implication was clear. *As opposed to being a prostitute.*

Torn between laughter and frustration, Zoe massaged her temples. She shouldn't have gone to the diner, but she'd been so damned hungry.

"Hello?" Margo sounded uncertain. She probably didn't remember the Vera Parsons name switch.

Or had Zoe remembered to tell her? Life was getting way too complicated. "Margo, it's me, Zoe. I found out the name of the hotel in Chicago. It's . . ." She saw Flynn coming out of the food mart. "Shit."

"The hotel is named Shit? What is that, some Asian chain?"

"Sheraton. On Lake Shore Drive," Zoe murmured. "Gotta go." Snapping her phone closed, she tucked it back in her purse.

Flynn climbed in the car and tossed a plastic grocery

bag into the backseat. "So you decided to call Trace after all?"

"No, I . . . uh, called my mother."

"That's nothing to be ashamed about. When I came out you put the phone away like I'd caught you doing something wrong. I believe in checking in with moms. I call home every couple of weeks."

Zoe felt like such a rat for getting into this cloak-and-dagger business. A guy who called home every couple of weeks wasn't the type to be hooked up with a stalker. Kristen was probably registered at the hotel and the bees were the work of a prankster who had no idea someone in the cabin was allergic.

"So where's home?" she asked, wanting to talk about normal things.

"A little mining town in Arizona." Flynn started the car. "You never would have heard of it. I grew up there. Mom runs a B and B and Dad stages mock gunfights for the tourists."

"Really?" Just as she'd never picture Flynn having a girlfriend, she'd never pictured him with interesting parents, either. "Was your dad an actor?"

"Nope. Miner. But the mine played out, and the town stayed alive through tourism, so my folks got into that. I can relate to the struggles here in Long Shaft. It's a similar situation." He made a U-turn at the end of the street, which wasn't difficult because no traffic was coming into town.

"Is the B and B one of those Victorian places with all the gingerbread?"

"Uh-huh. And my mom puts on a high-necked dress with a hoopskirt."

"I'd love to see that." She was suddenly taken with the

idea of visiting Flynn's parents and looking at scrapbook pictures of him when he was a little boy. Maybe there would be one of him in his eggplant costume.

"My hometown would love to have you. You'd be the star attraction."

"I was thinking more along the lines of quietly sneaking in by the back."

Flynn glanced over at her. "Zoe, I don't think that's your destiny." He found a parking space in front of the Long Shaft Trading Post. "I have one more stop to make. I want to buy a flashlight."

"In case Bigfoot shows up again?"

"Right. I'll be back in no time."

"Okay." After he left, Zoe pulled out her cell phone again and called the diner. This time she was in luck. Margo answered.

"Margo, it's me. Did you call yet?"

"I called. She's not there, Zoe."

Chapter Fifteen

Flynn had been so intent on getting a flashlight that he temporarily forgot that Jeff worked at the trading post and Luanne had asked to be dropped off there. He remembered both things when he spotted Luanne sitting on the floor over by the magazine rack, an open copy of *People* on her lap. She was so engrossed she didn't look up.

He was free to study the rest of the store, which turned out to be a bewildering combination of snack food, junk jewelry, discounted CDs and videos, T-shirts and sweatshirts, plastic toys, and souvenir mugs. It could have been a truck-stop convenience store anywhere in the country except for the overriding theme of Bigfoot. Flynn spotted some of the same merchandise he'd seen in the Sasquatch Diner.

"Hey, dude!" Jeff appeared from around the end of an aisle featuring stuffed versions of Sasquatch in varying sizes. "Welcome to the Long Shaft Trading Post. We're all Bigfoot, all the time."

"I can see that." Flynn glanced around, not finding what he'd come in for. "I need a flashlight, but you might not carry—"

"Oh, but we do, we do! Walk this way." Lumbering along in a great imitation of a Sasquatch, Jeff disappeared around the end of the same aisle.

Flynn followed him and came upon an aisle of camping supplies. Only these weren't ordinary camping supplies. All of them had been molded, stamped, or otherwise branded with the image of Bigfoot.

Sleeping bags were covered in fur and had huge fake feet sticking out the end. Tents had oversize footprints all over them. Supports for a camp stove were made of metal painted to look like two hairy legs with oversize feet.

"Who manufactures all this stuff?" Flynn had never been camping in his life, but if he could camp with this gear, he'd consider it. What a hoot.

"Some dude in San Francisco. I think he did a lot of LSD back in the sixties, so he's kind of whacked. But he inherited a bunch of money and he's having fun with it, like designing Bigfoot camping gear. He doesn't even, like, care if we sell it. Every once in a while he drives over to look at it on the shelves. He nods and smiles and goes away again."

Flynn walked up and down the aisle, finding new treasures by the second. He'd also been around Hollywood long enough to know this kind of crazy merchandise might catch on.

"What you need is a write-up in the *LA Times*," he said. "I can imagine this becoming the next new thing, with people making a pilgrimage to Long Shaft to buy a Bigfoot sleeping bag."

"Are you serious?" Jeff walked over and stroked the

fur on a rolled-up sleeping bag. "Could you, like, make that happen?"

"I'm not sure. Maybe." Flynn had a soft spot in his heart for struggling little mining towns. "I'm not in the cool crowd, so I can't promise anything, but I know a few people." Like the one sitting out in the car right now. "When I get back I could see if anybody's excited about the concept."

"That would be awesome, dude." Jeff gazed at him with reverence. "Because I don't know if you noticed, but this town is in trouble."

Flynn nodded. "I noticed. So where are the flashlights?"

"Right here!" Jeff lunged forward and plucked a statue of Bigfoot from a shelf. "Wa-la!" As he twisted the feet, light poured from Bigfoot's open mouth.

"Excellent." Flynn took the flashlight and twisted the feet to make the mouth light up. Apparently the kid who had craved toys like this was still alive and kicking inside him. "Tell you what, I'll take a sleeping bag, too, so people can see what I'm talking about."

It was the best excuse he could come up with to justify buying something he wanted anyway. He wasn't even sure what he'd do with it, but he couldn't leave the store without having one.

"Outstanding." Jeff tucked a sleeping bag under one long arm and started up toward the cash register. "Syd, that's my boss, is gonna be, like, doing the bunny hop in the aisles when I tell him about this."

"Maybe you should hold off." Flynn hated to get anyone's hopes up and not deliver. "I could be wrong. Like I said, I'm not one of the cool people."

"I know."

Flynn wished Jeff hadn't said that so quickly.

"But I don't think you're wrong," Jeff added. "You look like you have your shit together, with your cell phone and everything. If you think that LA people would go for this, I believe you." He plopped the sleeping bag on the counter. "I can give you a discount on your purchases because you're local."

"We're only renting for the weekend."

"That's good enough for me." As Jeff keyed in the sale, Luanne appeared at the counter.

"Tony, tell me you're not buying one of those mangy sleeping bags."

"Sis, I'm warning you. Back off." Jeff punched the last button and the receipt started printing. "We're executing a transaction here."

By the time Jeff finished lecturing his sister, Flynn remembered his name was supposed to be Tony. "You don't like the sleeping bags?" he asked.

Luanne rolled her eyes. "No offense, but I think they're dorky. I mean, what's the point in Bigfoot anyway? Is Bigfoot cute? *No.* Does he run around fighting bad guys like Spider-Man? *No.* Bigfoot is plain useless if you ask me, which nobody ever does."

"That shows what you know," Jeff said. "Bigfoot is, like, a major tourist attraction."

"Then where are all the tourists?" Luanne planted her hands on her skinny hips. "We've had exactly two this year, Tony and Vera!"

"But my man Tony has a plan." Jeff beamed at him. "Right, Tony?"

"A possibility, at least." Flynn pulled cash from his wallet to pay for the flashlight and sleeping bag. His credit card happened to be issued to Flynn Granger, which would cause some problems.

Luanne plopped her *People* magazine on the counter and flipped it open to a picture of Zoe and Trace at a Hollywood party. "I want you to see this, Tony." She pointed to the picture. "Doesn't Vera look exactly like her?"

"There's definitely a resemblance." Flynn should probably buy a copy of the magazine and tack that picture of Zoe with Trace on his bedroom wall at the cabin, to remind himself that she was involved with someone. He didn't care what she said about the level of involvement. Trespassing was trespassing and he didn't want to do it.

"Zoe and Vera could be twins. Even the smile is the same, and that's the part that usually is so different. When you see a movie where a person is playing the part of somebody famous who died, when they smile it really looks fake."

Flynn thought this munchkin was getting too close to the truth and needed to be diverted. "They say everyone has a perfect double somewhere in the world. That means that somewhere an exact replica of Luanne Dunwoodie is walking around this very minute."

Jeff snorted. "There's a sickening thought. One is bad enough. If there are two like her, I'll have to kill myself."

"You're in a heap of trouble anyway," Luanne shot back. "Janice called this morning after you went to work."

Jeff tensed and his glance shifted. "What did she want?"

"To tell you that she couldn't go out until eight tonight on account of she has to watch her little brother until then."

"Oh. Okay. No problem." Jeff's expression relaxed again.

"There's a problem all right. I asked her if you guys had fun last night, and she said you guys didn't go out."

Jeff groaned. "Luanne, you have a really big mouth, you know that? And how come you didn't tell me this when you first came in here this morning? Now Janice is probably madder than ever!"

"She thinks you're two-timing her with Becky. So are you?"

"No! No, I am not. Becky is nothing to me. Wow, I need to call Janice and explain." He reached for the phone behind the counter.

"This I want to hear." Luanne crossed her arms. "You told Mom and Dad you were out with Janice last night. Something fishy is going on."

And Flynn didn't really care what. At least Luanne was off the subject of Zoe look-alikes. He also didn't want to leave Zoe out in the car for too much longer. Somebody might proposition her, for one thing.

He picked up the flashlight and sleeping bag. "Thanks for the help. I need to be going."

"Wait." Jeff looked distraught. "I didn't put it in a bag or anything."

"That's okay. I don't need a bag." He wanted to leave before Luanne asked for a ride back to her house. Much more time with Zoe, and Luanne was going to figure out the disguise. "See you later."

As he went out the door of the trading post, he wondered if he should be concerned about where Jeff had been last night, after all. He'd met the guy out in the woods. Jeff could have come back later and put the bees under the porch, which would explain why they'd suddenly appeared first thing in the morning.

But suspecting Jeff of such a thing made no sense. Unless Flynn had become a lousy judge of character, Jeff wasn't a vandal, and he'd have no other motivation for doing something like that. Early that morning, though, Flynn had heard soft footsteps right next to the cabin. Someone could have been out there.

Ah, he might as well forget it. Nothing was adding up. And he had more important things to worry about, like why Zoe was in deep conversation with some bald guy who was leaning down to talk with her through the car window. Sunlight glinted off the top of the guy's head as he nodded enthusiastically.

Flynn was surprised by his surge of protectiveness. If Zoe had some dirty old man trying to convince her to have sex with him, Flynn was ready to haul the guy up by his shirtfront and tell him to leave well enough alone. This woman was with *him*.

Determination in every step, he walked up to the guy. "Can I help you?"

The man glanced around, took note of the sleeping bag tucked under Flynn's arm and the flashlight in his other hand, and smiled. "Glad to see you're supporting our cause."

"Um, right. Sorry to cut your conversation short, but we have to get back to the cabin, Mr. . . ."

"This is Ray," Zoe said. "He owns the Sasquatch Diner, plus he's the mayor of Long Shaft."

"Oh. I see." Flynn still didn't feel like being friendly, even though he now knew the guy's credentials. Ray also was married to Fiona, who only gave him sex when the moon was full.

Granted, that wasn't very often, but he'd just had it, according to Margo, so he had no business trying to proposition Zoe this morning. And he was the mayor, for God's sake. How did that look? Zoe seemed to be trying hard not to laugh, but Flynn saw nothing funny about it.

"Ray has a proposition for me," Zoe said.

"What?" Flynn couldn't believe she'd say it straight out.

"He thinks I should leave my current profession and promote myself as a Zoe Tarleton look-alike."

Ray looked Flynn over. "From your expression, you don't cotton to the idea, and I'm not clear what your arrangement is with this young lady, but she could have a real career instead of selling herself to the highest bidder, if you know what I mean."

"I don't think that's—"

"Hear me out," Ray said. "As the duly elected mayor of this fine town, let me say that Long Shaft would love to launch that career. She'd be a great complement to our Bigfoot campaign. I've even thought of a slogan: '*Beauty and the Bigfoot.*' "

"I've told him I really can't consider the offer, wonderful as it sounds." Glints of laughter danced in Zoe's blue eyes.

"And I've been trying to convince her otherwise," Ray said. "I have the feeling that you, sir, are the obstacle to the plan." He glanced at the sleeping bag. "Notwithstanding your contribution to our coffers with your recent purchase. I do appreciate that, but I have my eye on a bigger prize."

Flynn still thought Ray could be angling for a chance to sleep with Zoe. The mayor might be going at it obliquely, but if he thought she was a prostitute, then he might figure on some fringe benefits if he could hire her to do this impersonation thing for the benefit of Long Shaft. No telling what Ray thought Flynn was, though.

"Actually," Flynn said, "I am an obstacle to your plan. Miss Parsons and I are business associates down in LA. We both have obligations there, so I'm afraid she's not available."

Ray appealed to Zoe. "Is it ironclad, this business arrangement? More important, is it legal?"

"Perfectly legal," Zoe said. "Tony's my legal counsel."

"He is?" Ray gazed skeptically at Flynn as if to say, *And I'm Bugs Bunny,* but kept his mouth shut. "Well, if you ever change your mind, you know where to find me. Have a good day." With one last disapproving glance at Flynn, he walked away.

Zoe grinned at Flynn. "What *is* that thing under your arm?"

"A sleeping bag."

"But it's furry, and it has feet sticking out the end."

"I know. Pretty cool, huh?" Flynn opened the back door and deposited the sleeping bag on the seat.

Zoe started to laugh. "It's a Bigfoot sleeping bag, isn't it?"

"Uh-huh." He walked around the back of the car and up to the driver's door. "And that's not all." After climbing behind the wheel, he held up the Bigfoot flashlight and twisted the feet.

"Oh, my God." Zoe whooped with glee. "That is too funny. Let me see it."

Flynn handed it over and stuck the key in the ignition.

"I love this." Zoe twisted the feet back and forth, turning the light on and off. "I want one." She grabbed her purse. "Don't leave yet. Let me give you some money so you can go back in and get—"

"Not right now. You can have that one if you want." Flynn started the car and backed out. If necessary, he'd return to the trading post later and buy another flashlight for himself.

"That's not fair. I'll bet you love it, too. I can't take your flashlight."

"We'll work it out. The bottom line is that I'm not leaving you alone again. No telling what might happen next time."

"I thought I did a very good job handling Ray's proposition. I did wonder what was taking you so long, though. I thought you were never coming out."

"I got caught up in the whole Bigfoot marketing thing. You should have seen the camping supplies they have. I think if they got some publicity, it might start a craze down in LA."

"I'll bet you're right." Zoe continued to play with the flashlight. "So Luanne's brother works in the trading post, huh? I'm curious about him, now, after hearing Luanne describe him as Frankenstein. Is he a big guy?"

"Pretty big." Uneasiness settled in Flynn's gut as he revisited the fact that Jeff had told his family he was going on a date with his steady girlfriend and then hadn't done that. But he didn't want to share those thoughts with Zoe, because there was no real proof that Jeff had had anything to do with the bees.

So he decided to talk about something else. "Luanne was in the store, too," he said. "She had a copy of the latest *People*."

"So?"

"So she slapped it down on the counter and pointed to a picture of you and Trace. She said you and Zoe Tarleton could be twins."

Zoe leaned her head back against the seat with a sigh. "This is getting very tricky. I didn't think it would be. I thought you and I could come up to this tiny place no one had heard about and I could get some nerd coaching. But it hasn't been that simple, has it?"

"Not exactly."

When Zoe didn't say anything more for quite a while, Flynn began to worry that she was depressed about how the trip had turned out so far. "Everything will be fine," he said. "I bought some microwave meals that can be heated in a regular oven, and I got us some cheese to replace what we used for George. Once we're back at the cabin we'll start working on the script."

As she turned her head to look at him, the flashlight lay forgotten in her lap. "I've been trying to think how to tell you this, but I guess I'll just have to tell you. We have a problem." No doubt about it, she was definitely upset about something.

He grasped the first thing that came to him. "If it's the sexual attraction, we'll deal with that, too. After seeing a picture of you with Trace, I'm back on track myself. We—"

"That's not the problem. Well, maybe it's part of the problem. When Margo had the bees removed, she found out they'd apparently been placed there deliberately, probably sometime last night."

Flynn's gut clenched. "Deliberately? Why?"

"Your guess is as good as mine."

"How did they know it was deliberate?"

"There was a man-made hive under there, and they checked with the landlord, who said in no uncertain terms there hadn't been a hive there yesterday, or any time that he'd owned this cabin."

Flynn wrestled with the concept. The soft footsteps he'd heard early this morning echoed in his head. If only he'd roused himself enough to go out there, he would know who had planted the bees. "So did they collect any evidence? Footprints or anything?"

"I didn't think to ask Margo about that."

"Well, we should ask, damn it! If somebody's playing pranks on us, then we need to get all the particulars." But it was too late to gather evidence now, after other people had walked around the area. "I might have an idea who it was," he said, "although I hate to think they would do something like that."

"You think it's Kristen, too?"

Flynn nearly drove off the road. "*Kristen?* Why in hell would I think it was Kristen? Besides the fact it's completely ridiculous, she's hundreds of miles away!"

"Maybe not," Zoe said.

"I don't know what you're saying." Flynn pulled up outside the cabin and turned off the engine. "You're making no sense. Kristen would no more put bees under somebody's porch than she would dance naked on Sunset Boulevard. But even that doesn't matter, because she's at a convention in Chicago."

"At the Sheraton, right?"

"Right!"

"If you call there, you'll find she's not registered."

His eyes narrowed. "You called?"

"No, Margo did."

Flynn was ready to chew nails. "So that's why you were so interested in what hotel! You wanted to spy on her! That's a hell of a thing, suspecting someone you don't even know. And why should I believe what Margo said?"

Zoe shrugged. "So don't. Call the hotel yourself."

"I damned well will!" Flynn yanked his cell phone from his belt. But he didn't have the Sheraton's number there. For that, he had to pull out his PDA. He was so furious he nearly dropped it. Then he misdialed and got what sounded like an adult toy store.

Finally he managed to connect with the reception desk at the Sheraton. They told him Kristen Keebler was not registered with them. "But she has to be," he said. "You have a convention going on there, the New England Association of Legal Professionals. She's one of the presenters."

"Yes, we do have that convention this weekend," said the desk clerk. "But unfortunately I have no Kristen Keebler registered at the hotel."

Flynn thanked the clerk and hung up. "She changed hotels," he said. "That's the only explanation." *Or she's on her way here.*

"Maybe you're right," Zoe said. "Call her and see."

"I will." He speed-dialed her number, but all he got was her voice mail. Earlier he would have been happy about that, but now he wanted to talk to her. He wanted her to tell him that she'd changed hotels and hadn't thought it was important because they'd be communicating by cell phone.

He left a message for her to return his call and clipped his phone back on his belt. Then he stared out the window at the cabin and the porch where this morning bees had swarmed, bees that could have put Zoe in the hospital.

Kristen would never be involved in something like that, even if she had been a little upset about him spending the weekend with a movie star. She was a lawyer, someone who believed in coloring inside the lines. He'd never seen her lose her temper, let alone be capable of physical sabotage.

No, it hadn't been Kristen, and there was some explanation for the hotel situation. All he had to do was talk with her, and everything would be straightened out. He was certain of it. Almost certain anyway.

"If it helps any, I don't think it makes sense, either."

He glanced over at Zoe. "But somebody planted the hive of bees." He decided he'd better tell her about Jeff's mysterious behavior the night before.

When he'd finished, Zoe shook her head. "I can't see Jeff as the culprit, either. Why do that? What's the payoff? You'd have to go to a lot of trouble, and for what? I suppose he could be a mental case, but you didn't get that impression, did you?"

"No. He seems like a normal eighteen-year-old to me." He glanced at the porch again, then back at Zoe. "But if this weekend is getting too weird for you, we could head home."

"I've thought of that, but I really believe that you can help me get ready for the audition."

He felt honor-bound to give her alternatives. "We could work in LA."

"No, we couldn't. I can't make a move there without it becoming a big deal." She gazed at him. "If you're willing to stay, I'm willing to stay."

As he returned her gaze, he was forced to admit to himself that he didn't want the weekend to end just yet. Sure, part of that was the chance to catch a glimpse of Bigfoot. Most of it was about spending time with Zoe.

He cleared his throat. "I'll stay."

"Thanks." Gratitude shone in her eyes.

He accepted that gratitude with way too much pleasure. Maybe she only wanted him around to prep her for the audition, but he thought it might be more complicated than that. If they left now, he could pretty much guarantee nothing more would come of their attraction. But they weren't leaving.

Chapter Sixteen

Zoe wanted to believe that Kristen had simply changed hotels. God knows Zoe had changed hotels before, like when the media descended like gulls over a garbage dump. Kristen wouldn't have that reason, but she might have a perfectly good explanation.

She might have a picky, nerdlike reason. Zoe was willing to think that Kristen was picky because that eased her conscience about the sexual liberties she'd already taken with Kristen's main man, Flynn. Maybe the hotel shower massager didn't have enough settings. Maybe the Internet connection wasn't right for her laptop or the minibar had Keebler cookies, which gave her hives.

But speaking of hives, Kristen switching hotels didn't explain where the bees had come from. Zoe picked up the flashlight in her lap and twisted the feet a few times as she considered the matter and looked for answers.

"I can't figure this out," Flynn said.

"I can't either . . . unless . . . wait a minute. Luanne said there isn't anything to do in Long Shaft."

"You don't suspect Luanne, do you? I know she's a pain, but she wouldn't do something like that."

"I don't think so, either, but there must be other kids around here. Bored kids who had nothing to do last night, saw the lights on in the cabin, knew we were tourists, and decided to stir up the city folks." She was proud of her conclusion.

"I suppose they might have."

"Did I think that out like a nerd?"

He smiled at her. "You did. And you could be right, too." He opened the car door. "I would love to know the truth, but we may never find out."

"Maybe it was Bigfoot."

Flynn paused, his hand on the door. "I don't think there's ever been a recorded instance of Bigfoot playing that kind of prank, but maybe we need to consider that possibility. When you're asleep you lose your sense of smell."

"I was kidding!" The idea freaked her out. "You don't really think that's the explanation, do you?"

He glanced at her as if to say something more. Then he seemed to change his mind. "No, not really."

"You do so! I can see it on your face! You don't want to say because you can tell it's scaring the spit out of me, but you think it could be Bigfoot!"

"It's just that we don't know who or what did it, Zoe. I tend to look for all the possibilities when I'm trying to solve a problem." He brightened. "That's a nerd trait, by the way."

"Duly noted. But I'd like to eliminate that particular possibility from consideration. The idea that Bigfoot is creeping up to the cabin in the middle of the night, to deposit bees or . . . I don't know . . . *strangle us in our sleep* is not comforting to me. Go figure."

"Do you want to head home after all?"

"No, I want you to tell me that Bigfoot is not interested in sneaking around the cabin at night. I want you to say that he only runs through the woods howling and stinking up the place. Tell me that it was most likely bored kids playing a prank."

"Well, there's a ninety-nine percent chance that's the case."

Ninety-nine percent sounded pretty good to her. She would have preferred a hundred percent, but if she weighed going home because she was a weenie against a ninety-nine percent chance that Bigfoot wouldn't prowl around next to the cabin tonight, the odds were good enough to make her stick it out.

"I'll take ninety-nine percent." She opened her car door.

"Wait a minute. Let me scout the area before you go up there."

"To look for Bigfoot?" Maybe ninety-nine percent wasn't so great after all. "I thought he only roamed the woods at night."

"To make sure the bees are all gone."

"Oh!" She slumped back in her seat with relief. "Thanks. I'd appreciate that." She left her door open and sat in the car while she watched his long, lanky stride carry him up to the porch. Nice action on that man.

After all the buff bodies she'd known over the years, Flynn's more normal build was refreshing. She understood the demands of an acting career—she had to meet those demands herself. Unfortunately, it could lead to a touch of narcissism. Flynn was free of that, which made him extremely appealing.

She wondered what he had planned for that sleeping bag he'd bought. Although she hadn't dared say so at the time, sex had come to her mind the minute he'd walked out of the trading post with it under his arm. She hadn't known what it was other than a roll of soft furry stuff, but she could tell it was exactly the kind of surface made for naked bodies.

Without realizing it she began stroking the flashlight in a most erotic way. Oops. She needed to chill. Judging from the way Flynn had defended Kristen, he still cared about her. Therefore Zoe could forget about getting naked on Flynn's sleeping bag and concentrate on learning to be a nerd.

She had a perfect opportunity to observe him right now, and she was thinking about sex instead of doing her job. Unfortunately, observing Flynn seemed to lead to thoughts of sex. Maybe she should pretend he was really a transvestite. Nope. He looked too obviously male.

Exceedingly male. He climbed the steps with firm deliberation and paced the length of the porch. Twice. Then he came back down and walked around the perimeter. Whenever he came to an opening in the latticework surrounding the porch, he crouched and peered underneath. What a thorough guy. Thoroughness would be welcome in bed. *Stop that, Zoe!*

Finally he returned to the car. "As far as I can tell, the coast is clear. I didn't see a single bee. I found openings big enough to shove a small hive under there, but it looks like the pest people took off a section of lattice to get them back out and then nailed it in place again."

"How could you tell?" She wondered if he could read

her mind and see that she was mentally unbuttoning his shirt. She tried not to do that, but her mind had a mind of its own.

"Unpainted nail heads, shiny, with no rust."

"Interesting." She stepped out of the car. "You would have made a good detective."

"Thought about it. But I can't stand blood and I'm not crazy about dead bodies. Detectives seem to deal in those a lot." He moved around her to open the back door and haul out the groceries. "Besides, detectives are cool."

She would have thought he was putting himself down, except when she looked over at him, he was smiling. Such a sexy smile, too. "I do believe you're starting to get a kick out of this whole cool-guy-versus-nerd thing," she said.

"Maybe." He shifted the bag of groceries to his left arm and reached for the sleeping bag.

"Let me carry that in."

"I can get it." He scooped it up and tucked it under his arm.

"I know." She closed both car doors. "But I want to."

"First you covet my flashlight, and now you're after my sleeping bag. What next?"

She met his gaze, the answer on the tip of her tongue. But she didn't dare say it, not even as a joke.

His eyes darkened. Maybe he could read minds, after all. "You can carry the sleeping bag in. In fact, you can have it along with the flashlight."

"I'm not going to steal your flashlight or your sleeping bag." But she wouldn't mind stealing a night of sweaty sex. Only her conscience stood in her way. Unfortunately, her conscience looked like Rambo.

She took the sleeping bag from him. "I just wanted to

look it over to see if I want one myself." And she definitely did. It was even softer than she'd imagined. She rubbed her cheek against the black fur.

"Um, maybe we should leave it in the car after all."

She glanced up and discovered his gaze had turned from dark and potent to hot and superpotent. The obvious lust lurking there told her that he'd figured out how they could use the sleeping bag. It wouldn't involve sleeping.

Either she could pretend she didn't get his meaning or she could do the prudent thing and return the sleeping bag to the backseat. Her Rambo conscience made the decision for her. "You're right. There's no reason to take it in. It's not as if we need it for anything."

"We shouldn't need it."

Now there was a true statement. They really shouldn't need it. Or each other. They did, but they shouldn't.

"I'll put it back then," she said. "Once you get to the airport tomorrow night you can figure out how to ship it home." She didn't like the thought of leaving. Funny how fast she'd become used to having Flynn around.

"Good idea."

Pine needles crunching under her feet made the only sound as she walked to the car. Midday in the forest was quiet. Even the birds seemed to be taking a break. Opening the door, she dropped the sleeping bag on the seat, and closed the door again. There. One more temptation out of the way.

"I'm keeping the flashlight, though." She headed back in his direction. *Let's play hide the flashlight.* She gave herself a mental head slap. She had to derail this train of thought, because there was no relief in sight.

"Yeah, we need the flashlight." His eyes had returned to their normal deep gray color, as if he'd managed to recover his self-control. "That butane lighter wasn't cutting it."

"And if the electricity happened to go out, we'd be SOL." They'd have to feel their way around. Hey, not a bad idea! *Zoe, you're hopeless.*

"I'm surprised the landlord didn't give us a flashlight, now that you mention it."

Zoe glanced around at the peeling paint and the dilapidated rockers on the porch. "The landlord doesn't strike me as a concerned individual."

"Good point. Which means the bees could have been under there long before we arrived, even though he swears they weren't."

Zoe fished in her purse and found the front door key. "Yes, but isn't that a strange place to put a hive? I thought the idea was to harvest honey. That has to be a delicate operation to start with, let alone crawling under a porch to do it." She opened the door and walked inside.

"You're right." Flynn followed her in. "I'm just trying to find some logical explanation for all of this." He sniffed. "Does it smell funny in here?"

"A little." Zoe set down her purse and tossed her orange hat on the sofa. "Maybe the pest people sprayed something under the porch to keep the bees from coming back."

"Maybe." Flynn carried the groceries into the kitchen. "Except it's stronger in here, which doesn't make sense."

"Let's open a window." Zoe walked over to the dining nook and opened the window looking out on the forest. "It really is pretty here."

"Yeah."

Something in his voice made her turn, and the heat was back in his eyes. Poor guy, he was in serious lust with her. She wondered if he also had a bully for a conscience.

In case he did, she'd pretend not to notice his scorching glance. Food might help. She clapped her hands together like a Girl Scout leader at a cookout. "Let's warm up a couple of those microwave meals, shall we? I'm starving!"

He snapped out of his daze. "Okay," he said without much enthusiasm.

"You read the directions, since you're the directions guy, and I'll turn on this very old and decrepit stove." She walked over to it and noticed the dial was set on WARM. "That's funny. I wonder if it's on already?"

"Why would it be on already?" Flynn was engrossed in reading the directions on the chicken dinner and didn't look up.

"I don't know. Maybe I did it by accident last night." She turned the dial to OFF and opened the oven door. The hinges creaked, and although spatters from other meals speckled the oven, it was cold. "Okay, Margo warned me about this. Be right back." She went in search of the butane lighter.

Flynn glanced at her when she came back in. "Why do you have that?"

"The pilot light's gone out in the oven, so I need to—"

"No!" He dropped the chicken dinner on the floor and grabbed the lighter out of her hand.

"What's wrong?" She frowned at him in confusion.

"The smell! It's gas! A whole bunch of gas!"

She backed away from the oven so fast she bumped

into Flynn. "Omigod. You're right. What an idiot I am. I didn't even think."

"Let's get out of here." Clutching her hand, he headed out of the kitchen, stepping smack on the chicken dinner, which cracked open and spit peas and carrots all over the kitchen. "Shit."

"It doesn't matter." She pulled him away from the mess. "We need fresh air. We'll clean it up later."

"You're right." He took the lead again, tugging on her hand as he hurried through the living room. "Gas. I should have figured it out sooner."

"Me, too! But I was so fixated on the bees, and I know pest companies spray all kinds of junk around. I wasn't thinking of the gas."

Flynn threw open the door. "We'll leave it open. Between that and the back window, it'll clear out eventually." He drew her across the porch and down the steps, not stopping until they were yards away, standing among the pine trees. They were both breathing fast.

"I can't believe I almost blew us up." The blood throbbed in her temples. "Maybe I'm not cut out for country living."

Gulping for air, Flynn stared at the cabin. "Okay, let's reconstruct what happened."

"I said I'd turn on the oven while you read the directions on the chicken dinner. Which is now mushed on the floor." Zoe noticed that he hadn't let go of her hand, but she decided not to mention it. Under the circumstances, she liked his strong grip. It reminded her that she was in one piece and not burned to a crisp by an exploding oven.

"Yeah, sorry about that." He turned to her. "I'll eat the crushed one."

"No, you won't." The palm of her hand grew warm and tingly where his thumb stroked it. She shoved her conscience out of the way. She deserved to be comforted at a moment when she'd almost been blown to smithereens.

"I feel responsible. I should have identified that smell."

"Why was it your job? Are you some kind of expert on gas ovens?" Those lazy circles he was making with his thumb were getting to her. In a really good way.

"No. I've never been around a gas stove."

"Then why should you have guessed what the smell was?"

He shrugged. "Because the evidence was there. I knew we had a gas stove from cooking on it last night. We walked in and there was a funny smell in the house. I should have thought of gas as a possibility."

Zoe sighed, more from pleasure than exasperation. "Just because you're a nerd doesn't mean you have to be Mr. Answer Man all the time."

But he sure was Mr. Feel Good, even if he was only dealing with her palm at the moment. She remembered how he'd dealt with the rest of her in a previous episode and she began to heat up all over. She could probably defrost one of those frozen dinners between her thighs, no problem.

"I like having the answers." He swallowed. "You, um, said the oven was turned on."

"Yes. Very turned on." She was ready to purr from the gentle stroking. A person's hand was more sensitive than she'd realized.

"I'm . . . talking about the oven."

"I know." She struggled to breathe.

"We . . . we should . . . get to the bottom of this."

"Yes." She couldn't even remember what they were talking about.

With a groan he pulled her in tight. "I don't know what it is about you and the smell of pine trees." Then he kissed the living daylights out of her.

She'd always wondered what that expression meant, and now, thanks to Flynn, she knew. As he kissed her, the living daylights shot out of her like sparks from a blowtorch. He kissed her until her conscience collapsed into a heap on the forest floor.

Frug-a-dug! No explosion! And here they are, Tweedledee and Tweedledum, untouched. But they sure are touching each other, dammit. They're shameless, like dogs in heat. Flynn has the self-control of a rabbit—can't keep his hands to himself for five minutes.

You can bet his tongue is massaging her tonsils like crazy. He wants to run that tongue all over the rest of her, too. You can take that to the bank. He's dreaming of giving Zoe Tarleton some massage therapy where it counts. She wants some of that stuff, too. Look at how she moves her hips! Hussy.

They wouldn't chance it out in the open in the middle of the day, would they? Sure looks like that's what he has in mind, though. And she's stuck to him like a magnet to a refrigerator door. They're plastered together so tight I can't tell if his salami is ready for the oven, but I'll assume it is, from the heavy breathing going on. Now he's got both hands on her butt. What cojones, *doing that where anybody can see.*

I can't believe they're out here sucking face and rubbing bodies like nothing happened. It wasn't supposed to turn out that way. Where was the damned explosion?

• • •

Winding both arms around Flynn's neck, Zoe moved in closer so she could feel that big old flashlight of his. She knew exactly where she wanted to hide it, too. Judging from the restless motion of his hips, he had similar ideas.

He lifted his mouth from hers. "I want you." He was panting. "I want you every which way there is to want a woman."

"Same here. Switching genders." She went back to the glorious business of kissing him.

He pulled away again, his breath hot against her face. "But we're in the middle of the forest. And the house is full of gas."

"There's a backseat nearby."

"And the sleeping bag . . ." He kissed her throat and nipped at her earlobe.

"Yes, the soft . . . furry . . . sleeping bag."

"I want you naked on that fur. I want to—damn it."

"Damn what?"

"No condoms."

She knew he could go get them, even with the gas in the house, but once he left, her conscience would spring to life faster than Flynn's erection. Doggone it.

She couldn't leave him in this condition a second time, though. That was criminal. "Let's improvise," she said. "Last night's offer is still open. I'll be glad to—" She stopped when she realized he was no longer gazing into her eyes in eager anticipation. Instead he was staring at a point beyond her left shoulder.

She tensed as all the possibilities ran through her mind—bees, Bigfoot, Kristen with a butcher knife. "What . . . what is it?"

"A living, breathing chastity belt."

Zoe turned to find Luanne leaning against the rental car's fender, her arms crossed and a huge grin on her face. She pushed away from the car and flipped her braid over her shoulder. "It's taken me a while, Vera, but I've finally figured out who you are."

Chapter Seventeen

As Flynn studied precocious, pain-in-the-butt Luanne, he wondered how much money it would take to bribe an eleven-year-old to keep her mouth shut for twenty-four hours. Maybe Zoe could promise to get her an audition or offer a trip to Hollywood for a makeover or a VIP pass to the Golden Globes or dinner with Justin Timberlake. Whatever it took.

Zoe untangled herself from Flynn and turned in place, shielding him with her body. Man, did he appreciate that. The woman had class, not to mention the hottest mouth he'd ever had the privilege to stick his tongue into. Ergo, he had a little problem that he didn't want Luanne to notice.

"Who do you think I am?" Zoe asked, cool as could be.

And that, Flynn concluded, was why Zoe Tarleton was on top. She had poise and presence. And speaking of Zoe on top, he wouldn't mind seeing how that worked out, horizontally speaking. He knew it would only be a fling. As of now he was okay with that.

But he and Zoe needed to have a heart-to-heart about their significant others. Kristen was fading fast in his mind, but he didn't know how Zoe viewed Trace at this moment. Taking her recent reaction into consideration, she might be ready to forget about Trace.

Earlier in the weekend, Flynn had been concerned about poaching on Trace's territory. He was no longer quite so concerned. A couple of kisses from Zoe could alter a person's viewpoint. Also his physical reactions. Fortunately, Flynn's most obvious physical reaction had begun to subside.

"I've thought and thought about it," Luanne said. "Your hair is *exactly* like Zoe Tarleton's hair, and your body looks like her body, too, except it's hard to tell for sure with the clothes you wear."

"But you do realize I'm not Zoe, right?"

Flynn thought Zoe was whistling in the wind. She'd been made, and that was that. Time to see what kind of price Luanne put on that info.

Luanne seemed to be enjoying the drama of the moment. She gave every indication of drawing it out as long as possible. "Well, as I walked back from town I was convinced you were her. Every once in a while I'd stop and look at the picture in *People*." She gestured toward the hood of the car, where the magazine lay, its pages flipping in the breeze.

"You can't go by that picture," Flynn said. "It was what, two inches square?"

"I went home and got a magnifying glass. And you—" She pointed a finger at Zoe. "Look exactly like the person in that picture. Don't deny it."

"I never did deny it," Zoe said.

"So you could be her, except then I get here and see

you two playing tonsil hockey. And I say to myself, 'Why would any woman in her right mind dump Trace Edwards for Bill Gates?' "

Flynn happened to think he was better looking than Bill Gates, though admittedly not as rich. In any case, he got the point. Trace Edwards was a catch and a half. He was maybe half a catch, on a good day.

"But Trace isn't my boyfriend," Zoe said.

How Flynn wished that were true.

"I can see that." Luanne waggled her eyebrows. "I can *so* see that. And here's my conclusion." She paused, keen anticipation shining in her eyes. "You're Zoe Tarleton's double!"

Flynn gulped. They might be able to work with that. Zoe didn't have a double, but so what? Vera Parsons could be her double for the weekend. He hoped Zoe agreed with him and went along with Luanne on this.

"You're very smart," Zoe said.

The tension seeped out of Flynn's shoulders. It would be okay.

"Did I guess it?" Luanne quivered with eagerness. "Are you really?"

"I do camera work for her."

"Yes, and she's good at it, too," Flynn said. He followed Zoe's lead of telling the truth without giving anything away.

"I get it, I get it! And you're between pictures, so you're taking a vacation with your boyfriend Tony!" Luanne gave a little hop of joy. "Omigod. You have to tell me all about Zoe. What's her favorite food? What's her favorite color? I'll bet it's red, 'cause she wears a lot of red. Does she have any pets? Who's her favorite singer? Or maybe she likes a group better. What's—"

"Actually, this is a working vacation," Flynn said,

"Vera's studying a new script, and we should be getting back to it, right, Vera?"

"Yes, we should."

"That's okay!" Luanne's enthusiasm remained at full power. "Tell me when you'll be taking a break, and I can come back then!"

"Well, we have quite a bit to accomplish," Flynn said. "I'm not sure when we might have time for a break."

"In two hours," Zoe said. "Come back in two hours and I'll give you all kinds of juicy information about Zoe Tarleton. But only on one condition."

"Anything. I'll do anything."

"You can't say a single word to anyone about this. Nobody's guessed it except you."

"I won't say anything. I promise!" Luanne danced a little jig in the pine needles. "This is so cool. So totally cool."

"I mean it, Luanne. I can't have the whole town bugging me for details about Zoe."

"I know." Luanne's eyes shone. "Two hours. I'll be back in two hours." Then she raced away through the woods, her braid flying out behind her.

"Why did you tell her to come back in two hours?" Flynn realized he was whining, but he couldn't help it. He didn't know what was ahead for him and Zoe, but Luanne certainly didn't figure into any of his potential plans.

Zoe turned to him. "First of all, because I feel sorry for her. I used to be that age and starstruck. And second of all, because we need to buy her silence. I thought if we offered her something, she'd promise to be quiet."

"And do you think she'll keep that promise?"

"Oh yeah." Zoe smiled. "At least for now. She wants Zoe Tarleton's double all to herself."

Flynn sighed. So did he.

• • •

Zoe didn't tell Flynn the third reason she'd told Luanne to come back in two hours. Luanne's impending arrival would keep them from getting completely carried away. From her reaction to him so far, Zoe worried that Flynn had the power to release every last one of her inhibitions.

While that sounded exciting, it wouldn't allow her to think, and she needed to think . . . a lot. Given uninterrupted time alone with Flynn, she might forget everything—Kristen, Trace, the script. That wouldn't be doing her or Flynn any favors. Except the obvious.

"Let's go find out if the gas is gone." She started toward the cabin.

"Then what?"

She knew what he was asking. He wanted to know if they'd pick up where they left off, only in the vicinity of condoms. "We need to make some kind of lunch," she said.

"Cheese and crackers. Oh, and I bought some lemonade."

"I can live with that. We could work on the script while we're eating."

"All right. Sounds good."

As they climbed the steps together, she glanced at him with suspicion. He'd agreed to the script reading much too easily. Something was going on in that supersized brain. "You're fine with reading the script?"

"Sure. Let's do it."

"Okay. And Flynn, about what happened out there in the woods . . ."

"I know. You invited Luanne to come back to put the brakes on what's going on between us."

She should have known he'd be two steps ahead of her.

"Yes, I did, because we . . . we seem to lose all perspective."

"You're right about that." Inside the living room, he caught her arm, but once he had her attention, he released her. "Zoe, if you want to keep the lid on, you have to stop offering to give me a blow job."

Instantly that was what she wanted to do. Now.

He held her gaze. "So, are we agreed on that?"

She fought to remember her earlier plan to concentrate on the work she'd come up here to do. "Um, yes. Agreed. No more offers of a blow job."

"Because I have to tell you, that weighs on a guy's mind. I'm trying like hell not to poach on Trace's territory, but—"

"Trace is nothing to me." Whoops. That had sort of slipped out unannounced.

His eyebrows lifted. "Nothing to you? What do you mean?"

"He's not actually my boyfriend."

"I don't get it. According to everything I read, you two are—"

"That's the whole idea. He's my boyfriend so far as the media is concerned, because it's good publicity. He's big box office; I'm big box office. The fans would love to think we're together." She paused. "And to be totally honest, I think Trace is getting into it."

"But you're not."

"No. We have nothing in common except the business."

Flynn looked at her with those warm gray eyes. "I wish you hadn't told me that."

"I wish I hadn't, either. Because now I'm the bad guy here, because I've been poaching on Kristen's territory."

"It's not like I've put up a whole lot of resistance."

"Of course not!" She spread her arms wide. "I'm Zoe

Tarleton, sex goddess! It's not a fair fight, not when we're secluded in this tiny cabin."

He shook his head. "You're not giving me a whole lot of credit. I like to think I have the power to say no, even to Zoe Tarleton."

"Then why haven't you?"

"I did, last night, when I desperately wanted to walk down the hall and climb into your bed. You notice I didn't."

"Believe me, I noticed."

He sighed and rubbed the back of his neck. Then he glanced at her with a lazy smile that made him look way too hot. "But I have to say, when you made a second offer today . . ."

"Okay! I won't say that ever again. The blow job offers have all expired, effective this minute."

"You need to know I'm rethinking my commitment to Kristen."

She flashed back to high school and how her presence had gone a long way to crush Margo's dreams. "Don't re-think it. She's not here to defend herself. Once you're to-gether again, you'll wonder why you ever doubted that commitment."

He gazed at her. "Let's get something to eat. I think the gas is gone."

She recognized that the discussion was over for the time being. "I think so, too, but I'm not eager to test it with the butane torch."

"Me, either. Let's stick with cheese and crackers and lemonade." He walked to the door of the kitchen, where the microwave dinner lay squashed in the middle of the floor, its veggies radiating out in a sunburst pattern. "I'll get the broom."

"And I'll slice some cheese." They'd reached détente.

• • •

At Flynn's suggestion they took their crackers, cheese, and lemonade out to the porch. He thought that might be a wiser venue than the sofa in the living room, now that he knew Trace wasn't part of the equation. That left him to make the decision about what would or wouldn't happen between them.

That was a lot of responsibility. When he'd imagined they were both being equally bad, that was one thing. But Zoe wasn't being bad at all. She was free to do anything she wanted this weekend.

He wasn't, unless he wanted to call Kristen and break up with her over the phone. Talk about insensitive. She believed they were moving toward marriage. He'd believed it, too, until last night.

Now he couldn't think of much else besides having sex with Zoe, which didn't fit very well with proposing to Kristen next weekend. Still, having sex with Zoe was completely illogical. She wouldn't ever consider *marrying* him, for God's sake. So was he prepared to throw away a viable marriage partner so he could have a night of sex with Zoe?

Then there was the lawyer–client relationship to consider. He was pretty sure having sex with your client violated a bunch of ethical codes, and he'd never crossed an ethical line in his career. Being a straight arrow suited him down to the ground.

Once they had sex, they'd never be able to regain their former business relationship. Maybe she'd be able to forget it ever happened, but he wouldn't forget for the rest of his life. If she wanted to remain his client, which she might not, the sex would be the elephant in the living room every time they met.

"Let's do this scene." Zoe put her lemonade on the rickety table between them and handed the script to Flynn. "It seems like a pivotal one, so it could well be the one they have me read next week. Besides, we'll both relate to the setting."

Flynn took the script while careful not to make any sudden movements as he sat in the ancient rocker. He expected it to collapse any minute under his weight. That would fit the general pattern of disasters they'd encountered so far.

He glanced at the scene Zoe had found. "Why are they in a cabin?"

"Tony convinced her they needed to hide out for a few days until the cops can get some leads on who's after her."

Glancing quickly over the dialogue, Flynn could tell the scene was a cozy one. Familiar, too.

"While they're hiding out in the cabin, a policewoman is impersonating Vera and working late in the lab to see if she can trick the kidnappers into showing their hand. But Vera has her computer containing all her notes with her at the cabin, so the formula's not in jeopardy."

"Unless the impersonation doesn't work and they track her to the cabin."

"Right." Zoe leaned over so she could see the script, too. She wore the wire-rimmed glasses and had her hair tucked under the floppy orange hat again. She would have looked fairly dorky except that at some point she'd unbuttoned the top two buttons of her blouse. It gaped open, revealing the scalloped top of her bra. There was nothing dorky about Zoe's cleavage.

He supposed she was wearing what she'd called a nerd bra, plain cotton with the hooks in the back. That didn't matter to him. He was still extremely interested. "Maybe you should fasten the top two buttons of your blouse."

She glanced down. "Thanks for the suggestion. That suits Vera's character more. I must have unfastened them out of habit." She buttoned up.

So she unbuttoned her blouse out of habit. Whew. Watching her button it again made his mouth water. It didn't take much imagination to reverse the process. He could see those slender fingers undoing what they'd just fastened before moving on down the line to give him an unobstructed view of the nerd bra and all the beauty it contained.

"Any other pointers?" she asked.

"You don't have to do it right now, but you should probably file down your fingernails. And take off the polish."

She studied her red nails. "Not even a French manicure?"

"I don't see Vera taking the time and trouble. Short nails, no polish."

"What does Kristen do with her nails?"

He wondered if she'd introduced Kristen into the conversation on purpose, so he wouldn't forget about her. "She gets a French manicure, but she's a lawyer and appears in public a lot. Vera's a scientist who spends all her time in a chemistry lab." He paused to look over at Zoe. "Besides, I never said Kristen was a nerd."

"So she's not?"

Picturing bookish, quiet Kristen, he realized she fit the profile. "I guess she is."

"That's what I thought. You two are probably perfect for each other."

He'd thought so twenty-four hours ago. Now he was afraid they'd bore each other silly. But he felt disloyal saying that. "I guess we are."

"There you go, Flynn." She smiled. "You have the first line."

"Yeah." Looking away from that smile wasn't easy, but he finally forced his attention back to the script. If he kept his focus on the dialogue, he might make it through without an incident, although she did have that spicy scent going on. "You might want to skip the perfume, too."

"You think?"

"She's not trying to attract a man. She's trying to perfect this formula."

"Okay, no perfume."

Flynn wondered if eliminating the manicure and the perfume would make Zoe less sexy to him. Probably not. As she leaned close, her arm brushing his, even her body heat called to him. He couldn't very well ask her to turn that down. So he concentrated on reading his lines.

TONY

I wish I could figure out what it is about you.

Vera looks up from her computer.

VERA

What do you mean?

TONY

You're the least seductive woman I've ever met. So why is it I want to jump your skinny bones?

TONY

VERA

I can think of two reasons.

TONY

Then by all means, enlighten me, because this urge is a real pain in the ass.

VERA

Reason number one: I'm different from other women you've taken to bed. I'm a mystery. You wonder how sex would be with a flat-chested nerd like me.

Flynn paused. "This 'flat-chested' description keeps coming up. How are you going to manage that?"

"Wrap my boobs in an Ace bandage. I brought one. Do you think I should do that? Would it make the read-through more authentic?"

"Uh, no. That's okay. I just wondered." He didn't want to think about her going into her bedroom and taking off her blouse and bra. For the good of the cause, she needed to keep all clothes on and all buttons fastened.

"Ready to continue, then?"

"Sure."

"Your line."

Yes, it was, and he could feel the tension mounting in the scene. And on the porch.

TONY

Yeah! You're an effing mystery. If I passed you on the street I wouldn't look twice, but I have to hang around, so I get curious. Like about your brains.

VERA

My brains? I thought we were talking about sex.

TONY

We are. I wanna know how your brains might figure
into the same ol', same ol'.

"I think about that, too," Zoe said in a soft voice.

Flynn's body tightened. He kept his gaze mostly on the
script. From the corner of his eye he could see she was
doing the same, as if she knew that if they looked at each
other, it would be all over.

"Well, don't think about it," he said. "Brains are not a
factor."

"I don't believe you."

"Sex isn't a thinking activity." Which was why he was in
so much trouble. His penis took over the controls, and all
his noble resolutions disappeared in a flood of testosterone.

"Flynn, I don't want to mess up your situation with
Kristen."

Too late. "I know you don't. I appreciate that." He was
glad the script covered his lap so she wouldn't see the obvious activity going on there.

"But I keep thinking about having sex with you. I don't
know what to do about that."

He knew exactly what to do about it, but they'd have to
hurry. Luanne was due to show up in less than an hour.

Chapter Eighteen

Zoe had never wanted anyone this much before, but reading the script explained a lot. Flynn was a mystery to her, a fascinating mystery. Despite what he'd said, she believed that a really smart guy would make love more creatively than a guy with average intelligence, but she didn't have enough sexual experience to know for sure. Part of the turn-on might be the unknown.

Flynn cleared his throat. "Maybe if we just did it, took all the guesswork out of it, we'd be better off." He gazed off into the trees, as if they were contemplating a deep philosophical question instead of whether they'd do the wild thing in a few minutes.

Zoe glanced off in the opposite direction, although she wasn't seeing the beauty of the forest; she was imagining Flynn naked . . . on the Bigfoot sleeping bag. She wanted to agree with him. She *so* wanted to agree with him.

But she couldn't. "If you're thinking we'd get it out of our system, I'm not so sure about that. Sometimes it works, if people are totally incompatible. They have bad sex and that's the end of that. It's over."

"We could have bad sex," he said hopefully.

"You didn't seem to think so the last time we discussed this."

"Well, it's possible. I don't think bad sex is entirely out of the question. Then we could laugh about it and go on with our lives. Most people have bad sex to start with, right?"

"I guess." She was no expert. The wind through the tops of the pines sounded like a lover's sigh. Zoe wouldn't mind having a reason to sigh like that. "But what if it's not so bad? What if it leans toward the good side? What then?"

"I'd rather go on the assumption that it will be bad."

"Hey, Flynn, now you're starting to sound like me. I'm the one who wants to go on limited information. You're supposed to be the guy who wants all available input." And speaking of input . . . oh yeah, she could imagine how great a certain type of input would be right now.

"Here's what I'm thinking. Luanne will be here in about forty-five minutes. That's a decent amount of time to have a round of bad sex."

Her eyes opened wide. *Forty-five minutes?* Slowly she turned to look at him. He'd just elevated himself to a whole new level of respect. From her limited experience, forty-five minutes was a long time. "Um, Flynn?"

"Yeah?" He glanced sideways at her.

"Is that an average time for you?"

"Oh, it's less time than I'd like, but—"

"Oh." She might combust on the spot.

"Not long enough?"

"I'm sure it's . . . long enough." She grew wet in all the right places.

His gaze scorched a path to hers. "Then maybe we should go inside."

This was it. She hung suspended between what was right and what was more tempting than she could stand.

His cell phone rang.

Zoe should have expected it. Her weekend had been going like this. She knew who was on the other end—the person who had enjoyed forty-five minutes in heaven with Flynn Granger. Kristen had impeccable timing.

Flynn grimaced. "Probably Kristen."

"You need to pick up. Otherwise she'll wonder why you didn't. She'll get suspicious."

"Right." Flynn unclipped his phone from his belt and answered it.

Zoe decided not to stay there and listen in on the conversation, which would probably end any chance of forty-five minutes with Flynn anyway. He wasn't the kind of guy who could talk to his girlfriend one minute and jump into the sack with another woman the next.

Therefore, she needed to shift down, stop revving her engine, and gently lower her rpms. Be a good girl after all. She stood and walked into the cabin, leaving the front door open. Fortunately, the gas smell was gone.

Maybe she'd brushed against the oven knob and accidentally turned on the gas last night. But that didn't make much sense. If the gas had been on all night, they would have smelled it this morning.

She walked into the kitchen, drawn to the stove that could have disfigured her if the gas had exploded. She hadn't been near the stove since cooking that assault on the digestive system they'd called dinner. The more she thought about it, the more she was convinced she hadn't accidentally turned that oven knob.

Flynn might have, though. He might have bumped it. But what if he hadn't? That meant that someone had come into the cabin and turned it on while she and Flynn were in town eating breakfast.

The bees could have been a prank, something that wouldn't have been dangerous except for her tendency to swell up like a balloon in the Macy's Thanksgiving Day Parade. But leaving gas on when someone might strike a match was heavy-duty stuff. Someone with more than pranks in mind might be after her.

She blew out a breath. Or not. Margo had been a drama queen in high school and would probably love to believe in some kind of plot against Zoe. The poor woman had nothing going on in her life other than Bigfoot sightings.

Flynn's footsteps sounded on the pine boards of the living room. "Zoe?"

"In here, trying to figure out why the gas ended up being turned on." *And making sure I'm turned all the way off.*

He appeared in the kitchen doorway, his expression worried. "I don't know why it was on, either. I admit it's suspicious." He blew out a breath and shook his head. "Damn, all of this is crazy. The bees, the gas, Kristen. . . ."

"What did she say?"

"She asked me whether I was attracted to you."

Guilt settled in Zoe's stomach. "What did you say?"

"I couldn't lie to her."

"Why the hell not? Okay, scratch that. I understand. So what did she say after you confessed to a teensy bit of lust?" She peered at him. "You did minimize the lust factor, right?"

"Sort of."

"Oh, Flynn. Tell me you didn't describe the moment on top of the Sasquatch footprint."

"No. I wouldn't do that. But she . . . seemed to get the picture."

Zoe took a deep breath. "And?"

"She reminded me that you were a movie star, and that I shouldn't do anything foolish. She's afraid I'll get hurt."

Hell and damnation. Zoe felt lower than whale poop. Had she considered whether Flynn would get hurt? No, she had not. She'd only been worried about the Kristen situation.

Well, she would mend her ways. "Then I'm glad she called, because she's right. Having sex would have been dumb."

"Maybe." But his gaze hadn't cooled all that much.

"No maybes about it. You have a good thing going with a woman who cares about your welfare. Sadly, it looks as if I was fixated on your body."

He smiled. "Nice to hear."

"The point is, I don't want you to get hurt, either, but I didn't exactly make that a top priority."

"Possibly because you give me credit for being able to take care of myself," he said quietly. "Kristen doesn't."

"Can you blame her? She's frantic with worry that I'll come between you two, so she uses the first thing she can think of to stop that from happening. She warns you that I'm a movie star and movie stars break hearts."

Flynn regarded her steadily. "Do they?"

"All the time! Don't you read the tabloids?"

"You can't break someone's heart unless he hands it over."

"What were you, the captain of the high school debate team?"

"Yep." He glanced at his watch. "But it's a moot point whether we have sex or not, because Luanne will be here soon. We might as well work on the script until she gets here."

"All right, but I want you to know that even if we weren't expecting Luanne to show up, we wouldn't be having sex."

The light in his eyes grew brighter and his chin came up. "Is that right?"

Uh-oh. She might have just challenged his masculine ego. "Flynn, be sensible. It's a bad idea. You're on track for the kind of life you want. Having sex with me would only confuse the issue."

"Only if I allow it to."

"You think you have that kind of mental discipline?"

"You think you have that kind of sexual power?"

Well, the movie magazines implied she did. She'd never really believed it, though.

He laughed. "You do think that, and for good reason. You have thousands of men at your feet worshipping you as a goddess." He gazed at her. "I might be a fool, but I think I can handle that."

She blinked in surprise. Could he deal with her stardom? If so, that made him a man among men. She'd watched the dynamics of other Hollywood couples. Usually the less-famous one was either intimidated or jealous.

Trace was definitely in the jealous camp, which was one of the reasons she wasn't attracted to him. If Flynn could handle her public image and not be bothered, then he might be. . . . uh-oh . . . *the one*.

Oh my. That changed the game considerably. But she didn't have any idea if it was true. She didn't know what

he could and couldn't handle because they weren't involved with each other yet. Talk was cheap. And yet she
didn't think Flynn made idle comments.

"Let's look at the script." Flynn turned and started
back through the living room. "We'll deal with this after
Luanne leaves."

Zoe gulped. She'd thought all she'd have to do was be
strong and Flynn would back down and agree with her.
But the captain of the debate team sounded as if he already had his next move all planned out.

Flynn was still thinking about Kristen's phone call as he
returned to the porch and settled carefully onto a rocking
chair. Something was going on with her, and he wasn't
sure what. He'd asked if she'd switched hotels, and she'd
admitted to checking out of the Sheraton, but then she'd
changed the subject without telling him why she'd done
that or where she was staying now.

Besides acting territorial, she was also being evasive.
Margo's suspicions were unfounded, and yet he'd feel
better if he knew for sure that Kristen was in a hotel
somewhere in Chicago or that she'd gone back to Massachusetts. He'd never given her a reason to be jealous before, so he had no idea how she might react in this
situation.

She wouldn't plot sabotage, but he couldn't swear she
wouldn't suddenly appear in Long Shaft to confront him
if she thought something might be happening. What a
mess. He only had one option for coming out of this the
good guy. He had to keep his hands off Zoe. And he
didn't want to.

As Zoe sat down, he picked up the script. This damned

script wasn't helping. As near as he could tell, Tony and Vera were about to do the deed.

Zoe leaned over to read her next line. *"I'm sure I would be a disappointment to you, Tony."*

"Too sexy," Flynn said.

Zoe glanced up. "What do you mean?"

He nearly got lost admiring the beauty of her blue eyes. The wire-framed glasses drew his attention to them even more.

He cleared his throat and forced himself to focus. "You said the line as if you didn't expect to be a disappointment at all. Your voice was sort of low and throaty, like a come-on. Vera would say it crisply, matter-of-factly. She doesn't play games."

Zoe nodded, which made her glasses slip. She pushed them back in place. "Good. Thanks. Let me try it again." She sat up straighter and narrowed her lips into a prim line. *"I'm sure I would be a disappointment to you, Tony."* She broke into a grin. "How's that?"

"Better." There would be no disappointments with Zoe. He couldn't explain how he knew that, but he did. He gave his attention back to the script.

TONY

You're probably right. It's a crazy idea anyway, you and me. We'd drive each other nuts.

VERA

We'd last about five minutes.

TONY

Speak for yourself, doll-face. I can last a lot longer than that.

Zoe giggled.

"What?" Flynn glanced up.

"Just thinking how appropriate the line was, considering our last discussion, and how lame you made it sound. Say it with more authority."

What the hell. He'd give the line swagger. He looked into those incredible blue eyes. *"Speak for yourself, dollface. I can last a lot longer than that."*

"Whew." Zoe fanned herself. "That was good. Vera would be toast."

"No, she wouldn't." The urge to lean closer and kiss her was almost more than he could stand. "Vera wouldn't crack. Not yet."

Her expression grew dreamy. "Right. Because she thinks he wants to seduce her so he can steal the formula himself."

"Uh-huh." Maybe just one little kiss wouldn't hurt. Their glasses would get in the way, so that would keep them from getting into full lip-lock mode. But he wanted a little taste.

Zoe's voice softened. "But she finally does crack."

"Yeah." He couldn't stop looking at her mouth. Her lips were the perfect shape for kissing, and right now they were parted about a sixteenth of an inch, which was so damned sexy he forgot to breathe.

"Because she can't help herself."

"That happens." He drifted closer.

"Tell me about it."

A horn tooted in the driveway and they backed away from each other so fast they almost tipped both rocking chairs. Flynn looked up and was not pleased to see Margo's neon car sitting next to the rental sedan. Margo herself climbed out a second later.

"Hi there!" She pranced up to the porch in the UGG boots that seemed to be her favorite footwear. "I got some interesting news and I had a break at the diner, so I thought I'd come out and deliver it in person."

Flynn's jaw clenched. This was the person who'd planted the idea that Kristen was stalking them. He stood, because he'd been taught to be polite, but he didn't feel polite.

"What's up?" Zoe stood, too.

At the bottom of the porch steps Margo paused and glanced at Flynn. "Did you tell him that Kristen wasn't registered at the Sheraton anymore?"

"Yes, she told me," Flynn said, not bothering to disguise his irritation. "I don't appreciate what you're trying to do, Margo."

"She's only trying to help," Zoe said.

"She's casting suspicion on an innocent person." Flynn kept his attention on Margo, who seemed unaffected by his anger. "And Kristen isn't the type to—"

"I'm afraid that's not true," Margo said easily, not a single feather ruffled. "The rental agency called to say that someone had asked about renting this cabin and wanted to know exactly where it was located here in Long Shaft. Nobody ever calls about this cabin."

"So the Bigfoot campaign is finally working," Flynn said.

Margo shook her head. "Too much of a coincidence. I'd told the agency to let me know if anyone asked about the cabin because I wanted to make sure no reporters were nosing around."

"It probably *was* a reporter," Flynn said.

Margo smiled as if exceedingly proud of herself. "Not unless she has the same name as your girlfriend."

Flynn went very still. Apparently he didn't know Kristen as well as he'd thought. And it appeared as if she might be headed his way.

"So did the rental agent give information about the location of the cabin?" Zoe asked.

"No, he didn't, because I'd told him to be on the lookout for people wanting that information and not to give it out during this weekend."

"Thank you." Zoe turned to Flynn. "I wonder if this is worth it, after all. I could charter a plane and have us back in LA by dinnertime."

The possibility made Flynn realize how much he'd been counting on one more night with Zoe. But ultimately, that decision was hers. "It's up to you."

"Leaving like that would blow your cover," Margo said. "I thought you didn't want anyone to know you'd gone away to learn how to be a nerd."

"They wouldn't have to know that," Zoe said. "But you make a good point. Flynn and I would have to go back separately." She sighed. "And I don't feel ready for that audition. I need more time."

Margo gazed up at Zoe. "It was such a neat plan you had. I hate to see it go down the tubes because of a freaked-out girlfriend."

Flynn decided he'd had enough. "Listen, Kristen is not a threat. Even if she were to come to Long Shaft, which I doubt, she'd be coming to talk to me and find out what the story is regarding Zoe." He reached for his cell phone. "I'm going to call her right now and make sure she doesn't do that."

Zoe put a restraining hand on his arm. "Wait a minute. What are you going to say?"

"I'll tell her I've agreed to help you with this audition

and I want to honor that commitment. Then I'll ask her to put any concerns she has on hold until tomorrow night, when we can talk."

Both Margo and Zoe laughed.

"What's wrong with that?"

Margo rocked back on her heels. "If I got a call like that, I'd be out here on the next plane, ready to shove that nice, logical statement down your throat."

"I have to agree with her." Zoe gave him a sympathetic smile. "No woman wants to be put on hold, especially when her emotions are involved."

"Look, maybe she won't come out here," Margo said. "I felt like I had to tell you both that she'd called, but she didn't get any information about how to find the cabin."

"I really can't picture her coming here, either," Flynn said.

"Still, if there's a chance she might . . ." Zoe paused and gazed at Flynn. "It's complicated either way."

"I know." He shouldn't have told Kristen about this weekend. He could see that now, but at the time he'd felt honor-bound to do it.

Margo snapped her fingers. "I have a great idea. I can put the word out that Kristen is Flynn's extremely jealous ex-wife. I'll tell everyone to alert me if she shows up. She probably won't, but in case she does, she'd have to stay at the motel and eat at the diner. It's a small town. She'd be seen."

Flynn hated the idea of putting out the equivalent of an APB on Kristen. The concept was ludicrous when applied to a conservative, polished professional like her. But he couldn't guarantee she wouldn't show up without warning. She was already acting erratically.

He also didn't want a nasty scene between Kristen and Zoe. He hoped to protect both women from going through that. Although a part of him stood aside watching in total amazement that he, Flynn Granger, was becoming part of a triangle, he couldn't ignore the potential for disaster. And he would never come to Long Shaft again, so whatever tale Margo spun wouldn't matter.

"Okay," he said. "I guess we could consider that."

"Do you have a picture I can show around?"

No, he didn't, thank God. Handing Margo a picture to circulate would be carrying this charade too far. He shook his head. "Sorry."

"Then can you describe her for me? I'll need to tell people something."

"Short brown hair, five-six, a hundred and twenty-five pounds."

Margo nodded. "Okay. What else?"

Frantically he tried to picture Kristen, but images of Zoe kept superimposing themselves over Kristen's face. "She has all her teeth."

"What?" Margo stared at him.

It was the only detail he could think of, but both women were looking at him as if he'd lost it. "I mean, she hasn't had any teeth pulled because of braces or anything." He thought of another detail. "She's right-handed."

Margo snorted. "Now there's a defining quality. How about her eyes?"

"Twenty-thirty and twenty-forty. Corrected with contacts."

Zoe groaned. "I think Margo wants to know what color they are."

"That would help," Margo said. "The teeth and the

right-handed thing won't make her any easier to spot. Plus I doubt anybody in Long Shaft has an eye chart handy."

For one panicky minute Flynn couldn't remember what color eyes Kristen had. All he could see was Zoe's eyes—blue as the Pacific when she was laughing, dark and stormy when she was aroused—but Margo was waiting, so he had to say something. "They're sort of brownish," he said. "I think."

Then he checked to see how that had gone over with Margo and Zoe. Not well. Their disapproving expressions told him clearly that a man should know the color of his almost-fiancée's eyes.

That was the moment when he faced the sorry truth. He'd been asked to describe a woman he'd considered proposing to. All he'd come up with was a bunch of statistics that would fit very well on a life insurance application. A guy in love should be able to do better than that. A hell of a lot better.

A guy in love would have a picture in his wallet, for God's sake. He'd never even thought to ask for one. Kristen hadn't asked for one of him, either, and maybe she should have.

For now, he could only speak for himself, and he knew beyond a shadow of a doubt that he'd been kidding himself about Kristen. Much as he wanted to believe otherwise, he wasn't even remotely in love with her.

Chapter Nineteen

As Zoe listened to Flynn struggling to describe the woman he'd planned to marry, she concluded that either he was the most unromantic guy in the universe or he didn't love Kristen. She might be able to find out the answer once Margo left.

But no sooner had Margo driven away to begin her new mission than Zoe spotted Luanne wearing a green nylon backpack as she hiked through the trees in their direction. When she saw Zoe looking her way, she waved wildly and moved faster.

"Luanne's coming," Flynn said.

"I know. I saw her. Is it me, or is this starting to feel like *Little House on the Prairie* with us standing on the porch and visitors always dropping by? I have the urge to put on an apron and start making biscuits."

"If you ask me, it's more like *Little House on the Prairie* meets *X-Files*."

"I should have known you'd be an *X-Files* guy. That

show was too scary for me." Zoe decided she only had time for one test before Luanne came within hearing distance. Clapping her hands over her eyes, she turned her face away from Flynn. "What color eyes do I have?"

"Depends."

"Are you waffling because you don't know?" Maybe he was just that unromantic. How disappointing.

"I'm not waffling. Depending on the circumstances, they change color."

"Yeah, you're waffling." With her hand over her eyes, her other senses tuned in, making her conscious of his breathing and the minty scent of his aftershave. He might be unromantic as a hedgehog, but he still flipped all her switches.

"I am not waffling. When you're feeling happy and relaxed, your eyes are this turquoisy-blue color, but when you're upset, they get kind of dull, almost gray. And when you're excited, they get a darker blue, like a really deep lake."

"Oh." She was afraid to take her hand away from her eyes because he'd be able to see that dark blue color and know how he'd affected her with that elaborate description of her moods. He was obviously into her, and the feeling was most definitely mutual.

"In case you were wondering, I'm fully aware that I should have been able to give at least that much detail about Kristen. Knowing that I couldn't do that, I'm wondering what the hell I was thinking with all these marriage plans."

"You haven't seen her in a while." Zoe felt obligated to say that.

"Doesn't matter. I should have memories of her eyes, and I don't. All I can remember about her eyes is the discussion we had when we were comparing our lens prescriptions. And that's pathetic."

"I'm afraid so."

"Vera!" Luanne called out. "Please say you don't have a headache!"

Zoe took her hand away from her eyes. "Nope!"

"Thank God." Luanne hurried the final few yards until she reached the porch steps, where she plopped down and took off her backpack. "Because I have my interview all structured and I'd be *devastated* if you weren't up to it."

"Interview?" Zoe sat down on the steps next to Luanne. To think she could have a daughter this age if she'd gotten married right out of high school, as Margo had planned to. But Margo wasn't married and neither was Zoe. From what Margo had said, they were the exceptions in the Class of '91.

Until recently, that had seemed about right, to be footloose and fancy-free. But she was enjoying having Luanne around. She didn't see all that many kids these days. Being a mother might not be such a bad thing.

Flynn walked over to the steps. "Luanne, did you ever find out what your brother was doing last night when he was supposed to be out with Janice?"

"Nope." Luanne unzipped her backpack. "But I'm working on it. It's been a while since I searched his room. I need to do that tonight."

Zoe, who had never had a sister or brother, was scandalized. "You search his room? That's an invasion of privacy!"

"Big brothers have no privacy," Luanne said. "That's the way it is."

"She's right," Flynn said. "My little sister knew everything there was to know about me. So, Luanne, if you find out anything interesting, I'd like to hear about it."

"Sure, Tony. You got it." Luanne pulled a thick white binder out of her backpack. "Here we go. This contains all the information I've collected on my favorite actors." She sounded like a college professor unveiling a thesis.

Sure enough, on the three-ring binder cover *Luanne Dunwoodie's Big Book of Most Excellent Actors* was written in elaborate red calligraphy. Luanne flipped the binder open to the title page, where *Hollywood's Best by Luanne Dunwoodie* was lettered in purple script.

Luanne smoothed her hand over the title page. "I couldn't decide which title was better, so I used them both. Which do you guys think is better?"

Flynn sat down on the other side of Luanne and examined the binder. "Are you putting only actors in there, or both actors and movies?"

"Just actors. I have another binder for movies."

"Then I like the front cover title best, because it fits the subject better," Flynn said.

"Of course! I can't believe I didn't see that." Luanne ripped the title page out of the binder.

"Luanne!" Zoe was horrified. "All that beautiful lettering!"

"No big deal." She crumpled the page and stuffed it in her backpack. "I can do that stuff in my sleep. Now, let's get down to business."

"Okay." Zoe exchanged a smile with Flynn over Luanne's head. It was a nice moment; one could even say a parental moment. Now that was scary.

"I've divided the notebook into sections," Luanne said. "First by female and male actors, and then each actor has several different categories of information."

Zoe gazed in wonder at the rows of colored tabs. She'd never been that exacting about anything . . . ever. "Amazing," she murmured.

"Thanks."

Flynn nodded in approval. "Nice job."

On the other hand, Zoe thought, Flynn was very exacting, especially about the things that interested him, like studio contracts and Bigfoot and . . . well . . . the color of her eyes. Every time she thought of that description she wanted to kiss him some more. But Luanne was sitting between them at the moment, which was probably for the best.

"I've put the female actors in the front," Luanne said. "And that's 'cause frankly, they get a raw deal most of the time in Hollywood. Take Sean Connery, for instance. Name me one woman of his age who gets the romantic lead! It's not fair."

Zoe leaned her chin on her fist. "I agree."

"I mean, Zoe Tarleton is already thirty-two. She's getting up there."

"I don't know about that." Zoe sat up straighter.

"Be realistic! How many years does she have left as a big box-office draw? Four, five, six years?" Luanne cast an assessing glance over Zoe. "You'd better rake in the money as her body double now, before she's all washed up."

"I'll keep that in mind."

"Zoe will last longer than another six years," Flynn said. "For one thing, she doesn't look her age."

"That's nice of you to say." Feeling tons better, Zoe winked at him.

"That may not be enough." Luanne shook her head slowly. She wore an Eeyore expression of doom. "Nobody looks their age in Hollywood. It's a tough town."

Zoe bit her lip to keep from laughing at Luanne's worldly attitude. "I suppose that's true."

"Don't get me wrong," Luanne said. "Zoe's already made enough money to live on until she's old and gray, but her peak earning years are mostly behind her."

Luanne's comments were starting to hit a little too close to home. "Maybe she'll start getting character parts and expand her repertoire."

"That would be good. I think she could do it, too. She's underrated as an actor, if you ask me."

Zoe wanted to hug her for that, but Vera wouldn't have a reason to hug her, so she restrained herself.

"Instead of arranging the actors in alphabetical order, I put them in order of my most favorite down to my least. I have an index in the back so anyone could cross-reference the names, if they need to."

"Looks like you thought of everything," Flynn said.

Zoe glanced at him and emotion put a major squeeze on her heart. He was loving this. She hoped someday he'd have a kid like Luanne who was into details.

"I've tried to," Luanne said. "I also rank each actor with stars. Five is the best, and I only have one ranked with five stars." Then she turned the divider page over to reveal that her first female actor in the book was Zoe Tarleton.

All Luanne's comments about Zoe being nearly washed up were forgotten. Zoe was ready to take her home. She and Flynn could share her.

"This is what I have so far in the picture section." Luanne proudly displayed pictures neatly cut from magazines or printed off the Internet, each with the date when it was taken or the movie it was from.

As Zoe looked at the pictures, which ranged from her early publicity shots to more recent ones, she could see herself aging, but she could also see a sameness there. She had to break away from the glamour-girl roles, both to keep her career fresh and to stay sane. The audition was taking on more importance by the minute.

"And here I have personal information." Luanne turned to a page she'd obviously created on the computer. At the top she'd typed *Tarleton's Traits*. Underneath was a list of things Zoe recognized as being mostly generated by her agent and publicist. Some of it was true and some of it wasn't.

For example, under a category called *Zoe's Taste in Men,* Luanne had written: *She likes her men to have muscles, a great smile, and star power. Evidence: Keanu Reeves, Ben Affleck, Trace Edwards.* Not true, it turned out. Lately she preferred guys with glasses and law degrees— one particular guy, as a matter of fact. She winced when she realized that Flynn was reading this page, too. She didn't want him to feel bad.

So she pointed to that entry. "You know, I've talked to Zoe about her boyfriends, and star power isn't such a big deal with her."

"But all she dates are famous stars," Luanne said.

"I know." Zoe didn't want to ruin Luanne's carefully constructed page. The girl was liable to rip it out and start over. "And she likes those guys, but she also likes men who aren't actors."

Luanne pulled a pen out of her backpack. "So how should I fix this?"

"You could add something to the part about what kind of man she likes. There's room."

"What should I add?" Luanne waited, pen poised over the page.

"How about: *She also likes brainy guys*?"

Luanne nodded and started to write.

"That's good to know," Flynn said.

Zoe glanced over at him. "I have it on good authority."

"I guess you'd know, being so close to her."

Zoe held up two fingers pressed together. "Zoe Tarleton and I are like that."

The corners of his mouth twitched, as if he wanted to laugh but knew he couldn't. "Must be nice to be that close." He was flirting, and she knew it.

She should pretend not to notice, but that would be tough when her cheeks felt blush-warm. He hadn't known the color of his girlfriend's eyes, she reminded herself. She wasn't stealing him if Kristen had never had him in the first place.

"O-*kay*." Luanne slapped the page. "Let's get some more information. What's her favorite color?"

Zoe and Flynn spoke at once. "Red."

"How did you know that, Tony?" Luanne looked puzzled.

Zoe was intrigued. "Yeah, how do you know that, Tony?"

"She's always wearing it."

"That doesn't mean anything if you're talking about movies and publicity pictures," Luanne said. "That's why I left the answer blank, because you can't tell from what you see. That's all decided by other people. I want to know what color she wears when she picks her own outfit."

"Red." Zoe wondered if Trace had ever noticed how much she liked it. But Flynn had. He'd been paying more attention to her than she'd realized.

"Excellent." Luanne wrote in the color. "Now we're getting somewhere. How about food? What does she like to eat?"

Zoe thought about the food she'd shared with Flynn.

None of it had been very good, but all of it had become her new personal favorite. "Hot dogs, and spaghetti, and eggs Benedict."

Luanne wrote furiously. "Hot dogs. That's very retro. Just plain spaghetti? Not some special pasta?"

"Nope." Zoe looked over at Flynn. "Plain spaghetti, with a sauce made from canned tomatoes, garlic, onion— you know."

"If you say so." Luanne sighed. "Not very original, though. I was expecting something sophisticated like frog legs sautéed in white wine sauce."

"Ick." Zoe had never ordered frog legs and never intended to.

"But the eggs Benedict is more like it. I hope you didn't try the eggs Benedict down at the Sasquatch Diner, though. I've never had the real thing, but I know that can't be right."

"It isn't," Zoe said.

"Oh no." Luanne let her head fall forward with a thump onto the page. "You *did* order it. I should have warned you." She lifted her head. "Wasn't it the grossest thing you've ever tasted?"

"Pretty much," Flynn said. Then he cleared his throat. "Listen, Luanne, this has been lots of fun, but Vera needs a break."

"A break? I just got here!"

"I know. But it's been a long day." Flynn sounded kind but firm. And he avoided looking at Zoe. "You're welcome to come back tomorrow morning to ask more questions. We won't be leaving until about four in the afternoon."

Zoe began to hyperventilate. Flynn was taking charge and sending Luanne home. She didn't have to search very

hard to find his motivation. To have or not to have sex—
that was the question.

Luanne closed her binder and turned to Flynn. "I know
what's going on," she said. "You two want to be *alone*."

He nodded. "Yes, we do."

"Well, that bites."

"Sorry, Luanne." Flynn didn't sound all that sorry.
"But we did come up here for some privacy."

"I know." With a martyred sigh, Luanne put her binder
into her backpack and zipped it closed. "I suppose someday I'll have a boyfriend, in about a trillion years. And
then I'll feel the same way."

"Thanks for understanding," Flynn said.

Zoe didn't trust herself to say a word. Her blood was
too busy racing through her body to send an adequate
amount to her brain. No telling what she might blurt out
in her current state.

Luanne pushed herself upright. "As for my potential
boyfriends, it doesn't look so good. You should see the
prospects I have to choose from." She rolled her eyes.
"Hopeless."

"I was hopeless when I was eleven," Flynn said.

Luanne studied him. "I can see that. You have that late
bloomer look."

"Thanks."

"And look at you now," Luanne said. "Spending the
weekend with Zoe Tarleton's body double. That's not too
shabby. Well, I'll see you guys tomorrow morning. Is
seven too early?"

"*Yes,*" Flynn and Zoe said together.

"All right, all right! I'll make it eight."

"Make it ten," Flynn said.

"Okay, ten." Luanne hoisted her backpack over her shoulder. "But you said if I found out something about my brother, I should let you know. Does that mean I shouldn't let you know until ten?"

"You can call my cell phone." Flynn rattled off the number.

Luanne repeated the number twice. "Got it. Cool. I have the cell phone number of the guy who's dating Zoe Tarleton's body double. That practically makes me part of the in crowd. I'm at least on the fringes of the in crowd. Excellent."

"I'm not part of the in crowd," Flynn said.

"I know that, but Vera is right on the border, having all that contact with Zoe, and you're with Vera, and I'm in touch with you." Luanne grinned. "That's only three degrees of separation from Zoe Tarleton. See you guys tomorrow morning." She crossed the driveway and started through the trees.

Flynn watched her go. "I'm afraid she's very close to figuring out who you are."

"You think so? She seems convinced of this body double thing."

"Give her a little more time and she'll have it." He turned to gaze at her. "Especially after you told her Zoe liked brainy types."

Yes, she certainly did. Especially the brainy type sitting on the porch steps with her. "I don't see a problem with telling her that."

"She's sharp. Eventually she'll make the connection that the supposed body double is up here with a brainy type. Then she'll start to wonder if Trace Edwards is history and whether she came to the wrong conclusion."

"I suppose."

"With luck she won't figure anything out until tomorrow, and even if she does, she'd want to keep it to herself."

"Uh-huh." Zoe hoped that was the right response. She'd become so engrossed in looking into his eyes that she'd lost track of the conversation. His eyes changed color, too.

Or maybe his eyes changed temperature more than color. They were definitely a cool gray, like a piece of slate or a storm cloud, whenever Margo was around. She couldn't blame him for being upset with poor Margo, who had made his girlfriend look like a psycho stalker.

But his eyes weren't cool now. They were warm, like a soft wool sweater or a gray kitten in a sunny windowsill. The longer Zoe fixated on those eyes, the more she knew the answer to the question they'd been debating endlessly.

The answer was *yes*.

Chapter Twenty

Flynn stopped talking as he realized what was happening. Sitting there on the porch steps in the warm afternoon sun, without him lifting a finger, he'd somehow managed to seduce Zoe Tarleton. He couldn't imagine how he'd accomplished that.

He'd never considered himself a very persuasive guy, which was why he'd gone into contract law instead of criminal law, where he might have ended up arguing cases in front of a jury. When it came to Zoe's decision to have sex with him, he'd thought the jury was still out. From the expression on her face and the deep blue of her eyes, the jury was in and a verdict had been rendered.

So he could stand on principle and pass up the opportunity, which he doubted would ever come again. Realistically, this was a once-in-a-lifetime chance, given his nerd status and her cool status. The odds of a guy like him ever having sex with a woman like her were at least one in a billion.

Somehow he'd beaten those odds. And yet he wasn't morally free to take advantage of this miracle. He should break up with Kristen first. Yeah, right. He'd call her on the cell phone and say that Zoe was giving him the green light and so sorry about that, he had to break up now.

Not only was that the tackiest and most insensitive move on the planet; it would change Zoe's green light to red immediately. If he so much as spoke Kristen's name, Zoe's green light would change. She had a pretty active conscience herself.

Therefore, he couldn't make that phone call, for a bunch of reasons. What then? He pictured himself doing the noble thing and gently declining the invitation Zoe was making with those flushed cheeks and parted lips. If he could turn away, then he could break up with Kristen later this week knowing he'd done everything in order.

Normally he preferred doing everything in order. He preferred a balanced approach to life. But when he weighed sex with Zoe against denying himself that chance, maybe forever, so that he'd have a clear conscience when he told Kirsten it was over . . . well, sex with Zoe tipped the scales. It practically broke the scales, to be honest.

He was about to sin. He was about to demonstrate that he was fallible, that when presented with a temptation of this magnitude, he couldn't resist. For such a momentous decision he would have expected thunder and lightning or at least a dramatic wind to blow across the porch, signaling that life as he knew it was about to change forever.

Instead, the moment was incredibly simple. No fanfare whatsoever. He stood, held out his hand, and said, "Let's go in."

Zoe put her hand in his, and that was when he realized she was trembling.

He began to shake, too, as he started toward the door. The porch was wide, yet he walked across it as if balancing on a tightrope. This was far from being a done deal. One mistake in judgment, one awkward moment, and she could change her mind. He knew that as surely as he knew that right now she was all systems go.

The mood breaker might not even be his fault. They had three telephones that could ring. If some idiot was playing tricks on them, another prank could interrupt them at any time. Margo could show up with more news about Kristen. Luanne might decide she couldn't wait until tomorrow morning to come back. Bigfoot could make a surprise daytime run through the forest.

The potential for sexual disaster was huge, and that wasn't even counting his own likelihood of screwing up. He had a decent record of making women happy in the bedroom, but because he was so eager to make this particular woman happy, he could easily do something stupid. In fact, the odds of him doing something stupid were way lower than the odds that he'd ever be in this situation in the first place. Way lower.

First of all, he had to decide the door issue. Hand in hand, they couldn't go through together or they'd get stuck. He'd read somewhere that under stress, people's bodies tended to swell. They could get stuck in the door and stay that way until Luanne showed up in the morning. Getting stuck in the door would pretty much rule out sex.

But how to proceed? A man was supposed to let the woman go through a door ahead of him, but that put Zoe in the lead, taking him by the hand through the door. That wasn't the optimal dynamic.

So he led the way through the door, because he also

had to figure out which bed to use. Hers had more room, but his was closer to the condoms. He couldn't imagine leading her down the hall, making a side trip to his room for condoms, and then setting off hand in hand for her room. Inelegant—too much like running errands.

So they'd have to use his bed, short and narrow though it might be. He'd work around that restriction and hope he wouldn't fall off the bed at some critical point in the action. This might have been the easiest seduction in his sexual history, but the follow-through was turning out to be damned complicated.

Then, as they started down the hall, she squeezed his hand.

He stopped breathing, sure that she was about to call it off. Well, if she did that, he'd back her up against the wall and kiss her until she changed her mind again. He'd come too close to give up that easily.

Glancing down at her, he braced himself for a battle. "What?"

She smiled, and her eyes were still that encouraging deep blue. "Which room?"

Thank God he'd figured that one out. "Mine."

"Mine's bigger."

"I know, but I have the—"

"I'll meet you in my room."

His breath came out in a rush. "Sure." His voice cracked, but at least he'd been able to speak. With his tongue feeling about twice its normal size, any speech at all was amazing. He wanted her way too much. Even knowing that, he couldn't seem to get any perspective on the matter.

Reluctantly he released her hand so she could continue on down the hall without him. Maybe letting go of her had been a bad move, though. Maybe he should have insisted on using his bed so he could keep that connection. He watched her start to go into her room and wondered if he'd blown it.

Then she turned, and of course he was still standing motionless as if someone had glued his shoes to the floor. He fully expected her next words to be *Forget it*. Instead he noticed something absolutely incredible. On the way down the hall she had *unbuttoned her blouse*.

It hung open, giving him a generous view of what lay beneath—heaven cradled gently in stretchy cotton. His erection, which had been making its presence known for the last few minutes, snapped immediately to attention.

She rested one hand against the door frame, which made the blouse gape open a tantalizing bit more. Then she took off her glasses and glanced at him, her color high. "Don't be long," she said.

And it dawned on him that he was wasting time. While he'd stood there like a kid playing a game of statues, she'd been making good progress, closing the distance to the party bed and starting on the undressing. He, however, had achieved nothing but a hard-on. If he didn't correct his tardiness, she might dump him for dawdling.

Charging into his bedroom, he wrenched open the closet door and pulled his suitcase down from the top shelf so fast that it hit him on the head. He didn't even flinch. Unfortunately, his coordination was off and it took two tries before he successfully unzipped the pouch containing the box of condoms.

Once he had the box in hand, he started to race out of the room again. Then a shred of reason floated through his fevered brain and brought him up short. Coordination was important for the activity he was about to engage in, so he'd better slow down and get a better grasp on his reactions.

Damn, he was usually much smoother than this. The thought of having sex with Zoe Tarleton had him rattled. Sure, he needed to hurry down to that bedroom, but he didn't want to slide through the door like Cosmo Kramer.

Taking several deep breaths, he finally had the oxygen his brain required to think rationally about the box of condoms in his hand. Taking the entire box down might send the wrong signal, not to mention that it might remind Zoe of when she'd first seen it. He'd rather she forget all about the origination of the condoms.

Easy enough to fix. Opening the box, he took out one and stuck it in his pocket. He could always come back for more if the first time went well, but arriving in her bedroom with a boxful, or even a handful, was presumptuous. If they should be unfortunate enough to have bad sex they might be able to laugh about it, as he'd said, but he wouldn't be needing any more condoms. Leftovers would be embarrassing.

All right. He was as ready as he'd ever be. Now-or-never time had arrived. Improbable though it still seemed to him, he was about to enter the bedroom of one of the world's great beauties. He prayed he'd make a good impression.

Heart thudding, he took the long walk from his room to hers. In reality it was only about fifteen feet, but it felt like fifteen miles. He wondered if she'd be in bed yet and, if so, whether she'd have the covers pulled up to her chin. If she had the covers up to her chin, would she still be wearing underwear?

Or maybe . . . His brain shut down as he stepped through the door and found her stretched on the bed, sans covers, sans clothes, sans everything except an allover tan and a come-hither smile. And she was waiting for him.

Zoe barely made it to the bed before she heard Flynn coming down the hall. When he walked in and found her there, the expression on his face was worth all her efforts to strip before he arrived. Her dramatic training had prompted her to do it, although she'd never tried such a bold move.

Flynn looked like a man who had accidentally grabbed hold of a high-voltage wire, the ones the electric companies warned people not to touch. His eyes widened and his body shook. She even imagined his hair stood up a little. As for the action going on below his slender silver belt buckle—very gratifying.

She should probably say something, something sultry, but she couldn't think what. Frantically she tried to remember a movie scene she could draw from. A snatch of dialogue came to her, and she used it.

She propped herself up on one elbow. "I decided to get the party started."

He swallowed. "So I see."

"You, uh, might want to do the same." If he undressed himself, then he wouldn't find out that she was shaking and might fumble the job. Having him do it would preserve her image as the cool babe.

He nodded, reached into his shirt pocket, and pulled out his PDA.

"You have an appointment?"

"No." He seemed to be having trouble concentrating

on what he was doing, though. He kept glancing from her to the PDA in his hand. "I need a place . . . a place to put it."

She was incredibly touched. He really cherished that PDA she'd given him. "On the chair, maybe." A ratty wicker chair next to him was piled high with her clothes, but there was room for his PDA and his clothes on top. She hadn't had time to neaten up the room. She hoped he wasn't turned off by the mess.

Judging by the jut of his penis under his slacks, he wasn't even slightly turned off. He laid the PDA on top of her clothes and started on the buttons of his shirt. He kept his gaze firmly on her as he progressed. "You look . . ." He paused to clear his throat. "Incredible."

"Thank you. I work out." It occurred to her that the actors she'd dated mostly took it for granted that the women in their bed would have a toned body. Flynn didn't seem to take anything for granted.

"I've . . . uh . . . been to gyms before," he said. "Nobody I've seen . . . looks like that." He took off his shirt. Underneath that was a regulation white T-shirt.

By observation Zoe had figured out there would be a T-shirt layer to get through, and she waited for him to peel it off over his head. Instead he reached for the buckle of his belt.

Most Hollywood types could hardly wait to show off their manly pecs. But Flynn seemed to be getting undressed in the same order he got dressed—outer clothes, then inner. But once his belt was unbuckled, he stopped and frowned.

"Is something wrong?"

"Shoes." He leaned over and glanced down at his feet, as if he'd forgotten he had any.

She could see how that could happen, given the bulge that currently blocked his view. Of course he wore lace-ups. He'd probably have to sit down somewhere to take them off, and he couldn't very well sit on the chair piled with clothes and his precious PDA.

Desperate to solve his problem, she patted the bed beside her. "You can sit here."

He shook his head. "If I come over there, I'm liable to climb right in there with you, shoes and all." Instead he dropped to one knee and untied the first shoe.

Seeing him like that had the oddest impact on her. Flynn would be the kind of man who would get on his knee to propose. And the thought of him doing that with another woman made her heart turn over. She'd thought lust was the only emotion driving her. Maybe not.

He managed to get his shoes off without too much delay. When he stood and reached for his belt buckle, her pulse rate picked up. Then he stopped again and put one hand in his pocket. That's when she realized that he hadn't come into the room holding a box of condoms. Obviously he'd transferred some to his pocket and he wanted them available.

"I can take those," she said.

"I only brought one."

"One?" Disappointment washed over her.

"I thought that might be my limit." His gaze grew hotter the longer he looked at her. "I can get more later."

"Good." She swallowed. "That's good."

"In the meantime . . ." He seemed uncertain what to do with the condom.

"Throw it to me. I'll keep it."

He tossed it over and somehow she managed to catch

it. Then she had to decide what to do with it. The logical place seemed to be tucked between her thighs, so she put it there.

He stared at the foil packet pressed between her thighs as he unbuckled his belt and pulled it through the loops. She would have expected him to move faster, but he seemed mesmerized by her. After dropping the belt on the chair, he unfastened his slacks.

Now they were getting somewhere. She licked her lips as he pulled down the zipper and stepped out of his slacks. Oo-whee, the man sure filled out his tighty whities. If Flynn would be willing to model the retro-styled briefs, they could well come back into fashion. Zoe's heart beat faster with every second she gazed upon that form-fitting cotton.

He still wore his black socks, reminding her of some sleazy videos she'd seen, which only served to crank up her response. The black-sock-wearing guys in those videos always had an impressive package.

Next came his glasses. Once he'd taken those off and set them on top of his slacks on the chair, she was treated to a whole new version of Flynn. The only other time she'd seen him without his glasses he'd been a few inches from her face.

Now she had the whole man to gape at, and she visually devoured every bit of his long, lean body. Flynn with his glasses was sexy in a Wall Streetish sort of way. But Flynn without his glasses was . . . amazing.

The socks came off next. At last he reached for the back of his T-shirt, pulling it up and over his head. His dark hair came out mussed, and she loved that look. Then he peeled the shirt from his arms and tossed it on the chair.

Predictably, he combed his fingers through his hair, but that didn't completely tame it. He still looked sufficiently rumpled to be sexy as hell, plus now she had a full view of his chest.

Yum. Exactly the right amount of hair and the perfect muscle definition to make the view interesting. The more clothes Flynn took off, the less he looked like her lawyer.

And now for the main event. He shoved his thumbs under the waistband of his briefs. She held her breath and said nothing, although inside she was yelling like a customer at Chippendales: *Take it off; take it off; take it off.*

But he didn't. Instead he paused, let go of the waistband, and started toward the bed.

"But . . . but you're not done."

He stopped moving. "It seemed safer to leave them on."

"I'm not sure I want safe."

"I thought women weren't visually stimulated. All the research says that."

She gulped and gathered her courage. "Visually stimulate me, Flynn. Please."

"If you say so." He shoved down his briefs.

She had no idea what happened to the briefs after that. He might have picked them up off the floor and put them on the chair. He might have left them lying there. He might have grabbed the butane lighter and set fire to them.

She didn't notice. All her attention was fixed on the impressive equipment he'd unveiled. If the lawyer trade didn't work out for Flynn, he could have a fine career in the X-rated film industry. The camera would love him.

Someone let out a soft sigh. A moment later she figured out it was her. Sighs were understandable, when faced with such an exciting prospect. In all the years she'd been going to Flynn's office for legal consultation, she'd never suspected the treasure he'd kept hidden behind his desk.

He cleared his throat. "I . . . uh . . . guess the research was wrong. You look . . . very visually stimulated."

She raised her hot gaze to his, lust making her bold. "Damned straight. Now let's get this thing done."

Chapter Twenty-One

Flynn was trying not to feel intimidated, but from the moment he'd stepped into Zoe's bedroom and found her naked, he'd worried that he might not be experienced enough for her. Maybe naked wasn't such a big deal for her. After all, she'd acted in nude scenes, so lying here in her birthday suit with a man she'd never had sex with wasn't so unusual.

But her willingness to display her body had driven him to a frenzy of lust that might make him clumsy. Or too quick. If only he hadn't opened his big mouth and mentioned the concept of a forty-five-minute session. The way he felt right now, three minutes would be a miracle of self-control.

He'd thought leaving on his briefs would be of some help, but she hadn't wanted that. And whatever Zoe wanted she would get if he had anything to do with it. But he had to be careful not to overstimulate himself. He needed to maintain a certain amount of objectivity.

Oh, sure. Just look at those breasts, so plump, so golden, and tipped with raspberry nipples. He knew what her nipples felt like in his mouth. He wanted more of that, but he was afraid even the slightest nipple nuzzle would make him come.

Only one option seemed open if he planned to keep his forty-five-minute timetable intact. There was a small clock on the bedside table. She could see it easily if she wanted to keep track.

Too bad he hadn't thrown his briefs over it. The trick was to keep her so busy she wouldn't think to look at the clock. But first he'd need to remove that condom she held between her thighs.

Leaning down, he braced one hand beside her head as he lowered his mouth to hers. She tasted so good—too good. He could come just from kissing that full mouth and feeling her tongue slide against his.

She leaned back on the pillow and cupped his head in both hands. He became so involved in kissing her that he forgot his goal of getting the condom and putting it safely on the bedside table before he instituted his plan. Instead he found himself stroking her breast, which felt like velvet and would taste like honey. He remembered that.

But he mustn't taste. Yet how he wanted to. Besides, that was the logical order of things, the natural progression, to kiss her lips and her breasts before moving south. He had to forget about order. Forty-five minutes was a long time. Maybe if—

He gasped as her hand strayed toward his penis. His eyes flew open. This would never do. She'd bring him off in no time flat. Stern measures were called for.

Grabbing her wrist, he pulled it away from the detonation zone. Then he straddled her and took hold of her other wrist for good measure. Lifting his mouth from hers, he pinned her to the bed and looked into those blue, blue eyes. "We're going to take it slow."

Her reply was breathless but encouraging. "Okay."

"You're probably used to being in charge, but this time—"

"I'm not used to anything." Her breasts quivered with each shallow breath.

That gave him pause. "Meaning?"

"Meaning . . ." Her cheeks grew pinker. "I don't do this much."

He stared at her in disbelief. "But you're Zoe Tarleton."

"Sex symbol. I know."

A combination of heat and tenderness washed over him. "But . . . why now?"

"I can't seem to help it."

He got that. He couldn't, either.

"And I feel safe," she murmured. "I trust you, Flynn."

He gulped. "I'm glad, but . . . I'm afraid I'll let you down."

"Does that happen a lot, you letting women down in bed?"

He thought about the women he'd made love to. "No." But they hadn't been Zoe.

"Ever?"

"No." But this was *Zoe.*

She smiled at him. "Then I'll chance it. Kiss me, Flynn."

With a groan he lowered his mouth to hers. It wasn't like he had a choice, even considering the potential for disaster. Kissing Zoe was a given.

And once the kissing started, there was no stopping anything. His blood ran hot, and possibilities sparkled in his brain. He was inspired. He would do this.

Releasing her wrists, he slid down her warm, supple body. With her allover tan she was like a golden river carrying him south to the glory land of natural redheads and Brazilian wax jobs.

His weight forced her thighs apart, although they didn't seem to take much forcing. The condom packet fell and scratched against his chest, but he didn't have time to secure it now. She needed him to give her satisfaction, and he planned to do exactly that.

She smelled glorious, and with the first lap of his tongue he confirmed that she tasted even better. He took a brief second to congratulate himself. After all, it wasn't every day that a guy like Flynn ended up with his head between the thighs of a world-famous goddess like Zoe.

Then the importance of that factoid disappeared. They were no longer Flynn Granger, nerd, and Zoe Tarleton, superstar. Stripped of their roles, they were free to become lovers—a very eager man working to give pleasure to a more-than-willing woman. From the change in her breathing and her little cries of delight, he seemed to be succeeding.

He didn't rush it. The forty-five-minute boast hung over his head, taunting him to make good on it. So he'd give it his best shot.

If that meant hanging out here for a while, pacing himself, pacing her, that was okay with him. She hadn't started to beg yet, so he figured she was happy with the roller coaster he'd put her on. He switched from intense to lazy, taking her almost to the top, then easing off and letting her zoom back to earth.

Maybe she'd forgotten about the forty-five minutes. He got excited thinking about that. If she had, then he could move faster. If she had, he needed to find the damned condom, which was somewhere in the bed with them, but he wasn't sure exactly where.

He teased her some more, building the tension, waiting to see if she'd beg him to finish it. If she didn't, that was fine, too. He loved his work, loved making her wiggle and moan.

She gasped for breath. "Flynn."

"Mm?" He circled his tongue around her flash point.

"Are you trying . . . for . . . forty-five . . . minutes?"

So she hadn't forgotten. "Could be." He let his breath tickle her damp skin and she gasped again. She was so hot. Between the two of them, they could probably power a town the size of Long Shaft.

"I don't . . . care about . . . that, anymore. Make . . . me . . . come."

"Sure thing." And he settled into a task that was ridiculously easy. In no time her cries had escalated to wails, and he had to clutch her hips to keep her from thrashing around and dislodging him.

Apparently she didn't want any disconnect, either, because she grabbed his head so that he wouldn't stray from the target. Her enthusiasm sent a surge of lust through him that resulted in an even more painful erection, but those were the breaks. His time would come, and soon. Assuming he could find the blasted condom.

Jeez, Louise! After all those golden opportunities to do it outside where I could watch, they choose the damned bedroom for their boinkathon. No imagination whatsoever, plus my viewing angle is terrible and I can't hear worth a shit.

Flynn doesn't have a clue how dangerous that bedroom could get, either. He was better off sleeping in his

*own beddie-bye, but no, he has to take his throbbing man-
hood, as they used to say in the old romance novels, and
park it in Zoe's bed.*

*Those two idiots are such a cliché. She strips and he
climbs in and starts his program. Where's the mystery, the
intrigue, in that? Too easy. Make 'em beg for it, I say.
Withhold, then give in a little. Then back off. Work on
yourself for a while and make them watch.*

*Wouldn't Flynn be surprised if he looked out this win-
dow right now. He won't, though, because his head is
wedged between her legs for the duration. You'd think she
was serving hot fudge, the way he's going at it. But if he
did happen to glance this way, he'd get turned on by what
he saw, no question. If things were different, we could
make it a threesome.*

*But things aren't different. They are what they are. And
by tomorrow we couldn't make a threesome even if we
tried, because Zoe will be indisposed. Or disposed of, I
should say. I get hot thinking about that. Very hot.*

When Zoe climaxed, she nearly levitated. Had Flynn not
been holding her down, he could imagine her flying
around the room like a helium balloon as she cried out his
name. *His name*. That fact wasn't lost on him. He wasn't
just another talented tongue.

As she sank back to the mattress, still panting, she
whispered a word. It sounded like *more*. He could do that.
But when he settled in for round two, she dug her fingers
into his scalp and lifted him away from the target.

She said something else, but unfortunately she had her
hands covering his ears. Besides, his heart was beating so
loud he had trouble hearing anyway. Sliding back up her

body, he gazed down at her, prepared to read her lips, if necessary. He didn't want a communications glitch to ruin what was turning out to be an excellent episode.

He was struck by how much more beautiful she was than he'd ever seen her before, and that was saying something. Her skin was flushed and her eyes glowed with satisfaction. "You look great," he said. "You should come more often."

She nodded, a soft smile on her face.

"I couldn't hear what you said before."

Pulling his head down so that her mouth was right next to his ear, she murmured her very direct, very explicit request. It required only two words, and Flynn decided they were his two favorite words in the world.

And he would do what she'd asked . . . as soon as he found the condom. He started to ease back down between her thighs.

She grabbed his head again. "Where are you going?"

"To get the condom."

"Where is it?"

"I'm . . . not sure."

"You lost it?"

"Of course not." He hoped. Running back to his room for one at this critical juncture would not be smooth. "I'm sure it's right here." Wiggling back down between her legs, he began to search for the little foil packet, but he kept getting distracted by the beauty that surrounded him.

Then there was the problem with his eyesight. Without his glasses he couldn't see all that well. And the covers had bunched down at the end of the bed. He felt under those. No luck.

Zoe sat up. "I'll help." On her hands and knees, she searched the mattress. "Not here. Maybe it fell on the floor." She crawled to the far edge of the mattress and looked down.

Flynn might have trouble seeing a small square package without his glasses, but he had no trouble at all noticing how great Zoe looked on all fours. He must have whimpered with longing, because she glanced back over her shoulder at him.

"What?" she asked.

He swallowed. "You look . . . wonderful like that."

"Oh." Her eyes glowed with blue fire. "Would you like—"

"Yes."

"Just a minute." She dropped her shoulders to the edge of the mattress, which gave him an even more incredible view as she scooped something off the floor.

Raising up on all fours again, she tossed a foil packet in his direction. "I made my request. The position is up to you."

Zoe had never felt so free with a man. She was willing to try anything with Flynn, and the sooner the better. He brought out all the fantasies she'd kept locked away for so long.

That might be all tied in with his excellence at oral sex. In her estimation, any man who gave that subject his full attention had established the necessary credentials to do whatever he wanted with her. She didn't know whether Flynn read a lot, practiced a lot, or had a natural gift, but he obviously gave a woman's satisfaction top priority. That was exactly what she needed to shed her inhibitions.

She glanced over her shoulder and noticed that progress had been made. He nearly had the raincoat covering that bad boy of his. With any other man she'd be afraid to be this vulnerable, to present her backside and invite him to take what he wanted. But even though Flynn was well-endowed, she knew he'd never hurt her.

His chest heaved as he moved closer and put his hands on her hips. "You're sure?"

She was more than sure. "I can hardly wait."

"Spread . . . spread your legs a little more."

She did. And loved that he was giving her directions. "Anything else?"

"Lift up a little. Like that. Right there. Oh, God. I'm trembling like a leaf."

"Me, too." Anticipation made the blood pound in her ears. "I want you, Flynn. I want you bad."

"Then here goes." He eased forward, finding her casily, sliding in with a sweet, slow motion.

If he could patent that technique, he'd make a fortune. She closed her eyes to better savor the sensation. Pure wonderfulness.

He groaned. "Ah, Zoe."

"Mm." Eyes still closed, she let her head hang as she gripped the cdge of the mattress. The room was quiet except for the sound of labored breathing, both his and hers.

He groaned again. "This feels so . . . good. Are you . . . ?"

"Yes. Good." Her vocabulary wasn't up to the task of describing how she felt, but having Flynn glide deep inside her was now on her list of peak experiences. He managed to rub against everything that was worth rubbing against.

"I'm . . . I should warn you. I don't how long I can . . . last."

"That's okay." His mere presence there was almost enough to do the job. He wouldn't have to move much to hand over a helping of paradise. A little friction would be all she required.

And then he started giving her that necessary friction. His movements were gentle, but oh, so effective. He pushed forward with enough force to make the magic connection, but not so much that he threw them both off-balance. The bedsprings squeaked in an easy tempo. They were making beautiful music together.

"Stop me if you need to," he murmured.

"Don't . . . stop." She met his steady rhythm with a rocking motion of her own. Her breasts jiggled with each contact, and the vibration felt deliciously wicked. "I'm happy." And her G-spot was extremely happy.

He managed to keep the same rhythm for a little longer, but then he moaned and picked up speed, rocketing her into serious climax mode. She tightened her grip on the mattress and braced herself for the rush.

His thighs slapped against hers ever faster, and her body shuddered with each thrust as he powered her closer to nirvana. Little yelps of pleasure rose in her throat, marking time with his pistonlike movements. As her cries grew louder, he matched her with groans of pleasure.

Her orgasm crashed upon her, taking her breath away with its force. Through it all he continued to stroke, hitting the crest of every wave. Then with a deep moan, he plunged into her one last time and stayed there, gasping and quivering, as he pulsed to the tune of his own climax.

Once her body stopped quivering and her brain started to work again, she marveled at what had happened so far in this bed. She didn't have enough experience to know for sure, but it looked like she was in the hands of an incredible lover. Talk about lucky. Talk about totally satisfied. Talk about anticipation for more of the same.

But not right now. She was dizzy with all that pleasure. How nice it would be to plop down on the mattress and take a siesta to rest up in preparation for more thrills. But she and Flynn were still connected, and although she liked that feeling a lot, she didn't think they could fall over in unison with much success. If she fell without warning him, she might injure the precious equipment that had just given her the best orgasm of her life.

She wasn't about to let that happen. "Flynn?"

"Hmm?" He sounded completely zoned out.

"I'm about to fall over." Not the most tender thing to say after such an amazing sexual experience, but she'd be hard-pressed to find words powerful enough to describe how he'd made her feel.

His grip tightened. "I've got you."

"But I *want* to fall over."

"Oh." He sounded disappointed.

"I love this hookup, but I don't think we can maintain it and get horizontal at the same time."

"I guess not." Still he didn't move.

She had a hunch she understood the problem. He'd found his favorite spot and didn't want to give it up. He needed some serious motivation to get moving again.

She had the answer, though, for both of them. Oh, did she ever. "I think we need more condoms."

"You do?" He sounded more cheerful. Even his penis gave a happy twitch.

"Definitely. Unless . . . you're worn out." She sure hoped not.

"Nope. Not worn out. But . . . what about working on your script?"

She'd rationalized that, too. Incredible sex with a man who knew what he was doing made rationalizing a breeze. "My goal is to find out how you operate. Don't you think this qualifies?"

He laughed. "If it works for you, it works for me." Slowly he eased away from her. Still holding her hips, he guided her down to the mattress. Then he leaned over and nuzzled behind her ear, giving her a quick kiss there. "Don't go away. I'll be right back with more tips on being a nerd in bed."

"I'll be waiting." As she lay curled on the mattress imagining a whole afternoon of sex with her designated nerd, she smiled. Who would have guessed that preparing for an audition would be so much fun?

When the phone rang in the kitchen, she hoped he'd ignore it. After all, if it had rung earlier, he definitely wouldn't have answered. Then she remembered that it could be Margo with news of Kristen. If Kristen actually came to Long Shaft . . .

Flynn picked up the phone and Zoe could hear him talking to someone, but she couldn't make out what he was saying. She had a bad feeling that the conversation was about Kristen, though.

Zoe was convinced that Flynn didn't love Kristen, at least not enough to commit to marriage. Otherwise he never would have climbed into this bed today. And Rob hadn't loved Margo that much, either, come to think of it.

But without Zoe in the picture, would that love have eventually blossomed in either case? That was the part that nagged at her. She didn't like to think that she was a spoiler, but it was possible.

Her dad had a term for anything that tempted people to do things they shouldn't. He called those objects *an at-*

tractive nuisance. Diving boards in backyard pools fit her dad's criteria, plus climbable sculptures in public places. Zoe hadn't thought that people could be called attractive nuisances. Yet maybe that's exactly what she was.

Chapter Twenty-Two

Flynn hung up the phone and stared out the window, although the view was fuzzy without his glasses. He shouldn't be standing here naked in the kitchen with the curtains open and an incriminating box of condoms in his hand. It wasn't like him at all.

But he had the illogical feeling that if he couldn't see outside that clearly, no one could see inside that clearly, either. Besides, even if they could, he couldn't bring himself to care. From the time Zoe had requested more condoms, life as he knew it had changed.

If a woman like Zoe thought he was worth rounding up more condoms, then he'd seriously underestimated himself. With that knowledge, something had shifted deep in his psyche. Her validation had rocketed him from conservative to risk taker, and he knew the transformation was permanent.

Two days ago his life had been organized and predictable. He'd had a workable plan for the future. Now the whole carefully constructed scenario seemed naive. He was, to his great surprise, more complicated than that.

"Flynn?"

It was the voice of his new obsession, a voice with the power to send his blood racing through his body and then heading, with great precision, to his dick. He couldn't imagine how he'd lived without her.

"Be right there!" he called back. Their recent activity had made him both hungry and thirsty. As long as he was standing in the kitchen, he might as well get lemonade, plus the cheese and a knife to cut it with.

He used the breadboard as a tray to carry two glasses of lemonade, a couple of paper napkins, a wedge of cheese, a knife, and—in center stage on the breadboard— the box of condoms.

She was sitting cross-legged on the bed, and when she saw the presentation she laughed. "I've never seen a box of condoms presented on a tray with cheese and lemonade before, let alone by a naked waiter."

"And yet what else would a naked waiter be bringing you? The condoms should be sitting in the middle of a silver tray, considering the significance."

"No doubt. Who was that on the phone?"

"Your friend Margo. If you'll take the glasses, I'll put the rest of this on the mattress." He walked around the bed and held out the breadboard so she could grab the lemonade.

"What did she want?"

"I'll tell you in a minute. Let's get our snack organized first." He made sure the breadboard was steady on the mattress before he climbed into bed with her.

She handed him his lemonade. "Thank you for bringing this. The service in this cabin is outstanding."

His new persona allowed him to wink at her. "It's all because of the big tits . . . I mean *tips*."

She thrust out her chest. "I'm not all that big. I know lots of women who are bigger than I am."

"That's because you live in Hollywood, the land of big tits." He took a long swallow of lemonade. He would never have dreamed of saying that to her before, but they'd crossed a line, and he liked being on the other side of the line. He also liked sitting propped up in bed, naked with Zoe.

"I suppose." She cradled a breast in her free hand. "I considered augmentation, but I decided these would work well enough for now."

He winced at the idea of a knife cutting that golden skin. "The tanning beds are bad enough. Please promise you won't get into cosmetic surgery."

"I can't promise that. And this color isn't from a tanning bed. It's the spray thing, where you step in naked and they hit you all over with the color."

He would have loved to see a video of that. "Why can't you promise not to have cosmetic surgery?"

"Because I might need it." She picked up the knife and cut herself a slice of cheese. "You heard Luanne. I'm on the downhill slope. I've already tried dermabrasion."

"I don't know what that is, but it doesn't sound good. I picture sandpaper."

"That's the general idea."

"Zoe!"

"Don't look so shocked. I'll do whatever it takes to stay in the game."

He put his lemonade on the bedside table and turned to her. "You're gorgeous. You don't need surgery and sandpaper to stay that way."

Following his lead, she put down her lemonade and turned to him, her expression serious. "Flynn, you're in denial. I probably will have surgery eventually. It's a culture of youth out there."

"I've heard of actors who said they wouldn't get face-lifts. I know I have."

"Me, too. I'm not that secure, I guess."

And that was when he realized that Zoe needed him. He would love her so completely, so thoroughly, that she would accept herself as she was. But it was a little soon for that kind of declaration. "Just so you know, a nerd would scoff at cosmetic surgery."

"Of course they would. Because they don't need it. They live by their wits, not their looks."

"I thought that's why you wanted the part in this movie, so that you could escape the glam-girl reputation."

She took a bite of her cheese and chewed it while she gazed at him. Then she swallowed. "You really were the debate champion, weren't you?"

He shrugged. "Yeah."

"And you're forcing me to think this through. I suppose that's a good thing."

"Thinking has its place." But sometimes it was better not to think at all, like when he was deep inside her. And he was looking forward to that moment happening again soon.

"Well, here's your answer, Mr. Smarty-pants. Yes, I want a role that doesn't depend on glamour to see how that goes. I hope it gets me more respect as an actor. But I didn't say I wanted to give up on glamour completely."

"Why not?"

She looked at him in amazement. "Because it's fun to be cool!"

"Is it? Last time I checked you were having trouble meeting me for lunch because you were about to be mobbed. So far nobody's recognized you up here, but you've been paranoid that it would happen and ruin your weekend."

"True." She gazed at him thoughtfully for several seconds. Then she nodded. "Yes, that certainly is true."

He decided not to push his advantage. He'd planted the idea of moving into a different phase, but she was the one who'd have to make that decision. If she did, he'd be there for her. If she wanted to keep her image, then she wouldn't want to hang around with the likes of him.

So he cut himself a piece of cheese and began to eat. He needed his strength for the next round. Maybe if he made her happy enough in this bedroom, she'd figure out that they shared something better than being cool.

"You never told me what Margo called about."

And he didn't want to tell her now, either. But she deserved to know. "The manager of the Bigfoot Motel called her to report that Kristen had made a reservation for tonight."

Zoe stiffened. "I was so hoping that was a false alarm."

"Yeah, me, too. According to the motel manager, she guaranteed it with a credit card and told him she wouldn't make it in until late, probably after midnight."

Zoe was quiet for several seconds. Finally she turned to him. "Look, you know her. I don't. Could she possibly be behind the incident with the bees or the gas stove?"

He sighed and leaned against the headboard. "I don't see how. She'd have had to orchestrate those things from Chicago, and that means contacting someone locally. That's very far-fetched."

Actually, his overactive brain had already figured out

how she might have done it. Lawyers knew people on both sides of the law. Through various connections she could have found someone in the area willing to do her dirty work. But he couldn't believe she was capable of that.

"Plus it makes no sense for her to show up here if she's been sabotaging us," Zoe said.

"I guess not." And yet it did make sense. Although he hadn't specialized in criminal law, he'd learned something about the criminal mind. Criminals tended to be proud of their handiwork. They liked to admire the results. Kristen couldn't do that if she stayed in Chicago.

What was he thinking? Kristen wasn't a criminal! She was simply a woman afraid of losing her man. And she was losing him. It looked like he'd be telling her so in person.

"Do you think she'll out me?" Zoe asked.

"God, I hadn't thought of that. I hope not." Damn, if only he hadn't felt obligated to tell Kristen about this weekend. "I'm sorry, Zoe. It's my fault if that happens."

"Don't blame yourself." She picked up her lemonade. "You were doing what you thought was right."

"I'm sure she's only coming here to confront me. It's me she's upset with, not you, so maybe she won't say a word." He glanced over at Zoe. "And I don't think she's had anything to do with either the bees or the gas."

"I don't think so, either. I'm probably letting Margo's sense of melodrama get the best of me. She was like that back in high school and she hasn't changed."

"You two hung out together in high school?" He still couldn't picture it.

"Not really. We were both on the cheer squad. We sat together in some classes. We're both *T*'s." Zoe took a sip of her drink. "I sort of hate to tell you the history. I'm afraid you'll think there's a pattern there."

"What kind of pattern?"

"Her boyfriend dumped her to take me to the prom. I always felt guilty about that. Now that I see her life went nowhere after high school, I feel even more guilty. Maybe if she'd gone to the prom with Rob—"

"Hold it." He set the breadboard on the floor so he could scoot closer and wrap his arm around her. Doing that made him want to have sex again, but he planned to complete this little discussion first. It was important. "You're feeling responsible for how her life turned out?"

Still holding her lemonade, she glanced up at him. "Little differences can have a huge impact. For example, I couldn't get the art class I wanted as an elective so I took drama instead. It changed the whole direction of my life."

"In a positive way. A nurturing way." He forced his mind away from thoughts of kissing her. Kissing could wait.

"Sure, but bad things can have the opposite effect."

"Not necessarily. Don't tell me you never had a big disappointment, because I don't believe it."

She took a sip of lemonade. "I didn't get the lead in the play my senior year. I wanted that lead so bad I could taste it. Angie Leavenworth got that part, and I was better."

Now her kiss would taste of lemonade. But he wouldn't dwell on that. "Did losing the part ruin your life?"

"No. It made me want to show that drama teacher what's what." She grinned. "I did, too."

"I would say so." He loved watching her breathing naked, because then he could watch her breasts quiver with each inhalation. But he couldn't dwell on that, either.

"I get your point, though. Margo didn't have to let that ruin her life. But I still don't like being the one who took away her prom date." She put down her lemonade and turned toward him to wrap her arms around his neck. "And now here I am doing the same thing to Kristen."

He looked into her eyes. He couldn't help getting an erection when she was so close, but that didn't mean he couldn't tell her what was in his heart at the same time. "You've shown me that I wasn't ready to commit to her. You've done me a favor, and Kristen, too. Marrying her would have been a mistake for me and for her."

"I'm not so sure. I could be your last fling before you settle down."

He cupped her cheek in his hand, loving the softness and the way her eyes started changing color again. He'd pretty much finished the discussion, so he could let go of logic for now and start thinking of sex. "Until you came along, I didn't know the meaning of the word *fling*."

"So I've corrupted you?"

"Yeah. And I'm loving it."

"In that case, I might as well corrupt you some more." And with that she wrapped her fingers around his penis.

Life didn't get any better than this.

Zoe had always thought blow jobs were performance art, and she was, after all, a performer. But she wished she'd had more practice at this to be sure she was doing it right. Now that Flynn had decided to have sex with her she wanted to make sure he didn't regret it later when he had the not-fun job of dealing with Kristen.

Therefore she threw herself into the moment. She licked, she sucked, and she nibbled with such enthusiasm that Flynn lost all dignity. He clenched his teeth and writhed on the bed until the sheets came untucked and started sliding toward the floor, leaving the mattress exposed.

She must be doing something right. Maybe she should draw out the moment, the way he had with her. So she paused. After he settled down some, she'd start in teasing him again. Anyone listening would think he was being tortured, but whenever she took a break and saw his glazed, pleasure-filled eyes, she knew he was on a sexual high.

Her contribution was all the sweeter because she didn't think Flynn was used to this. She'd bet he was more about pleasing than being pleased. From what she'd heard, not every woman enjoyed the experience, either, which made no sense to her at all. What woman wouldn't enjoy reducing a guy to a quivering hunk of desperation?

Most of the sounds he made weren't words, only parts of words followed by a gasp when she really got him good. So when he babbled something that sounded like *can come,* she thought he finally wanted her to finish the job. But she decided to check.

"You want me to make you come?"

"No." He gritted his teeth and arched his back. "Condom . . . please."

Knowing he longed for that ultimate connection thrilled her. Maybe some men would have gladly let her lick them right into oblivion, but Flynn wanted more. In his current state of frenzy, he'd never be able to put the condom on for himself, either.

She leaned over the edge of the bed once again to snag the condoms, but at least she had a box to grab on to instead of a small packet. She and Flynn needed to organize this condom business differently so they were handy instead of having to dive down to the floor after them. Next time.

And she had no doubt there would be a next time. And

a next. Kristen's imminent arrival, whether they'd talked about it or not, meant that their privacy would end even sooner than they'd thought. That knowledge brought a sense of urgency to everything, especially this. Most especially this.

Despite some fumbling on her part, she had Flynn's penis dressed and ready to go in short order. Once Flynn was ready for action, she climbed aboard. He seemed to like that.

She did, too, for that matter. She was more than ready for a game of hide the flashlight. Once she was settled, she wiggled a little because it felt so good to do that. Working on him all that time had charged her up, too.

He circled her waist with both hands and held her still. "Better . . . take it easy."

She leaned forward and rubbed him with her breasts as she gave him a long, slow kiss. "I'll take it any way I can get it." It was their first chest-to-breast encounter, and she gave it an A-plus. The soft mat of hair cushioned her tits exactly right.

He trembled beneath her. "I have . . . zero control."

"And you're not used to losing control, are you?" She rotated her hips. Flynn's response gave her the courage to be flamboyant, and she was loving that.

He gasped and tried to hold her still. "No."

"I'm going to make you come." She rotated her hips in the opposite direction. "And you can't stop me. You're not in control of this one, Flynn, baby."

"Zoe, let me—"

"No. My turn." She started to ride him.

At first he tried to restrain her. His gaze burned with stubborn determination as he fought the onset of his climax. "You first," he said, his voice hoarse.

"Not this time. We're doing this out of order for a change."

He swore softly.

"Give it up," she murmured. "Give it up for me." She was very close, too, but she didn't want him to know or he'd keep trying to hold off. For once in his sexual life he was going to lose it first, and she was the woman who would make him.

Gradually the pressure of his hands underwent a subtle change. Instead of holding her in place, he began to urge her on.

She smiled in triumph. "Like that?"

"Yes. God, yes." He began to pant.

She turned on the speed and bit her lip against the orgasm pounding at her door. She wouldn't bow to it yet. Not until—

"You . . . win!" With a groan of surrender, he arched upward.

She bore down, and his spasms triggered her response. Rocking against him, she milked his every shudder, taking the spasms inside her body to blend with the waves of sensation spilling over her. What a rush. What a feeling of power and unity.

At last she drifted down onto his chest and nestled her cheek against his. Tenderness flowed through her as she thought of how vulnerable he'd become in that orgasmic moment. She felt incredibly proud of her ability to make that happen. No wonder guys liked to be in charge.

Chapter Twenty-Three

𝐹lynn was wiped. After very little sleep the night before and the mother of all orgasms a minute ago, he couldn't move. Vaguely he was aware that Zoe was taking care of things, things he should be dealing with in the aftermath. He shouldn't let her do that.

He shouldn't allow himself to fall asleep on the slippery surface of the mattress with the sheets gone who-knows-where and cheese on the floor that should be refrigerated and after-sex cuddling that hadn't been accomplished. In that jumble of thoughts, only one kept rising to the surface. *Flynn loves Zoe.*

If he ever left this bed, which at the moment seemed highly unlikely, he would take the knife he'd used for the cheese and go outside to carve that into a tree. Maybe he'd put clothes on first. Or maybe not. In his current state, clothes didn't seem all that important to the scheme of things.

Then Zoe returned to the bed, arranged her soft body

so that it touched his at many outstanding points, and pulled one of the tangled sheets up over them. He tried to say *Thank you*, but his mouth and tongue and vocal cords had taken a vacation. The rest of him was pretty much on temporary leave, too.

He hoped he wouldn't sleep all night. Something was about to happen around midnight, but damned if he could remember what. For now he had Zoe nestled against him, and a man couldn't ask for any more than that. He slept.

He woke up with a start. The room was mostly dark except for the patch of moonlight shining on the wicker chair containing his clothes, his glasses, and his PDA. Outside, the forest was quiet, eerily so. And then a smell like a battalion of skunks came through the window. *Sasquatch!*

Adrenaline shot through him. He shook Zoe awake. "We have to get up. He's out there."

"Who?" She sounded groggy. "Phew! What stinks? One of us needs to hit the shower, and I don't think it's—"

"Bigfoot." Flynn was already out of bed and pulling on his clothes. "I'm going out there."

"If you're going, I'm going." She scrambled out of bed and tripped on a section of sheet.

He caught her before she went down. Holding her luscious body reminded him of all he hadn't done after their last round of incredible sex. No acknowledgment had been made.

"Zoe, when we get back, I'll say all those things I should have said after we had such great sex. I apologize for zonking out like that."

"Don't worry about it." She gave him a quick kiss. "Right now you want a Bigfoot sighting."

"Yeah, I do." Although the longer he held her, the less

important it became. Maybe they should just go back to bed. If he gave his dick a vote, that's exactly what they'd do.

She wriggled out of his arms. "Come on. Don't let yourself get distracted. We can do that anytime."

He wished he could believe that. But she was rummaging around in the dark looking for her clothes, so he might as well do the same.

"Can we turn on a light?" she asked.

"Better not." Flynn thought he heard heavy footsteps on the pine needles and paused to listen. Maybe just the wind. "In fact, we'd better keep our voices down. I don't want him to know we're awake."

Zoe lowered her voice. "Are you sure it's not a family of skunks? We haven't heard that howl yet."

As if on cue, a haunting whistle echoed through the forest.

Flynn caught his breath. "There's your answer. That whistle is a trademark sound, too."

Zoe shivered. "Creeps me out."

"You don't have to come. You can stay here." He buttoned his shirt, and the holes and buttons came out wrong. He wasn't going to worry about it. And there was no point in searching for his socks, either. He did pick up his PDA, though, and put it in his shirt pocket. He liked knowing where it was.

"I'm not letting you go out there by yourself."

"Zoe, they're harmless."

"Easy for you to say. You've never met one. Listen, should we take it anything? Cheese, crackers, beads, trinkets . . . a Mennen Speed Stick?"

"I don't think we want to lure it closer."

"I was thinking more along the lines of appeasing it." She stepped into a pool of moonlight and grabbed her Einstein sweatshirt. "I thought maybe we should demonstrate our friendly intentions, like they show in the movies when the aliens land."

"Uh, I don't think we have to worry about that." In the moon's glow he could see her breasts. Even though his view was fuzzy, he could tell she hadn't put on a bra. He waited to see if she'd go braless under the sweatshirt. She did choose that option, which gave him all sorts of friendly intentions. He'd have to work hard to concentrate on Bigfoot.

"I'm ready." She glanced at him. "Are you ready?"

"Yeah. No, wait, my glasses." He fumbled around on the chair but couldn't find them.

"Here, let me." Zoe pawed through the stack of clothes and came up with them. "I'm sure you're not used to working with messes."

"Not so much." He put on the glasses.

"You've been very tolerant of mine."

"It was easy." If she only knew that being allowed in this bedroom, messes and all, had been the highlight of his whole damned life—but now wasn't the right time to tell her all that. "Okay, let's go."

"We should take the flashlight."

He'd forgotten all about the flashlight. Between Zoe and Bigfoot, his brain was mush. "Where is it?"

"I left it in the living room." She started down the hall. Then she turned, her voice hushed. "Are we going out the front or back?"

"Out the back. It's closer to—"

A long-drawn-out howl cut him off. The hairs on the back of his neck stood at attention. Sasquatch was definitely still in the neighborhood.

Zoe clutched his arm. "Omigod. This is so scary."

"You should stay here." He gently removed her hand and headed toward the living room.

"No way." She hurried after him. "I'm not letting you get eaten by Bigfoot."

"They don't eat people." He scanned the shadowy living room, hoping to see the flashlight.

"No one you know about. I mean, nobody's ever done a dissection of one, right? People disappear. You don't know what you might find in Bigfoot's tummy. Jimmy Hoffa maybe."

"I don't see the flashlight."

"Right here." She picked it up from the end table. "I'll be in charge of it." She started toward the kitchen.

"Wait. Let me have that. You stay inside. You can lock the door after me."

"Nope. My flashlight. You gave it to me."

"Zoe, there's no reason for you to go out there. You don't have a lifelong dream of sighting Bigfoot."

She unlocked the back door. "You shouldn't go looking for Bigfoot by yourself. You need me."

Well, he did, but not for chasing after Bigfoot. "I'll be fine."

"No, you won't. What if you lose your glasses?"

"I won't lose them."

She turned, blocking the doorway. "Answer me this. Have you ever had a Bigfoot sighting before?"

"No."

"Then you have no idea what will happen. You don't know if you'll end up running away, or jumping in surprise, or what. You don't have a leash for those glasses, so losing them is not out of the question."

He couldn't help grinning.

"Are you laughing at me? I can't see your face too well, but I thought I saw the flash of your pearly whites."

He had such an urge to kiss her, but he controlled it. "Zoe, that was one of the finest nerd speeches I've ever heard. You attacked the problem with pure logic. I think you're getting the idea."

"Glad to hear it. And now that I've passed that test, I'm also going with you and I'm keeping this flashlight."

"But you're scared."

"I'm scared, but I'm going. I am Plucky Girl."

Yep, the votes were in and the tally was confirmed. Flynn loved Zoe. "Don't turn the flashlight on yet, okay? I want to try and go out there undetected."

"I think undetected is great. I wouldn't mind being permanently undetected."

"Good. Me, either. I just want a good look. I don't have to have an encounter."

She nodded. "Agreed. So, I won't turn on the flashlight unless absolutely necessary, like when Bigfoot is running straight toward us and we have to blind him with it to give us that crucial five seconds to get away. And if that doesn't work, I'll throw it at him, and maybe he'll be intrigued because it's an itty-bitty version of—"

"Zoe."

"What?"

"You're babbling."

"Right." She took a deep breath. "Let's go." Opening the door slowly, she peered out. "Do you see anything?" she murmured. "Because I don't see anything."

"I can't see anything because you're still blocking the door."

"Oh." She edged out onto the small cement stoop, but she kept her hand on the doorknob.

"Maybe you should come back inside. I can tell you're very frightened."

"No, I'm good."

"Then you'll have to move away from the door. I can't get out."

"Sure." Keeping hold of the doorknob, she inched a little farther out onto the stoop, but she was still blocking his way with her outstretched arm.

"You'll have to let go of the door."

"Okay. I'll—" A shriek from the woods sent her hurtling back inside. Something clattered to the cement as she almost knocked him over trying to shut the door.

Flynn sighed. "This is silly. Just let me go by myself."

"No. I'm going now." She threw back her shoulders and opened the door wide. "And I won't hold on to the door this time. And I'm staying out there, no matter what awful noises that thing makes."

"What fell a minute ago?"

"The flashlight. I'm sure it's fine."

Flynn wasn't so sure. It was a novelty flashlight to begin with, not a heavy-duty kind that could take some hard knocks. But he wasn't going out with a butane lighter, not this time. At least the moon was bright.

He stepped out onto the stoop. Zoe was already standing below him holding the flashlight.

"Come here," she murmured.

He tried to see what she might be looking at, but nothing seemed to be moving in the shadows of the forest. He took the steps slowly, not wanting to accidentally trip and make extra noise. The wind had picked up, though, which should help disguise any sounds they made. But it would be harder to hear Sasquatch, too.

Standing next to Zoe, he leaned down so he wouldn't have to raise his voice to be heard. "Did you see something?"

"No." She moved so that she was facing him. "Put your arms around me."

He should have known she'd start to freak out the minute he closed the door. Maybe he'd have to resign himself to not seeing Bigfoot after all. She wouldn't let him go alone, but she was too scared to go with him. With a sigh he wrapped his arms around her.

"Good. Now hold on a minute while I shove the flashlight up under my sweatshirt."

"While you do *what*?"

"Flynn, pipe down. I need to test the flashlight. I'm putting it right between my boobs, so they'll shield the light from the side. Hunch your shoulders over mine so you can block it from the top. I'll see if any light comes up from my shirt."

He groaned.

"What's wrong?"

"Now I'm thinking about you with a flashlight tucked in your cleavage. Do you have any idea how suggestive that is?"

"I didn't look at it that way, but maybe you have a one-track mind."

"I wouldn't be surprised."

"I guess that means you've also heard of a game called hide the flashlight. I wondered if it was a universal kid's code for sex."

"I've heard of it, and thanks to that association, I'm getting hard. Happy now?"

She pressed her mouth against his shoulder to muffle her laughter.

"Zoe, turn the damned thing on, okay?"

She cleared her throat. "Sorry. I didn't mean to turn you on at the same time. At least I'm not so scared now. Whoops, this will take two hands. I forgot you have to swivel his feet."

So maybe it didn't matter if he never saw Bigfoot. He would always have the memory of standing in the dark holding on to Zoe while she played with a flashlight under her shirt. Not every guy could say that.

"Ah. Einstein's hair lights up. We're in business. You can let me go now."

"Maybe I don't want to."

"Yes, you do." She pulled the flashlight out and stroked it over the bulge in his pants. "After we find Bigfoot, we can go inside and have after-the-Bigfoot-sighting sex. All that adrenaline has to go somewhere. We might as well use it to boink our brains out."

"To hell with Bigfoot." He slipped both hands up the back of her sweatshirt. "Let's go insi—"

"Nope." She pushed him away. "We're doing this, Flynn. You'll regret it for the rest of your life if you don't."

An earsplitting shriek made them both jump.

Zoe gulped. "Wh-where do you think that came from?"

"Over there." Flynn pointed into the dark woods.

"Then that's where we're headed." Clutching the flashlight in both hands, Zoe started off.

Flynn had to hand it to her. That shriek had made him think twice about tracking down Sasquatch. Fortunately, it had also taken care of his erection problem. Heart racing, he caught up with Zoe as she walked bravely into the forest.

• • •

Zoe didn't know what the hell she was doing, charging off after some fourteen-foot monster she didn't want to find. This was so not her style. She didn't like monsters and things that went bump in the night, which was why she'd turned down every single horror role that had come her way.

She didn't belong here. She belonged in her beach house surrounded by all the luxuries and a state-of-the-art alarm system. But whenever she tried to imagine Flynn going into the woods without her, she got a really bad feeling in her tummy.

Could be she was falling for him. That would explain this irresistible urge to make sure nothing happened to his nerdy, Sasquatch-loving self. She wasn't quite sure where to put this new emotion that might be love, though.

Concepts such as marriage and babies were popping up in her brain, and she didn't know what to do about that, either. She'd assumed that those things would eventually become part of her life, but not *now*, for heaven's sake, when she needed to pour all her energy into getting this breakout role. Later, after she'd nailed the role and won a Golden Globe—that would be time enough to think about settling down with someone.

Unfortunately, the only someone she could imagine settling down with was currently walking beside her through the forest, pine needles crunching under his shoes. He had a girlfriend to deal with, and even if that got straightened out, he might not have any interest in a long-term relationship with a movie star. He liked an ordered existence, and her life was anything but.

"There." He put out a hand to stop her progress.

Immediately her thoughts stalled and the hum of her

fight-or-flight mechanism buzzed in her ears. The smell, she realized, had gotten worse. She swallowed. "I don't see anything."

"In that small clearing."

"Where?" She had to strain to hear him over the wind in the trees. She prayed he was imagining things.

"Through there, in that small clearing. About a hundred yards away. Sitting on a log."

Peering into the darkness, she saw an area where the trees gave way and moonlight spilled down like a spotlight. On the edge of that space was a shadow darker than the surrounding tree trunks. As she focused on that shadow, which did seem to be sitting on something, the shadow moved.

She stopped breathing. This whole episode felt like a bad dream, but the cool night air on her face told her it was real. "You're sure it's not a bear?"

"Yeah."

She didn't question that. Flynn knew his Sasquatches. "Why didn't it hear us?"

"The wind. It's blowing toward us, too, which is why it didn't smell us, but we can smell it."

"No kidding. This is a perfect place for a Glade stickup."

"I want to get a little closer."

Hadn't she just known that would happen? And if he was going closer, so was she. Love was not only blind, apparently, but terminally stupid, too. "First we should name him. Like we did George, the mouse."

"Okay. What?"

She pondered that a moment. Then she pondered another moment. Pondering meant they weren't moving closer yet, which was a good thing. But finally she couldn't stall anymore. "I think . . . Stanley."

"Stanley?"

"Nobody's afraid of a guy named Stanley."

"Then Stanley it is. Let's go." Flynn started through the trees.

She followed, both hands on the flashlight and one gripping its feet in case she had to switch it on in a hurry. She tried to move silently, but the pine needles crunching under her shoes sounded like someone breaking up pieces of Styrofoam and she was breathing like an asthmatic. Sheesh. She kept trying to think of the monster as Stanley, but it wasn't as much comfort as she would have liked.

Flynn cut the distance in half. Then he stopped.

Zoe stood there trembling. Now that they were within fifty yards, she had no doubt that the creature in the clearing was something she'd never seen before except in her nightmares. Huge and hairy, it nevertheless had a humanoid quality about it, sort of like a Neanderthal on steroids.

Flynn reached for her, drawing her into the circle of his arm. "It's Sasquatch," he said, his voice quivering with excitement.

Stanley. But she didn't say the name out loud. She didn't want to risk the slightest sound carrying across to the clearing. The stench was so bad she longed to cover her nose, but she was afraid to make any movements that might give them away, so she breathed through her mouth as quietly as panic would allow.

One good thing—the smell was coming at them, because the wind was blowing in their direction. The wind was her friend right now, and she'd put up with the horrendous odor.

Then the wind died. The creature stood and sniffed the air. As Zoe stood paralyzed, it turned and looked in their direction.

Chapter Twenty-Four

The Sasquatch knew they were there! Flynn had no idea what would happen next, whether it would come to investigate or run away. He wasn't sure which he wanted to happen, either. In spite of all his assurances to Zoe, he couldn't guarantee that Bigfoot was harmless.

Zoe. In his excitement he'd nearly forgotten about her, but he was painfully reminded as her fingernails dug into his arm. From the corner of his eye he could see that in her other hand she wielded the flashlight like a club. It wouldn't be much protection. And neither would he, really.

She was obviously terrified, and for her sake they should get out of here. Yet neither of them could run 35 miles an hour. If Bigfoot decided to chase them . . . Flynn seriously regretted putting Zoe in harm's way.

The creature took a step in their direction.

Zoe moaned softly.

Sasquatch hesitated, then took another step toward them.

Flynn came to a decision. "Let's go." Grabbing her hand, he clapped his free hand over his shirt pocket to keep his PDA from falling out. Then he took off running. That's when he discovered something he'd known as a kid and forgotten as an adult. Running away from the scary thing only makes you more scared.

But he wasn't about to turn around now. He doubted Zoe would let him anyway. Because of all the racket they were creating as they tore through the forest, he couldn't tell whether Sasquatch was following them or not. He imagined he heard the creature's labored breathing, but then he realized it was not Sasquatch doing all the heavy lung work. It was him.

Not knowing whether they were being chased increased his panic. But he couldn't look back. If he did, they'd lose time, and if Sasquatch was on their tail, they couldn't afford to lose even a second. So he continued to dash toward the cabin clutching Zoe's hand as they both smacked against low-hanging branches and tripped over roots.

By the time they reached the cement steps leading up to the back door, Flynn's lungs burned. He shoved Zoe up first. She fumbled with the doorknob and finally pushed the door open so hard she nearly fell down. Flynn barreled in after her and slammed the door shut. He also locked it, although a creature that large wouldn't be stopped with a flimsy lock.

Then he listened as best he could, considering that his breath rattled in his throat louder than a street rod at an intersection. "I don't . . . hear anything," he said. His panic began to ebb.

"Me . . . either." Zoe had collapsed into a sitting position on the floor. "Thank God."

From a distance came a mournful howl.

The faintness of the howl told Flynn that Bigfoot was moving away from them, not toward them. Unexpectedly, he felt sad about that. "He didn't follow us. But he sounds so lonesome."

"Good! Lonesome is excellent! That means he's not camped on our front porch hoping for an invite!"

"Maybe . . . maybe he was trying to communicate with us. And instead of responding, we ran away."

"I'm sure Stanley gets that a lot." Still gripping the flashlight, Zoe got unsteadily to her feet. "I mean, he's very scary and he has no sense of personal hygiene. That's bound to put people off."

Flynn kept picturing Sasquatch sitting alone in the small clearing. "If I were going to stay here, I'd try to make contact."

Zoe came over and laid her hand on his chest. "You don't have to feel sorry for Stanley. He has relatives. He has a family. Remember what Margo said? She's seen a female and a baby Bigfoot."

"Yeah, she did say that." Flynn wasn't ready to trust anything that Margo claimed, though. She was using Bigfoot for personal glory. Flynn would never do that.

The howl came again, even fainter this time.

"See, I'll bet Stanley's going home now," Zoe said. "He probably had a little spat with Mrs. Stanley. He couldn't very well walk into the local bar and have a beer, so he spent some time in that clearing, thinking things over."

Flynn smiled. "He did look like he was doing exactly that."

"He certainly did. Now he's back home with the missus. And they're having Sasquatch makeup sex." She shuddered. "Although the idea of sex with a body that smelly is extremely revolting."

"She probably likes the way he smells." Listening to the word *sex* come out of Zoe's mouth was having a predictable effect on Flynn. He wrapped his arms around her and remembered what she'd said about putting their adrenaline rush to good use. "Thanks for going with me on a Sasquatch hunt. You were very brave."

"You're welcome, but if it's all the same to you, I'd rather not do it again anytime soon."

He pulled her in close. "What would you rather do?"

"Make out on your Bigfoot sleeping bag."

The more Zoe thought about the sleeping bag, the more she wanted to turn the experience into a real adventure, the kind she'd always imagined and never had the nerve to do. When Flynn left to get the sleeping bag out of the car, she hurried into the bedroom and grabbed a condom from the box. Then she went out the front door, too.

The forest smelled of fresh pine, which was proof positive that Bigfoot had taken his smelly self far away. Moonlight filtered through the trees, an owl hooted nearby, and Jiminy Cricket chirped in the bushes.

The place had become a Disney set again, which was exactly how Zoe liked it. She felt like singing "Someday My Prince Will Come." Actually, he might come within the next twenty minutes or so, assuming he liked her plan.

He was lifting the sleeping bag out of the backseat as she approached, her footsteps crunching on dry pine needles. He turned with the sleeping bag in his arms. "What, you've changed your mind? Wait, I know. You want to carry it."

"No." She stepped closer and lowered her voice. No point in letting the whole neighborhood know about her intentions. "I want you to unroll it, fur side up, on the backseat."

He looked puzzled. "I thought you wanted—"

"I do."

"In there?"

"Uh-huh."

He glanced from the backseat to Zoe and to the backseat again. "Interesting idea."

"I thought it might be."

"One problem. I don't have a—"

"Right here." She pulled the condom out of her pants pocket.

He gazed at the condom for a moment. Then he looked at Zoe. "You have one hell of a sexual imagination, lady."

She wondered if he'd tell her that she was crazy, wanting to have sex in the backseat of the car when they had a perfectly good bed inside. "And?"

"And I really like that about you." He quickly took off the elastic strap holding the sleeping bag together and flipped the bag neatly onto the seat, fur side up.

She was pleasantly surprised that he was willing and eager to fall in with her plans. She wouldn't have guessed it judging from their interactions over the past five years. But as of this weekend, her picture of him had totally changed.

"Let me get in first." She handed him the condom.

"I figured." His voice was husky with excitement. "You're the one who went bonkers over the fur."

"When I was a teenager I had furry seat covers on my car." She climbed into the backseat and immediately pulled off her sweatshirt. The cool air hitting her breasts made her nipples tighten. She was already loving this concept.

He leaned down and draped one arm over the open door as he peered inside. "So you've done this before?"

"No. I wanted to, but I didn't trust high school boys to be careful about the pregnancy thing." She kicked off her shoes and shimmied out of her sweatpants. "You're bringing out all my repressed fantasies."

"I'm flattered. Unfortunately, I've never done this."

"Never? I thought all boys tried it at least once." She adjusted the sleeping bag on the seat.

"What can I say? I'm a late bloomer."

"Well, you sure did blossom nicely." She leaned back against the fur and pretended she was an Indian maiden about to be ravished by the local bad-boy warrior. "You're willing to give this a try, though, right?"

"*Oh* yeah." He climbed into the car and closed the door with a soft click. Then he handed her the condom. "Hold on to that."

She wondered if bad-boy warriors carried condoms. Probably not, but she didn't mind an anachronism or two. "This time I promise not to hide it between my thighs."

"I recommend holding it between your teeth." He took his PDA from his shirt pocket and laid it in the back window.

"I might need my mouth for other things. I'll put it up in the back window next to your PDA." Scooching over to make room for him to sit, Zoe realized how small the space truly was. "This might be trickier than I thought."

"I suppose about now you're wishing I'd stuck with the Town Car." He laid his glasses beside the PDA and started unbuttoning his shirt.

"Actually, no. I've changed my mind about that." The longer they were closed in here together, the more she liked it, even though the logistics would be challenging. He was right within touching distance. She ran a finger down the ridge of his spine.

He shivered. "Mm, nice." He pulled off his shoes without untying the laces. "What's that about changing your mind?"

"I think you should have whatever car suits your personality."

"I'm thinking about a red Ferrari." He unzipped his pants.

"You're not!"

"I am." Because he hadn't put on his belt when they'd left for the Sasquatch hunt, all he had to do was wiggle out of his pants. That left him wearing his briefs, and those disappeared within seconds, too. "Where's the condom?"

"Here." She handed it to him. Although he was close enough for her to put it on, she wanted to watch him do it, and he was right at eye level. But she acted as though she weren't watching, in case she made him self-conscious. "A Ferrari?"

"Yeah."

Moisture pooled in her mouth as he rolled the condom down over his penis. If she had a video of that, she'd put it on a continuous loop. Oh, baby.

He completed the job with a snap of latex. Then he glanced down at her. "This could take some maneuvering."

"How about if you kneel here, between my legs?" She squirmed with eagerness as she guided him to the right position and flopped back on the furry surface. Squirming felt so good while she was lying on soft fur.

"I think I get the idea." He leaned forward, bracing his arms on either side of her head. Dipping down, he nibbled on her lips. "Wasn't this one of the gold medal moves in gymnastics?"

"Want to give up?" She didn't think so. Judging from the musky scent of male arousal, he was as excited about this prospect as she was. Pheromones swirled through the interior of the little car.

"Hell, no. I'm almost there. At least I think I am. I can't see a damned thing."

"Leave the rest to me." She had no trouble finding his condom-covered penis. It was the most rigid thing within reach. When she took hold, he gasped. "Don't worry," she said. "I've got you."

"It better be you. I hear there are raccoons in these woods."

"It's me." She lifted her hips and reached for her sweatshirt on the floor. Once she bunched it under her, she was tilted at the perfect angle. Plus she was ultra-wet and ready to go. She made sure he was pointed in the right direction. "Rock forward."

"I thought you'd never ask." He pushed in slowly at first, and then with more confidence. "Not bad. Not bad at all."

"I would agree. I'd go so far as to say it's very good."

"That's nice to know." He eased back and shoved home again.

She felt the beginnings of an orgasm, one of those Flynn-inspired world-changing orgasms.

"I'm guessing we shouldn't make too much noise out here."

Although she loved making noise, especially with him, she decided he was right. It was, after all, the middle of the night, and Bigfoot had recently made an appearance. She didn't want Bigfoot hunters to mistake the sounds and come to investigate.

"Guess not," she said. "But if I don't make noise, how will you know when I'm—"

"Believe me, I'll know." He began to pump, slowly at first, and then with more speed. "I can feel when it happens."

"Good." His rhythm made her think of a well-oiled machine, which made her think of expensive cars, which made her think of . . . "A Ferrari?"

"Uh-huh." He stroked faster. "Not a Town Car. That's stodgy. A Ferrari."

"Amazing." She wasn't talking about the car anymore. She was too busy being swept away by the pleasure he was giving her with both barrels.

"Don't you think . . . it fits?"

Everything fit. Him with her. Her with him. "You betcha." As she felt the waves of another glorious climax roll over her, a climax he had engineered, she wondered if even a Ferrari was good enough for this incredible man.

I can't bleepin' believe this. I get all my ducks in a row, everything arranged for the big moment, and these two sex maniacs are horizontal in the rental. Or mostly horizontal. I can see Flynn's feet sticking up, which guarantees that his johnson is sticking somewhere else, and we all know where that is, don't we, boys and girls?

Why in hell aren't they zonked out in the bedroom? Or at least porking each other in that bed, oblivious to everything? Their timing sucks dead donkeys. They're going to ruin everything unless they get back in that bedroom pronto. I should go over there and open the door, give them a freaking heart attack.

On second thought, they'd never notice, not the way that car's rockin' and rollin'. He's giving it to her good all right. I can guarantee little miss movie queen has no clue how to make the most of it, though. It's all in the hips. I might come just thinking about it.

Hallelujah, the car's rocking harder. Hey, dummies, could you come a little faster? Then get your butts back in the house where they belong. If you make it quick, I'll have a little surprise waiting for you.

Once Flynn felt Zoe pulsing around him, he gave himself up to the demands of his own climax. When he came, he had to clench his jaw to keep from bellowing out his satisfaction.

The blood roared in his ears, and the world seemed to crash down around him. He imagined planets colliding, volcanoes erupting, earthquakes . . . wait a minute. Something big really *had* crashed to the ground. The sound was still echoing in his ears.

Beneath him, Zoe tensed. "What was that?"

"I don't know." Flynn pulled himself from his orgasm-induced lethargy. And this time he'd planned to finish the episode with all the cuddling and sweet talk Zoe could handle. So much for that idea. "I think we'd better find out."

"It isn't Bigfoot. No smell."

"Right." As he carefully disentangled himself from Zoe, he got a quick course in the shortcomings of car sex. He'd had heaps of fun, but now he was bare-assed and vulnerable while something unknown had made a really loud noise outside in the woods.

And he had condom issues. Because he wasn't about to leave a used condom in a rental car, he was forced to litter. And he had to roll down the car window to do it.

Rolling down the window right after something had crashed in the woods didn't seem wise. He remembered the old story about high school kids making out in parked cars while a guy with a hook for a hand prowled the night.

He rolled up the window quickly and reached for his clothes.

"Move over a little," Zoe said, "so I can get dressed, too."

He scooted to one side as he struggled into his briefs. "I think you should stay here with the doors locked until I find out what this is all about."

"Guess again."

"No, really." He shoved one leg into his pants. "I'd feel better investigating if I didn't have to worry about whether you were safe."

"Forget it, Flynn." She paused. "Or is there another reason you don't want me out there?"

"Like what?" He lifted his hips long enough to quickly pull his pants up. Now he knew why he didn't camp. Getting dressed in confined spaces was a real pain. He leaned back so he could zip his fly.

"Maybe you think it's Kristen and you want to deal with her alone."

He stopped in mid-zip. He'd forgotten all about Kristen. Although he wasn't wearing his watch, he had to guess it was well after midnight. "That crash we heard has nothing to do with Kristen." He said it with conviction, zipping his fly for emphasis. He hoped it was true. In the middle of the night after a recent Bigfoot sighting, anything seemed possible.

"Then I'm going with you." Zoe popped her sweatshirt over her head. "If it's a bear, two people will be more likely to scare it off than one."

He hoped to God it wasn't a bear. He'd heard that they could become used to people food and invade cabins to get it. Sometimes if they couldn't get people food they had to settle for just plain people. Flynn would like to skip that situation altogether.

As he untied his shoelaces, he marveled that he'd put shoes on without socks to hunt for Bigfoot and pulled them off still tied in order to have sex with Zoe. Apparently some sea change was going on inside him. Maybe he really would get that Ferrari.

Finally he was dressed with his glasses on and his PDA tucked in his shirt pocket. He was ready. Scared, but ready. He turned to Zoe. "What can I do to convince you to stay in the car?"

"Nothing. I'm going." She reached for the door handle on her side.

"All right. But keep close." He opened his door at the same time she opened hers, so at least she wouldn't get the jump on him. If he ended up hanging out with Zoe on a regular basis, and who knew if that would happen, he'd have to get used to the fact that caution wasn't in her vocabulary.

Until this weekend, it had been a favorite part of his. And what had that gotten him? A lucrative career but the wrong girlfriend. Apparently he couldn't use the same criteria in picking a wife that he'd used in building his law practice. Lesson learned.

Zoe started toward the cabin. "I think the sound came from behind the cabin."

"Hold it." He caught her arm. "Not so fast. Let's approach slowly until we know what we're dealing with."

"But if it's a bear, we should make a lot of noise so maybe we'll scare it away."

He had to admit she had a point. "Okay, slow approach, with lots of noise. Hey, you! Whoever's back there, we're coming around! And we're big, and mean, and we have . . . weapons!"

"And one of us in this group thinks you speak English! Don't mind him! He's seen *Brother Bear* once too often!"

Flynn glanced at her. "You're very loud, you know that?"

She took a deep breath and belted out another line. "I'm projecting! That's what actors do!"

"I hope it works. Mostly I hope we don't find a—" He stopped and stared at the cabin. "I know what made the noise."

"What?" She glanced around. "I don't see anything."

"Look at the roofline. See anything unusual about it?"

She glanced up. "Oh . . . my . . . God. A tree fell on the cabin."

"A big tree." Flynn kept looking, thinking maybe the scene would dissolve and he'd wake up, but nothing changed. A huge branch sprouted from the roof, and the rest of the tree had obviously crushed the back end of the cabin.

Zoe swallowed. "This could put a real dent in my damage deposit."

"Let's go see what it looks like from the back." But Flynn already had a hunch what the back would look like. Sure enough, the bedroom where they would have been sleeping if they hadn't been having car sex was demolished. The trunk lying in the midst of the rubble was as thick as an oil drum.

When Zoe saw the crushed bedroom, she put her hand to her mouth.

Flynn stepped closer and wrapped his arm around her. "I'm really glad you decided we should have sex in the car."

Zoe began to tremble. "Do . . . do you think . . . it was an accident?"

"Wouldn't be hard to find out. Let's go see what the bottom of it looks like." He kept his arm around her shoulders as they followed the line of the trunk to the base of the giant tree.

Sometime, certainly not tonight or they would have heard it, the tree had been sawed three-quarters of the way through. After that, a couple of well-placed shims and some solid blows from a sledgehammer would have been enough to send it toppling straight for Zoe's bedroom.

Flynn's blood ran cold. This was no spur-of-the-minute prank. It had taken advance planning. And if he and Zoe hadn't been in the car a few minutes ago, they might both be dead.

Chapter Twenty-Five

Okay, now I'm pissed." The more Zoe looked at that sawed-off tree trunk, the madder she got. All she'd wanted was a quiet weekend to prepare for her upcoming audition. "I don't know if this is the work of your girl-friend or some other nutcase, but I'm—"

"Kristen sure as hell didn't cut down this tree!"

Zoe faced him, ready to battle with somebody. He was handy. Too bad it was so dark out. A good fight was best conducted under full-spectrum lighting. "She could have hired it done, and don't tell me she couldn't."

His jaw worked. "Of course it's possible, but she's not that kind of person. She's not a *nutcase,* as you put it."

"How do I know that? She's the only one with a motive, Flynn. Exactly how long have you known her, anyway?"

"Just a year, but that doesn't mean I don't know what kind of person—"

"Only a year?" She crossed her arms. "And pray tell, how much of that was face-to-face?"

"Several weekends' worth. But it doesn't matter." His mouth thinned into a mutinous line. "We've been in constant communication."

"Yeah, with e-mail and phone calls, am I right? And there's an important element missing there, something that is an actor's stock-in-trade. It's called body language. Without that, you have no idea what people are really thinking."

"My friend Josh likes her!"

"Bully for your friend Josh. Did he grow up with her? Work with her for years? What's the basis of this friendship?"

"He . . . he met her when she was hired last summer. But he's a great judge of character. If there was something off about Kristen he would have picked up on it."

She rocked back on her heels. "I'm sorry, Flynn. That's not good enough. We have a situation here and the finger points at Kristen. I don't think either you or your friend Josh knows her well enough to vouch for her character."

"I know her as well as I know you!"

She glared at him. "Oh yeah? How many Bigfoot hunts has she been on with you? How many times has she risked her body in the interests of your particular passion for Sasquatch? We are bonded, buddy!"

He glared back at her, his mouth clamped tight in rebellion. Then, slowly, his mouth widened into a grin that became a chuckle and finally morphed into a full-blown laugh. "I guess we are."

She blew out a breath. "You're not supposed to laugh. We're fighting here."

"You're fighting. I'm laughing."

"I feel like punching something."

He kept smiling at her. "Want to punch me?"

"I can't. You're too happy. Besides, I don't believe in violence."

"Good. Me, either."

"Flynn, you have to admit Kristen's a suspect. She had advance notice of us coming here. Plus I know she's smart or you wouldn't be dating her."

"Sure she's smart." His tone was reasonable. "That doesn't automatically incriminate her."

Zoe couldn't very well yell at a man who sounded so civilized, so she lowered her voice. "But she's capable of organizing all of these incidents."

"She could have, but she didn't."

"Are you absolutely positive? You're the logic guy. Somebody's been doing this, and we can rule out Bigfoot, who couldn't do anything without leaving a trail of stink behind. It could be someone local, but they don't know who I am, so that makes no sense. Logically, Kristen's the most likely person."

Flynn rubbed the back of his neck. "I admit it looks bad, but I'm telling you, she didn't do it." He gazed at her in silence. Finally he sighed. "What do you want to do? Call the police? Have me try to get in touch with Kristen?"

His resigned expression eliminated the last of her anger. He was in a terrible position. Because of her, his romance with Kristen was in shambles, and now Kristen looked like the prime suspect for the "accidents" that had taken place since they'd arrived. Although Flynn needed to know if his potential bride was a psycho stalker, Zoe didn't much like her own role in the drama.

Calling the police, or whatever law enforcement agency held sway in Long Shaft, could be a nightmare. Of course she'd have to report the damage to the cabin eventually, but if they dialed 911 right now the media would come running. She could read the tabloid headlines—*Zoe Tarleton Almost Killed by Falling Tree! Lover's Girlfriend Implicated!*

No, thanks. There had to be another way out of this mess. But having Flynn call Kristen seemed like asking for trouble, too. Even if she wasn't the person who'd masterminded everything, she was an upset woman about to become an ex-girlfriend. If Flynn contacted her, the rodeo could start.

"I don't want you to call Kristen," she said.

"I don't want to, either. Confrontations don't go well at two A.M."

"Is that what time you think it is? I've lost all track."

Flynn pulled out his PDA and flipped it open. "It's two fifty-five. So what about the police? Even if nobody intended to harm you, we have evidence of intentional property damage."

"I know, but I don't want to call the police, either. If we could keep the lid on until we can get out of here tomorrow, that would be my choice."

He returned his PDA to his shirt pocket. "And in the meantime?"

She wished they could get back to having sex, but she didn't think they could afford the luxury. Vigilance was required, now that someone might actually be trying to snuff her out. "If the kitchen's still in operating condition, I think we need to make some coffee and eat some food. Even if the tree hadn't smashed my bed, I don't think I could sleep now."

"Zoe, if you're tired, I'll stand guard. You can sleep in my bed."

That earnest offer took care of whatever resentment she had left. It wasn't his fault that his girlfriend was going off the deep end. Well, it sort of was his fault for telling her where he'd be and then making her jealous, but Zoe had to share some of that blame.

In any case, Kristen's reaction was way out of proportion. Screaming and hurling insults was one thing. Arranging to have a giant tree land on top of your rival was a whole different ball game.

"I don't want to sleep," she said. "But I know exactly what we can do."

"Zoe, I don't think we can chance that, much as I'd love it. Once we get involved, we're lost to the world. We have to stay alert."

She stepped forward and cupped his lovable face in both hands. His chin was prickly with the beginnings of his beard, and she wondered what it would be like to wake up together every morning. The idea appealed to her. A lot.

"I agree that we have to stay alert," she said. "I wasn't talking about sex, although it's really nice that you assumed I was."

"You're probably not as fixated on it as I am."

"I might be more fixated than you." She stood on tiptoe and kissed him. The privilege of doing that might be coming to an end soon, so she needed to take advantage of the opportunity. "I've loved every minute of having sex with you. But now I think we need to concentrate on something else."

"What's that?"

"The script."

Before starting on the cooking and script-reading program, Flynn suggested they at least survey the damage. He didn't mention that the condoms were probably buried under a shower of pine needles, because he wasn't supposed to be needing them anymore. Still, he thought about them.

Taking Zoe's hand, he walked with her to the front porch, and together they climbed the steps. Inside the front door, nothing seemed wrong with the cabin. Flynn switched on a lamp and the room looked exactly as it had before.

But once they headed down the hall, everything changed. Where the roof had been, stars shone through, and the end of the hallway was nothing but a mass of tangled branches. Ironically, the house smelled like Christmas.

To say that Flynn deeply regretted telling Kristen his whereabouts this weekend would be a gross understatement. What had he been thinking? No woman would take that kind of news well, and on top of it, Kristen's worst fears had come true. He was now in love with Zoe.

Even so, he couldn't believe that Kristen, who had graduated magna cum laude from Columbia, would plot to seriously maim or even kill her perceived rival. He'd never felt that kind of intensity from her. She was a cautious person, or at least he'd perceived her that way.

Maybe he'd been wrong about her, though. Zoe had made a good point. He didn't know her all that well. If she'd actually hired someone to create havoc, she should be jailed or hospitalized.

And if she wasn't the culprit, who was? Flynn knew he should be solving this riddle with his usual mental dexterity, but lack of sleep, and mind-blowing sex, had eroded his usual capabilities. All he really wanted to do was cuddle with Zoe in her queen-size bed and then make love to her some more.

Unfortunately, as they discovered upon peering through the branches blocking their way, the bed had been reduced to rubble. Not only had Flynn lost a pair of socks and the box of condoms, but the tree could have destroyed everything Zoe had brought on this trip, with the exception of the script, which she'd left in the living room.

He put a comforting arm around her shoulders. "I'm sorry. You're pretty much wiped out."

"Yep. No loss on my nerd clothes, but my cell phone's buried under that mess. And then there's the essential stuff—soap, whitening toothpaste, mouthwash, toothbrush, deodorant, shampoo, conditioner, blow-dryer, styling brush, hair gel, exfoliant, night cream, body lotion, sunscreen, makeup, nail polish remover, cuticle cream, eye cream." She tapped her finger against her chin. "I know I'm forgetting something."

"You're welcome to share any of my stuff."

She looked skeptical. "And what kind of selection would you have?"

"Shampoo, toothbrush, toothpaste, and deodorant, mostly. A razor and some Aqua Velva."

"I love the Aqua Velva on you, but I think I'll pass on sharing it. That would be too weird. No blow-dryer?"

"Sorry." He wished he could be of more help. "I'd let you use my razor on your legs, but I'm guessing you do the waxing thing."

She smiled up at him. "And what makes you think that?"

"Well, it stands to reason that if you wax your . . . um . . ." He realized that he was venturing into a discussion they shouldn't be having.

First of all, he couldn't pull it off. Maybe after he'd been driving a red Ferrari for a while he could talk about Brazilian wax jobs with panache, but he wasn't there yet. And second of all, any reference to this topic would only remind both of them of the fun times they'd had with oral sex.

"You are so sweet and sexy. I could just eat you up."

And didn't he wish she would. "Let's not go there, okay?"

She laughed, took him by the arm, and pulled him toward the kitchen. "I can't help thinking about that topic and neither can you. But we won't act on it. I'm not about to let some stalker catch me with my pants down."

Zoe had eaten worse meals than the microwave dinners Flynn had bought, but not many. She was grateful for the energy the food gave her, though, and it turned out that Flynn made excellent coffee. She felt fueled up and ready to tackle the script again.

"Let's skip to a scene near the end," she said.

Flynn sat beside her on the sofa. "Good idea. We need to avoid the heavy-breathing scenes for now."

"Exactly." Zoe flipped through the pages. "To sum up, Tony and Vera have decided to destroy the formula because the company wants to rush the pill to market without enough testing."

"Good for them."

Zoe glanced up from the script. "It kills both their careers, though."

"That's okay. They did the right thing."

"Yeah, I thought so, too. When I read the treatment I liked the way it ended." She returned her attention to the scene. "So Vera has to leave the country and take on a different identity, which Tony helped her with. This is their good-bye scene. I have the first line." She cleared her throat.

VERA

So this is it.

TONY

Guess so. What are you going to do once you get to Chile?

Vera laughs, trying to keep the mood light.

VERA

Probably wait tables. I'll survive. I'm more worried about you.

TONY

Ah, I'll be fine. I'll wait tables, too, if it comes to that. Anyway, you take care of yourself. Send me a postcard.

VERA

I will.

TONY

I'd kiss you good-bye, but that would be a sappy Holly-wood ending. You're not into that sappy stuff.

VERA

No, of course not.

TONY

Me, either.

VERA

You'd actually wait tables?

TONY

Sure, why not? It's good honest work.

VERA

Okay, then I have a really, really stupid idea. I'm sure you won't like it.

TONY

Lay it on me, sweetheart.

VERA

I was thinking that . . . maybe we . . . maybe we should wait tables together. But you'd probably hate Chile.

TONY

I like the food. Why wouldn't I like the country?

VERA

Really?

TONY

Why not? Besides, you'll need me to supplement your income. I'd make more money than you.

VERA

What makes you think that?

TONY

I'd wear tight pants and get bigger tips. You have that flat-chested problem to deal with.

Vera makes a face.

VERA

Maybe I don't want you coming down to Chile after all.

TONY

Yeah, you do, because you happen to love me.

VERA

I never said that!

TONY

If you don't love me, what are you doing inviting me down to Chile to wait tables with you?

VERA

I just thought—

TONY

Be quiet, Vera. You know you love me, and I love you, including your flat chest. In fact, I'm crazy about your flat chest, and your skinny legs, and your juicy—

VERA

Tony! We're in a public place!

TONY

Doesn't bother me a bit.

VERA

You're making a scene.

TONY

You're lucky I don't throw you down right here. That's how much you flip my switches, baby.

VERA

I . . . do?

TONY

Damn straight. So brace yourself, doll-face, 'cause I'm
about to plant one on you, sappy ending or not.

Zoe sat very still after Flynn finished reading the last
line. He'd done a terrific job. They were lines he was supposed to read, lines she'd asked him to read, so why
should she give them any significance?

Even so, her heart was pounding as if the words had
meaning beyond the script. She kept hearing him say *I
love you* in that deep, resonating way that sounded so sincere. But maybe her coaching had transformed him into a
convincing actor.

"How did I do?" he asked.

"Great." Her voice came out raspy, so she cleared her
throat and tried again. "Really good." She still didn't dare
look at him for fear her emotions would be written all
over her face. "Did I sound nerdy enough?"

"You needed to be a little more hesitant and awkward
when you invited him to wait tables with you. Vera doesn't
know how to be seductive. You'll have to work hard to
keep that sexual invitation out of your voice." He sounded
very matter-of-fact. Not emotionally involved at all.

All right. Apparently reading the scene hadn't affected
him the way it had affected her. "Then let me try that line
again."

"As long as you're doing that, you might as well do the
we're in a public place line again, because it could use
more indignation. Even if they've had sex, she's not prepared to put on a display."

"Then maybe we should redo the whole scene."

"Fine with me." He shifted slightly on the sofa.

She wondered if he'd intentionally moved closer or if the fact that their hips were touching was an accident. She didn't move away. If they read through the scene again, he'd be saying those words of love one more time, and she wanted to hear them again, even if they were meaningless to him.

"Okay then," she said. "Let's take it from the top."

About two lines into the scene, she became aware of the warmth generated where their bodies touched. She tried to ignore it as she concentrated on acting like a nerd instead of the hot leading lady she was normally. After she delivered the line, Flynn didn't stop her, so she assumed she'd done a better job.

Then they came to his *I love you* line. He read it smoothly, without a hitch, and with exactly the right emotional depth. Much as she tried to downplay the effect, the words sang in her head. She forgot to read her next line.

"Zoe? You're up."

"Oh! Right." She delivered the line, hoping she put in enough indignation. They continued reading through to the end.

"You need one more run-through," Flynn said. "To solidify it."

The combination of his body heat and his voice seduced her more than she could let him know. Add in words of love, and she would be a puddle in no time. "Maybe we should try another scene instead."

"No, I think this one's good."

Smiling, she glanced over at him. "Since when did you become the expert on which scenes to read?"

He shrugged, which jiggled his body against hers

enough to ignite some serious fires. "I'm not. I just like this scene."

"Why?"

His gaze was even warmer than his body. "I just do."

Shivers of delight ran through her. Possibly, just possibly, he was sending her a subtle signal, the only signal he felt capable of right now. They'd been lovers a very short time and he had a girlfriend to deal with.

Under those circumstances, a man like Flynn would want to proceed carefully before he blurted out anything significant. But if he should have the opportunity to send a coded message through something like this script, then he might do it. What an electrifying concept.

"Then I guess we should go over it again," she said.

His gaze locked with hers. "As many times as it takes."

Chapter Twenty-Six

Flynn hoped Zoe was receiving what he was putting out there. In trying to avoid a sexually charged scene, she'd managed to find an emotionally charged one. He knew it was too soon to say straight out that he loved her. But Tony could say it to Vera. That appealed to him.

So he'd delivered the line with as much feeling as he dared. Then he'd used his job as nerd coach to convince her they should go over it again. And again. Each time Tony said *I love you* to Vera, the air seemed to vibrate. Flynn thought Zoe might be getting the message, because her cheeks turned very pink and her eyes sparkled.

How he'd love to kiss her right now, but they didn't dare start that routine with the back of the house open to the night and some weirdo playing dangerous games. So he had to be content with reading the final scene in the script and sitting close enough to Zoe that he could feel her breathing.

What a cozy situation. Flynn imagined what life

would be like if he could sit like this with Zoe every night for the next fifty or sixty years. Sounded like a great deal to him, but he couldn't speak for Zoe. Too bad the last scene in the script didn't give her a chance to say how she felt about him through Vera the way he was using Tony's dialogue.

After they'd finished a fourth go-round on the scene, Flynn decided he couldn't keep making her go over lines that she'd delivered perfectly. "That was excellent," he said.

"Thank you." She leaned her head against the sofa. "I need more coffee. I'm starting to get sleepy."

"Forget the coffee. Put your feet up and go to sleep. I'll make sure we don't get any nasty surprises."

She turned her head to look at him. "That doesn't seem fair. You must be as zonked as I am."

"I don't really need that much sleep."

"Man, I do. Eight hours is the bare minimum for me."

He stretched an arm across the back of the sofa. "Then lean on me and get some rest. We still don't know what we'll have to deal with tomorrow."

"I'll feel guilty."

"Don't. Come on. I'm not the least bit sleepy." That wasn't quite true, but he liked the idea of sacrificing himself a little. He didn't think the stalker was his fault, but he wasn't a hundred percent sure. Besides, having Zoe trust him to keep watch seemed significant somehow.

"If you insist." She kicked off her shoes and swung her feet up on the sofa. Then she nestled against him. "If I weren't so tired, this would turn me on."

Flynn wrapped his arm around her, careful to tuck it under her breasts and not make arm-to-breast contact.

This close proximity was bad enough, but if he got involved with breast contact, he'd be in trouble. "You'd think we'd have had enough sex by now."

Zoe yawned. "I'm beginning to think that with you and me, there's no such thing."

"Yeah, me, too. I've never been in such a constant state of arousal." He expected some sort of comeback. When she said nothing, he leaned closer. "Zoe?"

Her steady breathing was the only sound he heard. Just that fast, she'd fallen asleep. His heart expanded with the knowledge that she trusted him enough to fall asleep in the face of whatever danger lurked in the darkness. He wouldn't betray that trust, either.

About a half hour later he thought he heard something outside the cabin. He tensed, waiting to see if it was an animal scurrying by or something more ominous. After a while the noise stopped. When several minutes went by and nothing had happened, he began to relax. No one would harm Zoe while he was on guard. No one.

He laid his cheek against her hair. Now that she was fully asleep, he could say anything he wanted. There was only one thing on his mind. "I love you, Zoe," he murmured.

Zoe woke up when a cell phone rang. The sound brought her straight out of an erotic dream about Flynn and into sharp contact with his chin. "Ouch! Sorry!"

"Me, too. That's my cell. I left it in my bedroom."

She sat up and rubbed the sleep from her eyes. "You'd better get it."

"Yeah." He pushed himself off the sofa and walked stiffly into the bedroom.

Zoe peered out through the cabin's front windows and noticed early-morning sunlight filtering through the trees and gilding the porch railing. Their long eventful night was over, and their long eventful day was about to begin. She assumed Kristen was on the phone.

When Flynn returned, the phone still in one hand and his shoulders slumped, she took that as a sure sign he'd been talking to his girlfriend. "What did she say?"

"She found a Bigfoot costume in a bag in Jeff's closet."

"Huh?" Her thoughts screeched to a stop and made an abrupt U-turn. This woman was way more squirrelly than she'd ever imagined. "What the hell was Kristen doing in Jeff's closet?" And where was a can of Mace when she needed it?

"Not Kristen. Luanne."

"Oh!" Now the comment made sense, and she understood why Flynn looked so unhappy. His Bigfoot sighting had been trashed. "When did she find it?"

"Around midnight." He sighed. "She timed the search for after her parents went to bed and before Jeff got home from his date. She would have called us, but she didn't want to interrupt anything."

His disappointment became her disappointment. No matter how the weekend would ultimately turn out, she'd felt good knowing he'd had a Bigfoot experience. Now that had been taken away.

She stood and walked over to him. "Listen, maybe it wasn't Jeff we saw last night. What she found could be a Halloween costume, right? And besides, how would he make the noises and the smell? That was all darned realistic."

"He had a tape recorder tucked in with the costume. Luanne turned the volume way down and closed herself in the closet so she could check out the tape. Sure enough, it was screeches and howls."

"Damn it."

"As for the smell, she said his gym socks would have done the trick, but she found a recipe for making stink bombs in the bag with the costume. She didn't try the recipe, but she's sure it would work great."

Yesterday Luanne's cleverness had intrigued and fascinated Zoe. Today she wished the girl were a little on the slow side. Then Flynn could have gone home thinking he'd achieved a lifelong dream and Jeff could have continued playing Bigfoot for the tourists.

"I'm really sorry," she said. "I suppose she's going to tell on him. I've never had a big brother, but that seems like what little sisters live for."

"She hasn't told anybody except me, and I asked her to keep quiet. I think Jeff's having fun with this, but he might also figure it'll help the town. He shouldn't be ridiculed for trying to help, but if she blows his cover, he might be."

Zoe stepped closer and wound her arms around his neck. "That was thoughtful. Considering how he messed with your head, you could feel like getting revenge."

"Nah." Still holding his cell phone, Flynn looped his arms around her waist. "He's just a kid. He sure had me fooled, though. I was ready to believe."

"Don't forget that he's fooled a bunch of other people, too. Margo, for one." Then Zoe remembered something. "Wait a minute. Margo said she'd seen a whole family. How could Jeff pull that off?"

"I don't know. Maybe he walked on his knees to look like the baby. His natural size would be about right for a female, and then he could use lifts and an extension of the head part when he was supposed to be the male."

Zoe wasn't buying it. "That seems like more work than the average eighteen-year-old would put into it. I can imagine him running around in a costume once in a while. I can imagine him putting together the tape and the stink bombs. But trying to imitate different sizes and genders? Uh-uh."

"Maybe Margo has a good imagination."

"Or maybe there really is a Bigfoot family out there and Jeff is like an auxiliary Bigfoot."

He smiled. "You're just trying to make me feel better. I appreciate that, but it's okay. I'm a grown-up. I can deal."

"I'm *not* just trying to make you feel better." Although she was. "Margo was very convincing when she was describing her sightings."

"And they're her claim to fame in Long Shaft, right? I saw her picture on the wall in the diner along with the record of her Bigfoot sightings. The woman has no life, Zoe. I know she's your friend, but I can easily believe that she'd make up a Sasquatch family to get some recognition."

Zoe leaned her head against his chest. "Me, too. But I would like to think she really saw Bigfoot, for your sake. And hers."

"Thanks." He rubbed her back. "Um, Luanne mentioned something else on the phone."

"Let me guess." She felt the imprint of something hard against her forehead and realized it was the PDA in Flynn's shirt pocket. His devotion to that thing really touched her. "She begged to come over right now instead of waiting until ten o'clock. But we can't let her. She'd freak about the tree."

"I know, but she's going to be hard to put off. She's figured out that you're Zoe Tarleton."

Zoe's head came up with a snap. "Yikes." She looked into Flynn's eyes. "My fault. You warned me she'd work it out after I told her I like brainy guys."

"Yeah, that was the wrong thing to say. I still don't understand why you did."

"Because . . ." She wondered how much to reveal. "Luanne was focusing on the guys I've gone with in the past, and I didn't want you to think . . . that I wouldn't be interested in . . . someone like you."

His eyes darkened. "Are you saying that you could be interested in someone like me?"

"It's possible." Her heart raced as she thought of the implications of what she was saying. She was skirting close to a declaration, which scared her. He might not feel the same. In the dark of night and the heat of sex, people could think one way. In the morning they could think a whole different way.

He cleared his throat. "Interesting."

Talk about noncommittal. But she didn't blame him. The stakes were pretty high. "The thing is, I don't know if someone like you could be interested in someone like me."

"It's possible."

Her tummy gave a little leap. Maybe she should simply take the plunge. "Flynn, I—" The kitchen phone rang, cutting her off. And maybe that was for the best. They should probably table this discussion until after he'd dealt with Kristen.

Zoe slipped out of his arms. "I'll get that. It's probably Margo with news about Kristen's whereabouts."

"Just so you know," Flynn called after her, "Luanne said she'd keep her mouth shut on one condition."

"Yeah, and what's her price?"

"She wants to be invited for a sleepover at your house in Malibu. I'm supposed to call her back after I talk to you."

Zoe laughed. Only an eleven-year-old girl would settle for a sleepover. "You can promise her the sleepover. Just keep her from showing up here today." She picked up the phone. "Hello?"

"Zoe, it's Margo. Are you okay? When you took so long to answer, I started hyperventilating. I've been worried sick now that Kristen is in town."

Zoe was determined not to fall in with Margo's love of melodrama. "We're okay, but the cabin isn't in such great shape."

"Omigod. What happened?"

"A tree fell on it." She decided not to mention right away that it didn't look like an accident.

"Oh no! On the cabin? What part?"

"The master bedroom and bath got the worst of it."

"And you weren't hurt? Zoe, you could have been *killed.*"

She was trying not to think about that. "Maybe. Fortunately, Flynn and I were outside at the time."

"Whew, that is so scary. I wonder if it was on purpose."

"I . . . um . . . maybe."

"It was! Did you call anybody, like the police or the fire department?"

"I suppose we should have, and we will before we leave, but I don't dare call the cops while I'm still here. It would end up in the papers."

"I understand," Margo said. "But I'm really afraid this Kristen person is out to get you. Now that I've heard about this, I'm glad I did what I did."

Zoe told herself not to panic, but visions of knife-wielding maniacs danced in her brain. "What did you do, Margo?"

"Fifteen minutes ago, I went to the Bigfoot Motel and talked to her."

"Margo!" Zoe could imagine how Flynn would react to that news. "What in God's name did you say?"

"I told her that it looked like someone was out to get Zoe Tarleton, and that because she had a motive for that, she was being watched. I said I was your friend and she'd better not do anything to you, or she'd have to answer to me."

Zoe groaned. "I appreciate the sentiment, but we don't know that Kristen's involved in any of this."

"You're too trusting. You always have been. What would you say if I told you she's been in touch with Trace?"

"*What?*"

"You heard me. She used some connections she had and got his private number. She found out that he didn't know about this trip."

Zoe's stomach began to churn. If Kristen had gone so far as to get Trace's number, she certainly could have arranged a few accidents, too. And now Trace knew about this weekend and he'd be pissed that she hadn't told him.

"Kristen's weird, Zoe. No telling what she's up to. I'm glad I said something to her. Maybe she'll think twice now."

"Did she say anything more about Trace?"

"Just that Trace didn't seem happy about you and Flynn spending the weekend together."

"I'm sure he isn't. Listen, Margo, I need to go. I should talk to Flynn." Then she had to decide whether to call Trace or wait until she got back to LA.

"Which reminds me," Margo said. "Kristen wants Flynn

to come to the motel to talk. She's in room fifteen. I said I'd pass the message along."

"If she's skilled enough to get Trace's private number, she could easily find out where the cabin is. She could come here herself."

"Unless she'd rather not see him with you around."

Zoe sighed. "Good point."

"When he goes, I think he should be careful, but as long as they stay out in the open, he should be okay."

Zoe shivered. "You really think she might get violent with him?"

"Who knows? Oh, I almost forgot. She's also been in communication with Jeff."

"Jeff?" Panic became a real possibility. If Jeff was involved . . .

"She had some story about wanting to get Flynn a Bigfoot souvenir as a joke, but I think there's more to it. Flynn needs to check out what's going on."

"I'll tell him she wants to see him." Zoe wasn't crazy about the idea of Flynn going to the motel, but he would probably want to. She'd make him promise to have the conversation outside, not in the room.

"I think he should go right away, before she has a chance to pull anything else. Or do damage to herself."

"I'm sure he'll want to do that. Thanks, Margo."

"Let me know how it goes, okay?"

"Sure. Talk to you soon." Zoe hung up the phone and turned. Flynn was standing in the kitchen doorway. "Margo went to see Kristen at the motel."

He frowned. "Shit."

"I knew you wouldn't like it. But Flynn, Kristen's been in touch with Trace." Zoe discovered she was trembling.

She wrapped her arms about her middle to steady herself.

"How?"

"According to Margo, she pulled in some favors and tracked down his private number so she could find out what he knew about this weekend."

Flynn looked shaken. As he adjusted the position of his glasses, his hand quivered. "I . . . wouldn't have thought she'd do something like that."

"But she did. That took some real effort, and some ingenuity. And she also contacted Jeff."

"That's crazy! Why would she . . ." His voice trailed off and he looked stricken. "He lied to his parents about where he was Friday night."

"She might have hired him. I thought the same thing."

"I hope to hell that's not the explanation."

"But you're not so sure, are you?"

He shook his head, and his gaze was haunted. "No. No, I'm not so sure."

"She wants to see you at the motel. She's in room fifteen. She asked Margo to pass on the message."

"I'll go right now." He ran a hand over his bristly chin. "I was planning to get cleaned up before I went to see her, but I think I'd better just leave."

"Do me a favor. Have the conversation out in the parking lot, not inside her room. And take your cell phone."

Flynn opened his mouth as if to say something, but then he closed it again. "Okay, I'll do that. I won't be gone long, but maybe you should start packing up. Once you're out of here, we can get the police involved."

She felt the urge to laugh, which was bizarre considering the circumstances. Maybe she was getting hysterical.

"What's wrong? What did I say?"

"You told me to start packing." She swallowed a giggle.

"So what? It's a good idea. Get a jump on it so Margo can take you back to Sacramento."

"Flynn, in order to pack up my stuff, I'd need a chain saw."

He blinked. "Oh. Right." Pausing, he took a deep breath. "I apologize, Zoe. I know an apology doesn't cut it considering everything that's happened, but I take full responsibility. If I hadn't told Kristen where I was going this weekend, none of this would have happened."

She stepped closer, until they were almost touching. "I wouldn't change a thing."

"Are you kidding? You've risked getting stung, blown to bits, and flattened. I would sure as hell think you'd like to change some of that!"

"Not if it means changing the rest of what happened." She put all the things she couldn't say into her eyes as she looked up at him.

His expression softened. "I think that would have happened without all the scary stuff."

"You never know. Change one thing, change everything. Besides, what if you hadn't found out about Kristen? What if you'd married her?"

He cupped her face in both hands. "I figured out yesterday that wasn't an option anymore."

"When yesterday?"

"After I realized that I didn't know the color of her eyes, but I had a dozen different ways to describe the color of yours."

She grew warm and shivery at his implication. "Oh."

"Yeah. Now I really need to go. I'll let her know it's over between us, and warn her that she'd better not retaliate in any way."

"Margo already said something along those lines. Long Shaft's a small town. I don't think she'll get away with anything else."

"But we need to bring an investigative team in here. If she's responsible, then she needs to be charged, along with whoever's been helping her."

"Don't tell her that." Zoe was still worried about his safety.

"I won't." His kiss was gentle. "I'll be back soon."

"Good."

With another quick kiss, he released her and walked quickly through the living room and out the door.

"Be careful!" she called after him.

"I always am!" he called back.

And she loved that about him. A girl wanted to know that a man was careful when she was about to hand him her heart.

Now that she realized that Kristen was all wrong for him and might even be a psycho stalker, Zoe didn't feel so guilty about the sex. In fact, she believed that she'd saved him, in a way. Without having sex with her, he might have married Kristen, only to find out too late that he'd hitched up with a loony.

What if they'd had kids? What if the kids had inherited the psycho gene? Yep, she'd done Flynn a huge favor. The favor had been more than returned, though, because she had a much better idea of how to tackle the nerd role, and then there was the whole sexual compatibility thing combined with a possible happily-ever-after thing. In the area of favors, she still owed him, big-time.

Because she couldn't pack, she decided to make another pot of coffee and open up the cornflakes Flynn had bought yesterday. When he got back they could each have a bowl while they discussed how to leave Long Shaft with as little fanfare as possible.

She was setting the table when she heard Margo's "hello" drift through the front door. Apparently she had decided to come over and inspect the tree damage for herself. Zoe couldn't blame her. It wasn't every day you saw a bedroom full of tree branches and pine needles.

"I'm back in the kitchen," Zoe called out. "I started a pot of coffee, if you want some."

"No, thanks," Margo said as she walked through the kitchen door. "I don't have the time." She had on a white vinyl mini and a white stretch top this morning. A sparkly headband held her hair away from her face, and her makeup was gaudy but perfect.

"Are you headed to work?" Zoe couldn't imagine slogging off to the Sasquatch Diner on Sunday morning to wait tables. She felt sorry for Margo, whether Flynn thought she should or not.

"No, I have the day off, remember?" Margo carried a pink vinyl satchel over her shoulder. "You were supposed to need a ride back to the airport."

"Oh, right! I still do need one. But as you can imagine, I won't be hauling along any luggage this time. Wait until you see the bedroom. It's a mess." She put down the two cereal bowls she'd brought over to the table. "We can go look now, if you want."

"Not now."

Zoe glanced at her in confusion. Something about Margo's behavior wasn't right. "So did you change your mind about the coffee?"

"No. I haven't changed my mind about anything." She pulled something that looked very much like a gun out of her satchel.

Zoe didn't like guns, and if Margo thought she needed one to defend herself from Kristen, well, too bad. "If you brought that for me, I'm not comfortable taking it," she said. "Flynn will be back soon, and I don't know how to use guns anyway."

"That's okay. I do." Her dark eyes gleamed.

Alarmed, Zoe shook her head. "No, Margo. I won't have you standing guard over me with a gun. That's too weird." And she noticed something else. Margo was wearing little white gloves, like the kind they used to use for some of their cheer routines. Zoe couldn't figure out why, unless . . .

Margo lifted the gun and pointed it at her. "Then how about if I just shoot you with it? Would that be a little less weird?"

Zoe's eyes widened and she found breathing was a real chore. "Don't even kid around about something like that!"

"Believe me, I'm not kidding."

Zoe hadn't thought she was kidding, either. From the moment she saw the gloves, she'd begun to figure it out.

Kristen Keebler, Harvard law professor, might not like Zoe very much, especially now that Flynn was no longer a viable marriage prospect. Kristen might be delighted if Zoe suddenly had to go on location for several months in the crocodile-infested waters of the Amazon.

But Margo fit in a whole other category. Margo didn't like Zoe at all, not even a little bit. In fact, Margo wanted her dead.

Chapter Twenty-Seven

Flynn had barely arrived at the motel when his cell phone rang. He pulled into the parking lot and shut off the engine. Might as well answer his cell before heading to room fifteen. Zoe might be calling him. Or even Kristen. At times like this, he couldn't ignore his cell phone.

"Tony!" Luanne sounded as if she'd been running.

Flynn groaned. "Luanne, I'm sorry I didn't call you back. But I don't have time to talk now."

"Me, either! You have to come back to the cabin!" She was panting.

"Luanne, if this is about the tree, I know about the tree."

"No! It's about Miss Taggart!"

An alarm buzzed in his brain. "What about her?"

"I was going over there to see you guys because I figured you forgot to call, and I saw Miss Taggart's car there instead of yours. Well, I don't like her, which is why I never asked if I could call her by her first name, so I started walking around the house, and then I saw the tree, and—"

"Get to the point, Luanne." Tension was building in his gut.

"I'm trying to! I heard loud voices, so I went sneaking up to the kitchen window and peeked in. Tony, Miss Taggart was pointing a gun at Zoe! So I ran home to call you!"

The world tilted, and when it settled back onto its axis, Flynn saw everything with complete clarity. *Of course.* He reached for the ignition. "Call nine-one-one."

"I did! They put me on hold, so I hung up! Tony, you have to come back and save Zoe!"

"I will." His body felt as if it had been chiseled from a block of ice, but he would get there and he would save her. He had to. Peeling out of the parking lot, he gunned the motor on his way down the main drag. Then he deliberately ran the red light. Maybe he'd attract the attention of a cop who would follow him to the cabin.

But the street was deserted this early on a Sunday morning, so he was free to drive 80 miles an hour past the Sasquatch Diner and the Bigfoot Trading Post. The road to the cabin was filled with potholes and he hit them all at speeds guaranteed to ruin the shocks.

He should have trusted his gut with Margo. He'd known she was bad news. He'd *known.* She'd thrown suspicion onto poor Kristen, who might or might not be at the Bigfoot Motel. Kristen had been a pawn in Margo's scheme to get Zoe. But why? Revenge for a missed prom? That just didn't seem right.

As he neared the cabin he slowed down. If he had a chance of saving Zoe, he'd have to sneak up on Margo. Several yards from the clearing he pulled over, turned off the engine, and got out of the car. Margo's neon green car still sat in front of the cabin.

He tried to listen for voices, but the blood rushing in his ears made hearing tough. God, he had to be in time. And if he was in time, what then? He was unarmed. He didn't know martial arts. Where the hell were the cops in this town? He'd broken the speed limit by 50 miles an hour, for crissake!

As he crept around the side of the house, he heard them talking and sent up a silent prayer of thanks. Although he couldn't make out what either of them was saying, Zoe had managed to keep herself from being shot, at least so far. Maybe she'd convinced Margo to put away the gun.

He had to climb over the tree and snagged the back pocket of his pants on a branch. Rather than bother to untangle himself, he ripped the material free. Cool air blew on his ass, and he didn't care.

On the far side of the tree he came face-to-face with Luanne and Bigfoot. In broad daylight it was easy to identify Jeff in a costume, but at night, in the shadows, Jeff could have fooled anyone, including him.

Flynn panicked. He wasn't sure why Jeff was in costume, but neither of these kids had any business being here, putting themselves in the possible path of a woman with a gun. Where the hell were their parents? He mouthed, *Go home.*

Jeff shook his head. "We're backup, dude," he said in a low voice.

Shaking, Flynn walked closer. He was getting rid of these two before they got hurt. "Go," he said. "Now."

Luanne lifted her chin. "We have a plan."

"Take her home," Flynn said, appealing to Jeff.

"Dude, maybe you should listen. She's smart."

So was Flynn, but he had no plan. He'd never envisioned a situation like this. So he leaned over and put his face close to Luanne's. "Okay, I'm listening. Make it fast."

Zoe couldn't believe that she hadn't seen the hatred in Margo's eyes long before this. Surely the woman had given off clues, clues Zoe had totally missed. So now she was in a hell of a fix.

Fortunately, Margo had a laundry list of grievances and apparently wanted Zoe to hear them all before pulling the trigger. She'd started with elementary school. Zoe didn't remember Margo from elementary school, and that seemed to be part of the problem. Their alphabetical pairing up had started then, but Zoe had been oblivious to Margo, probably because she'd had a crush on Jimmy Switzer, who'd sat in front of her.

From Margo's standpoint, Zoe had ignored her all through elementary and had barely noticed her in middle school. Margo had worked to get on the cheerleading squad just so she could become friends with Zoe, and even then it hadn't really happened.

"But now we're friends!" Zoe said. "Or at least we were, until you pulled a gun on me. I have to tell you, Margo, pulling a gun on someone really puts a crimp in the relationship."

"We're not *friends*." Margo sneered at her. "You never once invited me to come and see you in that fancy house in Malibu, now did you?"

"You want to come to Malibu? Hey, we can arrange that. Let's get out the calendar and—"

"Don't move!" Margo raised the gun and pointed it in Zoe's face.

In the course of her career Zoe had done a few movies that involved guns. She'd never much liked them, even as props. She especially didn't like them when they looked loaded. This one did, although loaded and unloaded guns probably looked the same. Still, Zoe imagined the chambers seemed fatter somehow.

Her job was to avoid having one of those fat chambers discharge a bullet in her direction. In the movies, characters always tried to talk their way out of a situation like this, or at least stall until help arrived. Zoe knew that Flynn would be coming back. She had to stay alive until then.

She took a deep breath, which always calmed her before a scene. "So you're going to shoot me because I didn't become your friend? Maybe it's me, but that seems a little extreme, Margo."

"Oh, there's a lot more to it than that. Do you remember Rob?"

"Of course I do. I feel horrible about the prom, if it's any consolation." Judging from the gun in Margo's hand, it wasn't.

"The prom?" Margo laughed. "The prom is chump change. I hated not going, but I'll tell you what I hated worse. Zoe, have you ever been pregnant?"

"Uh, no." She had a bad feeling about where this discussion was going. "I take it you have?"

"Briefly." Margo's gaze hardened. "When the father refused to marry me, I got rid of it."

Zoe swallowed. "The father was Rob."

"Yeah, Rob."

"So why aren't you shooting him?" Then she felt instantly guilty for putting ideas in a crazy woman's head. "Scratch that. Shooting is not the answer. Shooting is never the answer."

"I could never shoot Rob. I love him."

Oh, boy. Zoe was dealing with a total fruitcake. "What about Bob? Aren't you engaged to be married to Bob?"

"There's no Bob."

"Sure there's a Bob!" Hysteria nibbled at her, threatening to take over. "You said he's crazy about blueberry cobbler!"

"I made him up." Margo raised the gun. "I think it's time to shoot you."

"You know, maybe you should reconsider that idea. It'll end badly, with you going to jail. I've never been to jail, but I've seen movies, and the wardrobe options are not good."

Margo shook her head. "I'm thinking Kristen will go to jail. While I was in her motel room I snagged a couple of personal items which I can leave at the scene of the crime. Everybody in town knows Kristen is crazy with jealousy. Even your precious Flynn thinks so."

"But Flynn went to see her at the motel! He'll be her alibi!"

"She's not there." Margo aimed the gun right between Zoe's eyes and squinted down the barrel. "I told her Flynn wanted to meet her at a little picnic area by Bigfoot Lake."

"There's a lake around here?"

"No, but I gave her directions that should keep her busy for a while. She'll have no alibi."

"Then Flynn will be back any minute." Zoe struggled to breathe. "Once he finds out she's not there, he'll come back here."

"Maybe, except he's a thorough guy. When he gets no answer, he'll go to the motel office and ask about Kristen. The motel office will call the room. The manager might even decide to check the room. I stopped by the office and said Kristen was depressed and might be a danger to herself."

"Sounds like you planned this very carefully."

"I tried to." Margo sounded quite proud of herself. "But I've also made use of the good luck that came my way at the last minute. Let me tell you, I was thrilled to find out Kristen was in the picture. We've had several long talks."

"You convinced her to come out here, didn't you?"

"Of course. She didn't want to, but I explained how you'd stolen my boyfriend and then ditched him, so you'd for sure do the same with hers."

"I didn't ditch Rob! I quit going with him because he lied about you!"

Margo's eyes glittered. "Yeah, and he blamed me for the breakup. I couldn't win. But now I have you where I want you, and that's all I care about. People don't often get a chance to ruin the life of the person who ruined theirs."

"Margo, let me make it up to you. Come to the beach house in Malibu with me. We'll sit on the deck and drink cosmos. I'll invite Matt Damon and Ben Affleck over. We'll have a party. You'll be the guest of honor."

"Like that would ever happen. You can't make it up to me, so don't even try. The baby Rob and I were supposed to have is dead, and he's married to somebody else."

Zoe felt herself getting sucked into the quicksand of Margo's insanity. "Give yourself a chance to find someone else, too. Someone better than Rob."

"There's nobody better than Rob. He's perfect, and if it hadn't been for you, he would have married me and my life would be perfect right now, too. I had everything planned—my wedding colors, pink and silver, my bridesmaids . . . I was planning to ask you to be a bridesmaid. Funny, huh?"

"Yeah. Funny. I look really bad in pink and silver." How bizarre. Other than the cheerleading activities, Zoe had spent no time with Margo, and yet Margo had scripted her into her wedding. The woman was a genuine wacko. No wonder Rob had dumped her.

"Pretty soon it won't matter what color you wear," Margo said. "You'll look bad in everything, because you'll be *dead.*" She put her finger on the trigger. "Let's do a little cheer, shall we? Give me a *D*!"

Zoe began to shake. "What about the noise?"

"We're in the woods. Everyone around here has guns. They shoot to scare off whatever wildlife is bothering them—bears, skunks, whatever. A gunshot in these woods is like a car horn in New York City. Give me an *E*!"

"So guns are a total cliché, right? Surely you don't want to do the obvious thing. Maybe you should think about a more creative way to do me in."

Margo groaned. "Trust me, I tried. I poisoned your food, I planted the bees you're so allergic to, I raced back here while you were eating and turned on the gas so you could blow yourself up, and nothing happened! So I had to console myself up by watching you boinking your precious lawyer."

"You watched us?" Zoe's tummy rolled.

"I deserved to have some fun. Now I can say I saw the great Zoe Tarleton getting it on. And you looked as sweaty

and stupid as the rest of us. I have to say, though, he'
hung real nice . . . for a nerd."

"You're sick, Margo. You need help."

"No, I don't. I manage fine up here in Long Shaft. I'l
manage even better once you're taken care of. Too ba
the tree didn't do the job for me, though. That would'v
been cleaner. Now I'm stuck with shooting you. Give m
an *A*!"

"Margo, don't you see?" Zoe worked to keep her teetl
from chattering. "All those missed opportunities are jus
God's way of telling you not to kill me."

"I have to, Zoe. I couldn't live with myself if I didn'
Give me another *D*! What does it spell? *DEAD!*" Sh
pulled the trigger.

As Zoe braced herself for the impact, an empty cham
ber clicked. She nearly collapsed on the floor in relief.

"Damn it all! One empty chamber, and you luck ou
and get it. Trust me, it won't happen twice." She started t
squeeze the trigger again and paused as a howl sounded
next to the house. "What the hell is that?"

It sounded like the cavalry to Zoe. "Bigfoot?"

"Can't be. There's no smell."

The howl was followed by a shriek.

Margo's glance shifted to the window but moved
quickly back to Zoe. "Okay, so something's out there."

"I think you should investigate," Zoe said. "You coul
add another sighting to your list."

"You'd like that, wouldn't you? Sorry. Bigfoot is im
portant, but shooting you is on the top of my To Do list
even above Bigfoot sightings." She two-handed the gu
she leveled at Zoe.

Zoe wondered if she could dive out of the way in time
Probably not at such close range. Maybe she should rusl

her. It looked like she was going to die anyway, and at least she'd go down swinging.

Bigfoot howled again.

Margo darted a quick look out the window again. "Damn it, why did he have to show up now? I've never had a daylight sighting."

"That could make history." Zoe thought she heard a noise on the cement stoop outside the back door. She took a tiny step toward the back door.

"Stay where you are!" Margo repositioned her finger on the trigger. "I'm afraid the sound of the gun will scare him away, but I'll have to take my chances on that." She began to squeeze the trigger again.

The back door slammed back on its hinges and Flynn knocked Zoe out of the way as the gun went off.

At the moment she realized Flynn had been hit by the bullet meant for her, something snapped in Zoe. With a roar of rage she flung herself at Margo, who fired off another shot that missed Zoe and slammed into the wall next to the window.

Before Margo could shoot again, Zoe was on her, knocking her to the floor with a thud that shook the dishes in the cupboards. Then Zoe proceeded to give Margo the biggest girl fight of the century. She pinched, she gouged, she pulled hair, while Margo shrieked louder than Bigfoot.

"I'll take over." The voice sounded young, but the costumed body that inserted itself into the fight and pushed Zoe away was substantial. Bigfoot looked like he could handle Margo, which left Zoe to check on Flynn.

She turned and crawled back to where he lay crumpled on the floor, his glasses lying several feet away and a blackened bullet hole piercing the material of his shirt, right over his heart. *No!* screamed a voice in her head. A whimper came from the open doorway. Zoe glanced u and saw Luanne standing there, hands to her mouth, eye shining with tears.

Zoe gulped. "He'll . . . be . . . okay."

"Yeah . . . I will." Flynn opened his eyes.

"You're alive!" Zoe felt dizzy with joy.

"So far."

"Don't move," Zoe said. "Don't try to be brave. You'v been shot."

"I feel like I've been shot." He lifted his head. "Jeff you got Margo under control?"

"You betcha, dude. Like, I got her in a choke hold."

A moan of discomfort verified his statement.

"Don't worry about Margo," Zoe said. "Just sta quiet." She spied the cell phone clipped to his belt. Unfas tening it, she stared at him, expecting blood to start gush ing out of his chest any minute. Keeping her attention o that bullet hole, she held out the phone to Luanne. "Cal nine-one-one."

"I'll try."

"What do you mean, *try*? Just dial it!"

"Out here in Long Shaft, it doesn't always work."

"Well, keep trying!" Zoe clutched Flynn's hand. It fel so warm, but any minute he could go into shock. Wh hadn't she ever taken a first-aid course? She knew noth ing about injured people. And now the injured person wa the man she loved.

"Am I bleeding?" Flynn looked up at her.

"Not that I can see." She was afraid it was all internal She didn't know how it worked with bullet wounds Maybe he was bleeding from the back.

"I think I should sit up."

"No, don't sit up! Wait for the paramedics."

"Seriously, I don't feel so bad."

Zoe tightened her grip on his hand. "Don't talk like that. In the movies, whenever somebody starts talking like that, they—" She realized Luanne could be listening, so she leaned closer and murmured the rest. "They croak."

"I'm not gonna croak." He looked into her eyes. "I'm glad you're not shot."

She swallowed a sob. "I'm sorry you are. You shouldn't have jumped in front of me."

"We were hoping she'd get distracted enough by Bigfoot that I could shove both of us out of the way."

"She was distracted, but she shot you anyway." Zoe blinked back tears.

"Unbutton my shirt. Tell me how bad it is."

"O-okay." That was probably what she should do, anyway. Then she could rip up some clothing and make a pressure bandage. That sounded right. With trembling fingers she unbuttoned his shirt.

Ordinarily he'd be wearing an undershirt, but they'd had a wild night and certain clothing options had been eliminated, like her bra and his undershirt. Taking a deep breath, she pulled the shirt aside and found . . . no bullet hole. Instead there was the beginnings of a bad bruise, but no hole.

"You're not shot," she said, marveling at the sight of his unbroken skin.

"I'm not?"

"No." And then she figured out why. Reaching into his shirt pocket, she pulled out his PDA, which had a bullet embedded smack-dab in the middle of the titanium cover. "Look at this."

Flynn struggled to a sitting position and took it from her. "That damned Margo killed my PDA! I loved that thing! All my appointments are in there, and some case notes, and my address book, and my phone numbers!"

Laughing, Zoe reached over and caught his face in both hands. "Who cares? You're alive! You're not shot!"

He looked at her and his grin was sheepish. "Well, there's that."

"You crazy idiot." She leaned forward and kissed him.

"What in God's name is going on here? And what's the deal with Chewbacca?"

The voice, a famous one at that, got Zoe's attention immediately. She stopped kissing Flynn and swiveled so that she could see past where Jeff had Margo pinned to the floor. Standing in the kitchen doorway was a blond, exceptionally tan guy who'd made *People*'s fifty most beautiful list. Twice.

He looked upset. Behind him stood a brunette in a tailored pantsuit. She didn't look too cheerful, either.

"Everyone stay calm and we'll work this out," said a uniformed officer who appeared at the back door.

Luanne squealed. "Calm? You expect me to be calm? I'm standing in the same house with Zoe Tarleton and Trace Edwards! My dreams have come true!"

Zoe feared that her nightmare had just begun.

Chapter Twenty-Eight

Flynn would have preferred that Kristen hadn't come on the scene at the very moment Zoe had decided to kiss him. And he didn't have a chance to talk to Kristen for quite a while. Eventually the squad car left with Margo in the backseat. Luanne immediately started rounding up scraps of paper and getting both Trace and Zoe to sign autographs.

Flynn took that as his cue. He glanced at Kristen. "Let's go out on the porch."

"Okay." Her well-modulated voice didn't crack, although there were definite signs of strain around her eyes. Her short brown hair was as neat and tidy as ever, though, and there wasn't a visible wrinkle in her pantsuit.

Her eyes were hazel. Flynn made a mental note. And she wasn't a crazed stalker. He was ashamed of the thoughts he'd had about her, disgusted with himself for letting Margo twist things in his mind. But that didn't change his basic belief that Kristen wasn't the woman for him.

On his way out to the porch he was aware of Zoe's gaze. He would have liked to send her a signal, but he couldn't do that without Kristen noticing, and that would be unkind. So he left with Kristen, all the while feeling the tug of Zoe pulling him back.

The porch held memories of Zoe, too. When Kristen sat in the same dilapidated rocker Zoe had used when they'd read the script together, Flynn wanted to suggest a different place. But that would be silly. They needed to have this conversation, and Kristen should be sitting down.

Flynn steadied his glasses on the bridge of his nose. The impact of hitting the floor had loosened one of the earpieces and the glasses needed some adjusting, but he didn't want to take the time. He sat down beside her and cleared his throat. "A year ago—"

"We were different people." Kristen folded her hands in her lap and studied her fingernails.

She had that French manicure Zoe had thought would fit in with a nerd image. Flynn thought of Zoe's glasses and her crazy outfits. She'd be better off studying Kristen instead of him. But he was glad she'd chosen him for her role model.

"It was too neat," Kristen said. "We met, got along, thought we could move right into a suitable marriage."

"Kristen . . ." This was hard for him, but he thought it had to be said. "I led you to believe that I was in love with you. That was wrong. I thought I was, but now I realize I just . . ." He paused and looked at her. "I just wanted to be."

Her throat moved. "Me, too."

He wondered if she was saying that to salvage her

pride. If so, he'd let her do it. "Then I guess you must have flown out here to tell me that."

"I did." She met his gaze. "I realized that you were getting involved with Zoe and, knowing you, you'd be conscience-stricken about it. I didn't think talking on the phone would convince you, so I came out here to make sure there were no doubts. We need to break it off. For both our sakes."

"Did you really call Trace then? I don't know what to believe anymore."

"Actually, I did. I have a friend-of-a-friend who got me the number."

"Why?"

She smiled. "I was curious about how Zoe was playing this. What I said on the phone is true. I like you. I might not love you, but I like you and I'd hate to see you get hurt. Trace admitted to me that he and Zoe aren't as committed as the media let us think."

Flynn had been wondering if Trace would challenge him to a duel at sunset, darts at dawn, or whatever was the in thing these days between romantic rivals. Maybe a drink-off at noon. "How is Trace taking this?"

"He wishes Zoe had told him about it. He's not all that invested, but he doesn't want to look like a fool in front of the Hollywood crowd." Kristen glanced away and a flush crept into her cheeks. "He and I had some long talks."

"Really." Now here was an interesting development. Flynn gazed at the orange Lamborghini sitting in the clearing next to his rental and Margo's neon Taurus. Trace had driven Kristen here. Flynn hadn't put that together before.

"He doesn't get to talk to very many people who aren't in the business. I think . . . maybe it was a refreshing change for him."

Well, well. And that clinched it for Flynn. He was definitely not in love with Kristen. Trace Edwards might be interested, and Flynn felt no jealousy whatsoever. Nada. "Trace would be wise to take a closer look," he said.

"Thank you." Her color deepened. "That's nice of you to say."

"Hey, I recognize that you're a terrific person. But between the two of us, there's no . . ."

"Right. We were kidding ourselves."

Relief loosened his tongue. "And to think I thought you were some stalker! What a riot."

"You did?"

Maybe he shouldn't have said that. Judging from her expression, he should have kept his big mouth shut. "Not for very long. Mostly I didn't. Maybe for a tiny moment, this morning, after all the things that had happened, and then Margo said you'd called Trace. But deep down I knew you weren't trying to kill Zoe."

She laughed. "Oh, Flynn, you're priceless. If I ever needed proof that you weren't in love with me, that would be it. You actually thought I might commit murder. Too funny."

"Only for maybe an hour, tops. The rest of the time—"

"Save it." She laughed again and put her hand on his arm. "And good luck with Zoe. These Hollywood romances can get dicey, even with the best of intentions."

"Maybe I should say the same to you."

"No, that would be incredibly premature." But Kristen's eyes sparkled, nonetheless. "After all, I'm heading back to Massachusetts, and—" She stopped talking as

Luanne and Jeff came out on the porch. Jeff had pulled off his Bigfoot mask, but he still wore the suit.

Flynn stood. "Taking off?"

"Yeah, dude." Jeff extended a hairy paw to shake Flynn's hand. Then he nodded to Kristen. "Ma'am."

"Thanks for the help with Margo," Flynn said.

"No problem. And I guess you figured out why I have this costume."

"Uh-huh." Flynn looked him over. "I have to say, the impersonation in that clearing last night was amazing."

"But that's just it," Luanne said. "He says he wasn't out there last night!"

Flynn clapped a hand on Jeff's shoulder. "Hey, it's okay. You don't have to spare my feelings."

"I'm not sparing your feelings, man. I wasn't there. The night before, yeah, I was, like, running around in my costume, doing the Sasquatch shuffle. Last night, I was with Janice."

Flynn glanced at Luanne. "You told him to say that, right?"

"Swear to God, I didn't. And I promise you he's not lying. He's lousy at lying. The 'rents can't tell, but I can, in a heartbeat."

Flynn didn't know if the two of them were conning him or not, but he decided to accept what they said at face value, because that meant he'd really had a Bigfoot sighting to his credit.

"Listen," Jeff said. "Are you still gonna, like, mention the Bigfoot items when you get back to LA?"

"Sure. Be glad to."

"Great." Jeff smiled. "Well, we gotta go. The folks will be back from church any minute. And we have to be all '*oh yeah, we slept in.*'"

"So you won't be telling them about this?" Flynn realized that Zoe needed to get out of town soon. Trace did,
too, but Flynn wasn't so worried about Trace.

"We won't be telling anything," Luanne said. "I can't
say what will happen with the sheriff's deputy, though.
You might want to make tracks."

"Probably." Flynn nodded. "So long, then."

"Oh, you'll be seeing me again," Luanne said. "Zoe invited me for that sleepover. She said the three of us could
have lunch, too."

"She did?" That was encouraging.

"Come on, brat." Jeff ushered Luanne down the steps.
"Let's leave these folks alone so they can make a quick
exit." He waved at Kristen. "Bye now."

"Good-bye," Kristen said. Then she glanced at Flynn.
"So that kid impersonates Bigfoot?"

Flynn nodded.

"It almost sounded as if you believe in that nonsense."

He hesitated. Then he realized he had no reputation to
protect with Kristen. "Yes, as a matter of fact, I do."

"My, my." She chuckled. "And I was planning to get
you a Bigfoot souvenir as a gag gift. I don't know you at
all, Flynn Granger."

No, he thought, *but Zoe does.*

Zoe heard Kristen laughing on the front porch with Flynn
and her hopes died. So much for those happily-ever-after
dreams. Kristen was back in town and having a grand old
time with the guy Zoe had thought might be her one-and-
only. Zoe might have temporarily bewitched him, but
Kristen truly understood the way to his nerd heart.

The minute Zoe had seen Kristen, she'd recognized
how perfect this lawyer babe was for Flynn. No wonder

he'd planned his whole future around her. From her conservative pantsuit to her practical haircut she was perfect for him. They could live in a house where the daily chores were color coded and the clocks were all synchronized.

"Zoe, we need to get the hell out of here."

She looked at Trace sitting on the sofa where she and Flynn had spent so many special moments. She'd been unable to sit down at all. "I know." She continued to pace the small room. "Before long the word will be out."

"Right. But before we go, do you want your people to make the announcement of our breakup or should I have my people do it?"

Her heart ached for him. "Trace, spin this any way you want it. Say you've found someone else. Say I'm an ice queen. Whatever you want. I feel awful to have put you in this position."

He gazed at her. "Ah, it wasn't going to work out. I kept thinking it would, but I could feel you pulling away. I mean, shit, you wouldn't even go to bed with me. How crazy is that?"

"Pretty crazy." Women all over the world fantasized about going to bed with Trace Edwards and she had avoided doing it.

"Okay then." He pushed himself up from the sofa. "I'll have my people say that I've become interested in someone else." He glanced toward the porch. "A lawyer from Massachusetts, maybe."

"Oh, Trace, don't do that to yourself. They're a matched set of bookends. Can't you see that?"

"I must need the prescription changed on my contacts, because all I see out there is opportunity."

"I know you're used to getting any woman you want, but—"

"Not any woman. I couldn't get you."

She looked into his eyes. They were brown, but she wouldn't have been able to tell anyone that on cue, either. "You wouldn't have wanted me," she said.

"Maybe not."

"But I'm afraid Kristen isn't your answer, either. She's taken."

He jingled the keys in his pocket. "Let's see."

"Trace, don't humiliate yourself." *And don't force me to face the truth right this minute, either. Give me a little time to get used to the facts.*

"Wish me luck."

"Trace—"

But he bolted out the door and was soon standing in front of Kristen, working that bad-boy smile of his. "I'm ready to hit the road. Can I give you a ride?"

Zoe braced herself for Kristen's refusal. She hadn't stopped to figure out the consequences, either. If Kristen said no, then Zoe had to race out and either grab the empty seat in Trace's Lamborghini or hitch a ride with Flynn and Kristen in the rental sedan. That would be cozy, Flynn and Kristen in the front and Zoe the reject in the back.

Then the most amazing thing happened. Kristen got out of her chair and walked down the porch steps with Trace. Zoe rubbed her eyes and looked again to make sure she wasn't hallucinating. After they drove away she was still standing there trying to adjust her thinking when Flynn came inside.

"We should take off, too," he said. "Let me grab my stuff."

We? He'd said that so matter-of-factly, as if it didn't happen to be the most important pronoun in the English language. While she was still digesting the impact of that pronoun, he returned with his small suitcase in one hand and his laptop over his shoulder.

"Is there anything else you want to bring?" he asked. "It'll be a long trip."

"It will?" She was confused. "Aren't you taking us both to the airport?"

He shook his head. "Your ticket is buried somewhere under that pine tree, and besides, I don't want to take separate planes. I'd rather drive down to LA. It'll give us time to talk."

"About . . . what?"

He smiled at her. Then he put his suitcase and laptop on the floor and closed the distance between them. "Don't you know?"

Her heart began to hammer. "I hope I know."

"Yeah, you know." He pulled her close. "We've been on a Bigfoot hunt together. We're bonded."

She looked into those soft gray eyes and saw everything she needed to see there. "It really might have been Bigfoot, you know."

"I've decided it was."

"Me, too."

He kissed her lightly. "We have to go. Otherwise the good citizens of Long Shaft are liable to mob you and we'll never get out of here."

"I don't want to leave."

"We could come back on our honeymoon."

Her breath caught. "But you haven't even asked me—"

"I didn't think there was time."

"Take the time."

In an instant he was on one knee. "Zoe Tarleton, will you marry me?"

Her pulse was beating so fast she was afraid she might pass out. "You're all out of order, Flynn."

"I am?"

"First you're supposed to say you love me."

"You know that already."

"Say it."

"I love you. I love you more than I've ever believed I could love anyone. Now will you marry me?"

"First I have to say I love you back."

"But I know you do!"

"Let me say it anyway. I love you, Flynn Granger. I love you desperately and completely." She paused. "Now propose again."

He started grinning. "Zoe Tarleton, will you marry me?"

"Yes, I will. What's so funny?"

"You. All this doing-it-in-order stuff. You're acting like a nerd!"

"Then I guess you'd have to say the weekend was a success."

He stood and drew her into his arms. "Most definitely. Now kiss me quick, and let's go."

Her kiss wasn't all that quick, but eventually they managed to get themselves out the door. At the last minute she remembered to grab the script and the Bigfoot flashlight. As they were jumping into the car, a far-off howl drifted through the trees.

Zoe looked at Flynn. "Do you think that was Jeff's tape recorder?"

"No. Do you?"

"No." They exchanged one last secret smile, and Flynn put the car in gear.

Epilogue

At the Golden Globe Awards ceremony Flynn sat with Zoe at a linen-draped table that included Zoe's parents, her agent, and Luanne. Zoe's parents looked completely out of their element, but Luanne was completely in hers. When she wasn't star gazing, she was busily talking to Leon. Flynn predicted she'd fulfill her goals in no time.

During the first half of the awards, Zoe laughed and smiled a lot, but Flynn was the guy holding her hand under the table. He could feel the tension running through her. A glass of wine would have helped, but she wasn't allowed. He had to hope that the stress of being here tonight wouldn't bring on her contractions.

She liked to joke that she was fifteen months pregnant. By rights she shouldn't even be here, but he wouldn't have tried to talk her out of it. She'd worked too hard, wished too long. If she made it, then no one else had the right to go up there and accept for her. She deserved all the limelight she could get.

The program had never seemed this lengthy before. But then, he'd never had a stake in it before. The closer they came to Zoe's category, the tighter her grip on his hand. When they finally announced the actresses up for leading roles in a comedy, the camera swung to each in turn. He thought she'd cut off his circulation for sure when the camera found their table.

"I love you," he murmured. *And if I have to lose a hand tonight, the sacrifice will be worth it. At least it's my left.*

"I love you, too." She didn't look at him.

His heart was pounding very fast, so he could only imagine how hers was reacting. "Just don't go into labor."

That made her laugh, but it was a breathy, nervous sound.

The two idiots on the stage made a three-act play out of opening the envelope. Flynn was ready to leap up there and do it for them by the time they finally pulled the card from the envelope.

"And the Golden Globe goes to . . . Zoe Tarleton!"

Flynn jumped to his feet, effectively yanking Zoe up with him. She stumbled, but he caught her and steadied her as best he could, considering how shaky he felt. Then, with applause beating against his eardrums like surf, he kissed her. He felt her lipstick going all over him and he didn't care. He could barely breathe, he was so happy.

Dazed and clapping like a maniac, he watched as she hugged her parents, her agent, and Luanne before making her way to the stage. The satisfaction he felt at this moment was almost better than sex. Almost. He hadn't had any of that for a while, because she was very close to her due date and he hadn't wanted to screw up the process. So he'd take this as a substitute.

At last she was standing in front of the microphone,

her smile dazzling the cheering crowd. She wore a red chiffon dress that billowed around her big belly. To see her wear a dress for a change was a treat. These days she practically lived in her Sasquatch Diner XXL T-shirt, special-ordered after the second trimester.

The crowd continued to clap, and he marveled that the woman they were applauding was his wife. He still woke up every day in disbelief that he was married to her. She even seemed to *like* the fact. Go figure.

Then she started her acceptance speech, and he strained to catch every word. She'd rehearsed it with him, just in case, and he hoped she'd remember all the people she'd wanted to thank. She sailed right through the list like a champ. He would've been so rattled he would have forgotten half of them, but she didn't.

She also remembered to thank the citizens of Long Shaft. That little mention would boost their tourism even more, although after the Bigfoot craze had hit LA a year ago Long Shaft was already a popular destination. Zoe had even made a guest appearance at Long Shaft's first annual Beauty and the Bigfoot Festival.

When Long Shaft had been duly thanked, Flynn thought that would be it, so he brought his hands up in preparation for more enthusiastic clapping.

Only she had more to say, something she hadn't rehearsed with him. "And I especially want to thank the most important person in my life, the man who's taught me what's important, the man who put me in this condition, so that I could barely waddle up here, my favorite nerd, Flynn Granger!"

Flynn stood there with a goofy grin on his face as the camera moved in. At one time he would have been horrified at the idea of a camera trained on him, a camera beaming his face to millions of viewers around the world. But he wasn't the same guy he used to be. He acted spontaneously once in a while. He sometimes took things out of order. And he drove a red Ferrari.

So instead of being embarrassed by the attention, he blew Zoe a kiss.

She blew it back to him. Then she leaned toward the microphone. "Get your ass backstage, Granger. I'm having contractions."

He launched himself from the seat.

"We'll bring Luanne to the hospital!" Zoe's mother said. "Just go!"

With a quick nod of gratitude, he hurtled backstage. Then he, Zoe, and the Golden Globe Award took a wild ride in the Ferrari. On the way to the hospital Zoe called her doctor, who'd been watching the awards and was on her way. Then Zoe took a call from her parents, who were stuck in traffic and would get there the minute they could.

Her parents hadn't made it by the time Flynn screeched the Ferrari to a stop at the hospital's emergency entrance. Okay, so he'd handle this by himself. He'd taken the birthing classes. He'd be fine.

Zoe wanted to haul the award into the delivery room, and in the end, they scrubbed it down and let it stay, along with Flynn. She delivered their baby daughter the same way she made love, with great enthusiasm and lots of noise. In the process she ended up cutting off the circulation to Flynn's right hand.

Fortunately, his left hand had almost recovered from her grip during the Golden Globes, so when he finally had a chance to hold baby Luanne, only one hand was completely numb. Most of the rest of him felt a little on the numb side, actually. All that joy was a bit much to take in.

But he'd work on it. Holding Luanne, he smiled down at Zoe, who still had sparkles in her hair from the fancy updo she'd had created for the awards. "Nice timing."

That famous Zoe Tarleton smile was a little wobbly as she gazed at Flynn holding their new daughter. "Thanks. I was feeling the contractions during the ceremony, but I didn't want to tell you."

"I'm glad you didn't."

"I wanted things to go in order, Flynn. First the Golden Globe, then the baby."

He couldn't decide where to look. They were both so beautiful and he didn't want to miss anything. "Zoe, you are becoming such a nerd."

"I know. Isn't it great?"

"It's scary, is what it is." He kept staring at his daughter, unable to grasp that he was truly a dad. "Next thing you know, little Luanne will become a nerd."

"I'll bet she will, especially if my devious plan works and we get her namesake to make trips to Malibu so she can babysit."

"That girl is going to be over the moon. First you get her a bit part in a movie, then you invite her to the awards, and now you name our kid after her."

"I want to keep my five-star, front-of-the-album rating. Flynn, back to the nerd thing. We need a different car."

"Yeah, I know." He gazed into the unblinking stare of his daughter. "Something that will hold a baby seat. We don't have to get a nerd car, though. We can get a Town Car, or maybe a Beemer."

"I don't want a Town Car or a Beemer."

"You don't?" He was falling in love with this little cherub. Completely and irrevocably in love.

"I was thinking . . . a Civic."

That made him redirect his attention to Zoe. "You're kidding."

"Nope. It would do the job, so why not?"

Flynn groaned. "I've created a monster. What about looking cool?"

"I don't care." She gazed up at him, her eyes filled with love. "Besides, I have a husband I'm crazy about, a gorgeous baby, and a Golden Globe. What could be cooler than that?"

"I have no idea." He wondered if a person could explode from too much happiness. He hoped not, because if so, he was a walking time bomb.

Zoe had apparently recovered enough to give him the full wattage of her Zoe Tarleton smile. "Then buy us a Civic, Granger. We're gonna set us a trend."